# Legends of Erin:

## Beyond the Castle Door

TO Noah,

Thank you so
much for coming
to my Boot camp
at Tustin! I hope
you like the Story!

*[signature]*

Meadow Griffin's love for all things fantastical and large imagination moved her to write her debut novel, *Legends of Erin: beyond the Castle Door*. She was homeschooled her whole life along with her two younger brothers, (the inspiration for Fadin and Tase) and currently lives in California with her family.

# Legends of Erin:

## Beyond the Castle Door

Meadow Griffin

# Legends of Erin:

## Beyond the Castle Door

Olympia Publishers
*London*

www.olympiapublishers.com
OLYMPIA PAPERBACK EDITION

A CIP catalogue record for this title is
available from the British Library.

ISBN: 978-1-84897-152-3

This is a work of fiction.
Names, characters, places and incidents originate from the writer's
imagination. Any resemblance to actual persons, living or dead, is purely
coincidental.

First Published in 2011

Olympia Publishers
60 Cannon Street
London
EC4N 6NP

Printed in Great Britain

## Dedication

I dedicate this book to Betty Martinson, my beloved grandmother, without whom this book would not be a reality.

## Acknowledgments

Firstly, to the Lord who has blessed me with such a story.

Mom, for taking the time to listen to me read and re-read my book every time I changed something and for pushing me forward when things got so complicated I was ready to give up.

Dad, for loving my characters, my ideas and giving me a schedule to follow so this story didn't end up as unfinished.

My brothers, Logan and Tristian, for being my Tase and Fadin and doing things in life that inspire me to write them.

My dearest friend, Chanel, for supporting me in my every move.

Olympia Publishers for taking a chance on an unknown author.

Thank you sincerely everyone!

*"Oh the tangled webs we weave, when first we practice to deceive."*

"Marmion", 1808, Sir Walter Scott.

# PRONUNCIATION GUIDE

Many of the names and words in this book are hard to pronounce, and nearly all of them are spelled quite differently than how they are spoken. The following is a guide for some of the difficult names and words.

## Names

Aednat = Ey-nit
Afanasii = A- fan-a- see (long e)
Ailín = Ah-leen
Aimirgin = Av-er-yin
Aislinn = Esh-leeng
Alroy = All-roy
Bojin = Boe-jean (long o)
Caoimhe = Kee-va
Ciaran = Keer-awn
Clearie = Clear-ee (long e as in cutie)
Colmcille = Colm-cill
Cormick = Kor-mick
Daireann = Dar-rawn
Desmond = Dez-mond
Dia = Di-a (long i)
Dubhlainn = Dove-lin
Etain = E-tane
Enda = En- dah
Fadin = Fae-din
Faolan = Fwail-awn
Fintan = Fin-tan
Feidhelm = Fail-im
Glendan = Glen-dan
Kyna = Key-na
Lorcan = Lor-can
Puceula = Puke- u -la (long u)
Quinlan = Quin- lan
Saoirse = Sear-sha
Tase = Tae-z (long a)
Teagan = Tee-gan (long e)

# Words

Ainobhach = Ain-o-VAKH
Ainondall = Ain-on- dhall (Ain = long a)
Cavan = Cav-in
Corr = cor
Dalbhach = Dul-VAKH
Diabhalta = Dia-va-luh-tah
Erin = Erynn
Faróg = Far-UG
Fitheal = Fee-hul
Geartú = Gear-TOO
Glomhan = Glom-han (long o)
Killeen = Kul-EEN
Mayog Xukk Clape = May-oog Zook Clae-p (long a)
Mcayog lolo = Mick-ay-aug (as in august) loo-loo
Muirín = MIR-een (roll the r)
Orthanach = ur-han-ach
Uair = U-air (long u)
Vayyokc = Vay-ah-K (hard k)
Xoor = Zoor (roll the r)

# Chapter 1

## *The O'Callaghans*

Tase Mathew O'Callaghan, a boy of no more than twelve years old, stood in the middle of his messy room feeling perplexed and quite angry.

"Where is it?" he cried. "I know I put it on the desk before I fell asleep!"

He knew he had his homework sheet before he went to bed the night before, now it was nowhere to be found.

"Guess you didn't," Tase's twin brother Fadin said.

Tase looked at him, at his red hair that was the same texture as his own, his pale skin, and facial features that were nearly identical to his own. He and Fadin nearly looked like the same person, except that Fadin wore his hair longer, and his eyes were blue-green while Tase's were sky-blue.

Though they did look very much alike, he and Fadin were not identical twins. Their mother said that as they grew, they would begin to look less and less like each other. Tase happily waited that day, for they were always getting mixed up. Their teachers could never figure out who was who, and even their friends, such as they were, got confused.

Not that Tase minded being a twin, in fact he liked it very much, but sometimes it was hard when people called you by the wrong name, or you got into trouble because of your brother. He and Fadin had had many an argument about that, though for the most part, he and Fadin got along. They were always together and had never once been apart, and that was the way Tase liked it. He felt whole and complete with Fadin around, and he knew Fadin felt the same way, although at this particular moment, Tase wouldn't have minded being apart from him.

"Thanks for all the help," he cried.

Fadin began tying his shoe and yawned deeply. "Well I'm not the one who lost my homework sheet, now am I?"

Tase felt anger boil up inside him. That was just like Fadin, if Tase lost something he couldn't care less, but if it was he who was the owner of the lost thing, then Tase would be digging through drawers and crawling on the ground beside him.

Tase rolled his eyes and began pulling out all his night shirts from his dresser. It had to be in here somewhere, it just had to. Tase did not want to have to face his substitution maths teacher, Mr. Donovan, without it.

Mr. Donovan was a rather boring and easygoing person most of the time, but if a student came in without the homework sheet, well then, that was an immediate detention. Tase had been in enough of those because of Fadin, he was not about to get into trouble because he couldn't find a lousy piece of paper.

He slammed the dresser drawer in frustration and yanked out another.

"Boys!" the voice of their mother was unmistakable.

Tase picked his head up.

"Yea, Ma?" he and Fadin cried in unison.

"Keep it down up there, and don't you two start a fight this morning, we don't want to be late again."

"Okay, Ma," they cried.

"Oh, and, Tase."

"Yes, Ma?"

"You had better find that homework sheet you're looking for, because I'm not driving down to that school later to pick you up from detention. You can sleep in that school if you like it so much."

"Okay, Ma," Tase cried rolling his eyes.

He looked back at Fadin who had his mouth wide open. "How did she know that? How does she always know everything?"

Fadin had always been fascinated by the way their mother seemed to constantly know when they were doing something wrong. Tase had given up figuring it out years before. He assumed she had eyes in the back of her head, or a sixth sense when it came to him and his brother, but Fadin wouldn't relent, and often got into trouble to see if their mother would find out. She always did.

Tase shrugged. "I don't know, but you get your lazy bum off that bed and help me find it."

"No," Fadin said, laying back on the bed. "I don't think I will."

"You bloody eejit!" Tase yelled, quiet enough so that his mother couldn't hear. "If this were you, you know I'd be looking with you."

Fadin lifted a finger.

"Ah," Tase said, "don't you even try and lie about it."

Tase saw him think for a moment, then nod.

"Fine, I'll help you find your stupid homework. Where did you say you put it?"

"On the desk," Tase yelped, "but it's gone."

Fadin snapped his fingers. "Ma, she must have moved it when she took our dirty laundry this morning."

"But I don't put my clothes on the dresser."

Fadin smiled. "I did."

Tase arched his eyebrow.

"To make it easier for her."

Tase shook his head. "Okay, fine, where would she have moved it to?"

"The hamper, in Da's office."

Tase shrugged. "Worth a try."

Fadin popped off the bed and led the way into the narrow hall and into the tiny room that served as their father's office.

It was quite messy, the most cluttered room in the house, and the only room that their mother didn't clean every day. There were mountains of paperwork on the small desk, trash on the floor, the wastebasket was overflowing, and the bookshelves had dust covering them.

On the wall, to the left, was a large map of Ireland, and a big red dot to indicate the city, Waterford, where they lived.

It was located in the Southeast region of their great island, as Tase had heard his father say, and they lived right in the heart of the large city. Though it paled in comparison to Dublin, the largest city and capital of Ireland, Tase still felt his home was a considerably large place.

Tase turned his attention away from the map and spotted the laundry basket near the desk, filled to the brim with dirty clothes and on the top of the pile, sat Fadin' s green shirt, the same shirt he had worn the day before.

"There," Tase said, "If she accidently took it with the clothes it would be here in this pile."

He and Fadin pulled their dirty clothes out and tried in vain to find Tase's lost homework. It was nowhere to be found.

"Great," Tase cried flinging the clothes back into the hamper. "Where could it be?"

Fadin looked over to their father's desk. "Maybe she didn't look at the paper well enough and thought it was Da's."

"You think she put my homework on Da's desk?"

Fadin shrugged.

"Fine," Tase said, getting up and moving to the desk, "come on, let's look."

He and Fadin looked through the mountains of paper and pencils and trash.

Most of the paper on the desk was from their father's job at the bank. He worked at O'Leary's Savings, not five minutes from their house. He had worked there for as long as Tase could remember and now that he thought about it, Tase had never actually been to his father's work or met any of the people he worked with.

That seemed a little odd now that Tase had it on his mind. Most of the other children in his school had been to their father or mother's work at least once, and all of them had met at least one co-worker.

Tase was about to say something to this effect when he saw a small green envelope on the desk. It had been sealed with red wax, and was now torn open. Tase picked it up and flipped it over.

*To Alroy O'Callaghan*

This was all it said, in curved, definitely female, handwriting.

Tase's interest was piqued, he pulled a piece of small green parchment from the envelope and opened it slowly.

*Dear Alroy,*

*How are you? Well I hope. I know this is a bit strange and out of the ordinary, and believe me if there wasn't cause for concern I wouldn't write, yet, as it is, there is a reason I am contacting you.*

*Strange things are happening here in Glas-Cavan, not the normal strange either, dark things are stirring again, and I can't help but feel a sense of déjà vu at the way things are taking place.*

*If you remember it was a subtle change that began everything last time. Little oddities here and there, and that is what is taking place now.*

*I implore you, please come to see me today at ten o'clock. I know it is an hour earlier then you usually leave, but please do it for me, and for your family. I wouldn't ask unless something was seriously wrong.*

*I look forward to seeing you. Stay safe and send Teagan my love in any way that you can.*

*Sincerely Yours,*

*Kyna*

Tase lowered the paper and swallowed hard. What an odd letter. What strange and dark things could be taking place? Why couldn't she send her love directly to their mother? And where was Glas-Cavan? Tase had of course heard of Cavan, a little town a few hours away from Waterford. But Glas-Cavan?

Even though the contents of the letter were unusual, the oddest thing about the correspondence was whom it was from. Why would Aunt Kyna be sending their father a letter like this? In fact, why would she be sending him a letter at all? They never saw her. In fact, Tase and his brother had never even met her.

If it hadn't been for he and Fadin accidently walking in on a private conversation between their parents, they wouldn't even have known she existed.

Their parents hardly ever talked about her, and when they did, they always got into an argument. From what Tase had listened in on, he knew that she lived far away, was very wealthy, was his mother's sister, and hadn't been spoken to in over fourteen years. This was not only peculiar because she was their mother's sister, but strange because they had no other living relatives.

Their father had no siblings, and his mother and father had died in a tragic accident before Fadin and Tase were born. The rest of his family lived far away and weren't close to him.

Their mother had only one sister, Kyna, and due to some fallout, failed to communicate with her. Her parents, too, had died, in a car crash, and the rest of her family had moved, and no longer wished to see her.

It was odd, Tase thought, that he and Fadin had no aunts, no uncles, and no grandparents that they knew or saw. All the other children in their school had aunts, uncles, grandparents, and cousins. But Tase and his brother did not, and the fact that all their parents' family had died and moved away before they were born, seemed awfully coincidental.

Tase had tried countless times to explain this to Fadin, but Fadin didn't really care. He seemed to think there was nothing out of the ordinary about it. This letter, however, was sure to get his attention.

"Hey," Tase said handing him the parchment, "look at this."

Fadin looked up. "Is it your homework?"

"No, but look at it."

Fadin took the paper and read it. His face became concerned and he looked up at Tase. "Aunt Kyna? Why would she write, Da?"

"I don't know," Tase said, "but she did. I wonder what could be happening where she is. I wonder what's so strange about it."

"I wonder if Da went to see her," Fadin said, looking back down at the note.

Now that Fadin mentioned it, Tase wondered that too.

"It doesn't say when she sent it," Fadin said looking at the envelope.

"No, it doesn't."

Tase took the envelope and turned it from side to side. He suddenly saw something glow out of the corner of his eye. He looked down and saw that a drawer of his father's desk was slightly open. He pulled it out further and saw a small golden crest glimmering inside.

Tase picked it up.

It was quite beautiful with moldings and carvings placed on the golden rim. Along the sides of the crest there lay seven gleaming emeralds, and in the middle, two letters overlapped each other: D. A.

"What do you think that stands for?" Fadin asked, fingering the object.

"I don't know," Tase said. "I've never seen this before, have you?"

Fadin shook his head. "I wonder where Da got it?"

"I wonder too."

Tase and Fadin stared at the crest, each holding an end of it, entranced by its beauty.

"BOYS!" Their mother shouted.

Tase and Fadin jumped, dropped the crest, and watched as it rolled on the floor and out of sight.

"Yes, Ma?" they cried.

"Will you hurry up? Breakfast is almost ready. Tell Clearie and your father it's time to come down as well, and you'd better have that homework with you."

"Okay, Ma."

Fadin turned to Tase. "You eejit, you dropped it!"

"I dropped it?" Tase gasped. "You're the one who dropped it."

"I did not."

"Oh, shut your gob. It doesn't matter, let's just find it so Da doesn't know we've been in here."

Fadin grunted in agreement and dropped to the floor to help Tase look.

It wasn't under the desk or by the chair, it wasn't under the trash or by the door. It was gone.

"Great," Fadin shouted, "you lost it, you lost Da's crest!"

"I did not," Tase yelled back. "If it was anyone's fault it was yours, you're the one who decided to hold half of it. If it had been in my hands it would have been just fine!"

"Just fine?" Fadin laughed. "You jumped nearly ten feet in the air, you plonker."

"So did you. You even went higher then I did, you right thick caffler."

Fadin lunged forward but Tase was ready.

He braced himself for the impact but Fadin had too much thrust and they both toppled to the floor.

"Get off me you bloody eejit!" Tase cried.

He smacked Fadin in the face, causing him to loose focus for a second.

Tase pounced on the advantage.

He pushed with all his might and forced Fadin to lose balance and topple next to him.

Tase jumped on top of Fadin's stomach and began bouncing up and down.

"Ug," Fadin cried. "Ge-et off."

"Not till you say it was your fault, Tase billowed.

"Okay, okay," Fadin said.

Tase stopped bouncing for a moment and watched as Fadin took a deep breath.

"Well?" Tase said.

Fadin looked at him. "Alright, it was your fault."

Fadin smiled and Tase bounced on his stomach once more.

Fadin had been waiting for the bounce. When Tase was up in the air, he shoved him to the side and tried to get on top again.

Tase blocked his attempt and they both began rolling all over the floor.

Suddenly Tase felt the earth drop away and he and Fadin went rolling right down the stairs.

One, two, three, four, they hit each stair with a sickening bump.

Tase felt his head hit, then his arm, and his knee.

Finally they landed on the carpeted entranceway and all the anger Tase had felt was forgotten to be replaced by numerous aches and pains.

"Oh," their mother said, sticking her head out of the kitchen. "Good to see you boys finally decided to come down the stairs."

Tase and Fadin grunted in agony.

Their mother looked on at them, her electric blue eyes showing no pity.

She had told them countless times not to fight on the stairs, and Tase now remembered all her warnings quite well.

She watched them angrily for a moment, stamping her foot and furrowing her brow, but then her mothering instinct took over and the pity that had been missing flooded her expression.

She shook her long, raven, curly hair and folded her arms, cloaked in a brilliant blue shawl. "Are you two alright?"

Tase and Fadin nodded.

She locked her eyes on them and arched a dark eyebrow. "I hope you two have learned something. Perhaps now when I tell you not to fight on the stairs you'll both listen to me?"

Again Tase and his brother nodded in agreement.

"You two had better behave yourselves," their mother said, "because I'm not kidding, if you get into detention today, you two can walk home."

Her eyes lingered on Fadin's face.

"Why do you look at me when you say that?" Fadin asked reproachfully.

"You know very well why," she said, unfolding her arms and turning back to the kitchen. "Now get up off the floor and come and eat your breakfast."

Fadin looked at Tase and rolled his eyes.

Tase smiled. He didn't need words to know what Fadin was thinking.

Tase watched Ma's dark-curly hair flip around the corner. Even when she was upset with them, it was hard to deny her beauty. She was the most gorgeous woman he had ever seen. He knew many children thought their mother was the most beautiful woman in the world, but in his and Fadin's case, it was true. Everyone always commented on her striking features, and many men gaped at her when they were out. How his father ever caught Ma was a mystery to Tase.

"Hey," a voice from up the stairs called, "why don't you both get off the floor so I can walk."

Tase and Fadin looked up to see their elder brother, Clearie, coming down the narrow staircase.

He had his school clothes on, his blond hair combed, his shoes tied tight, and a pile of books in his arms. Clearie never went anywhere without a book, they were his closest friends and his life. Fadin and Tase teased him more often then not about his obsession with reading, but Clearie really didn't care.

It was funny, at least in Tase's mind, that Clearie, a fourteen-year-old young man, really had no friends at school. For he was not only smart and witty, but also quite good looking and was always noticed by the girls.

He had been born with eyes that were two different colors. The right eye was the same electric-blue of their mother's, and the left was violet. This fact alone would get anyone noticed, but beside that Clearie had his blond hair that he wore longer to cover ears that were a bit too large, and strong features that would make any girl swoon.

Yet he refused any and all who tried to get to know him. He was much happier alone in his book world that was filled with adventures that could not really affect or harm him. So alone he stayed, with no real human contact besides that of his teachers and family.

Tase looked up at him now, as he came down the stairs, his head held high, and turned to see what it was Fadin was thinking.

The sparkle in Fadin's eye told Tase what to do.

They waited till Clearie was at just the right spot, then they grasped both of his legs and watched as he crashed to the floor and his books flew in all directions.

"Ouch," Clearie cried.

He turned, livid, to Fadin and Tase and grasped the book nearest to him. He swung it at Fadin's head, but Fadin ducked, narrowly missing the heavy mathematics volume.

"Boys!"

Tase cringed at his mother's tone.

Now she was really angry.

"I told you to get up off the floor and stop all that fighting," she shouted at them from her spot in the kitchen. "Clearie, I expected more from you since you are the eldest. Now pick up your books and help set the table, Fadin and Tase," her tone was harsher with them. "Last warning!"

It astounded Tase that she didn't even have to peek over the corner to know everything that had just happened, but he didn't argue or waste time.

He got up off the floor and watched as Fadin silently shoved Clearie down once more.

Once Clearie had righted himself, the three of them dashed into the kitchen, set the table, and sat down to await whatever it was their mother had made for breakfast.

She turned away from the stove, gathered enough plates, and began serving helpings of Sausage Meat Patties.

Tase felt his stomach rumble as his was placed in front of him.

"Good morning," their father sang as he entered the kitchen.

He had a suit on and his curly bright red hair was combed as best it could be. He moved from side to side, showing off his nice clothes and his short but thin frame.

He walked directly to their mother and laid a kiss on her cheek.

"How are you, Teagan, my darling?"

Their mother smiled. "Good, Alroy dear, except for the fact that our sons nearly killed each other on the stairs this morning."

He looked straight to Tase and Fadin. "Boys, how many times has your mother told you about that?"

It was a question not really meant to be answered.

"Now you two had better behave yourselves, I don't want your mother having to come down to school to pick you up from detention again."

His brown eyes lingered on Fadin.

"I always get the blame," Fadin said, throwing his hands in the air.

"Because it is you who is always in trouble," their father said.

Fadin folded his arms.

"Now you three," he said looking at each of them, "behave yourselves."

Fadin made a nasty face when their father turned away.

Tase had to cover his mouth to suppress a laugh.

There was a sudden whining from the door that led into their small backyard.

Tase popped his head up and dashed to the door.

"Oh dear, I forgot to let Pathos in."

As soon as the knob was turned, a large black, white, and tan Bernese came running inside. He moved quickly past Tase and his father and made his way under the table. Once there, he lopped himself onto Fadin's lap and began to cry for a bit of his breakfast.

Fadin giggled.

"Pathos!" Their father smiled. "Get down boy. No begging."

Tase grinned at the long-snouted dog. He was getting a bit of white around his face now, beginning to show old age. It was about time, Tase thought, for he was awfully old for a canine, especially a large one. He had been around for as long as Tase could remember. Since before he and Fadin were born.

He had asked his mother once where they had gotten him, but all she said was, "He found us. I don't really know how it happened."

All Tase knew for sure was that he was around Clearie's age. That was quite a long life for a Bernese, for any dog really.

Pathos looked sorrowfully up at their father, but when he wouldn't relent, Pathos decided to remove himself from Fadin's lap. He moved everything off Fadin's chair except for a single paw, which he kept clinging to his pants just in case Fadin forgot he was there.

"So," Ma said, handing over more plates full of breakfast. "You'll be seeing Lorcan this morning then?"

Tase smiled.

Lorcan was a man Tase heard his father talk of often from his work. Tase had, of course, never met this person, but he did hear a lot about him.

Tase assumed he was a partner of his father, and they seemed, obviously, to be close friends.

"Yes I will." Da grinned. "But unfortunately I have to leave a bit early today."

Tase stopped eating, his fork halfway between his plate and his mouth.

"Oh?" Ma said looking at him oddly.

"Yes, I wish I didn't, but there's been a problem at the bank, and my manager has asked me to come in ahead of schedule."

Tase looked at Fadin. He had stopped eating as well.

"How early?" Ma asked, quite concerned.

"I have to leave by ten," their father nodded. "An hour earlier then normal, but there's no need to worry, I'm sure everything will be right as rain in no time."

He smiled broadly and continued eating his patty.

Tase stared wide-eyed at Fadin.

Their father was leaving at ten? An hour ahead of schedule? He was going to see their Aunt Kyna. He was going to see her today.

Ma stood still by Da's side for a moment, then seemed to decide the news was not cause for concern, and sat herself down and began eating her own breakfast.

Tase tried to act normally, but his appetite was gone.

Why was he lying to their mother? Why didn't he tell her he was going to see her sister? Why should he feel the need to hide it from her? What was really going on?

Tase jumped, spilling his juice, as a knock was placed upon the front door.

"Oh, Tase!" Ma cried. "Hurry and clean it up."

He noticed no one had heard the door, so he leapt to his feet and wiped the mess up quickly.

Another knock was placed upon the door and this time everyone turned.

"I'll get it," Fadin yelled.

"So will I," Tase shouted back.

He threw his rag in the sink and attempted to beat Fadin to the door.

It was a sort of game they always played. Who could answer the knocker first? Fadin nearly always won.

Fadin shoved Tase out of the way and held the door open wide.

"Hello," he said with a big smile.

"Good-day," the blond-headed postman said. "Post for you, young sirs."

Fadin snatched the mail up before Tase could even get a peek.

"Thank you, Tom," Fadin smiled.

Tom, the postman, held his hat up to them and briskly walked away.

Fadin closed the door and promptly stuck his tong out at Tase.

Tase smacked him on the back of the head.

"Boys," Ma said warningly.

They stopped their fighting immediately.

Fadin walked back to the table and flipped through the mail.

"Oh," he said, coming across a rather thick envelope. "A letter from Saoirse!"

Tase's heart jumped.

Saoirse, their elder sister, had written to them. She was nineteen years old and away in America for school. It wasn't uncommon for young people to do this before they settled down, especially a young adult as smart and talented as their sister. But she was still terribly missed at home and a letter from her was reason to celebrate in the O'Callaghan house.

"Let me see, let me see!" Ma squealed.

Tase stood on his tip toes and read the front of the envelope.

It said:

*Saoirse M. O'Callaghan*
*2021, Lancaster Avenue*
*New York*
*10029 New York*
*United States*
To:
*Alroy C. O'Callaghan*
*109 Little Hallow Rd.*
*Waterford City*
*Co. Waterford*
*Ireland*

"Oh, I do hope it's good news!" Ma cried.

"Of course it'll be," Da smiled. "Our girl always has good news."

He grabbed up the envelope and tore it open.

"Hold on a second, Teagan," he giggled as their mother made a grab for the letter.

"Oh, just give it to me," she whined.

He held it up high teasingly, and when it looked as though she could stand it no longer, handed it over to her so she could read aloud.

"Dear Ma and Da," she began smiling wide. "How are you? I'm fine. I really like it here in New York but feel rather suffocated sometimes with how many people live here. It's always busy, and there are no rolling Irish hills to set your mind to wander, at least the hills I live by don't.

"I like my job. It's hard but keeps my interest. School is good, challenging but I'm getting all good grades. Speaking of A's how are the boys' grades?

"I am very happy here, but I'm excited to come home on holiday. I will be home for Christmas, and I already have all your presents picked out. Tell the boys not to try and guess, they never will.

"Give Pathos a kiss for me and tell everyone I love them.

"Talk to you soon. Write back A.S.A.P.

"Love you, Saoirse.

"P.S. Thank you for the presents, they made my birthday! And my roommate says hi."

Ma smiled wide and kissed the letter.

"See, great news," Da smiled. "And look, she's sent us some pictures."

He pulled out several photos, which he flicked through, and handed to Tase and Fadin when he was finished.

Tase held them in his hands.

They were of two girls—one with dark, raven, curly hair, like his Ma and piercing green eyes. The other, Saoirse's roommate, had long blonde hair and freckles.

The photos contained his sister and her friend dancing, jumping, laughing, writing, kissing a small black cat, and snorting milk out of their noses. There were also a few pictures of buildings and people sitting on the side of the road with guitars and other musical instruments.

Tase smiled at a photo of his sister making a silly face next to her blonde friend.

She looked like a younger version of Ma, except she was shorter, and on the left side of her neck, where Saoirse was always sure it was visible, lay a paw-shaped birthmark. It was her favorite physical feature about herself, and it was nicknamed her "little wolf mark."

"Looks like they're having a lot of fun. When does she have time for work or school?" Da asked, looking at his watch. "Speaking of work," he kissed their mother. "I have to go."

"Drive carefully," Ma demanded, as he grabbed his coat and walked to the door.

He stopped just before he opened it, and turned to the archway between the kitchen and the living room.

He touched the spot where he and their mother had carved their names into the wood. This was a tradition he always completed before going anywhere.

He muttered something to himself with his hand upon the carving, as he continuously did, and then took one last look at his family.

"I love you all very much. You know that, don't you?"

Tase was a bit startled by the way he said this. Why was he looking at them all like that? Like he was afraid he'd never see them again?

"Of course we do, Alroy," Ma smiled a little weakly.

Tase felt a strange constricting in his chest. He felt like he had to say something, something important to his father before he left. He didn't understand why, but he needed to.

He racked his brain for something important to say, but all he could think of was "We love you too, Da."

It seemed to be important enough.

His father smiled wide, and blinked back what appeared to be tears.

Why was he acting like this?

"I'll see you all after work," he grinned. "Goodbye."

Tase wanted to make him stop, he had a terrible feeling, but he did nothing.

"Goodbye," he whispered back.

And that was it, his father smiled, waved, closed the door, and was gone.

"Alright," Ma said, clapping her hands together and snapping Tase back into reality. "Finish your breakfasts and then it's time to head to school."

As she said this, Pathos jumped upward and grabbed Clearie's patty from the table.

"Pathos," Clearie cried. "No, no, drop it."

But the Bernese had no interest in listening. He dodged all hands that flew toward him and gobbled the patty down within three seconds flat.

"Oh, never mind," Ma shouted. She looked at the clock in the kitchen. "Oh dear, we're going to be late. Hurry up, boys. Go and grab your books, Fadin and Tase. Clearie, feed Pathos and I'll make the lunches. If we hurry, we'll make it in plenty of time."

# Chapter 2

## *The Hooded Woman*

Up in their room, Tase tore apart drawers and curtains, shoes and clothes.

"Where is my darn homework sheet?" he wailed.

Fadin glared at him. "I don't know where your stupid sheet is, but you had better find your books and get your socks on."

Tase muttered a few choice words under his breath and gathered his books from beneath the bed and inside the closet.

"Oh, I need socks and I don't have any clean ones."

Fadin pulled his history book from under his top-bunked mattress and glanced down at Tase.

"Well then put on the ones you were wearing last night."

Tase threw his covers back and dug down deep until he found one of his runaway socks.

"Katy Berry, where's the other one?"

He felt around and looked behind the mattress.

"Where did I . . ."

Tase turned and looked back at his pillow. He snapped his fingers in remembrance. He had forgotten that he had awoken wrong-side-up that morning.

He pulled the pillow up and found not only his sock but his missing homework sheet as well.

"Fadin," he cried. "Look."

Fadin peered at the sheet as he waved it in front of his face.

"You finally found it. It was under your pillow the whole time?"

"Yea," Tase said with a smile. "I forgot I put it under there last night so I wouldn't lose it."

"Lot of good that did you," Fadin said rolling his eyes. "Sometimes Tase, you're about as sharp as a beach ball."

Tase held his fist up. "Why you bloody—"

"Boys, are you almost ready? I don't want to be late," Ma called.

"Yea, coming Ma," they both answered.

Tase blew a raspberry Fadin's way, and hopped out of the door and down the stairs, trying to throw on his shoes and socks.

Their mother was shoving their lunches in their bags just as they entered the kitchen.

"Good," she said, looking up. "Five minutes to spare. Now, if we get right in the car, we'll be there on time.

They opened the front door, reached their car, and were nearly ready to get inside when old Mrs. Cunningham yelled at them from next door.

Tase clamped his eyes shut.

They were going to be late now for sure.

Mrs. Cunningham could talk the leg off a horse and she was heading up the small hill that separated their two houses, ready to, as she called it, "chat."

"Hurry, get in the car, and buckle up," Ma whispered harshly. "I'll just tell her we have to—"

"Teagan dear!" Mrs. Cunningham said loudly. She was up the hill grinning widely and out of breath. "I thought I might," she inhaled loudly, "miss you."

"Well, you know," their mother smiled, "you almost did. I have to get my kids off to school now."

"Oh, that's nice dear," Mrs. Cunningham said brushing the remark aside. "But did you hear that horrible noise last night?"

Tase watched his mother's shoulders sag and her eyes close in hopelessness. "No," she said despairingly. "What noise?"

"That almost scream, darling. Oh my, it gave me a fright, and it was so loud. How could you not have heard it?"

"A scream?" Ma said looking back at the car. She got Tase and his brother's attention and mouthed, "Start fighting in a few minutes. Give me a reason to leave."

Tase and Fadin nodded.

Their mother turned back to old Mrs. Cunningham. "I didn't hear anything last night."

"No?" Mrs. Cunningham said, seemingly shocked. "Well then, did you see the hooded woman running around your yard at all hours of the night?"

Fadin made a circle with his fingers near the side of his head.

Tase laughed silently.

It was a well known fact that Mrs. Cunningham had been in a mental institution a few years back because she had been "seeing" things.

"Mrs. Cunningham," Ma said sounding concerned, "have you taken your medicine lately?"

Mrs. Cunningham gasped and covered her heart with her hand.

"Why, of course I have! How dare you insinuate that I am losing my mind. I take my pills every day, and that woman was not an illusion."

"That isn't what I meant," Ma said. "I know you're not mental, but I certainly didn't see anyone or hear anything last night." She turned and gave Tase the look.

"You eejit." Tase yelled at Fadin with a smile. "Don't you touch my, uh, my, uh—puh-pen. Yea, pen. Get away from my things!"

He playfully shoved Fadin, who laughed aloud and cried.

"You plonker! That pen is mine!"

They began to playfully argue, and anyone with half a mind could see they were putting on a show, but Mrs. Cunningham became instantly worried.

"Oh, Teagan dear," she fussed, "you must control your children. What a sight."

Ma turned to them and smiled. "Yes, I am sorry. I'll deal with them." She walked toward the car, half laughing. "Boys," she yelled. "You are both grounded for a month."

Mrs. Cunningham gasped. "Oh, dear, not too harsh!"

"Oh no," their mother said turning to her, "they must be punished." She smiled back at Tase and Fadin and pointed to the door. "Shut the door, face forward, and no talking."

Tase tried desperately to suppress a laugh.

"Y-yes ma." Fadin said pretending to cry.

He closed the door and covered his mouth, for the giggles would not stop.

"I am sorry, Mrs. Cunningham, but I must take them to school. I'll see you later."

"Wait, Teagan dear."

But their mother already shut the door. "I hope everyone's buckled," she cried, and sped out of the driveway.

They all giggled most of the way to school until Tase realized they were going to be quite late. He began to get nervous, and watched as Clearie nearly lost his mind fretting over getting caught, and his grade point average being affected.

"I can't let being tardy affect my perfect report card, I just can't."

Tase watched Fadin roll his eyes. He couldn't have cared less.

~~~

As they pulled up to their school, Ardan Secondary, Ma blew them all a kiss and nearly shoved them out of the door.

"Sorry for being late. If you do get into trouble, please tell Headmaster Walsh to call me. This one wasn't your fault, but Fadin," she looked hard at him, "don't be a problem."

Fadin flung his hands in the air but she already had begun to drive off.

"It's always me," Fadin complained.

Tase mustered up a smile, but inside he felt quite nervous about Headmaster Walsh noticing their tardiness. All he could do, however, was be calm, wait, and hope that the Headmaster wouldn't see them strolling in.

Fadin walked ahead, and pushed both the swinging front doors open.

Tase watched Clearie give him a nasty look. "Why don't you just go on the loudspeaker and announce that we're late, huh?"

Fadin looked back at him. "Oh dry up you whiny maggot. There's no one here."

"Really?" the familiar voice said from behind them.

Tase swallowed hard. He turned around and felt his heart skip a beat, as he was faced with the large and terrible form of Headmaster Walsh.

He was a rather short and rotund man in general with a balding head as well as a small white goatee and mustache. But he had the cruelest eyes Tase had ever seen, and he was sure that all the children in his school felt their icy glare.

Though Walsh could really be no taller then his father, Tase realized, it felt to him like he was three meters high, armed with the deadliest weapon known to man. The way he carried and conducted himself made you feel like you were no bigger then an ant. And when he locked you with those dreadful, chilly eyes, you felt like you would rather sink into the floor and vanish from existence than stand before him and be judged.

Tase could hear his heart pounding deep inside his ears as he looked up into Walsh's furious face.

"Three O'Callaghan boys," said the headmaster in his low grumble. "What a surprise this is."

Tase gulped again, and tried to stop himself from shaking. He would rather get a week full of detention than have to stand in front of this man for one more second.

Tase had heard the stories in the lunch hall and recess before. Horrendous tall tales of children getting locked in small rooms lined with nails, being hung upside-down by their toes for hours, and getting fed canfuls of motor oil in Walsh's early days. He had apparently had a very bad temper when he was younger, and no one would oppose him for fear of what he would do to them.

Tase knew these were just stories, but standing in front of him now, looking into his horrid eyes, he had to wonder.

"Oh right," Fadin whispered in Tase's ear, "I'm sure it is since we've been so early these last two weeks."

Tase snapped his head in Fadin's direction and stared at him, aghast.

Did he want to get locked in a room filled with nails?

"Want to say something, Fadin?" asked the headmaster as he bounced on the balls of his toes.

Tase clenched his hands into fists and tried to will Fadin not to be a smart aleck.

"Don't say something dense, don't say something dense, don't say something dense," he whispered to himself.

"No, sir," Fadin answered, sneaking a meaningful glance at Tase.

Tase exhaled the breath he had been holding.

"Oh, good because you already have after-school activities and I'd hate to add onto the list." Headmaster Walsh said.

"Katty Barry," Fadin grumbled under his breath.

Clearie knocked him in the shoulder.

"We are sorry sir," Clearie said in his most sincere voice. "Our mother said you could call her, it wasn't our fault."

"As true as that may be, I cannot allow this tardiness to go unpunished, this is the third time this month, you realize, and we are only in the second week."

Clearie nodded and stepped on Tase's foot, causing him to nod too.

"Well," Headmaster Walsh said, circling the three boys, "Why don't you all go to your classes, which have already started," he added sounding annoyed, "and then all three of you meet me in my office after school." He locked all of them with one last evil stare. "We can then discuss your punishment for your repetitive tardiness."

Tase and the others nodded, Fadin with the most difficulty.

The Headmaster raised his finger, and pointed it at them warningly. He nodded, satisfied with himself, and then turned on his heels and walked down the hall.

As soon as he was gone, Fadin burst. "What a thick, lousy eejit. He lives for this kind of thing you know."

"Will you shut your gob?" Clearie shouted through clenched teeth. "You are amazingly uncaring about anyone or anything but yourself. Some of us have reputations and grades to keep up without any help from you."

"Oh, give it a rest will you, bookworm? Not all of us are obsessed with school like you are."

"You'd be smart to take a lesson or two from me. I'm not the one with almost all bad marks, am I?"

"No," Fadin answered smiling at Tase. "But we're not the ones wasting away behind dusty old pages not having any fun either."

Clearie lifted his English book high but Tase yanked it away.

"All right that's enough," Tase cried looking from one to the other. "Now let's just get into class before we get into any more trouble."

"You're on his side?" Fadin asked, mouth wide open.

"Of course I'm not. I don't care much about school, but I do care about having to be here all night long because the two of you got into a stupid fight. We survived our meeting with the headmaster, so please, let's just get to class before he comes back."

Fadin and Clearie exchanged menacing glances before finally agreeing.

"I need my book," Clearie said coolly.

"Catch," Tase said, flinging it at him.

Clearie caught the book, took one last look at the two of them, and briskly walked away.

~~~

Mr. Donovan's lazy voice carried on for what seemed like hours.

Tase stared out of the window into the courtyard and completely blocked out of the mathematics lesson. He didn't particularly care about the square root of something or another or that 'x' stands for this or that. He didn't like maths, in fact he didn't like school. Half the things he learned he figured he'd never use, except for what he learned in English. He enjoyed writing very much, it was the best part of the whole day, unfortunately the day was just beginning, and he still had three more classes before he got to enjoy anything.

The day had not been a very successful one so far. What with finding that odd letter from Aunt Kyna, and getting into trouble with Headmaster Walsh. At least he hadn't gotten punished for losing his homework.

He handed his mathematics page to Mr. Donovan, a rather tall, skinny, dreary-looking man, about the age of fifty, with big thick eyebrows and a mustache that he always fiddled with. He nodded, which meant his work was not "F" material. At the very worst he would get a "C," so the day was not completely lost.

He peered two desks over and spotted Fadin.

He appeared to be taking notes, but Tase knew better. He was probably just scribbling a picture of his favorite football team.

Fadin hated school even more then Tase did. He felt that it was a complete waste of his day and counted the seconds until it was all over.

"O'Callaghan," said Mr. Donovan, directing his scolding at Fadin. "Are you paying attention?"

As the two of them were always getting mixed up, most of their teachers just said their last name and looked at the one they were addressing.

Fadin glanced up.

"Yes sir," he lied.

Mr. Donovan looked at him over his half-moon spectacles. "Really?"

Mr. Donovan may have been a substitute but Tase knew he was no fool. He had been teaching their class for nearly six-and-a-half months now. Six months at the end of last year and the first two weeks of this year.

He had seen Fadin's concentration and work and he knew good and well that he was not paying attention.

"Well then, perhaps you would like to come up here and show me how to solve this problem. Huh?"

He stared at Fadin and nodded to the blackboard.

Fadin hid his rolling blue-green eyes and went reluctantly up to the front of the class. He glanced at the problem, took the chalk sarcastically in his hands, and began writing.

In only a few seconds he was done.

Mr. Donovan pushed his glasses up his rather large nose, combed back his long, graying hair, and looked over the problem.

He turned quite stunned to Fadin. His eyes were wide and his mouth was open. He re-read the problem and solved it himself several times before stating in a voice full of confusion, "Cor—correct."

He nodded to Fadin's empty chair and began fingering his moustache.

Fadin slid a smile to Tase before nestling in his desk and again picking up his pencil.

This demonstration didn't surprise Tase at all. In fact, he was surprised he didn't show off more.

Fadin was rather smart in maths and science; he just didn't care enough to get good grades. Actually Fadin was good at almost everything. He was a fair football player, he understood history, he could do a maths problem in a matter of seconds, and he was an expert at making the Headmaster angry.

Tase had to turn away at this thought so that he didn't laugh at the picture of Mr. Walsh's furious purple face that came to mind.

He again took up looking out of the window and thinking about the letter from Aunt Kyna.

Why would she have written, their Da? Why was he lying to their mother about it? And why had he acted so oddly this morning?

His concentration was broken as a bird flew by the window with a twig in its beak. A butterfly perched on a flower near the tree where it had landed and fluttered lazily. A small woman, with bright red hair, stood in the middle of the courtyard, cloaked in a black wrap, and a spider began spinning its web near the top of the classroom…

Tase paused. A woman in a black cloak?

He stared. There she was; he hadn't imagined it.

Standing not one-and-a-half meters from him was a bright-red-headed, hooded woman.

She just stood there still.

Tase wondered if she was sick or hurt.

Then the woman lifted a white bony finger and pointed it directly at him.

The noise that came next was unlike any Tase had ever heard. It was a deafening high-pitched scream.

The windows and all the glass in the classroom shattered. The students leaped from their desks and tried in vain to block out the horrid sound.

Mr. Donovan fell backward in his chair and huddled under his own desk.

As abruptly as it had started, the noise suddenly stopped.

"What was that?" Derry Dillon, a rather round, dark-skinned, freckly boy asked.

"I don't know," said Iona Roche. "What do you reckon Mr. Donovan?"

Mr. Donovan had gone pure white. His hands were still clamped over his ears and he was staring dreamily at his class.

"W-what?" he asked, coming out of the daze and staring at Iona.

"What do you think that was, Sir?" she asked, looking at him hopefully.

He stared out at the place where the window had been. He looked horrified and yet strangely understanding.

His expression made Tase nervous.

"I—I don't know," he said finally. "We need to go," he stammered. "Yes, that's what we need to do, go. Come along class, follow me into the hall."

Tase was pushed along with the crowd of students as they all tried to make their way out of the door.

He looked for Fadin but did not see him. Tase figured he was already out in the hall. After they all squeezed themselves out of the tiny classroom, Tase found him.

"What do you think made that awful…" he began.

But Fadin stopped him.

"There's no one else here," he said dumfounded.

Tase looked around.

He was right. All the other class doors were still shut.

Tase moved through the other students and pushed his face up against a classroom window. "They're all sitting there like nothing's happened," he said to Fadin.

Mr. Donovan was whiter than ever. He kept mumbling under his breath, fiddled with his moustache, and cleaned his glasses over and over.

Tase heard the sound of footsteps and Clearie came bounding around the corner.

"You heard it too?" he asked, staring at his brothers as well as the confused class.

"Yea," Fadin said. "What do you suppose it was?"

"I don't know," he said, eyeing Mr. Donovan."But all the other classes haven't seemed to notice." He paused, staring at the classrooms. "All the windows and glass in our room shattered."

"Ours did too," Fadin nodded.

"Attention," the speakers in the hall suddenly boomed.

Tase recognized the voice of Headmaster Walsh.

"Would Clearie, Fadin, and Tase O'Callaghan, please report to my office… immediately!"

The boys exchanged puzzled looks.

"Maybe he heard it too?" Fadin suggested.

"I don't know," Clearie answered. "But we'd better find out what he wants."

Tase took one last look at Mr. Donovan, who still seemed incoherent, and turned to catch up with his brothers.

~~~

As they entered the cold, nicely kept office, Tase saw his mother sitting hunched in the Headmaster's chair.

He was startled to see her. Whatever they had done couldn't be bad enough to have her here.

Then she turned to them and he saw that she had been crying.

A horrible feeling crept up Tase's spine, stinging him in the stomach and the heart. He thought he knew what was coming, but he couldn't believe it, he wouldn't.

He watched as his mother stood. Her legs wobbled beneath her and a handkerchief fell from her lap. She looked at them with waterlogged blue eyes, eyes that had a horrifying truth in them, a truth Tase would not accept.

"Boys," she said in a voice that Tase had never heard before.

He felt like screaming out, begging her to stop. But he could say and do nothing, he was powerless to stop the news he knew was coming.

"Something, something terrible has happened," she said in a gasp of pain.

Tase closed his eyes, he wanted it all to go away, he didn't want to know.

"Your father," she sobbed.

Tase began chanting inside his head, "No, no, no."

"Your father is—" she broke down in a sob and then gasped for air and willed herself to speak. "Your father is, he's, well he's—dead. Boys, your father was in an auto accident. A head-on collision, and he's gone, he's just gone!" She broke down into horrible sobs and fell to the floor.

Headmaster Walsh ran over to her and tried to comfort her with a softness Tase had never seen.

But Tase did not run to her. He stood there, still and lifeless. He felt as though the bottom had dropped out of his world and he no longer knew his place in it.

This couldn't be real, it just couldn't. Things like this didn't happen to him, to his family. This had to be a dream, a horrible nightmare. But as he watched his mother bawl and weep, and stared as Clearie and Headmaster Walsh tried to help her stand as her legs shook and would not hold her up, he realized it was not a dream.

Why hadn't he stopped his father from leaving that morning? Why had his father lied to him? To all of them? Did he ever actually know who his father was? Could this actually be happening?

Tase felt like the room was spinning and that he was going to be sick. This was indeed real and his father was gone, gone forever. He was never going to see him again. Never.

# Chapter 3

## *Funerals, Cars, and Castles*

The visitation was long and terrible, and the day of the funeral was even worse.

Buckets-full of meaningless people telling you how sorry they are, and how bad they feel.

Tase knew they meant well, but their words were empty. They meant nothing.

The person who had really helped them the most was old Mrs. Cunningham. She had helped set up the funeral, picked out the casket, flowers, and called up everyone who could attend. And because they were short on funds, she insisted that she pay for it all.

Ma did not have much in her to argue, so she gave into their neighbour relatively quickly, and Mrs. Cunningham had handled everything.

When they returned home from the burial, four days after their father had died, all Tase wanted to do was curl up in bed and let the world go on without him, but he knew he couldn't. His mother needed him too much.

He and his brothers were all she had now because Saoirse couldn't come back from America. She hadn't enough money.

And so that was that. They were alone with Ma. Her only comfort.

Tase had never seen her sad like this before. It was even hard for her to catch her breath without bursting into tears.

Over the past few days she would just stay in bed till noon only getting up to help make them lunch and dinner, if she could even will herself to do that.

Most days Mrs. Cunningham brought food over for them, which was very much appreciated, since Ma's cooking abilities had very much deteriorated.

As they entered the house, Pathos jumped up to greet them.

He wagged his tail and pawed at their legs. When they closed the door, he still sat there waiting.

"He's not coming home, boy," Clearie told him in a raspy voice.

Tase could tell he was fighting back tears.

His blue eye looked more glossy than usual.

Tase stopped at the spot where his father had carved his name in the door. He stroked it, and looked around the house.

It felt so empty without him in it. So...not like home.

He inhaled deeply at the thought of the terrible car crash that had claimed his life.

It had been a freak accident, apparently.

There had been a policeman, or as his father had called them, a garda, at the scene when the accident had occurred. He told their mother what happened when she had arrived.

"The car just hit what appeared to be an invisible wall, or bump, or something," he had said. "It was the craziest thing I'd ever seen ma'am, the most extraordinary thing. Then the car simply flipped and was hurtled nearly three meters in the air, then the gas tank caught fire and—"

That was the end of his explanation, the other garda at the scene had shut him up for being so insensitive.

It was strange all right, Tase couldn't deny that. He didn't understand how a car could simply flip over of its own accord, or be thrown three meters high. But the oddest thing about the whole incident, at least in Tase's mind, was how his mother had been at the exact spot where the accident had occurred five minutes after the car had overturned.

No one had called her, no one had identified his father's body, and the garda who had been notified of the accident hadn't even shown up yet. But his mother was there, screaming and crying and trying to pull his father from the burning vehicle.

Tase had wanted to ask her how she had known, how she had gotten there so fast, but she was so fragile now, he didn't want to upset her, so he had let things be for now.

"You want anything, Ma?" Tase asked, now watching her nervously.

She just shook her head and collapsed on the couch.

Fadin sat by her feet and helped pull off her shoes. "Do you want me to go grab it for you?" he asked, trying his best to keep a brave face.

She nodded, fingering their father's Claddagh Ring on her thumb.

Fadin ran up the stairs and in a few moments returned with their father's jacket. He handed it to her and she clutched it tight.

Tase saw her breathe it in as fresh tears streamed down the side of her face.

She stroked the sleeves and straightened the collar. "I miss him so much," she said, again taking in the jacket's smell.

All three boys came to sit by the couch.

Tase crouched on the floor near the jacket.

Clearie sat by her head and stroked her hair.

"We all do, Ma," he said. This time, Clearie could not stop the tears from coming.

Pathos came and put his head on her lap.

She stroked his ears and sat up.

"There's something I need to talk to you boys about," she said wiping away the drops on her cheeks and clutching the jacket to her chest.

Fadin nodded, moved closer, and twirled his fingers in her black curls.

"You know that I didn't work," Ma said, swallowing hard, "I stayed home and took care of the house and you. Your Da was the one who always provided the money for us."

They all nodded.

Tase could guess where this was going.

"Well, I have to get a job now, but the jobs I can get don't pay as much as your Da's did," she paused and suppressed a sob. "So, we can't afford this house anymore."

Tase swallowed hard. He had been right. He knew that they hadn't been poor when their father was alive, but they weren't rolling around in money either. They had depended upon their father's weekly pay, and without it there would be no more water, electricity, clothes, shoes, food, house, there would be no more anything.

"Didn't Da have money saved?" Clearie asked.

"Some," she said looking down at the jacket, "but not enough."

Fadin stared at her. "What are we going to do then?"

Tase glanced first at Fadin, nodded, then turned his attention to his mother.

That was a good question. A question Tase really could not see the answer to. Unless of course they wanted to move into Old Mrs. Cunningham's, whom he was sure would not object, yet whose house smelt powerfully of mothballs.

Ma looked up at Fadin. "I've had a talk with your Aunt Kyna."

Tase nearly felt his heart stop.

He snuck a meaningful look at Fadin, who responded with furrowed brows.

Aunt Kyna. So she had called her sister. How strange that after all these years, their mother had finally gotten in contact with her not a week after their father had died. Not to mention that before he left for work the morning of the accident, he had received that odd letter from their aunt. Was this just a coincidence? Did that letter have anything to do with their father's accident? Or did all this have more meaning? Was there more to this story than met the eye? Tase seriously thought there was. And then, there was that cloaked red-headed woman. Who had she been? And why had she screamed at him? Didn't Old Mrs. Cunningham say something about seeing a cloaked woman the night before?

Tase swallowed hard, and shook his head of the troubling thoughts. He needed to focus on here and now. There would be plenty of time for questions later.

"Rich, Aunt Kyna?" Fadin asked, playing it off as though this was all he knew of her.

"She isn't rich," Ma answered, sounding slightly aggravated.

Tase blinked. He couldn't figure out why she should be angry about this, but now that he thought about it, Ma had talked about her being wealthy quite a bit, whenever Kyna was brought up in private conversations. She had always seemed aggravated at this point. Was it because she was jealous that her sister was rich while she lived in a normal little house in a normal little neighbourhood? Tase decided that had to be the reason.

Fadin cocked his head and looked up with his blue-green eyes, as if he were pondering a very confusing fact. "She does live in a castle, doesn't she?"

"Yes, she does, but she isn't rich. The castle belonged to her husband and he left it to her when he died, along with all of his possessions. *She*,"

Ma emphasized the she, "on the other hand, is anything but rich."

Tase gulped. Ma seemed quite hostile. He wondered how well this talk could have possibly gone between his aunt and Ma.

"So she lives in a castle but she isn't wealthy?" Fadin asked. "Sure," he paused and shrugged sarcastically, "makes sense."

Tase gaped at him, and ran a hand through his own light-red hair. Sometimes Fadin didn't know when to shut his fat gob.

Their mother gave him a serious and stern look. "Just because someone owns a castle doesn't mean they have money. Your Aunt Kyna doesn't. The money is all tied up in the house. If she wanted to, she could sell it, but she won't, so therefore she doesn't have piles and piles of money lying around like I know you think she does. She has to work and live just like everyone else. But she has offered for us to come and stay with her for awhile, and I agreed."

Tase knew his mouth fell open. Go and live with Aunt Kyna? The aunt they didn't know? Really? Was this the best idea? Ma really didn't seem too happy with her at the moment. Could they really all live under the same roof as her? And what about their school? Their friends? Not that they really had any great ones, but still. Move somewhere they knew no one?

Tase wasn't so sure he liked this idea.

"I know it will be a big change," Ma said, shaking her curly, raven head, "and that it's a bit far, but we don't have a lot of options at the moment."

Tase nodded. That was true. It was either Aunt Kyna's castle or mothball Mrs. Cunningham's.

Clearie looked down thoughtfully and asked, "How long will she let us stay?"

"As long as we want," Ma said. "She lives alone except for a cook and butler."

"You mean her servants," Fadin replied.

Tase gave him a stupid look. Why did he always pick times like this to be obstinate and, well, a bloody eejit?

Tase studied his face better and saw that it had gone quite red.

Fadin was angry, not at Ma, but at everything. He was angry about leaving, about Da dying, about all the unanswered questions, and about the fact that it seemed Da had lied to them and kept secrets. Tase could almost hear the emotions pouring out of him.

Truthfully, Tase was upset too, but he knew his Ma was right and she needed them right now. They should not be sarcastic and problematic, but supportive and helpful.

Fadin was being neither, though Tase understood why.

"I don't need you to be difficult, Fadin Michael O'Callaghan," Ma said irritably.

She always used their full names when she was extremely upset. This is hard for everyone," she finished.

There was a long pause.

Tase looked from one to the other, waiting for Fadin to say something.

Apologize Fadin, Tase pleaded in his head. Just say you're sorry.

"I'm sorry," Fadin finally responded.

Tase didn't think he looked so in the slightest.

Ma acknowledged the apology, such as it was, with a smile. "Well, now that we know where we're going, I think we should start getting things ready for packing."

"Now?" said all three in unison.

Ma nodded. "We only have a few weeks," she said, looking around regretfully. "Someone has already purchased the house and they want this thing done as soon as possible."

Tase let his mouth hang low. What?

He looked at Fadin who gaped back.

This didn't make any sense. He hadn't seen a sign up, or people come and look at the house. How could it be sold? How in the world could a house be put up for sale and four days later be bought by someone? It wasn't possible. Besides, houses didn't sell that fast anyway. And when was it she had talked to Aunt Kyna? Didn't he see her on the phone yesterday? She had made and had no other calls since then, at least none he had been privy to.

"I know it's fast, but the family fell in love with the house and they are very excited about it. So we have to move out quickly."

"When in the world did you have time to put the house up for sale?" Clearie asked.

"Oh," Ma seemed to be covering something, "I already knew someone who was interested in buying it." She stood and looked about the room. "A friend of mine actually had been telling me for awhile how much she loved the house, and that if we ever decided to sell, she'd buy it in a heartbeat."

That sounded awfully fishy to Tase. A friend bought the house? And this friend had talked about wanting the house for a long time? Odd, to say the least. Besides, his Ma didn't have too many friends, and he had never heard anyone she had talked about wanting the house.

"What friend does she have?" Fadin whispered.

Tase shrugged.

"So," she said, walking over to their father's name carved into the wood, "it's time to box it up, move on, and start over."

She became very quiet, and stroked the carving. She muttered something under her breath as her and Da had always done. Tears begun to tumble down her cheeks.

Tase got up to hug her, but stopped as she started speaking quietly to their father's carved name.

"It's been too long, far too long, Alroy. We can't run anymore, there's nowhere else to go. It's time—time to go back."

Tase felt his heart jump. What?

"Back?" Tase asked, watching her closely.

"I said pack," she answered, wiping away her tears and turning to look at her children. "Yes, time to pack."

Tase looked at Fadin.

Fadin shook his head and arched an eyebrow.

Why did Tase have the funny feeling their mother wasn't telling them everything? Was she, too, keeping secrets? What was she talking about, can't run anymore? When had they ran? Why would they need to? Did he really not know his parents like he thought he did?

He shuddered at the answer he did not want to hear. The answer that kept popping in front of eyes, like fireworks in July. *You don't know anything,* it said.

Ma clapped her hands together, causing Tase to jump, startled out of self-conversation.

"So let's get started, shall we?" Ma said. "I think the first thing we should do is get boxes."

~~~

Fadin rushed inside the house for one more bathroom break before he and his family hit the road.

He ran through the empty living room and up the stairs that creaked loudly and echoed through the now very empty house.

It really didn't feel much like home anymore, now that everything was packed.

It had taken them four weeks to get everything done. It really shouldn't have taken that long, but Ma was so down that they often only worked half days and then sat all together in her bed, eating the sweets that Mrs. Cunningham brought over, watching Da's favorite movies and TV shows.

They had bought box after packing-box, filled each one to the brim, and still had quite a few belongings left over.

Ma had gone through every one of their possessions, and had given away all the unimportant stuff, like furniture and old clothes. Then she had made them all clean the entire house, top to bottom, which Fadin had hated.

When all that was said and done, they stuffed their van as full as it could be stuffed and prepared for the trip to Aunt Kyna's castle.

It was a few hours away, which is why Fadin was running down the hall to the toilet.

Ma had made him "go back inside and try," because it was a far trip and they wouldn't be stopping.

He went inside the bathroom, relieved himself, flushed the toilet, forgot to wash his hands, and tromped back out into the hall.

He began to run toward the stairs when he suddenly stopped for no apparent reason. His feet wouldn't move. His legs wouldn't budge. He was stuck.

He turned his head slowly and saw that his father's office was next to him. No wonder he was stuck, he hadn't been in there since the day Da died.

The door was closed, and he knew that inside it, there was nothing but the old desk they hadn't been able to take. All of his paperwork and other important things had been removed by Ma and put in a special box she kept with her at all times.

He knew he should just go down the stairs and meet his family in the van, but he couldn't. Part of him had to go into that office. He had to see it one last time before they left. It was part of his Da, the place he had spent most of his time in this house.

He swallowed hard and moved towards the door. He turned the handle and pushed it open.

The familiar scent of his father rushed up to meet him. The smell of paper, the morning, and cologne—like a crisp letter.

He breathed in deeply as memories flooded into his mind. Memories of laughter, silliness, feeling safe, and being home. He hadn't felt any of those things since the accident.

He walked inside the now big-looking room. The wooden desk sat lonely in the clean emptiness. A sad reminder of how the office used to be.

Fadin walked up to the desk and caressed it.

How many times had he come home from school and ran up to this office? How many times had he seen his father smiling at this desk? He had always known that he could find him here. Always known that he'd be here smiling. But no more.

There would never again be any, "How was your day at school, son?" or "Come on Fay, let's drive to our fishing spot."

Da was dead, he was gone. He had left them—him. He had left Fadin all alone. He had abandoned him, and done so without answering any of his questions. Questions about things Da had been hiding, like that letter. What had he been keeping that letter hidden for anyway? Why had he lied? Because he was a Liar, that's why. A capital L—I—A—R—liar. And Fadin didn't think he could ever forgive him for that.

There was a sudden shining from the floor that caught Fadin's eye.

He squinted in its direction.

The light was coming from inside the floor air vent. He bent down and peered into the vent. Whatever it was, it was catching the sunlight perfectly, and sending a beautiful glow in all directions.

Fadin stood up and looked about the room.

There had to be something left he could use to get it out.

He spotted something silver in the top drawer of his father's desk. He opened the drawer and saw a letter opener.

*Perfect.* He thought.

Fadin grabbed it and moved back to the vent. He slid the silver opener down through the holes in the grid. He tried over and over until he finally slipped the end through some part of the glowing thing, and slowly brought it up.

When it was in reach, he grabbed it and looked at it closely.

It was his father's golden crest. The crest he and Tase had found the day of the accident. That's where it had gone to. It had rolled on the floor and fallen into the ventilation shaft.

Fadin turned it over in his hands and traced the small letters carved in gold, D.A. He wondered what that meant. D. A., what could that possibly stand for? Doughnut Army? Dark Amphibian? Daft Apples?

Fadin jumped as his mother honked the car's horn.

He had taken too long.

"Alright, Ma. I'm coming," he muttered.

He stuffed the crest inside his trousers pocket and dashed down the stairs.

At the door, he stopped and stroked the carving of his father's name. "It's not really home anymore," he said. He began to turn and leave when something caught his eye. There was a word inscribed beneath his father's name, a word he had never remembered seeing there before.

X-O-O-R.

Fadin blinked. What did that mean? He tapped the wall and found, to his surprise, that it was hollow.

Ma honked again.

"Okay, I'm coming," Fadin grumbled. He looked at the wall and decided it was nothing, just some wiring for the house, that was all, a hollow spot for electrical purposes.

Fadin took one last look at the house and with yet another honk, ran out to meet Ma, closing the front door one last time.

~~~

The car bounced and Fadin hit his head on the windshield.

He sat up and rubbed it gingerly.

*So much for trying to sleep.*

He arched his back and stretched his legs forward a bit. He felt like he was getting a cramp in his legs, and the right one had begun to tingle.

Fadin grabbed his leg and patted it over and over, while looking out of the window.

He checked for signs of progress, to see if it looked as though they had gotten any further since he had closed his eyes.

*Nope.*

It appeared as though they hadn't moved at all. There was nothing but trees and rolling green hills, basking in the September sun, which was bright, but not warm, with a slight drizzle of rain.

The cold was already starting to set in, cold and rain. Summer was dying and the autumn was ready to take over. When the short autumn ended, along would come winter. Not that there was really all that much difference between fall and winter. Not in Ireland anyway. Just clouds and rain, and more clouds and more rain.

Fadin had heard Saoirse talk about the autumn in New York. Hundreds of trees turning colours, making it all look like magic, and then the snow that covered everything in the winter. She said the white made everything look so different, and that Christmas wasn't really Christmas without snow.

Fadin had never seen snow, well perhaps once, when he wasn't big enough to remember it. Snow rarely fell in Ireland, even a sprinkle would cause panic among the adults. They did not like to drive in it.

Oh, it got cold in the winter, yes, in fact it was cold for the majority of the year. It never got much over 20° C in June and July, and the coldest months were January and February, which didn't go much below 0°C. There were the rare freezing spells, but it was mostly rain, always rain.

Fadin turned his head away from the window. It was depressing looking at the same view over and over. It felt like they still had an eternity to go.

He looked over at Clearie.

He had his nose buried in a book as usual. That was all he ever did or talked about, books and school. It wasn't like there were other important things to do with your time, like actually live.

Fadin did not understand his older brother in the slightest, and he honestly did not want to. If Clearie wanted to live in the pages of his smelly old books, then he would let him.

Besides, he had Tase.

Fadin pretended to have an itch on his shoulder, and glanced at his twin sitting in the back seat.

Tase was sitting silently, peering out of the window with his light blue eyes. His fingers were swaying, as if he were listening to some kind of tune in his head.

Fadin saw Tase notice him looking back, but he pretended not to see, and instead twisted his finger in his red hair, as he did often from force of habit.

Even without the sideways glance, Fadin would have known Tase had seen him. They had the ability to read each other very well, and sometimes, even feel what the other was feeling or hear what they were thinking. But those occasions had been rare.

Tase continued to look out of the window, not giving Fadin an ounce of his attention.

So Fadin turned forward again, now upset and confused.

Tase had been acting odd lately. In fact, he had been acting odd since their father had died.

Not that Fadin blamed him.

Their Da dying had been the worst thing either of them had ever gone through.

It had been, and was, very hard on Fadin. He loved his father, and wished he were back, but he was also angry with him. And Fadin allowed that anger to help the sadness go away.

But Tase did not have that ability. He was the softer one, always had been. He seemed to feel things more deeply, and he was most definitely feeling this deeper then Fadin did. He seemed to be nearly consumed by it, and it was affecting everything.

Tase had not been eating well, Fadin had noticed. He hardly touched his meals, which he used to scarf down. He had not been wanting to wake up in the mornings, instead he just wanted to stay in bed all day.

Fadin had made him wake up each sun-up, jumping on his head or legs.

Tase would say, "I'm up, I'm up already."

But Fadin seriously wondered if Tase would have gotten up, if it hadn't been for him.

And then there were the nightmares.

Tase had been having horrible dreams lately. He would call out in the middle of the night, kick the walls, throw his blankets off, and scream hysterically.

Fadin had awoken him from these terrors on more than one occasion, begging him to tell what the dream had been about.

Tase would just stare at him with those terrified blue eyes and say, "Nothing, it was nothing. Just a nightmare is all."

But they were more than just nightmares.

Fadin had heard him call out their Da's name, and beg some woman to get away from him.

Fadin didn't know what his dreams meant, or what they were all about, but the day after these nightmares, Tase was always cold and cool with him, and Fadin could not understand why.

He tried over and over to talk with his twin, but Tase refused to fess up. He was not going to let Fadin in on the truth. And that worried Fadin.

In all honesty he was afraid for Tase, but his pride nearly always got in the way, and he knew it.

*Well,* Fadin thought, *if he's going to treat me like I don't matter then I'll treat him like he doesn't matter.*

But that idea had only made things worse.

Now they weren't talking at all, and Tase was pretending like Fadin didn't exist. This not only made Fadin angry, but more concerned and confused than ever. He seriously wondered if Tase was going to be okay.

He had to be okay. He would be.

Fadin squirmed in his seat, trying to get comfortable, and turned to look out of his window again.

He wondered how much longer they had to go. It seemed like they had been driving for hours.

He moved around again. He felt that his left leg had also fallen asleep, and it began to tingle all the way up to his thigh.

Fadin stretched his legs straight out in front of him, careful not to hit the head of Pathos just below, and turned from side to side trying to crack his back.

"Don't do that," Clearie almost shouted.

Fadin turned and looked over at him. "What?"

"You know I can't stand that sound," he whined.

Fadin smiled.

Clearie's abnormally large ears, which he hid under his longer blond hair, were very sensitive to sound. He could hear things from very far away, and sometimes, things no one else could.

For example, when they were pulling away from the driveway that morning, Clearie said he heard an odd clicking sound as the car started. Ma ignored him, for he was always hearing odd things. But as they pulled out, a large and very fat rat ran out from underneath the car. It had a strip of red wire wedged in its teeth.

Ma had gotten out, making sure the car was okay. It had been. But how Clearie had heard the rat gnawing could not be explained. And Ma did not push the issue.

Now, sitting in front of a cringing Clearie, Fadin couldn't resist.

"Oh, you mean this?" he asked, and turned quite far to the right. His back made a horrible crackly noise.

Clearie's purple eye twitched. "I said don't."

Fadin cracked his knuckles.

"Stop."

He turned his neck in a big circle.

"I said stop."

He took his shoe off and yanked his toes one by one.

"Fadin!"

"THAT'S ENOUGH!"

Fadin felt himself flung forward and the seatbelt strap nearly choked him.

Ma had slammed on the brakes and was now completely turned around staring at them.

Fadin gulped and shrunk down in his seat. He had gone too far.

"Both of you stop fighting this instant," Ma yelled. Her blue eyes were wide and fiery, and her black curls bounced with each shake of her head. "You two know that all four of us are stuck in this little car and every noise and yell hits like a ton of bricks. We have *all* been in this car for a long time, and the two of you are not the only people who are tired of sitting in one spot. This is your only warning. Fight again and so help me, I'm not even going to turn my head around."

Fadin did not need an explanation.

Their mother had never been one to hit them but he didn't put it past her in this state.

Ma sat forward, and began to start the car up again. She suddenly stopped, and leaned forward.

"Are you okay, Ma?" Clearie asked.

"Fine," she answered.

Fadin didn't think she looked fine. Her face had gone quite pale.

Clearie leaned forward to look at her. "Ma?"

She held her hand up to indicate for them to hold on. She put her hand to her mouth and opened up the car door.

Fadin saw her body heave, heard her gagging, and the sound of something liquid hit the asphalt.

Fadin crinkled his nose. The smell was awful, sour and rotten.

Ma sat up and grabbed a tissue from her purse. She wiped her mouth and sat still for a moment, gathering herself.

Fadin watched her tensely.

She had been sick like this since Da had died. She would go into the bathroom often, and Fadin could hear what she was doing.

He hoped it was just the flu, but it had lasted a long while.

Ma let out a deep sigh, straightened her mirror and began to drive again.

Fadin watched her a moment, and when he was sure she was alright, turned to the side and looked out of the window.

He should have known better then to pick a fight, but this drive was taking forever.

He knocked his head on the window trying to think of a way to amuse himself. He heard Pathos snore as he lay on the floor beneath his feet. He looked down and gave the Bernese a pat on the head.

Pathos looked up, yawned, and snuggled back onto the floor mat.

Fadin sighed. He fiddled with his fingers and thought of as many songs as he could. He hummed them quietly to himself, trying to do anything to make the trip seem less boring.

He turned to look at Tase again.

He had stopped looking out of the window and was now reading a book.

Fadin furrowed his brows.

A book? He would rather die of boredom then read a book.

He whispered to Tase. "Ma was really angry, huh?"

Tase didn't even look up. "You shouldn't have picked a fight. That was stupid."

Fadin stared at him for a minute and then plopped himself forward.

Tase had never taken their mother's side over his. In fact Tase had always supported him even when Fadin could tell he didn't agree.

Fadin leaned his head on the armrest.

He felt hurt and more confused. What had made Tase treat him this way? They had of course fought before, but they were always little fights and they made up the same day. This, however, was different. Something had to be very wrong. He just couldn't figure out what it was.

Did Tase want him to figure it out? If so, how did he expect him to do so when he wouldn't even talk to him? He couldn't read minds. Well, he could hear Tase's sometimes, but that wasn't happening now. And it was stupid for him to have to try.

He flung his head on his fist and glared out of the window.

This whole thing was stupid. Moving away from their home. Going to Aunt Kyna's. Ha, he bet she didn't even live in a castle. It was probably just a stupid little shack, with flies and rats and—his eyes widened and his mouth fell open.

In plain view, not five meters away, was the biggest castle he had ever seen.

It had large stone pillars, beautiful stained glass windows, and two towers that sat on either side.

In certain areas of the castle's walls and towers, there were vines that grew up and completely covered the stone front. And here and there, Fadin saw signs that there had possibly once been a fire, many years ago. For the stone in some places was blackened and in several areas it looked as though the castle had been rebuilt.

The yard was open and had several hedges, trees, roses, ponds, and acres and acres of grass surrounded by a dark forest that was beginning to turn colour.

As they pulled up, Pathos moved to the door, shoving his muzzle at the crack.

"In a minute, boy," Fadin said, looking at the double-door that stood nearly three meters tall.

It had large silver knockers, was made of cherry wood, and was surrounded by what looked like iron.

There was a fair-haired woman standing in front of the double-door. She looked pleasant enough with a bright smile on her face and kind eyes. She held a light blue umbrella to keep out of the rain which was beginning to pick up steam.

Fadin stared at her, trying to see some resemblance to his mother, but he found none. The woman's blonde straight hair contrasted with their mother's black curly locks. Her button-like nose appeared small compared to their mother's long, regal-looking nose. Her thin, pink lips did not have the plump, red brightness their mother's held. Her lime-green eyes paled in comparison to their mother's electric blue. She stood wispy and short next to their mother's tall, average-set figure. Fadin wondered if this woman was their aunt or just a maid coming to help them with their luggage.

As soon as their car stopped moving, she walked up to greet them. Her shoulder-length hair and pale blue dress blew in the wind as she came up the stone path.

Fadin noticed a rather tall man walking along behind her.

The man was thin, had a bit of a large nose, longer graying hair, and very thick eyebrows. His eyes, too, were grey and he had fuller lips, for a male, which made a low curving M. He was dressed in what looked like a butler's outfit—a black suit with a high white collar, and had his own grey umbrella, clutched in his large hands.

The man appeared to be in his fifties, and looked oddly familiar somehow. It was as though Fadin had seen him somewhere before, but he couldn't place him. It wasn't like he could have actually met him anyway, so he disregarded it.

They all managed to get out of the car and open their shields from the rain before the two strangers reached them.

Fadin looked out toward the surrounding forest, taking a deep breath to prepare himself to meet these—people. This was all so odd. Meeting his aunt for the first time. At twelve? Not normal. But what was normal anyhow?

He gazed at a swaying tree, which was moving more than all the rest, and then quickly looked down, as something caught his eye.

There, at the entrance into the woods, stood a large black dog. It just stood there, glaring his way, with very light, brilliant eyes.

If Fadin didn't know better, he'd say the animal was a wolf, but that was impossible. There were no wolves in Ireland. So that animal had to be a—Fadin blinked. The animal was gone.

Strange.

The sound of approaching footsteps snapped Fadin back into reality, and he quickly looked frontward.

Ma took a step forward as the two strangers came within a few centimetres of them.

"Hello, Kyna," Ma said a little coolly. "Enda," she nodded towards the man.

Fadin looked over to the man and what appeared to be his Aunt Kyna.

The butler seemed to be having a hard time containing himself. He kept fiddling with his fingers, and seemed to be holding back—were those tears? No, certainly not, not from the butler. It had to be a leak in his umbrella.

He shifted his vision to Aunt Kyna.

She stood there for a long moment. She seemed to be thinking. Her hands were folded, and Fadin thought he saw a slight quiver in her chin.

"Oh, Teagan," Kyna suddenly shouted. She rushed forward, dropped her light blue parasol, and threw her arms around Ma. "I've missed you so."

Ma seemed very surprised. She put her arms back around Aunt Kyna, holding her loosely, seeming unsure how to react. "I've missed you too."

"Oh, come here," the man Enda hollered. He put his large arms around both Ma and Aunt Kyna, knocking Ma's umbrella out of her arms, hugging them both up tight.

Fadin saw distinct tears streaming down his face. It was not just the rain droplets, which were now hitting them all freely.

So he had been trying not to cry. How odd. How did this butler know Ma besides being her sister's worker?

The hug lasted what seemed to be a long while. Ma seemed uncomfortable at first, but as Enda and Kyna did not let go, she settled in until finally she began to sob, in what seemed to be grief and happiness.

Finally Enda released both women and backed a little away.

Kyna picked up the parasols and took Ma by the shoulders, looking deep into her face. "It's been too long, Teagan. Far too long." Aunt Kyna wiped Ma's tears away and smiled up at her. "Still the most beautiful woman in all of Glas Cavan. Don't you think, Enda?"

Enda nodded. "Most definitely."

This caused Ma to cry harder and once again grip onto her sister.

"There, there," Kyna cooed, "it's alright, it's okay. You're here, you're safe. Shhhh."

Ma breathed in deep and got control of herself. She smiled up at her sister, then at Enda, who gave her a deep and understanding smile.

"These are my children," Ma said, turning to Fadin and his brothers. "Clearie, Fadin, and Tase."

Aunt Kyna smiled at them. "Hello boys, I'm your Aunt Kyna. My, how handsome you are." She turned to Ma. "You never said anything about twins. What a pair."

Ma laughed. "Wait till you really see them together."

Fadin shifted uneasily. He did not like to be talked about in the third person. Especially when he was right there in front of them.

"And where is dear Saoirse?" Enda asked, grinning at Fadin and his siblings.

"Yes," Kyna said. "Where is she?"

How did they know about Saoirse? Fadin wondered. They really didn't seem to know much about Ma and her life. Again, odd.

Ma shook her raven curls. "Oh, I forgot to tell you, she's in America, studying in college."

"Ah, what a wonderful thing to do," Aunt Kyna nodded. "But she didn't want to come back, to stay a while, after the—" she stopped herself, "after what happened?"

Fadin looked at his Ma, wondering if she would tell Aunt Kyna about Saoirse's money problems. About how she could not afford to come back, not right now.

"No," Ma smiled. "She has too much to do. Besides, I have my boys, and now the two of you."

Aunt Kyna seemed not to buy this, but she smiled and dropped the subject. "You certainly do. Well, come on inside. I can have Enda take care of your bags." She nodded to Enda, who courteously opened their trunk and began unloading.

Pathos jumped at Aunt Kyna's legs, as she led them down the long walkway.

She laughed pleasantly and scratched behind his ears.

"Oh yes," she said smiling. "I remember you. Pathos, you can definitely come too."

Pathos barked in happy agreement.

~~~

The inside of the castle was enormous.

Fadin had never seen anything so huge in his entire life. The front door alone had been big enough for a giant to get through.

As they entered, they were faced with long winding stairs, a hall to the left, and a large arch leading into an open yellow room to the right.

The floors were planked with dark wood and the walls were painted a cream colour with white trim. The furniture was extravagant, and one desk looked like it cost more than their whole house and car put together.

"This is the foyer," Aunt Kyna said, arm outstretched. "And over to the right is the Sun Room, the Tea Room, the Buff Room, two bathrooms, and the East Tower. To the left are the kitchen, the Dining Hall, the Rose Room, the West Room, and the West Tower, as well as the door to the garden.

"In front of us are the stairs leading to the Print Room, the Crichton Room, the Blue Room, and the Green Room, as well as bathrooms for each.

"If you get lost," she joked, "Just follow the smell of food, and you'll eventually find the kitchen."

"What's through there?" Clearie asked pointing to a door under the stairs.

"Just a broom cupboard," she smiled. "If you boys want, you can go and pick your rooms."

Fadin looked up the winding stairway. "Which one is yours?"

"I stay down here," she said smiling at them. Her lime-green eyes twinkled in the soft light.

"Go ahead and pick," Ma urged.

Fadin looked at his brothers. Clearie shrugged and Tase avoided his glance.

Fadin began to climb the winding stairs, his brothers fallowing suit. As Fadin ascended, he began to think about his suitcase and how glad he was Enda was bringing it up.

"Oh," Aunt Kyna called before they got too far. "The only rule about this house is never, ever, go into the dungeon. It's got its own door outside on the grounds. It's locked, but I still don't want any accidents. You never know what's in those things."

Fadin swallowed and Clearie looked at him nervously.

"It's not dangerous," she added quickly, seeing their response. "But you never know what's down in the dark, so it's just safer to stay out of it." She smiled, trying to reassure them.

Fadin nodded, turned away, and picked up his pace a little.

"I don't know about you," Fadin said looking at Tase, "but I don't think I'm going to feel very safe living in a house with someone who has a dungeon."

He looked to see if this had made any impact. "Well," he added seeing that Tase had made no response, "I just wouldn't make her angry if I were you."

# Chapter 4

## *The Face in the Ceiling*

Tase closed his sky-blue eyes and flung himself onto the bed. It was large and comfortable.

He gazed up at the green ceiling and allowed his eyes to survey the room. It was a bit larger than his and Fadin's used to be, and rectangular instead of square.

There was a dresser next to a large panelled window, which was pushed up against the back wall. The closet was large, and the bed was pushed up against the right side of the room, it had green covers and the foot of it faced the wooden door on the far left.

Tase noticed Fadin walking into his own room, suitcase in hand.

He kicked the door open to reveal a room almost identical to Tase's, but instead of being covered in green, it was draped in blue.

Tase turned to one side, making a point not to look at Fadin.

It wasn't that he was really angry with him, more frustrated. He wanted desperately to talk to him about the woman he had seen on the day of their father's accident, but wasn't sure how. He was afraid that Fadin wouldn't believe him, and that was the last thing he needed right now. That's why he never told him about the nightmares. He didn't need his own brother thinking he was crazy, so instead he decided to freeze him out.

He heard Fadin shut his door and decided to turn around, onto his back.

He fumbled with his shirt and pulled out his Da's necklace. The one he had given him on his birthday last year. Fadin had been given his old pocket knife so that things had been kept fair.

Tase caressed the necklace gently, and turned it over and over in his hands. It had a single tooth on it, about the size of a shark's, held up by a thick brown string. He imagined his Da sitting next to him in their old house, talking to him about how he had gotten the sharp molar.

*"I got it when I was about your age,"* he heard his father say, *"I was nearly killed, but I managed to beat the monster, and save the day."*

*"What was it?"* he would ask, knowing perfectly well what a tall tale his father was selling. But he didn't care.

*"That I can't tell you. It's a secret but one day when you're older, I'll*

*let you in on all the details."*

"Now I'll never know," Tase said softly, returning from the old, broken memory.

He heard footsteps and sat up.

He saw Enda carrying his large suitcase and a few boxes into his very green, very empty room.

"Where would you like these?" he asked.

Tase looked at him for a moment before answering.

He was quite an interesting-looking fellow. It would be effortless to pick him out of a crowd, and difficult to forget him. Yet Tase felt as though he'd seen this man before. Someplace but where? When? He lived here, away from Waterford. It was impossible for Tase to have seen him before. Yet that voice, deep, calming, and the strange sensation of hearing an eagle cry. He had heard it before. And the way he moved so silently, while being so tall, that was familiar. But when had he met this man? Tase could not remember.

"Over there, in the corner." Tase said pointing to the desk.

Enda nodded, and put the luggage down. He walked in front of Tase and bowed slightly.

"Is there anything else I can get for you?"

"No," Tase said glancing at his enormous gloved hands.

Strange for him to wear gloves in September, and inside the house? "That's all."

Enda bowed again and, oddly quiet for his large size, left the room.

Tase got off the bed and opened his boxes. He put his pictures up on the dresser as well as some of his play things.

He polished the picture of his Da on the sleeve of his shirt, and placed it on the desk. He tipped it so he could see his own reflection and was surprised to see a small green figure dart across the room.

Tase dropped the frame and turned to look behind him.

There was nothing moving, not a mouse, not a bug, nothing.

He stood up and walked around the room. He looked in the closet but all he found were cobwebs and empty hangers. He laid himself flat on the floor and peered under his bed. Only an old sock. He rolled over so he could look under the desk. Just a few balls of dust, nothing unusual at all.

He turned over and stared at the ceiling.

*"I wonder what that was,"* he thought dully.

"Fadin, Clearie, Tase, dinner," their mother's voice rang through the halls.

He pulled himself onto his feet and took one last glance around his room before turning to go down the winding staircase.

Fadin opened his door, nearly running Tase over. "Oops," he said stopping not five centimetres from Tase's face. "Sorry." He glanced into his room. "Unpacked?"

"Sort of," Tase answered coolly. He was still feeling frustrated with him.

"Oh," Fadin looked down at his feet. "Well good. Better get downstairs."

Tase nodded and went down first.

Fadin followed close behind.

They took several wrong turns and even after following Aunt Kyna's advice of trying to smell food, opened two doors that did not lead into the dining hall. When they finally reached the dining room, they found their mother, Clearie, and Aunt Kyna already sitting at the rather long table.

Tase moved himself in front of Fadin and took the seat nearest Aunt Kyna.

Fadin was then left with the seat next to Clearie. He walked to the chair and sat down without looking up.

"Everything all right?" Ma asked, unfolding a napkin.

"Fine," Tase answered.

Fadin simply grunted.

She eyed them nervously but said nothing.

"Well," Aunt Kyna rose from her seat and smiled. "Shall we eat? Good, let me just go and get the cook." She left the table and disappeared through the swinging doors, which apparently lead into the kitchen.

Ma kept looking from Fadin to Tase, clearly trying to figure out what was the matter. She bit her lower lip, as she usually did when she wanted to say something, but decided against it.

The wooden doors swung open and Aunt Kyna entered with a blond plump woman and several steaming plates.

"Dinner is served," she said with a smile. "Daireann has made us a wonderful Smoked Cod Pie." She gestured to the woman next to her who was smiling brightly.

Tase smiled back but didn't mean it.

The cook, Daireann, looked quite pretty for an older woman, with frizzy white-blond hair that had been put up in a messy bun. Her shape boasted of her profession, with many curves and plumpness.

She wore a long-sleeve shirt with the sleeves rolled up and an apron that had a little of this and a little of that covering it.

"The food looks lovely," Ma said shooting reproachful looks at all of her boys.

"Yes," Clearie piped up, seeming startled. "Looks delicious."

Aunt Kyna sat down and Daireann began serving up portions.

When she put some of the pie on Tase's plate he began to feel sick. It wasn't that the food didn't look good or that he wasn't hungry, he just felt overwhelmed, and the thought of eating made his stomach turn.

He glanced at Fadin who was practically stuffing his face. This made Tase feel even more nauseated. He had so much on his mind that he felt like his head might split in two.

He poked the cubes of cod with his fork and tried to force himself to take a bite. When he lifted the clump of food to his mouth, however, he felt as though he might vomit. He quickly put it back onto the plate before the gag reflex became too strong.

He took another glance at Fadin who was still packing it away as though he had never eaten before.

"You don't like fish?" Aunt Kyna asked softly.

"Oh," Tase said, surprised that she noticed. "No, I do, I'm just—not very hungry."

Ma put down her fork and looked at him oddly.

He wished he would have just taken the stupid bite. He knew his mother would worry about him now because he usually had a big appetite, especially after several hours of eating nothing.

"Are you feeling alright?" she asked making to get up from her seat.

"I'm fine Ma, really," he added, after seeing her disbelief. "I'm just tired, that's all."

"If you aren't feeling well," said Aunt Kyna. "You can go up to your room if you like. No reason to sit here and feel sick."

He smiled at her. "Thanks, I think I will if that's alright." He looked at his mother who nodded but still looked concerned.

He went to grab his plate but Aunt Kyna insisted that he go straight upstairs.

"Daireann can take care of it," she told him.

He nodded, smiled, and left the dining hall.

The climb up the stairs seemed much longer than last time. He actually found himself cursing the person who decided to make so many blasted steps and nearly fell at the top because he kicked at one.

He opened the door to his green-coloured room, and plopped himself on the bed.

He turned around and grabbed the picture of his Da from the desk, and covered himself in the thick blankets.

He wished more than anything to be back in his old room with Fadin next to him, and just have everything back to normal.

He heard the door creak open and sat up to see Fadin standing in the archway.

"Don't you ever hump off?" he said angrily.

"I just wanted to see if you're feeling alright," Fadin answered.

"I'm just a bit jaded, that's all," he tried to sound convincing but obviously wasn't.

"You sure you're not hungry?"

"Positive." He was feeling frustrated. Why didn't he just leave him alone?

"I could bring you some food up if you want."

Tase could tell Fadin was trying his best to help, but he didn't want to be friends again, he just wanted to be left alone.

"I'm fine."

"Are you sure? You don't look fine."

"No, you're right, I was just letting on," he said angrily. "I told you I'm fine."

"But…"

"Look, I just want to be left alone," he almost yelled. "Now just shove off will you?"

Fadin looked hurt. "Oh, okay," he said slowly. "I guess I'll go then."

"Good. I'm glad you finally got the message." Tase regretted saying it almost instantly.

Fadin looked at him wide eyed. "Alright."

Tase could see the anger boiling.

"But don't think I'll ever try and help you again, no matter how sick you look."

"Good," Tase shot back. He was too upset to say anything else.

"Fine."

"Fine!"

And with that, Fadin slammed the door and stomped down the stairs.

Tase flung himself backward and threw the covers over his head.

He couldn't remember a time when he had felt more angry or hurt. He hadn't meant to be to mean to Fadin, but he was angry with him. Why didn't he see the woman? Why couldn't he guess what was wrong? How could he act so normal when their entire lives had been turned upside-down?

He buried his head in the pillow and clung to his Da's picture.

His mind raced, giving him a terrible headache. He was sure he would never be able to calm down, but after a few minutes he worried himself to sleep.

~~~

Fadin romped down the stairs, through the foyer, and flung open the front door.

"Where are you going?" Clearie asked coming out of the hall.

Fadin turned to him, trying to control his outrage. "Out."

He didn't wait for a response. He was so upset he didn't care whether his mother would be angry or not.

Once the door was shut behind him, Fadin let out an angry sigh. He kicked a rock laying on the walkway and it flew across the lawn. He hopped up and down on one foot, clutching his smashed toe.

"Stupid," he mumbled, looking in the direction the rock had flown.

He put his throbbing foot down and began to walk across the acres of grass. He felt the heat rising in his cheeks and began muttering to himself.

"Shove off? Glad you finally got the message?" he kicked at the ground with his unharmed foot.

"After how nice I was… When all I was trying to do was help… What does he want me to do? Am I really supposed to read that gom's mind?" He smacked the root of a tree.

"What does he want from me? I try and be nice, and he tells me to leave him alone. I leave him alone, and he sulks." He picked up a stick and threw it.

"What am I suppose to do!"

He stood still glaring around the property. It was mostly grass and trees with the occasional puddle of water.

He looked up and yelled pointlessly to the heavens. Whether it was to God or his Da he didn't know, but he felt someone up there deserved a little bit of his anger.

He jumped up and down, kicking at the damp grass. He grabbed anything he could, twigs, grass, rocks, and threw them in all directions. He even sat on his knees and screamed curses at nothing and to no one in particular.

After a few minutes when his temper had subsided, he stood up and took a deep breath. He stared at the tree nearest to him and imagined his Da standing beneath it.

He felt the anger he had toward his father vanish a little, to be replaced by the hurt and sadness that was always beneath it. "I wish you were here," he whispered.

He wiped away a tear, and cleared his throat. He only allowed himself to feel sad when he was alone. It wasn't okay for Ma, or Tase, or even Clearie, to know how broken he actually was about the whole thing. They needed him to be strong, especially his Ma. He had to be strong for himself too.

He saw something move out of the corner of his eye and turned to see what it was. He looked but saw nothing unusual, only a small bush and a tree. He looked again.

The tree was wiggling in an odd fashion. It almost looked like it was shaking.

He licked his finger and thrust it into the air. There was no wind. He walked over to it, expecting to see someone standing behind it or something shaking it.

To his surprise, there was no one.

He stood back and watched with growing interest as the tree continued to wiggle and shake. He wondered what could be causing this tree to move so much without any help.

Then the tree gave a harsh shudder, and was suddenly sucked under the ground, with a slight popping noise.

Fadin stared, dumbfounded. He rubbed his eyes to make sure he was seeing correctly. He even gave himself a little pinch to make sure this wasn't a dream.

He walked over to the hole where the tree had been, and peered into it.

The dirt was upturned, so he couldn't see very far. He walked around it and tried to dig to get a clearer view.

The ground suddenly began to grumble and shudder.

Fadin jumped back and watched as the tree popped out of the ground like a geyser. It shook, almost like a dog, and removed the dirt from its branches and leaves. It swayed for a few moments and then became still just like any other tree.

Fadin stood, mouth open, mind spinning.

*"Trees can't move,"* He thought, *"and they certainly can't go underground."*

He laughed lightly, hoping he wasn't going crazy.

Something touched his shoulder and he jumped nearly a meter in the air. He flung himself around and stared into the face of his mother.

"Goodness," she said catching her own breath. "I came to see if you were alright." She put a hand on his face and forehead, checking his temperature. "You left the table without a word, and then stomped off outside."

He glanced at the tree, making sure it was still there.

Ma looked at him nervously. "Are you alright?"

He turned back to her, feeling the colour drain from his face. "Yep," he said, trying to sound sincere. "Yes, yup, fine." He put on the best smile he could. "Just wanted to explore the grounds, I'm fine though."

She looked at him disbelieving.

"Really, I'm okay Ma, I'm fine." He grabbed her hand trying to reassure her.

"Well," she said still keeping her gaze on him. "Come on in, it's getting cold."

"Okay," he answered, taking one last look at the tree. "I'm tired anyway."

They walked together, back to the castle, as the sun was beginning to set. As the sun's rays left the sky, the air began to get nippy.

Fadin hadn't realized how far he'd gone and was happy when they entered into the warmth of the castle.

"Oh, good," Aunt Kyna said as soon as the door swung open. "We were worried about where you had gone. You never know what lurks around at night."

Fadin smiled at her.

She really was a nice lady, much nicer then he had expected.

"I'm alright," he said. "Just exploring the grounds that's all."

"Well, I think there's plenty of time for that tomorrow when the sun is up," Ma said firmly.

Fadin nodded and felt himself display a big yawn.

"I think you'd better head to bed," Ma nodded, putting a hand on his shoulder. "Clearie and Tase are already asleep."

"And your pup went up into your Ma's room, he's snoring like a freight train." Enda added.

Fadin glanced over his shoulder. He hadn't even noticed him standing there or heard him walk up. He was too quiet for how big he was. In fact, he was too quiet period.

"Alright," Fadin answered, arching his back for a stretch.

He really didn't need much convincing, he was exhausted and wanted to be alone so he could think about what he had seen.

"I'll see you in the morning then?" he smiled.

"Goodnight." The three of them answered consecutively.

He climbed the mountain of stairs, and quietly opened his door.

He glanced at Tase's room and saw that his entire body was covered. He shrugged and entered his own very blue room.

Most of his things were unpacked and set on the dresser and desk, but he still had two boxes to go.

He flung himself onto the bed and stared at the high ceiling. He let his mind ponder and try and make sense of what he had seen. He could almost feel the wheels of his head turning, and could have sworn he heard his mind "ping" as if one of the wheels had come off its track.

After about an hour of trying to find a rational reason for a tree to disappear underground, Fadin decided it was time to call it a night.

So he got up, slipped on his nightclothes, and crawled into bed. To his surprise, falling asleep was not hard, and as soon as his head hit the pillow he could feel sleep crashing over him.

After a few moments he left reality behind and entered the land of dreams.

~~~

Thump.

Fadin shot up into the blackness. He felt his shirt, and realized it was soaked through. He had had a terrible nightmare about his father.

Fadin was running through the woods and saw him. He tried to run to his Da, but his legs would no longer move. He called out but Da didn't seem to hear him. A fire sprung up behind Fadin and he screamed, but Da kept walking away. There was the swift *thump* of gates opening up into what could only be described as a giant oven, and Fadin began to be dragged into it.

Then he had woken up.

He looked around his room and fell completely silent, trying to listen.

"Thump—thump—thump."

Fadin jumped out of his bed and flicked on the light. Where was that coming from?

"Thump—clack—thump—clack."

It was coming from the ceiling. He was sure of it. How odd. Who could be in the ceiling?

He heard the sound moving further away. He grabbed his jacket and quietly opened his door.

"Thump—clack."

The noise was much louder in the hall. And being so near it, he realized it sounded like someone limping. Someone limping with one leg, sounding like it was—wood?

He strained his neck to see if his mother or Clearie heard the noise. There didn't seem to be any sign of them.

How they could sleep through all the racket, he didn't know.

"Thump—clack, clack—thump."

The sound was moving towards the stairs. And it sounded as though the pace were quickening.

"Thump—clack, clack."

The door to Tase's room creaked open.

Fadin looked over, startled, and saw Tase standing in his own jacket, apparently wide awake.

"You hear it too?" Fadin asked, eyeing him apprehensively.

"Yea," Tase answered, glancing down the hall.

"They aren't awake," Fadin informed him.

Tase gaped at him, disbelieving. "How can they sleep through this?"

"Thump—clack, clack—thump, thump."

They both looked up.

"I think it's moving," Fadin whispered.

They looked at each other.

"What do you suppose it is?" Fadin asked.

"Rats?"

"Don't be thick, rats don't make that much noise."

"Thump, thump—clack, clack, clack—thump—CRASH!"

They jumped.

Tase shifted his gaze to Fadin. "That one was louder," he whispered.

"Yea, it was."

They both looked up again.

"Bam, bam, bam!"

"Little vayyokc!" Someone yelled.

Fadin gulped, and fixed his eyes upward.

Suddenly a face, hideous and livid, was thrust into the wood of the ceiling. It stretched down as if it were in rubber, nearly touching the two of them. It opened its mouth and shrieked, "Get out of my house!"

Fadin cried out.

Tase fell to the floor.

The face smiled, laughed, and then returned up into the ceiling.

The boys looked at each other, yelped, and ran into Tase's room.

They slammed the door and jumped onto the bed. The covers were thrown over them so quickly that they knocked heads throwing themselves backwards.

Fadin curled into a ball and shut his eyes tight. He panted and shook his head. That was impossible. That couldn't have been real, it couldn't.

He covered his eyes with his hands and rocked slightly. Oh, how he wanted the light on, but he was too afraid to leave the safety of the covers.

He could hear Tase breathing frantically and shaking his head over and over.

Fadin's heart was racing, and he could feel the thumping in his chest and hear it in his head. He shivered and tightened the ball he was in. He could honestly say he had never been so scared before in his life.

If only he and Tase hadn't fought. He wished he could talk to his brother so that he didn't feel so alone in this pitch blackness.

"I'm sorry," he wailed. "I didn't mean to be such a ruddy idiot before."

"So am I," Tase cried back. "I didn't mean what I said. Any of it."

Fadin felt slight warmth in the pit of his stomach. He removed his hands from his eyes and could see the slight outline of Tase.

"Friends?" he asked, teeth chattering.

Tase nodded.

A loud howl suddenly rose up from somewhere outside.

The noise sent shivers up Fadin's spine. He looked at his brother.

They grabbed onto one another and closed their eyes tight.

~~~

That night was the longest Fadin could ever remember.

The noises stopped soon after they entered Tase's room, but neither of them left the sanctuary of the blankets.

"What do you think it was?" Tase asked after things had been quiet a while.

"I don't know," Fadin replied in a whisper. "A ghost I suppose."

They looked at one another.

"Do you think Aunt Kyna knows about it?" Tase asked.

"No, she seems nice, and I don't think she would send us up to sleep where the ghost lives on purpose."

"I don't know," Tase said skeptically. "Maybe that's why she sleeps downstairs."

This thought had not occurred to Fadin, but it seemed very likely that this was the reason she didn't sleep upstairs. "Why would she have us sleep here then?" he asked.

"She may not be as nice as she seems. Or perhaps she didn't think it would bother us."

Fadin nodded. He hoped it was the latter, but there was no way to be sure. "Do you think we should tell her we saw it?"

"No," Tase replied. "If she doesn't know it's here, she'll think we're crazy."

"Yea, I suppose so." He turned to look at Tase. "Why have you been acting so funny lately?"

Tase didn't look at him. He instead glanced down and fiddled with his fingers. "I guess—well now that you've seen this, you won't think I'm such a header."

"I wouldn't think you were a header, no matter what you said or what you saw."

"You might have before," Tase said turning to him. "It's what you didn't see that's the problem."

Fadin cocked his head. "What are you talking about?"

"Well, you remember that day Ma told us about the accident?"

"Yea, the day all the glass shattered in Mr. Donovan's classroom?"

Tase nodded. "That day, before that terrible noise, I saw a woman."

"A woman?" Fadin arched an eyebrow.

"Yea, but she wasn't an ordinary woman. She was cloaked and pale with fire-red hair."

Fadin thought on this for a moment. "A hooded woman? You mean—like the woman Mrs. Cunningham said she saw?"

Tase nodded. "I thought the same thing. She said she saw a woman in our yard that day, right?"

Fadin nodded. "Yea, I remember thinking she was crazy."

"Apparently not. I saw her, and when I looked at her, the strangest thing happened."

"What?"

"She pointed a finger at me and screamed."

"She screamed?"

"She was what made that terrible noise and made all the glass break. I'm sure of it."

Tase was right. Fadin might have thought him a bit mad, if had he not seen a tree get sucked under the ground, and a face pushed out of the ceiling.

"I've been having terrible nightmares about her too," Tase continued. "Nightmares about her and—Da. I dream she comes for him, and no matter how hard I scream or try to warn him, he always runs right into her. And I can see his car, and she's there. She is what smashes and flips it while Da is inside, unable to get out. He tries to escape the smashed car and cries out for help. I struggle to get to him, but I can't move. And every time, I have to witness as the car goes up in flames, and the inferno eats him alive." Tase shivered, and gulped in several deep breaths to keep himself from crying.

Fadin felt his heart sink. What a horrible dream. Having to watch Da die? He felt a shiver go up his own spine. No wonder Tase had been screaming in the middle of the night.

"I've been having them almost every time I go to sleep," Tase answered.

Fadin felt very rotten about this. He wished he would have been more persistent in finding out what had been wrong. "Who do you think she was?" he asked, trying not to dwell on how dreadful he felt.

"Don't know," Tase said turning away from him. "I wish Da were here."

Fadin felt his stomach drop. He did too. Da would know how to explain what was going on. At least he hoped he would. Nevertheless, they wouldn't have to be living in a haunted castle hours away from their actual home.

"I'm glad we're talking again," Tase said.

Fadin smiled.

Even though they were under three blankets in the pitch black, too afraid to leave the room much less the bed, he felt a bubble of happiness rise in his chest. "I am too."

# Chapter 5

## Ciaran's Castle

Sunshine slapped Tase in the only part of his face that was not covered.

He shut his eyes tight and turned over. He spotted Fadin, and all the events of the night before came rushing back to him.

He flipped over and lay on his back.

How they had fallen asleep, he didn't know, but was he ever glad it was light out, and they didn't have to worry about any faces popping out of the walls. At least he hoped not.

The castle sounded quiet, but it was too light out for everyone to still be asleep. Besides, people could be playing football in the dining room and he would not be able to hear it.

Fadin stirred. He stretched his arms, expanded his legs, and yawned broadly.

"Morning," he said. His red hair was a mess, sticking up here and there in odd fashions.

Tase, feeling anxious, asked, "Do you suppose we could have dreamed it all?"

"No way," Fadin said sitting up. "It was too real. Besides, I wouldn't be in here if it had been a dream."

That was true.

Fadin flung the covers off them. "I guess the sun's up," he said squinting. "Want to go downstairs for breakfast? I'm starving."

*"How can he think of food after what we've seen?"* Tase thought. His stomach growled in answer to his question. It felt as though it had shrunk three sizes, and he began to feel very sick.

Tase rapidly remembered that he hadn't eaten anything the night before, and suddenly breakfast sounded like a very good idea.

They took off their nightclothes and dressed for the day before setting off down the long stairs.

"It's to the right, right?" Fadin asked, pointing.

"Uh," Tase answered. "I think. The second door, or was it the third?"

Fadin shrugged. "Well I know it's down that hall somewhere. Come on."

He led them down the right hall and opened up the second door.

"Whoops," he said, backing up and beginning to close the door.

"What?" Tase asked, pushing forward and shoving his head inside the room.

Fadin had apparently opened up the door to the West Room. And it looked to Tase like Daireann slept in it.

There was a small bed which was unmade, shoes all over the floor, loads of potted plants throughout the dwelling, and clothes strewn all over the place, including a very large, brown brassiere dangling from the nightstand.

Tase cupped his hands over his eyes. "Close it, close it," he billowed.

Fadin moved him out of the way and securely shut the door. "Like I said, whoops."

"Whoops indeed," a familiar, deep voice said.

Tase flipped around and froze as he saw Enda standing in front of them.

"That," Enda said, pointing to the now shut door, "is Daireann's bedroom."

Fadin smiled and laughed nervously. "We are—um—quite aware of that now."

"Hum," Enda nodded. "You certainly are. If you're looking for the dining hall, it is that-a-way." He pointed to the third door down.

Tase smiled. "Thanks, Eh-Enda."

He and Fadin sort of side-stepped their way past him, not taking their eyes away, till they were two doors apart. They then, turned round at the same time, and briskly walked to the dining room door.

"Weird, that one," Fadin said as he pushed the double-doors open.

They swung widely, revealing that the oddly long table was empty except for two place settings.

Almost immediately, Daireann popped through the opposite swinging doors, holding two plates of egg and bacon nests.

The smell floated over to them, making Tase's stomach grumble louder than ever.

"Here you go, dears," Daireann said, plopping the plates in front of them. Her white-blond hair was tossed up into a messy bun, and her shirt and apron were already covered in some sort of unrecognizable goop. "The others ate a few hours ago," she said. "You two certainly know how to sleep the day away." She smiled at them and left for the kitchen.

As soon as the doors swung shut, Tase sat down and began shoveling forkfuls of the egg and bacon nests into his mouth. He only stopped chewing to get a drink or to pause so he could catch his breath.

He finished his first plate as Fadin was halfway done with his own and helped himself to second and third servings.

When he had finished he leaned back, feeling very satisfied, and noticed Fadin gaping at him.

"What? I didn't eat at all last night."

Fadin just shook his head and picked up his plate. "I don't think I've ever seen a person eat that much. I thought you might explode."

Tase smiled and brought his plate into the kitchen too.

As they pushed the kitchen doors open, a parade of smells came galloping at them.

Tase recognized the scents of basil, parsley, cinnamon, lemon, fish, potato, and some sort of tangy spice. All together the sent was mouth-watering, even though Tase felt like he was ready to pop.

The kitchen was large, with several stoves, counters, sinks, and shelves. There were vegetables, meat, spices, eggs, and flour all about the counters. Dishes were piled high in the sink with this or that dripping to the floor. And, odd as it was, dozens of plants, sat, lined up on each ledge, counter, stool, and every nook and cranny of that kitchen. Just like the plants in Daireann's room.

Flowers, reeds, vines, and thorny rose bushes were all over the place. Some were in planting pots, others were in breakfast bowls and cups, and still more were growing right along on the floor.

Tase nearly tripped over a large creeper, as he moved towards the very dirty sink.

"Oh dears," Daireann nearly cried. "You mustn't do that. I appreciate the favour, but Kyna—er—the mistress—pays me to cook and clean. So if you're the ones doing it, what good am I?"

Tase smiled and handed over his plate. "Sorry. Just used to doing it ourselves I guess."

Daireann smiled back, taking Fadin's plate as well. "Like I said, I appreciate it, but there is no need. You dears and your Ma have been through a lot as of late, and you need to take it easy. There will be plenty of time for cleaning and whatnot later." She put the plates in the large dish pile, and turned back to them. "Alright, off with you now. Why don't you two look in the garden? I'm sure that's where your Ma went."

"Thank you, Daireann," Tase said, pushing through the swinging doors.

"Yea, thanks," Fadin nodded.

Daireann smiled and shooed them out.

"She a little batty, isn't she?" Fadin said once they were clear of the dining room.

"I think she's nice," Tase grinned.

"Nice, sure," Fadin agreed. "But what about all those plants? Why in the world would someone want that much foliage?"

Tase shrugged. "She's got a green thumb?"

Fadin cocked his head sarcastically. "Sure, Tase, sure."

They stopped as the glass door to the garden came into view.

"At least this one is easy to spot," Fadin said turning the knob.

The sweet smell of morning grass and flowers settled over Tase, as the air from the garden swept him up. It was a truly glorious day outside. The air was crisp and the sun shone brightly, although its ability to actually warm anything was minimal.

The castle garden was quite a sight. It was nestled in its own little nook between the castle and an opposing wall, which separated it from the outside world, beside a black iron gate, which rested to the far right. The foliage was wonderfully kept, with beautiful flowers, patterns, and pictures. Benches lined the edges of the stone walkway here and there with a tree or two standing proudly overhead. And in the middle, there sat a large fountain fashioned in the image of a mermaid seated upon a rock. Water poured from her eyes and her hand, creating a pool which twinkled lively in the sunshine.

Tase spotted Ma and Aunt Kyna sitting on a bench in a rounded corner of the garden. They had a blue and green blanket lying upon their laps and were sipping a cup of tea, talking quietly about something or other. Ma looked pale, like she was getting sick, and had a handkerchief clutched in her left hand.

Pathos sat silently beneath their feet, enjoying what warmth the sunshine was bringing.

Aunt Kyna noticed them walk in and smiled. She waved them over and pointed to the bench opposite hers.

"Good morning," she said as they came to stand in front of her. "Did you sleep well?"

Tase wondered if she did know about the ghost and was just asking them as a joke. "Very good, thank you," he said.

She nodded happily. "No bad dreams? The bed bugs didn't bite?"

Fadin looked over at Tase.

Tase nodded in agreement. He did not need words to know Fadin was thinking the same as he. Tase was not going to sleep alone in this castle, not in a million years.

"We want to share a room," The two of them said in unison.

Ma looked as though she could have fallen off her chair. "Share a room?" she asked, looking from one to the other. "After all the complaints about having to share a room in the old house? After all the begging and pleading to turn Saoirse's room into a second bedroom for you? You want to share?"

"We do," Fadin said firmly.

Tase bobbed his head in agreement. If that ghost wasn't gone, they could at least be together when it stuck its ugly head out.

Ma looked at them, exasperated. "Well, okay then. If that's what you really want, you can go back to sharing."

Tase looked at Fadin, relieved.

"Why don't you tell Enda what room you two want to share, and he'll bunk the beds and transfer your things, for you." Aunt Kyna chimed in.

Tase smiled. "Thank you, we will."

He turned with Fadin to head back inside, but Ma stopped them.

"What are you two boys going to be up to today?"

Fadin turned around. "Exploring the castle."

Tase raised an eyebrow, but said nothing.

"Really?" Aunt Kyna said. "Well, that is quite a fun idea. Just be careful not to get lost, and remember, if you go out on the grounds, stay out of the forest and away from the dungeon."

"We will," Fadin answered for the both of them. "Goodbye."

Aunt Kyna and Ma waved to them as they walked away and went through the glass door.

"Exploring the castle, are we?" Tase asked as the door shut.

"I have an idea," Fadin said, an odd smile on his face.

Tase observed him nervously. "What?"

"It's in the middle of the day, in total sunshine."

"Yes, I can see that. Congratulations, you deserve a gold star for your keen eyesight there, Fadin."

Fadin disregarded his sarcasm. "Ghosts can only come out at night, genius."

This was what Tase had been afraid of.

"No, nope, no way," he shook his head. "I am not, do you hear me, not, going up into that creepy old— "

"We have to."

"No we don't. We can stay down here, be safe and choose life."

"Safe? Was last night what you'd call safe? The thing stuck its bloody face out at us. From the ceiling, no less! If it can stretch a wood-covered ceiling like it was made out of rubber, what else do you think it can do?"

"My point exactly. If it can do worse things, let's not go up into its home and make it easier for the monster to kill us. We might as well giftwrap ourselves and wish it a happy bloody birthday."

"I'm going up there to see what it is. If you want to stay down here and let me go alone, then you can forget about sharing a room."

"You're the one who asked," Tase said, trying to hide his fear.

"Come on, Tase. You know that if we don't go up there, we'll be thinking about it all night long. We'll probably have to hide under our covers again."

Tase thought for a moment. He really didn't want a repeat of last night, and if it had been a ghost they had seen, then it couldn't come out during daylight anyhow. At least he hoped it couldn't.

The plan seemed safe enough, so reluctantly, Tase agreed.

"Good," Fadin beamed. "Let's go and find that door then."

~~~

It was harder than they thought to find the way into the attic.

Fadin led them all over the upstairs trying to find the slightest clue as to where the door might be. They walked the entire length of it twice, three, four times, and still nothing.

Tase massaged the back of his neck. It hurt from staring up at the ceiling for nearly an hour.

"Let's forget it," he said, eyeing Fadin who was still looking up. "There obviously isn't an attic in this castle." He couldn't deny he was happy about that. He really had no desire to find whatever it was hiding inside the walls.

Fadin snapped his fingers. "Maybe there's no door here," he smiled broadly as if a lightbulb had flickered on. "But maybe there's a way in from one of the towers."

Tase stopped rubbing his neck. He hadn't thought of that. Crud.

"Come on."

Fadin grabbed his hand and they flew down the very long stairway.

Tase was amazed they didn't fall.

When they arrived at the bottom, Pathos came bounding around a corner to greet them. He jumped up on two legs, knocking them both over.

"Okay, okay boy," Tase laughed as he was bathed in Mountain Dog slobber.

Fadin gave him a pat on the head. "Go on, Path."

The Bernese moved himself off them, and sat back, wagging his tail happily.

"Which tower do you think?" Fadin asked looking from left to right.

Tase shrugged. "They might both have doors."

Pathos barked, and took off running to the right.

The boys exchanged glances.

"I guess right," Fadin nodded.

They fallowed Pathos through the Sun Room and into the Tea Room.

There, much to Tase's dismay, Clearie sat reading a rather large book. He lifted his head slightly so he could see who had entered.

"What are you two doing?" he asked, putting the book down. He surveyed them closely, with his unique colored eyes.

Tase shot Fadin a worried look. How were they going to keep Clearie out of this?

Fadin took the initiative. "Getting something for—" there was a slight pause, "for Aunt Kyna," he said.

"Right," Clearie said incredulously. "In the East Tower?"

"Just let us be, Clearie," Tase jumped in. He did not want to have to hide under the covers for a second night.

Clearie looked from one to the other. He shrugged and picked his book up again. "Whatever. Go find a present in the East Tower, or do whatever it is you are really doing."

Fadin smiled at Tase, and they headed for the small hallway ahead of them.

"Just don't get into any trouble," Clearie called to them.

Fadin rolled his eyes.

As they entered the very long, narrow hallway, Tase noticed several pictures hanging on the walls. He tried to look at one, but saw only a black portrait. He turned his attention to another, but that one was black as well. He stood as far back as he could from the wall. All the pictures were black and empty.

He turned to Fadin who was trying to open a door along the wall. "All the pictures are blank."

Fadin looked up. "Weird, why do you suppose she would have all these blank photos on the walls?"

Tase shrugged, still looking at them.

"I bet this is her room too," he pointed at the door he had been trying to open.

Tase nodded, and shifted his gaze to down the hall. "Hey, Pathos he's found something."

They walked to the end of it, where the black and brown dog sat in front of a rather fancy bookcase.

Fadin walked in a small circle, looking up and down as he did so. "Where's the door to the tower?"

Tase did the same thing. "I don't know. Why would she tell us there was a tower when there's no door?"

Fadin eyed the bookcase. "Maybe she doesn't want us in it. Maybe she does know about the ghost."

This sent a chill up Tase's spine. He certainly hoped not.

Fadin began pulling books off the shelves and tapping the wood back.

"What are you doing?" Tase asked, looking at the pile of books now on the floor.

"There might be a false book that opens the door."

"Why would a book open the door?"

Fadin stopped and gave him an irritated look. "Don't you watch the telly? Why would someone put a random bookcase at the end of a hall unless it was hiding something?" He raised both eyebrows and tucked in his bottom lip.

Tase made a similar face, only his was mocking. "I don't know, so they could read at night?"

Fadin stared at him for a moment.

Tase felt, rather than heard, him thinking what a complete idiot he was. After a moment or two, he kept removing books.

Soon there were no books left on the shelves and nothing at all had opened.

Tase folded his arms. "I told you."

"Oh, shut it," Fadin said, looking up and down.

Tase started picking up the books.

"Wait!" Fadin cried. "Let me see that."

He took a small blue book from Tase's hands. On the front cover it read "Yek Eht."

"Looks like a different language," Tase said, looking it over.

"Nope," Fadin smiled, "it's English. It's the key, look." He tried to open the book, but it remained tightly shut.

Tase tried too, but it didn't open. "Okay, so it doesn't open, but what makes you think it's the key?"

"Can't you read?" Fadin asked. "Look, Y-e-k E-h-t."

"So?"

"T-h-e K-e-y. It was spelt backwards."

Tase shook his head and looked at the cover again. "It is spelt backwards."

Fadin smiled. "Now all we have to do is find the keyhole."

They both looked up and down the bookcase, but there was no hole or any specific place that looked like it would open a door.

Pathos whined and scratched at the bottom of the wall.

"What's wrong, Path?" Fadin asked, patting the dog on the back.

"Look," Tase almost shouted. "That stone, there, it's the same size and shape as the book!"

Fadin put the book over the square stone. "It is," he pushed and the stone clanked itself inward, taking the book with it.

84

Tase heard a crack from behind them and saw a picture frame being pushed outwards from the opposing wall. He rushed over to it and pulled the frame and the black picture away. There, a stone of equal size was protruding from the wall.

Fadin grabbed it and it came off with a little "pop."

The space where it had been was quickly replaced with another stone that moved itself forward until you could no longer tell there had been a blank spot at all.

Fadin turned the stone around and revealed that it was hollow in the back. There was something wrapped in black cloth, stuck in the empty space. Fadin looked up and pulled out the wrapped thing. He slowly unraveled the black cloth and from it fell a wooden carving.

Tase picked it up, and turned it over in his hands.

The carved wooden thing looked like a big "K" with vines growing out of the side. The vines were covered in small golden leaves and connected to the vines lay two half-circle-looking things. Each half-circle had bright green emeralds carved into them—three on the left and four on the right. And in the middle of all this was a long sword with the word "Erin" etched into it. The "K" also had a word carved into its side, but Tase could not read it.

"What do you think it is?" Tase asked, looking up and handing it to Fadin.

Fadin gripped it tight, and looked over both sides. It fit easily in one hand with only the sword extending a little beyond his palm.

"Erin," he said quietly. "Why does that word sound familiar?"

"Because," Tase said, remembrance flooding him. "Mrs. McClain, our grammar teacher, used it in a poem the last week we were at school. It means Ireland, just a poetic name for it."

Fadin looked at him incredulously. "You actually remember what Mrs. McNain taught us?"

Tase smiled. "McClain, and I don't know, I suppose I do."

Fadin shook his head and turned his attention to the bookcase. "Let's find out what this thing is for."

They walked over to it and Fadin put the wooden carving on one of the shelves.

"Hum, I don't think anything's happening," Tase said, a little smug.

Fadin moved as though he would smack Tase and then stopped. His mouth dropped, and he pointed at the bookcase wall.

In front of their very eyes, a symbol exactly the size and shape of the wooden carving burned itself into the wood of the shelf.

Tase and Fadin exchanged frightened and excited glances.

Tase picked up the wood "K" and lined it up with its burned counterpart. He pushed hard, and the bookcase swung open with a clang.

Tase peered inside.

It was a long, narrow, winding stairway. The walls and steps were made from gray stone. The stone-covered walls, like the hall they were in, were covered in blank, black photos.

Fadin stepped in first, followed by Pathos.

Tase walked in cautiously and glanced up the twisting stairs.

"Maybe this isn't such a good idea," he said, taking a step back.

Fadin turned to him with one eyebrow raised. "After finding keys in walls and books spelt backwards? We have to."

Tase fiddled with his fingers. "Its dark up there, we should come back with a flashlight."

"Oh, come on—we have Pathos."

"Pathos doesn't come with a built-in light, does he? Because that would be news to me."

Fadin folded his arms. "Do you really want to sleep under three blankets again?"

Tase sighed. Darn him for knowing exactly how to push the right buttons. "Okay, fine—let's go."

Fadin smiled and grabbed the wooden carving from the bookcase.

"In case we need it," he said.

They walked slowly up the windy stairway. As they got higher, the temperature got colder.

"Isn't heat supposed to rise?" Tase asked, suppressing a shiver.

"Not in here, I guess," Fadin said.

Tase felt along the wall as the stairway got darker. He could hardly even see Fadin standing in front of him. Was that something moving up ahead?

"Ouch!"

Tase bumped into Fadin's back and nearly lost his footing. He clutched onto to Pathos to keep from tumbling down the stairs.

"Found the door," Fadin declared.

Again the symbol of the carving was burned into the wood.

Tase could see the light red outline upon what was apparently the door.

Fadin pressed the carving against it, and the door opened.

They entered into an incredibly dark, round room.

Fadin tripped over something hard, crying out.

Tase, not being able to see, kicked Fadin and the carving went sliding across the black floor.

"Oh no."

"Ouch, that was my hand."

"I can't see anything."

Tase noticed a sliver of light coming from the wall. He walked over to it and pulled at the curtain.

Sunlight flooded into the room, causing both boys to squint.

When the shock of going from complete darkness to sunshine wore off, Tase looked down and saw the hard thing that had caused Fadin to fall. He bent down to pick it up, and let his lips fall open in awe.

"It's a sword," he said, staring at its gold and jewel-covered handle.

Pathos trotted across the room and brought Fadin the wood carving, nuzzling him as he did so.

Fadin patted him on the head half-heartedly and admired the long weapon.

"It must be dull," he said stroking it. "Or my legs would be gone."

Tase nodded, letting his fingers dance over the cutting edge. It had pretty curved writing engraved into the blade. He couldn't read most of it, but there were two overlapping initials placed near the tip. D and A.

"Fadin," he said, pointing to the letters.

Fadin stared. "D. A. The same initials as on Da's crest. What do you suppose they stand for?"

Tase shook his head. "I don't know, but I want to find out. I want to know why those same letters are on a sword hidden up in Aunt Kyna's tower. And why Da had them on a crest he hid inside his desk."

Fadin nodded, but said nothing.

Tase swallowed the lump in his throat and looked about their surroundings.

The room was filled with the same black pictures. Nothing inside the frames, except for one large canvas with a big "D" hanging over the dust-covered bed. The ceiling and a single trunk were smothered in cobwebs, and a large wrapped thing hung up on the wall. The walls looked very old and worn, for the entire room was covered in grooves and indents, as if someone had gone to the walls with a knife. But as Tase looked closer, he saw it was words carved into the very stone of the walls. In fact it was the same word, carved over and over.

X-O-O-R.

Tase walked around the room, letting his fingers scamper along the sides, and in and out of the carved word. He bent down over the trunk and wiped some of the dust away. Big gold letters sat upon the lid. The inscription showed the same word that was carved into the wood "K."

Tase made an attempt at pronouncing it. "Dalb—hach? Dalbhach," he said.

Fadin turned. "What?"

"Oh," Tase looked down at the words again. "Nothing."

"Well, stop doing nothing and come and help me," Fadin made a grunting sound. "I think I've found something."

Tase moved over to where his brother stood, pushing against the wall.

"What are you doing?"

"I think there's a door here."

Tase looked again and saw what appeared to be a door etched into the wall. It had been covered by a red moth-eaten curtain.

"Well, why don't you use the carving?"

Fadin looked at him dully. "I already did. Would I be standing here, trying to push my way through, if I had a key?"

Tase shrugged. He leaned against the door and tried to force it open as well.

"It won't budge," he said breathlessly.

Fadin took a large breath. "There has to be another way."

They stood back and looked the wall up and down. Nothing.

Tase looked around and noticed something.

Pathos was staring very intently at the door frame, cocking his head from side to side.

"Look at this," Tase said, bending down.

When he got closer, he saw that there were words etched into it. He traced them with his finger and tried to make them out.

"Ig kde gave ow Dia Ailin oheg kdic mooj," he tried.

"What do you suppose it means?" Fadin asked.

There was a low rumble and both boys jumped back.

The door shook with surprising force and slid askew into the wall.

Tase looked at Fadin, who smiled and entered the hidden room.

It was a large, rectangular-shaped space and most certainly the attic they had been searching for. It was covered with broken objects, dust, and thousands of cobwebs.

Tase looked up and saw many old, cracked beams.

"I hope those hold up a bit longer," Fadin said, noticing them as well.

Tase felt a shiver go up his spine. "I don't see anything." He gazed around the dimly lighted area. "Maybe we did imagine it all."

"Oh come on, don't do this now. The hard part's over, besides, would we be up here if we did imagine it?"

"I don't know Fadin, I have a bad feeling. Can't we just go?"

"There's nothing up here," Fadin said, picking up a dust-covered box. "See, nothing to be afraid—"

"MINE!" A shrill voice cried.

Fadin leapt backwards as something wrestled the box out of his hands.

"It's mines, you oinseach! You tries to steal it, you gadia!"

A small olive-green colored creature yanked the box away and hopped to the table. The creature was very skinny and appeared to be a boy, for he was wearing what looked like torn, filthy rags, only on his bottom. His eyes were bright yellow, as well as the tips of his pointed ears. He clutched the little box with all his strength, eyeing the two of them angrily.

Tase stared at him and said the first thing that came to mind. "What are you?"

The creature gave a terrible scream, and his entire ears and hair became the yellow colour. "These things—ahhhh—these things come into my home, they tries to steal and they wants to know what I am?" He stamped his foot hard on the table, and Tase saw that it was getting bigger. "The vayyokc!"

"I'm sorry," Tase stammered. "We didn't know you lived here. We weren't trying to steal from you."

The yellow-eyed creature looked them up and down.

Tase saw the colour beginning to drain from his ears as they became olive-green again.

"You are the loud things, from the last dark?" he asked.

Tase cocked his head. "Oh, last night? Yes, that was us. Did we wake you?"

The creature shook his head, causing the long ears to flop from side to side. "My eyes were open, but you things were too noisy. You coulds have woken up the whole castle."

Tase glanced at Fadin, who was simply staring dumbfounded.

"I'm sorry we were so loud," Tase continued. "Was that you who yelled at us?"

The thing nodded its head.

Tase again glanced at Fadin for help, but he just stood still, eyes fixed upon the small creature.

"What's your name?" Tase finally managed.

"Ciaran," he said, giving a little bow. "And to answer your rudeness, I is a Fitheal."

Tase raised his eyebrows. "A what?"

"A Fitheal." Ciaran said again. He stared at him for a moment and repeated. "You know, a Fee-hul." He looked at him irritably. "A goblins."

Comprehension dawned in Tase. "Oh, a goblin." He smiled at Ciaran. "Well, my name is Tase, and this," he gestured toward his brother, "is Fadin."

Ciaran looked at them both. "Why are you things here?"

"Our mother brought us here. This is our Aunt Kyna's castle."

Ciaran shrieked. "Kyna's castle? Hers castle!" His ears and the tips of his fingers became yellow again. "This is nots her house, this is my house. I cleans it, I keeps the spiders out of it, I watch for strangers, I keeps the secret door secret. I keeps this castle safe while she sits in hers tea room and invites diabhalta muzzies into it."

Tase put his hands up. "I didn't mean—"

"And what's it mean your Aunt? Kyna cannot be its mother-sister. Is impossible! She coulds not have done this. She is unable to have little yamia's of her own. This thing cannot be!" Ciaran's entire body was now a piercing yellow, and his hands and feet were more than twice their normal size.

"Please," Tase tried. "We didn't want—"

"No, no, no, NO!" Ciaran turned to look at him, his eyes wide with fury. "What is mother's name?"

Tase stared. "My mother?"

"Yes, its mother."

"Teagan," he spluttered. "Teagan Rose O'Callaghan."

Almost immediately, Ciaran again became green. His feet and hands shrank, and his eyes turned a stunning hazel. "Teagan?" He cocked his head. "You are an O'Callaghan?"

"Y-yes." Tase stammered.

Ciaran burst into thunderous and slightly insane laughter. He released the dusty box and rolled along the table. "I was thinking..." he choked. "Worried for her..." He let out a half-scream, and continued to tumble on the old piece of furniture.

Tase turned, and saw Fadin was no longer in a daze, but was walking toward the hysterical Ciaran.

"What is he laughing about?" he asked Tase.

"Nothing," giggled Ciaran as he got up from his fit. "Stupid things I thinks about is all," he said with a smile.

Tase exchanged glances with Fadin.

"You is welcome here any time," he said, bowing a little. "You, with the same faces."

"Thanks," Fadin said. He added in a whisper, "I think."

Ciaran smiled. "So..." he jumped down to the floor. Tase noticed that he stood no more than a third of a meter off the ground. "You two are Dalbhach?"

"We are what?" Fadin asked.

"Dalbhach," said Ciaran. He looked from one to the other. "You things do not speak proper I see."

Fadin suppressed a laugh.

"I guess not," Tase answered. He wasn't exactly keen to make the goblin angry again.

"It is a…" Ciaran looked as though he was in deep thought. "Sorcery, wizards, magic?"

Tase furrowed his eyebrows. "What? You think we're magic?" He wrinkled his forehead. "No, we aren't."

Ciaran looked shocked. "Its shoulds be. After alls," he shrugged his shoulders. "Its mother is."

The two of them exchanged frightened looks.

"What do you mean, our mother is?" Fadin almost shouted.

"Not very quick, these things," Ciaran mumbled. "Your mother," he pointed at them, "is Dalbhach. Magical."

Tase felt the colour drain from his face.

"No," Fadin snorted. "She isn't. She can't be." He looked at Tase. "Can she?"

"She cans and is," Ciaran assured them. "Why is this bad thing?"

Fadin sat down on the cobweb covered floor. "Why would she lie? Why would they both lie?"

Tase sat next to him. "Why would he?" He nodded to the small goblin.

Tase saw that Fadin had gone very white. He was sure he had too, and his stomach felt like it was doing backflips.

"Do not be sad, little vayyokc. I is sure she hads reason for not to tell you." He smiled and showed his stained teeth.

Tase simply half-smiled back.

"Are you certain about this, Ciaran?" he asked hopeful.

"Oh yes," he smiled again. "I is very sure."

There was a sudden pounding noise that made Tase jump. He turned to Fadin.

"Clearie," they said simultaneously.

They both walked briskly over to the door and listened. There was another loud pounding and muffled cries.

"Ciaran," Tase said backing away, "is there another way out of here?"

"Oh, yes," the little goblin said happily. "Comes over here."

He scurried beneath their feet and led them to a curtain-covered wall. As he pulled back the tattered cloth, Tase saw a large hole. It was crudely covered by a frying pan that only concealed half of it.

"I haves to have more than one ways to get out of here," Ciaran said excitedly. "It would makes people nervous to see a fitheal running through house, I thinks." He gestured toward the hole.

There was another loud banging sound.

"Where does this lead to?" Tase asked quickly.

"The grounds, but don'ts worry, no one will see you things."

92

Tase didn't have time to ask questions. As he leaned down to crawl into the hole, he saw it was barely big enough for him.

He stopped, looked around the room, and realized for the first time that someone was missing.

He whirled his head around. "Where's Path?" he demanded.

Fadin simply shrugged. "I thought he was with us the whole time."

There was a muffled yell.

"You things better go, to get away from loud pest."

"Close the doors for us?" Tase asked, hopeful.

Ciaran looked a bit insulted, but nodded just the same.

Tase took a deep breath, turned forward, closed his eyes tight, and pushed off.

The hole was really more like a slide. He ran his hand along beside him as he fell, taking notice that the slide was metal and cool.

Tase could not see where he was going, making the ride more thrilling, for the tunnel was filled with inky blackness. The only way he knew he was not alone, was by the light sounds of Fadin yelling.

Quite suddenly, wind whipping through his red hair, things started to get hot. The metal he was sliding on became almost unbearable to touch, causing Tase to try and jump while he slid.

Someone was yelling.

Tase listened as he tried in vain to keep off the boiling surface.

"Let me outta here, let me outta here," the voice shrieked. "Ya wicked, fat, old cow. Let me out, I say. Ya can't keep me in here. Ya can't treat me like a hostage. Ya let me out. No one keeps Ruepricked Joshua Dylan Jordan Alex Cody Tanner—"

The shouts faded and were gone.

The slide cooled off considerably and started to become too cold.

Tase winced at the icy pain on his bare hands and tilted his head as he heard the distinct sound of running water. He tried to listen harder, but the slide gave a great lurch and he was hoisted upwards through the air. He gave a little yelp and was slammed back onto the slick ground.

When Tase could take no more, light began to snake its way in. He squinted. The floor dropped away, and he landed with a thud, face-first into the dirt. Gathering himself, he sat up to spit out a mouthful of dirt. He looked about and noticed a barrier of bushes surrounding him when suddenly, Fadin landed on top of him, planting Tase's head into the dirt once more.

Fadin grunted and rolled off.

Tase, hardly noticing the sharp pain in his back, popped up and stared out of the bush cover. Seeing no one, he gave a sigh of relief and winced at the soreness that overtook him.

"What was that?" Fadin almost shouted.

Tase nearly toppled over, surprised by this outburst.

"What was he talking about?" Fadin cried, beginning to pace back and forth. "Our mother is a Dalibahoosit or whatever? What does that little muppet know?"

"Maybe he confused her with someone else," Tase said hopefully. "He did get her mixed up with another person when he got so angry, remember?"

Fadin looked at him doubtfully. "Perhaps, but if it is true…"

"I know," Tase answered, dreading the very thought. "But we don't really have any proof."

"Yea," Fadin said incredulously. "Only a goblin living in the attic, magic carvings, and secret doors."

Tase felt his heart sink. Fadin was right. He couldn't even hope Ma hadn't lied to them, could he? It was all too real.

"We should get going before Clearie breaks the bookcase down," Tase said without much enthusiasm.

Fadin nodded but didn't say a word.

# Chapter 6

## *The Hogans*

Fadin sat at the window letting his blue-green eyes survey the grounds. The trees were swaying in the cool October wind, and small birds where trying their best to fight it.

The last week had been rather quiet.

After his and Tase's narrow escape from the attic, they had snuck up behind Clearie in the hall.

He claimed to have heard movement in the walls. He could have sworn he heard Fadin and Tase's voices clear as a bell.

Fadin and Tase had of course denied it, leaving Clearie to defend himself against Ma and Aunt Kyna.

Ma had said he hadn't gotten enough sleep and that he should go straight to bed. Aunt Kyna seemed only too ready to accept this explanation and agreed that he should go too.

If they did have any idea about a goblin living in the attic, neither one let on in the slightest. They acted as if Clearie was going crazy, and even whispered about it when they thought no one was listening.

They hadn't counted on Fadin and Tase sneaking about, trying to pick up on any and all conversations. Or had they?

This act of Ma's, or whatever it was, put a damper on how credible Fadin thought Ciaran was. Why would she talk about the possibility of Clearie being crazy if she knew full well what did live in the walls? Or perhaps she really did have no idea that a goblin inhabited the upstairs and really was worried about her eldest son's sanity.

Whatever the truth was, the trip up to the attic was treated like glass that might shatter if anyone mentioned it. Neither Fadin nor Tase said a word about it since they had walked away from the hidden slide. Though, Fadin knew, it was constantly on their minds.

Pathos came and sat by Fadin's feet. He looked up and whined.

Fadin looked down at the dog. He had been curious about how Pathos had managed to get out of the east tower and back behind the bookcase without being noticed. But after some thought, he decided it was unimportant. The door had probably closed before Path could get in. It was the only logical answer.

Fadin smiled, bent down, and scratched behind Pathos' ear.

The Bernese moved his foot like a propeller and Fadin scratched harder.

"Coming down?" he heard Clearie say.

Fadin turned.

Clearie had been a little nicer to them since the attic incident.

Fadin suspected he thought they knew something about the voices he had heard, though he never said anything.

"Yea," Fadin nodded. He took one last look at the rocking trees and stopped. His eyes widened as he looked near the edge of the forest. The same black dog, the one he had seen the day they had arrived, was standing in the tree's shadows. Its light eyes gleamed, and Fadin could have sworn it looked up at him.

"Hey, Fadin," Clearie said, annoyed.

Fadin jumped at the sound, and blinked. He ignored Clearie and looked back at the forest floor, but the dog was gone.

Fadin furrowed his brow.

"Fadin?" Clearie asked.

Fadin shook his head. He must have imagined the animal, that was the only explanation. He sighed. "Let's go."

They bounded down the stairs, Fadin taking two at a time.

Pathos ran ahead of them, wagging his tail happily.

Fadin saw Tase sitting at the bottom stair, looking at something in his lap. He wondered what was up.

"Hey," he said, unsure of what to say in front of Clearie.

Tase looked up and smiled.

Fadin saw he had a small wrapped thing in his hand.

"Ready to eat?" Tase asked, putting the thing in his pocket.

Fadin had a good idea of what he was holding and why he had been sitting alone. He was thinking about going back up into the attic, and Fadin was more than willing.

Clearie seemed to notice the strange behavior, because he was eyeing them suspiciously. "You two alright?"

"Fine," Tase smiled.

"Never better," Fadin lied.

Clearie's two different colored eyes twitched. "Well, let's go then."

Tase shot Fadin a meaningful look as they continued towards the dining hall.

"Good morning," Ma said as her three boys entered the room.

She looked pale and sicker than the day before. The bug, or whatever it was that seemed to be making her sick, hadn't left since they arrived. She had been vomiting more frequently and often clutched at her stomach, as she had on the ride over to the castle.

"Where's Aunt Kyna?" Fadin asked, noticing their mother was sitting all alone.

"She had to take care of a few things, go back to work. But I wanted to spend some time with you anyhow."

Fadin could tell she had been crying.

Her nose, red and puffy, always gave it away.

"Besides," she continued. "I've missed you all." She glanced around the table and Fadin saw tears forming. "I'm sorry," she spluttered, letting the tears tumble down her cheeks. "I haven't been a very good mother to you these past five weeks."

Over a month. Had it really been that long? Fadin felt a pain in his chest at the thought. Five weeks since Da had died.

She dabbed at her eyes with a napkin and continued. "I didn't mean to shut you out, or not be there for you. It has just been hard since your, Da..." she trailed off and covered her face in her hands.

All three boys jumped up from their seats and were at her side in an instant.

"No, no, you haven't been," Clearie cooed.

"We all miss him, Ma," Tase added.

Fadin tried to say something, but a lump formed in his throat, making it impossible to even swallow. He simply put a loving hand on her shoulder.

Ma lifted her head from her hands and smiled at them. Her blue eyes seemed to pop out as they always did when she cried. "Things have been hard," she said grabbing Tase's and Clearie's hands. "But it will get better. I'll get better." She breathed deeply trying to stop the tears. "I'm going to be the good mother, I used to be."

"No," they all started.

She put a hand up. "I know I haven't been myself. I haven't spent much time with you, but that's going to change." She grabbed Fadin's hands. "Just be patient, things will get more normal."

They all smiled at her.

Fadin wondered how normal things could really be. He wondered if he would ever feel normal again.

"Now," Ma said, adjusting herself in her chair. "Go and eat."

They did as they were told, but Fadin had really lost his appetite.

They all talked for a long time. They discussed moving, the castle, Aunt Kyna, and the great loss that had overtaken them. Nothing, of course, was said about the attic and what lurked there, but Fadin felt happiness bubble inside him once more. Even though he knew things could never be the way they were, this simple time made him feel at ease again.

"You know," Ma said, beginning to clear the plates. "You'll be starting school again soon. It is almost October Holiday."

Fadin had to suppress a groan. He knew they had had almost six weeks off, but he still didn't want to have to start all that up again. He tried not to feel awful as he thought about having to begin in a new school. As if the old one wasn't bad enough.

"So, I think we should start looking for a proper one," Ma said smiling. She surveyed them all and smiled even wider. She was obviously trying to make this sound more enjoyable then it truly was.

*I'd rather get shot*, Fadin thought dully.

"Don't be so glum," Ma said, putting her hands on the twins' shoulders. "It won't be so bad."

Fadin glanced at Clearie, who didn't seem to mind a new school in the slightest. He was grinning happily, more than likely dreaming about all the fun classes and books he'd be sure to get.

The eejit.

Fadin crinkled his nose, then put on his best fake smile and looked up at Ma. He saw oddness in her eyes. It seemed as though she was hiding something, something she wanted to tell them but didn't.

Could it be that she knew what lurked up in the attic? Or wanted to tell them the truth about what she was? Or just wanted to come clean for lying? But then again, that could all just be a misunderstanding. Couldn't it?

"Well," Ma said, clearing what was left on the table. "Why don't you all go outside for a bit. The fresh air would do you good." She glanced at each of them. "You've all been inside too much."

Fadin felt his heart sink a little. Even though he had been avoiding the attic incident, he had been looking forward to possibly going back with Tase. He was certain what Tase had been holding was the wooden carving, and he was sure the look Tase had given him meant they should go back, today. Now, however, there would be no way to sneak off if they were told to go outside.

"Can I bring a book as long as I'm in the sun?" Clearie asked.

Fadin rolled his eyes. What was the point of going outside if you just stuck your nose in a book?

"Fine," Ma answered incredulously, "as long as you're in the sun and outside."

He nodded and got up to go pick and his precious book.

"Go on you two," Ma smiled at them.

Fadin and Tase got up and left the dining hall as well.

"Teagan," the voice of Daireann cried, as the swinging doors closed.

"How many times am I going to have to tell you, stop clearing the table? Let me do that."

Fadin smiled. She was awfully forceful, you had to give her that.

Tase snapped his fingers in disappointment. "Now what?" he asked.

"I guess we'll do it tomorrow," Fadin answered, feeling thoroughly disheartened now.

"Do what tomorrow?" Clearie asked, popping up from behind the wall. He had a small book clutched in his hands.

"Nothing," Tase answered.

Clearie raised an eyebrow and lifted up the small blue book. "The Key," he said pointing at the black letters. "It was stuck inside the wall. You wouldn't know anything about that, would you?"

Fadin arched an eyebrow. "You feeling alright there, Clearie?"

Clearie snapped a fiery look at him. "I didn't imagine the voices, did I?"

The twins exchanged glances.

"Nope," Fadin said with a broad smile. "You're just a header, voices come with the territory. If you start talking back to them however," he lifted his hands, wrists together, "we'll have to have you committed."

"Stop being a gobdaw and tell me the truth. I heard you up there."

"I'd keep your voice down. You don't want Ma and Auntie to hear you. They might just bring out the handcuffs and straight-jacket."

"Oh, shut up," Clearie yelled, tossing the book at him. "I know you're lying. I'm going to watch you, and I'll find out what's really going on. Just wait." He turned and headed off in the direction of the east tower.

"Just be sure to tell the voices in your noggin hi for me," Fadin called after him.

He turned to Tase, who didn't look very happy.

"What?"

"Why didn't you just tell him?"

"That there's a goblin living in the attic? Oh yes, I'm sure that would go over really well. I saw the little maggot myself, and I still have a hard time believing it."

"He's going to find out anyway."

"How? He doesn't have this, does he?" Fadin grabbed the wrapped thing from Tase's pocket.

Tase snatched it back. "He's bound to hear him. Ciaran isn't exactly quiet."

"Then if he hears or sees him, we'll explain. But there's no reason to now."

They heard footsteps.

"Come on," Tase whispered.

They ran silently to the door and went out as quietly as possible. When they were outside, they began to walk around the castle.

"Do you think Ma knows?" Tase asked.

"No," Fadin said quietly. "I don't even think Aunt Kyna does."

Tase nodded. "I miss Da."

Fadin looked out at the swaying trees. "I wish there was a way to talk to him."

"Me too," admitted Tase. "He would know what we should do."

*Or how to lie to us*, Fadin thought. He shook his head. What an awful thing to think. He was their father after all. Hadn't he known best?

They turned the corner and Fadin was surprised to see a rather tall girl of about thirteen looking in the bush where the tunnel was hidden.

She had long, straight, blue-black hair, olive-tan skin, and very dark eyes. She was thin, lanky, and stood head and shoulders over Fadin and his brother.

"Hey!" Fadin shouted.

The girl turned and smiled at them. Looking at her head-on, there was no way to deny she was pretty. Her lips were quite plump for her being so young, and her dark eyes danced as she smiled kindly in their direction.

"Hello," she said sweetly. "Did you know there's a hole in your house?"

"Yes," Tase answered awkwardly. "It's—it's ours."

"Yours?" she asked sounding perplexed. She arched a black eyebrow and stuck a hand in the pocket of her jeans.

Fadin threw him an irritated look. "Yes, we made it," he fumbled. He tried to think of a good story. "To... hide things in." *Stupid.*

"Oh," she said sounding unconvinced. "Well, my name is Aimirgin, Aimirgin Hogan." She smiled again and stuck a long-fingered hand out.

"Uh..." Fadin started oddly, "I'm Fadin and this is my twin brother, Tase."

They both shook her hand.

"Are you Kavanaghs?" she asked.

"No, no, we're O'Callaghans," Fadin answered.

"Oh," she said with an even bigger smile. "So you're Miss Kavanagh's...?"

"Nephews," Tase answered.

She nodded.

There was a long, awkward silence. They all seemed to be fascinated with the sky, the trees, the grass.

"Well," Aimirgin said, "I guess I'll be off then." She began to walk away.

Tase looked at Fadin, his blue eyes urging him to say something.

"Wait," Fadin said feebly, "you don't have to leave."

"Okay," Aimirgin said turning around. Suddenly, she lurched forward and fell face-first into the grass.

"Are you alright?" Tase asked, rushing to her side.

Fadin bent down next to her too.

Aimirgin had her head back and was laughing. "Yes, yes, I'm alright. I always trip and fall and knock stuff over. My da calls me accident prone."

Fadin looked down at the tiny hole which had caused her to fall. It was no bigger than his thumb. "I'd say so," he giggled.

Aimirgin shot him a playful look. "Hey, no laughing at the gracefully challenged."

Tase chuckled.

The two of them helped her up and dusted the mud and grass off her.

"So," she said, once she was all clean and steady on her feet. "What were you two doing out here anyhow?"

"Nothing really," Tase answered. "Our ma wanted us to go outside."

"I see. Not much to do out here."

Tase nodded and looked at the castle wall.

Aimirgin let her eyes survey the bushes. She was looking intently at the hidden tunnel.

"So," Fadin began feeling awkward, wanting to get Aimirgin's attention away from the tunnel. He couldn't think of a thought to go along with the "So." The word hung in the air like a disgusting odor.

"Are the stories true?" Aimirgin asked quite abruptly.

"What stories?" Fadin asked, looking at her nervously.

"The," she looked around to be sure no one was listening, "ghost stories," she finished in a whisper.

Fadin saw Tase grin.

He really didn't find this amusing. The last thing they needed was this girl thinking they had ghosts in their castle. She just might find it interesting to check, and what would they do if Ciaran jumped out to greet her?

"I didn't know there were stories," Tase said, shifting his eyes for an instant at the tunnel.

"Oh yes," Aimirgin said. "Loads of stories. People seem to think a ghost lives in your attic."

Fadin gasped, and tried to cover for it by yawning.

"They do, huh?" Tase asked, looking up to the small round window.

Fadin wanted to slap him. He wasn't even trying to cover the secret. If anything he was making it seem more believable.

"Well Fadin and I have been in that attic…"

Fadin held his breath.

"…and I can assure you, no ghost lives up there."

Fadin felt relief rush over him. Tase had said the perfect thing, and the best part of all was he hadn't even lied. There was no ghost, only a little green goblin who could stick his face out of the ceiling.

Aimirgin didn't seem convinced. "When did you go?"

"A week ago," Tase answered.

"In the day or night?"

"Why does it matter?" Fadin asked.

"It matters because ghosts only come out at night."

"Who told you that?" he asked mockingly. "Not every ghost only comes out at night."

She gave him an irritated look. "Oh really? Who told you that?"

Tase suppressed a giggle. "We went in the day," he said, smiling.

"Well," Aimirgin nodded, gazing at the round window. "You can't know for sure then, can you?"

Fadin rolled his blue-green eyes.

"Maybe we could go up in the attic at night, and check—"

"No!" they yelled simultaneously.

She looked startled and Fadin wished he could take it back. If anything would make her suspicious, screaming at her for wanting to have a look at a rumored attic would certainly do it.

Aimirgin just stared at them for a moment looking confused. "Well," she said, glancing at a thing on her arm that looked like a watch. "I have to go." She smiled at them and began, once more, to walk away.

"Wait," Tase said, throwing Fadin a sideways glance. "I'm sorry, we didn't mean—"

"No, no," she smiled. "I actually do have to go. My da is taking me and my brothers out for a picnic."

"Oh, that's nice," Tase said. "So you're not leaving because we shouted at you?"

"No," she chuckled. "It would take a lot more than that to scare me away. Besides," she glanced at the window again, "I don't believe you."

"No?" Fadin asked.

"No," she answered. "I think you're hiding something."

Fadin swallowed. Great, that's all they needed.

"But since I have to go, I'll have to sneak into your attic later."

Fadin opened his mouth to shout at her, but Tase clapped his hand over it.

"You won't find anything," Tase said, raising his shoulders.

"We'll see." She gazed at the roof. "Hey, do you want to come to the picnic?"

"With you?" Fadin almost shouted.

"No, my da likes to lock me up in a coffin whenever he goes out," she mocked. "Yes, of course with me. And my family, obviously. You want to ask your parents? I know my da wouldn't mind."

They looked at one another.

"Alright," Tase said. "We'll be back in a tick."

She smiled and nodded.

When they turned the corner, Fadin turned to him.

"You really want to have a picnic with this girl? We don't even know who she is, and by the way, she's thinking about sneaking into our attic."

"She won't really," Tase said. "Besides, it's not like we really have anything to do now anyway."

"Maybe not, but..." Fadin said trying to think of an excuse. "...but we—just ate."

Tase shot him an irritable look. "I didn't eat much, and you didn't even touch your plate."

"But..."

"Come on," Tase said. "What happened to being brave? Besides, what's so terrible about a picnic?"

They had reached the door. Tase pulled it open and they went inside.

They found their mother in the Tea Room. Tase quickly explained about the girl and her request to have them picnic with her family.

"Yes, of course you can go. I'm so glad you found someone your age." Ma beamed. "Now go on, have fun."

*Yea, fun.* Fadin thought. He sulked all the way back to Aimirgin.

"You can come?" she asked, seeing them turn the corner.

"Yup," Tase nodded. "Where to now?"

"My house. It's not far. Follow me."

She lead them towards the woods that surrounded Kavanagh Castle, and once they reached them, started inside.

Fadin hesitated. He really didn't feel like going inside the woods. Not after what had happened with that tree, and seeing that dog. He looked at Tase and willed himself to enter.

"So you live in a house in the woods?" Tase asked, once they had penetrated the dense outer rim.

"Yea, but it's not like a shack or anything. I love it, and you have your own built-in-privacy with all these trees."

"What about animals?" Fadin asked, looking warily around.

"Nah, they don't seem to bother us much," Aimirgin smiled. "Ouch." She tumbled forward after tripping on the root of a tree.

"You okay?" Tase asked, giving her a hand up.

"Fine," she answered playfully.

Fadin rolled his eyes and folded his arms. Why did he have to be here? In these stupid woods with a girl who couldn't even walk? He wasn't really sure what he was so upset about, but he knew he really didn't want to go on any stupid picnic, especially with this girl, who thought they had something living up inside their attic.

The sound of crunching leaves caused Fadin to jump, startled, and look about.

"Oh, it's probably just a rat or something," Aimirgin grinned. "Nothing to be scared of."

Fadin rolled his eyes. Sure, a rat, but what about a giant dog?

There was another rustling sound.

He turned and could have sworn he saw something big and black dart behind a tree. He gulped.

*Just a rat, it was only a rat.* He thought unconvincingly.

Aimirgin's house really wasn't far from Kavanagh Castle. It took about fifteen minutes and was easy enough to find. All they had to do was cut through the woods to the south and go straight. Once you walked far enough, the Hogan House came into view.

The home was no castle, but it was still two times larger than their old home. It looked like an oversized cottage with a thatched roof and several square shuttered windows. It stood about three stories high, and the outside was tapered with leafless tendrils. Here and there a few obscure flowers were planted along the entrance. The patterns were erratic, and the effort put into the foliage looked poor, yet very strongly attempted.

A very tall, olive-skinned man came out to greet them. He had Aimirgin's dark eyes and jet-black hair. He smiled kindly, and his face displayed the wrinkles that followed many years of hearty grins.

"Hello my sweet," The man said, kissing Aimirgin on the head. "Who are your friends?"

"Fadin and Tase O'Callaghan," she said smiling at them.

The man got a strange look on his face and all the colour left him. He put a long-fingered hand to his chest and stared intently at Fadin and Tase. He seemed to lose his balance for a moment and swallowed hard. He shook his head and seemed to snap out of whatever had overcome him. He smiled at the boys again and put a large hand out.

Fadin and Tase exchanged odd glances, but took his hand, each in turn.

"Lee Hogan," he said pleasantly. "A pleasure to meet you. My daughter, you already know, and these," he added hearing the front door open, "are my sons— Colmcille, Quinlan, Desmond, and Cormick."

Four young men came bounding out of the house and gathered around Lee. They were all taller than their father, and he had to be over two meters.

There seemed to be a substantial age difference between Aimirgin and her brothers, because the one who looked the youngest had to be about twenty.

The one named Colmcille stepped in front of the others. He was the thinnest of the four and had the longest hair. It was pulled back into a low ponytail, and shone blue in the sunlight. "Nice to meet you…"

"Fadin and Tase." Lee finished.

Colmcille smiled. "Fadin and Tase." He turned to his father. "We'd better get going. I have to be back in two hours."

"Can't spare any time for your poor old Da, huh?" Lee joked.

"Aw, how could you, Col?" The son named Desmond asked, leaning on his brother's shoulders. He appeared to be the eldest and had a shaggy, shoulder-length mane atop his head. His eyebrows were thick and he had scraggly facial hair. Through the front of his shirt, you could see the beginning of chest curls and his arms were thickly covered. From far away this man could look shady, but once you got up close, you saw his kind, dark eyes.

"Oh?" Colmcille turned to look at him. "What about you? Mr. I-can't-even-come?"

"Hey, things changed. I'm here, aren't I?" Desmond smiled.

"Yea," the youngest, Quinlan, added. "Under duress." He towered over the others, and looked the most like his father out of the lot. His eyes squinted as he smiled and dimples stuck out, his hair fell to the nape of his neck, and a single strand swung to frame his face.

"Shove off," Desmond laughed.

"I think he's right though, Da." Cormick said grabbing a pack from the floor. "We should head out." Cormick was probably the best looking of the

106

four. He had a strong chin, firm high cheekbones and thick biceps.

*Sort of a dark version of Clearie,* Fadin thought.

"Alright then," Lee said happily. "Let us be off." He turned to the twins as they began walking. "Have you ever been on a lunch in the woods?"

They both shook their heads.

Fadin didn't know how good an idea a lunch in the woods was.

"Then you're in for a treat," he said, prodding Fadin in the side with his elbow.

Fadin turned to Tase staring at the trees. "Think it's safe?"

Tase leaned in. "What do you think's going to bother this lot? They're bloody giants."

As they walked the older boys made jokes and every now and then began to rustle. This was stopped almost immediately, however, with the reminder that they were on limited time.

They soon found themselves in the middle of a clearing that had a nice carpeting of grass. Mr. Hogan announced that this would be their picnicking spot.

"Can't find a nicer place out here," he said laying down the blanket.

Cormick sat the backpack down and pulled out several sandwiches.

To Fadin's surprise, there was enough for everyone to have three.

He felt a bit odd sitting down with the chatty family and wished desperately that Aimirgin had her mother there instead of her father.

"So," Mr. Hogan started after a sandwich or two. "You're awful quiet things, aren't you?"

Fadin resented being called a thing, especially after the visit to Ciaran's attic.

"Why did you decide to move to your aunt's home?"

"Her castle, you mean," Fadin snapped. He could feel the heat rising in his cheeks.

Lee ignored the comment, causing Fadin's toes to curl.

"We, um," Tase began throwing him a reproachful look. "Couldn't afford our house anymore."

Aimirgin popped her head up and became more attentive.

This enthusiasm made Fadin even angrier. Why should she care? Why should any of them care? They seemed very happy in their own perfect little family.

"Why couldn't you afford it?" Lee asked, looking concerned.

"We had a—um—loss," Tase fumbled.

Fadin could feel the anger boil.

"I'm sorry," Lee said, leaning forward to put a hand on Tase's shoulder. "I understand what it feels like to—"

"Oh do you?" Fadin burst. He couldn't take it any longer. How could they know? How could this man, who got to be alive with his children every day, understand anything? "Tell us then," he screamed. "Tell us how you know what it feels like to lose your da. What it feels like to watch your mother barely get out of bed. Tell us what it's like to see the house you grew up in be sold to complete strangers. To pack up your da's things, and never take them out again, because he isn't coming home. He's never coming back, not ever! You tell me what it's like to need him and know there is no possible way that you can ever talk to him again." Steaming tears were tumbling down his cheeks now. "You tell us exactly how it feels to be hopeless, and know that there's nothing you can do. Tell us how it feels to know your ma is hiding things from you, but won't say a word." He knew he had gone too far, but couldn't stop himself. All the hurt was simply pouring out of him, and there was no way to prevent the flow. "How hard it is to hide things from her too," he continued. "What it feels like to never say how you feel, because you're afraid you're going to set her off again, and all you want is to see her happy." He took a deep breath, and glared at Mr. Hogan. How dare he assume to know anything. "Tell us. Explain it to me, in detail, what it's like!"

Fadin let the tears of anger and hurt pour out of him. He stood his ground, glaring, and taking in deep breaths, as though he had just finished running a race. He waited for Mr. Hogan's response—mean, harsh, angry. Something, anything.

But Mr. Hogan just looked at him. His expression was anything but angry. Instead he looked quite sad. His almost-black eyes were glossy as if tears were waiting to tip out. His brow was furrowed in pain, and he seemed to be fighting back a lump in his throat.

Fadin suddenly felt terrible. He felt like dirt, lower than dirt. He really hadn't meant to go off. He didn't even know he had been that angry, that hurt. He hadn't known he had so many feelings, and many of the things he said were news even to him. Yet, now, looking into Mr. Hogan's eyes, he felt terrible for feeling them and taking them out on this man, who was just trying to be nice.

Fadin noticed Tase was staring at him, wide-eyed, and mouth open. It made him feel even worse.

"I can't pretend to understand how that must feel," Mr. Hogan said, staring into Fadin's eyes. "I don't know what it's like to lose your da at such a young age, or what it's like to try and put on a brave face for your mother." He stood up on his knees, a head taller than Fadin. "I do know, however, what it feels like to lose someone." He put a calming hand on Fadin's shoulder. "I lost my wife a while ago, Chanel, and I understand how hard it can be. I know what that empty feeling is like." He put a hand over his chest, and clamped his teeth down, at the pain. Tears rolled down his cheeks and off his chin. "I know," he said, nodding and patting the place where his heart resided. "I know."

Fadin couldn't keep the tears away. They tumbled out from him like a waterfall. He felt ashamed, stupid, but at the same time, strangely relieved.

Mr. Hogan grabbed him up in an embrace that made him cry even harder. It reminded him of the way Da used to hug him. He felt safe, protected, and for the first time since the accident, the very empty space that his father had left.

It took him quite a while to calm down, but Mr. Hogan never seemed impatient and never loosened his grip. Fadin was glad for that—not only did it feel comforting, but the giant hug hid his face and muffled his crying.

When the stream of tears did finally stop, Cormick, looking sad and sympathetic, grabbed a few pastries and some water.

They ate them quietly, without anyone saying a word, not even Tase, who looked as though he had been crying himself.

Everyone finished their dessert, and when reminded by the startled gasp of Colmcille, they had to hurry back.

"You four go on," Mr. Hogan said. "I'll say goodbye now."

No one asked questions, but simply said their goodbyes and nice meeting yous, and then promptly strolled off.

The walk back with Mr. Hogan was a much slower pace. He didn't try to hurry them along at all, in fact, he seemed to want to take his time.

"Does your mother have any idea about how you feel?" Mr. Hogan asked. Although he sounded as if he already knew the answer.

Fadin simply shook his head. He was afraid that if he said too much, he may start to cry again. That was the last thing he wanted. He had done enough crying for the whole year, as far as he was concerned.

Aimirgin and Tase walked along besides Fadin and Mr. Hogan in complete silence.

"I think you should tell her," Mr. Hogan said, putting a large hand on his shoulder. "She deserves to know."

Fadin shook his head again. "She has too much on her mind."

She also was hiding something, maybe even something as big as being a Dulbahoosit. If she didn't trust him, why should he trust her?

Mr. Hogan seemed to hear what he was thinking. "Sometimes adults don't tell their children everything for good reasons. All she wants to do is protect you."

Fadin shrugged. "She shouldn't hide things."

"Well, what makes you so sure she is?"

"I just know."

He saw Tase nod solemnly.

Mr. Hogan put his arm around Fadin. "If you ever need to talk, either one of you, my door is always open."

Fadin smiled, and he saw Tase grin too.

They reached the Hogan house. It looked very cozy in the afternoon sun, and a wonderful smell was wafting out.

Fadin seriously wondered how they could possibly eat again, but kept the thought to himself.

"Aimirgin," Mr. Hogan addressed his daughter. "Why don't you walk the boys home. I don't want them to get lost."

"I really don't think we will, Mr. Hogan..." Tase began.

He held his hand up. "It would make me feel better." He smiled, and gave both of them a warm hug. "I hope to see you soon." He let them go, and turned his gaze to Fadin. He beamed again, and turned to walk inside the house.

"Let's go then," Aimirgin said, and began to lead through the thinning woods.

The walk to the castle was very quiet. Except for Aimirgin stubbing her toe on a pointed rock, no one said a word and there were no imaginary dogs, either.

Fadin felt uncomfortable, and wished he could think of something to say.

"Well," Aimirgin said as they came up to the hidden tunnel, "here we are."

The two of them nodded.

She nodded too and stood by the bushes awkwardly. "Goodbye, then," she said after a few moments and turned to leave.

"Wait," Fadin blurted. He really didn't know what he was going to say, but knew he couldn't just let her leave like that. "Thank you for inviting us."

She grinned. "Thank you for coming." She paused for a moment then said, "I'm sorry about your da."

Fadin nodded, "I'm sorry about your mother."

She bobbed her head, seeming to struggle with something in her throat. "Well goodbye, O'Callaghan boys."

"See you soon," Fadin added.

She turned and grinned. "See you soon."And with that, she walked away.

"What was that?" Tase blurted when Aimirgin was well out of earshot.

Fadin shrugged. He didn't want to talk about it. The truth was he really didn't understand the freak-out himself.

"Well?" Tase asked when Fadin said nothing.

"I don't know, I just got mad."

"Got mad? That was way more than mad. I don't think I've ever seen anyone cry so much. Well, besides Ma."

Fadin kicked a rock.

"Why didn't you tell me?"

"Tell you what?" Fadin asked.

Tase gave him an irritable look.

"Don't give me that," Fadin said. "I know I didn't tell you, but I really didn't know I felt that way either. Besides, you weren't exactly honest with me about the woman at school and your nightmares. So I'd say we're about even now. Don't you think?"

Tase thought for a moment, finally he nodded. "Okay, fair is fair I suppose." He was quiet for no more than a second when he added, "You can always tell me things, you know that, don't you?"

Fadin picked up a rock and threw it into the vast open grass. "Yea, I know. I really didn't mean to flip out like that."

Tase let a small laugh trickle from him. "I didn't think you did."

They came up to the door, and Fadin grabbed the knob to open it. He jumped back in surprise as it turned itself in his hand.

The door swung open, revealing a very cheerful-looking Clearie.

"What do you want?" Fadin asked, a bit hostile.

Clearie simply lifted his hand in the air. He was holding something wrapped in a black cloth. He allowed the wrapping to slide away, and smiled at the shocked look on their faces as he showed them the wooden "K."

"I think," he said, gazing into the air before locking eyes with them, "we need to talk."

# Chapter 7

## *The Hidden Closet*

Tase stared at him, his mouth completely dry. He felt around in his pocket and found a large hole. He gulped quietly and remained motionless. He couldn't think of what to do or what to say. Maybe they should just tell him, but then he may think they were crazy and go and tell their ma. Having their ma know about Ciaran was the last thing they needed, especially because they didn't know if she was lying to them or not about being, well, whatever it is that she was.

He just stood there, still, the wheels in his head turning. There had to be something he could say to throw him off or make him unsuspicious. But before he had to think too hard, Fadin shot out his idea.

"About what, exactly?" Fadin asked, sounding completely uninterested.

Clearie looked a bit annoyed but remained calm. "Guess."

Fadin pointed at the wooden carving. "That?" He looked at Tase. "That piece of wood? Why?"

"I think you know why," Clearie answered, sounding more irritated now.

"No, I don't think I do."

Tase saw Clearie's bottom lip tighten.

"Okay then, if you want to do it this way," he closed the door and moved closer to them. "Why was Tase hiding this from me when we came down this morning?" He shifted his gaze over to him.

"I didn't see him hide anything."

Clearie looked up, obviously trying not to get too angry. "Well I did, and then you kept looking at each other like you were hiding some big secret. I also saw the two of you fiddling with it when you went outside."

Tase closed his eyes briefly. If only Fadin hadn't grabbed it away from him. Perhaps they should just tell him, they really weren't fooling him anyhow.

"That wasn't a piece of wood we were messing with," Fadin said surprisingly. "It was a key we found under our bed. We thought we'd try it out on the…" he smiled, "dungeon door. It's right around the corner."

Tase grinned. It was around the corner. They had seen it when they walked to Aimirgin's house.

Clearie seemed to be shaking a bit, and his lips were now very thin. "Oh, really?"

"Yes, r-e-a-l-l-y," Fadin mocked.

"Then where is it?" he asked, looking from one to the other. "Where is this imaginary key?"

Tase felt a lightbulb switch on in his head. "We lost it," he said smiling.

"Lost it?"

"Yea, when we went on the picnic," he lifted his pocket up so Clearie could see the hole. "I didn't realize it until we got back only a few minutes ago actually. Too bad, it probably would have worked."

Clearie was now visibly shaking with anger and disappointment. "Well then," he said, grinding his teeth. "If it's not important to you—"

"Nope," Fadin chimed in. "Not important at all."

Clearie glared at him. "Then there's no reason to keep it?"

Fadin looked a bit worried. "Well, right."

Clearie smiled. "Right, why would you want to keep an old, useless piece of rubbish?"

"We wouldn't," Fadin answered, sounding unsure.

"Of course you wouldn't. So..." he lifted his foot up and dropped the wooden carving.

"Wait!" Tase yelled.

But it was too late. Clearie's foot had come smashing down, and the carving lay on the floor in a heap of broken pieces.

"You plonker," Fadin yelled, staring at the smashed pile.

Clearie grinned. "I thought it didn't mean anything," he said happily.

"It... didn't," Tase fumbled.

"You didn't have to go and crush it though," Fadin whined hopelessly.

Clearie shrugged. "I just got rid of a piece of useless junk." He looked satisfyingly at them. "Well, see you inside."

The door shut with a light slam, leaving Fadin and Tase to stare at the sad broken heap.

"What now?" Tase asked, not looking up.

"Don't know," Fadin answered, in an equally hopeless tone. "That was the only way into the attic, and now it's gone..." he trailed off and bent down to fiddle with the squashed mess.

Tase felt a horrible sinking feeling in the pit of his stomach. Now they may never find out if their mother was just a human, or if she was something else. He gazed up into the attic window. "Maybe we could climb the tunnel?"

"No," Fadin said glumly. "It's far too steep and slippery. There's no way we could make it."

Tase hung his head. There had to be something. To his amazement, he saw the broken pieces of the "K" beginning to glow red.

Fadin shrieked and jumped up, sucking at his fingers.

"It's hot," he yelped.

Tase stared back at the pile and watched as the pieces pulled themselves back together. They seemed to just climb back into place. Out of the blue, the carving caught fire, but before either one of them could panic, it had put itself out, and was whole again.

Fadin bent down and touched it cautiously. "It's fine," he said, picking it up.

Tase took it from him. "It's like nothing happened to it." He turned it over in his hands. "That burn mark's still there, though," he said, examining it. "I wonder why it didn't fix itself with that too?"

Fadin looked as well. "Weird, maybe it's not a normal burn."

"What do you mean?"

"Well, all I'm saying is, we found it in a house that has goblins living upstairs. I think its safe to say the people this belonged to weren't normal."

Tase nodded. That was most certainly true. The carving itself certainly wasn't normal, and they did find it hidden inside a stone wall.

"What do you think the "K" stands for?" Tase asked.

Fadin shrugged. "A name or something?"

"Maybe," he agreed. "We'd better keep it hidden now that Clearie thinks he crushed the darn thing."

Fadin took it. "We probably shouldn't keep it in the house."

"Where then?" Tase asked thinking this was a foolish idea.

"The tunnel?"

"What if Aimirgin finds it?"

"I thought you liked her," Fadin said in a mock-girly voice.

"Shut up," he said taking the carving back. "You were the one who told her we'd 'see you soon.' " Fadin glanced at the floor. "Besides, I don't care if she is nice or not, she may take it and decide to really have a look in our attic."

"She'd have to figure out what it is first." Fadin pointed out.

"That's true, but I think it would be safer somewhere we could easily get to it. Somewhere we could keep an eye on it."

Fadin smiled. He took the wooden "K" back and walked over to a planter with a small tree growing out of it.

"Hand me that cloth," he demanded. Fadin took it, wrapped the carving inside, and dug a small hole, burying the carving.

"That'll work," Tase said, surprised at the suggestion.

"Now Clearie won't have any idea. But we have to act sulky the rest of the day, so we don't seem suspicious."

Tase looked up. "He'll think we know something then?"

"He'll know we know something if we don't," Fadin retorted. "Couldn't you tell he didn't believe us? He thinks he broke something important to us, and it would be better to make him think that was the truth. If we don't, he'll know something's up."

Tase nodded. "Well, we'd better get inside then. What do we tell him we did with it?"

Fadin cocked his head to think. "Tell him we threw it away. No sense in keeping 'an old useless piece of rubbish.' "

They smiled at each other and taking one last look at the planter, went inside.

~~~

It didn't surprise Tase to see him sitting in the sunroom reading a book. Clearie was obviously very happy with himself for causing them so much trouble. When they walked in, he poked his head up and smiled at them. The grin seemed totally innocent from the outside, but inside, Tase knew Clearie was gloating with his supposed triumph.

Ma and Aunt Kyna were there too, sitting on the patterned couches. Aunt Kyna, sipping a cup of tea, and Ma knitting.

*She never knits.* Tase thought. *How odd.*

Apparently their aunt had come back when they had gone with the Hogans. She was clad in a long, flowing-sleeved dress. The neck line was low and wide, and the material seemed almost to be made of silk or something like it. The colour was deep forest-green and brought out her eyes.

Inspecting it, Tase thought it looked like a piece that belonged in the middle ages. Everything she wore looked like that. And come to think of it, all he'd ever seen her in was these old-fashioned dresses. Although you couldn't deny they were beautiful.

"Hello, darlings," Ma said happily. "How did the picnic go?"

Tase saw that her nose was a little red and she was still very pale. She must have been crying. He hoped she would get better soon. Not everything Fadin had said to Mr. Hogan he disagreed with.

"Your mother was telling me you two met a friend?" Aunt Kyna asked before he or Fadin could answer their mother. She sounded positively delighted.

Tase nodded but felt a bit awkward. He wasn't used to having an aunt, especially one who cared about his "friends." Hearing her so excited gave him a strange cringing feeling, and although he was sure she meant well, her tone sounded as if she was interrogating someone. No, that was mental.

"The picnic went good, Ma," Fadin answered, stumbling on his words a little.

"Just good?" Ma asked, putting down her knitting. "Didn't you two have fun?"

Tase was sure Fadin did not want his crying fit out in the open, so he quickly jumped in. "Yea it was fun, a little odd though, new people. It takes some getting used to."

"Did her family come as well?" Ma asked.

"Her da and brothers."

"That's nice, her mother didn't want to?"

Tase felt his body stiffen. He didn't want to give her the answer. It would certainly make her feel worse. Oh why had she asked? "She—um—died a while back now."

"Oh," Ma said. She looked distant for a moment, like she had gone somewhere else, and only her body had stayed behind. "The poor thing." She picked up her sewing needles and began to knit slowly.

Aunt Kyna watched her warily as she spoke. "Sounds like she's a nice girl, what's her name?"

"Aimirgin," Fadin answered.

"Pretty name," Aunt Kyna said, turning to them. "I have a friend whose daughter's name is, Aimirgin. I've always liked it."

Tase nodded slowly. Aunt Kyna was trying to make conversation, but it was awkward. Not that Tase didn't like her, he did, but sometimes her warmth seemed—well—acted. Not genuine. But that could just be him as well. He wasn't used to having an aunt.

"I—I'll be back in a bit," Ma said unexpectedly. She stood up and allowed her sewing needles and thread to fall to the floor. "I'm glad you boys had a nice time," she said quickly, as an after-thought. She smiled at them, unconvincingly, and walked out towards the entrance.

Aunt Kyna watched her, got up, and paused at the arch, which lead into the entrance. "I'm just going to check on your ma. I'm glad you two met a friend." She grinned just as falsely and followed Ma, leaving Fadin and Tase alone with Clearie.

"So," Clearie said, laying down his book. "You going to try and glue the pieces back together, or did you just give up?"

"We didn't even know what it was, why should we want to put it back together?" Fadin asked, mixing in just the right amount of anger.

Clearie beamed. "So what did you do with it?"

"Threw it away," Tase answered. "Like you said, no use in keeping it."

He shrugged, positively glowing, and continued reading his book.

Fadin rolled his eyes and gestured towards the stairs.

~~~

When they reached the room that had temporarily been Tase's, Fadin closed the door.

Tase flopped himself on the bottom bunk and looked around.

Enda had moved all of Fadin's belongings into the space and bunked their beds a week before. Now the room had not only green but blue in it as well, which was alright because the green and blue complemented each other.

"What are we going to do?" Tase asked, staring at the ceiling. "We can't hide it forever."

"No?" Fadin asked, leaning against the closet. "Why not?"

Tase rolled over and stared at him. "What do you mean why not? We can't keep a secret like this, especially if Clearie is already suspicious. Not to mention the fact that our little secret has a mind of its own and could pop at anytime. This won't keep quiet for long."

"Well it's at least quiet for now."

"Yea, but for how long? We have to figure out what we're going to do next."

Fadin shifted his position a little. "We'll think of something."

Tase let his mouth drop. He gaped, wide-eyed, at the bizarre scene in front of him, not sure whether to be afraid or excited.

"What?" Fadin asked, looking at Tase's dumbfounded expression.

Tase simply lifted a finger and pointed.

The white wooden door to the closet had changed into a dark, slightly chipped one. The knob looked very worn, and in the centre of the beat up old door sat the same symbol from their wood carving. A large K.

They exchanged glances and moved closer.

"Do you think it's safe?" Tase asked, eyeing the knob.

"There's only one way to find out," Fadin said. He closed his eyes and grabbed the handle.

Tase clamped his eyes shut just as the door was beginning to open. He heard the sound of wood against wood and slowly opened one eye. Relief rushed over him as he saw the open door revealed only a closet. A very strange and unusual closet but a closet just the same. It appeared to have belonged to a young woman. There were several strange dresses hanging on the racks, dresses like Aunt Kyna wore, and at least two dark green cloaks.

There were also several pointed, round, and square hats sitting on the shelves along with oddly shaped shoes.

On the walls hung two pictures. One was black and empty like others they had seen around the castle. The other, old tattered, and hung with tape, contained a handsome green-eyed young man. He had a large smile, silvery hair, and appeared to be singing.

Tase cocked his head. "Who do you suppose that is?" he asked, gazing at it.

Fadin leaned over his shoulder. "Don't know, long-lost relative?"

Tase shot him an irritated look. "Seriously, who do you think that is?"

"I don't know. I haven't got the slightest idea, although it isn't exactly surprising, seeing how we really don't know who our ma is either."

Tase clenched his fist. Why were there so many secrets in this house? He spotted a faded piece of parchment tacked to the wall. It had curvy ink writing on it, splotched here and there with water stains.

Tase snatched it from the wall and looked it over.

"What's that?" Fadin asked, leaning over his shoulder.

"A letter," Tase said. "Listen:

*Dear DA,*

*Why? I don't understand? Why would you bring us to this point, only to vanish? Only to leave us? What happened to you'll always be there?*

*I don't understand. Why have you gone? Why did you choose what you chose? Why did you sacrifice yourself for us? We were willing. All of us, any of us, to take your place, to do what had to be done. Why then? We need you here. We cannot win this without you, we simply cannot.*

*We, I, did not deserve what you did. None of us.*

*Where are you now? What do you expect us, to do? We are alone now, so alone. Afanasii is strong. How do you expect us to carry on when you have vanished from our side?*

*I don't understand you, or why you've done this, but what choice do I, have now?*

*It is only us, who carry out this plan.*

*Why could it not have been me who died? I would rather it have been, oh how I wish it.*

*Love,*

*T.K. "*

Tase put the paper down and looked at Fadin.

Fadin raised an eyebrow. "Did you hear the word the writer used?"

Tase nodded. "DA, capitalized. Instead of the word Da, the writer could mean D.A. The letters on Da's crest."

Fadin pulled the crest from his jacket pocket.

Tase had seen it the night he and Fadin made up. Fadin always kept it on his person just as Tase kept the necklace under every shirt.

"What do you suppose it stands for?" Fadin asked.

"I think it's initials," Tase answered. "I think it's the initials of some person. Someone this writer loved very much." Tase paused for a moment and thought about all that had transpired since his da's death. Suddenly, he felt angry. "Why was this kept secret?" he asked, not really directly to anyone. "Why was the carving hidden?"

Fadin shrugged. "Maybe someone thought these things shouldn't be discovered."

"Or, are too dangerous to be revealed."

"What are you talking about?"

"Think about it, Fadin. Why are all these pictures blank?" he pointed at the black photo. "Why are we not allowed in the dungeon? Why is a dungeon even in this castle? Who is D. A.? Why did Da have a crest with their initials on it? What is so important that it needs to be kept a secret like this?"

Fadin simply looked back into the closet.

Tase continued. "I think Aunt Kyna knows, she has to, it's her castle. These things are being kept quiet for a reason, and I'd like to know what that reason is."

"It seems like we're not supposed to know," Fadin repeated.

Tase turned away from his brother and leaned forward to grab a wooden box sitting on one of the shelves. He brushed the dust off it and glanced down at the carved letters.

"T. K. Just like the letter," he said quietly. "Wasn't Aunt Kyna married?"

Fadin turned to him. "Yes, I think so. Why?"

"Yes, Ma said she was. She said her husband had left her this house, and it was all she had."

"Why?" Fadin repeated quietly.

"Has Ma ever told us her maiden name?"

"Kavanagh," Fadin answered, sounding perplexed.

"Don't widows usually keep their married name?"

"Yes I suppose."

"Aunt Kyna is Ma's sister, right?"

"Right."

"So why wouldn't Aunt Kyna keep her married name?"

"What are you talking about?"

"Aunt Kyna's last name now is Kavanagh, right?"

"Okay."

"So why didn't she keep her dead husband's last name?"

"What made you think of all this?"

He picked up the box and showed him the initials.

"T.K. So?"

"So, Teagan Kavanagh."

"There's no way to know whether or not there was another girl with the same initials living—"

"There wasn't. These clothes aren't more then twenty years old, and Aunt Kyna's husband didn't have any siblings. I heard Ma talking to Da about it once."

"How would you know how old these clothes are?"

Tase just looked at him for a brief moment. "Come on Fadin, there is no way these clothes belonged to Aunt Kyna's mother-in-law. This closet belonged to a teenager, young adult at best."

Fadin looked back at the closet. "I don't know why she would change her name back."

"Unless she didn't."

"What?"

"Ma said this was the husband's house."

"Yea, so?"

"It's named Kavanagh Castle. She wouldn't have been able to change the name of the estate if it had been her husband's property, especially if there were other living relatives."

"What are you getting at?"

"Why would Ma have a closet in her sister's husband's house? Or maybe it wasn't her brother-in-law's house at all. Maybe Aunt Kyna really isn't her sister, or this is really just their home, and there was no brother-in-law." He glanced around the closet again. "These are Ma's initials, it's her writing even on the parchment."

Fadin looked at the letter more closely.

"Someone isn't telling the truth, and it seems like these secrets run deeper then we thought. We don't even know whose house this is."

Fadin put his hands up. "Don't you think we're jumping to conclusions?"

"You really think that? Look at all the things we've already found."

"A house goblin and an undisclosed closet hardly prove this isn't Aunt Kyna's Castle, or that Ma is lying."

"Okay, let's put aside the fact that none of this adds up. Have you looked at Ma and Kyna together?"

"No, I usually keep my eyes shut when I'm around them."

"Stop trying to be smart. I'm talking about the fact that they look nothing alike."

Fadin glanced back at the closet. "You have a point I suppose, but we really don't have any proof or facts. We're guessing that this was Ma's closet, and if it was, then she really is lying about a lot more than we thought."

Tase nodded. "There is one way we could check."

"How?"

"Ciaran. We could ask him whose closet this was."

"You actually trust him? What if he lies?"

"What reason would he have to lie?"

Fadin shrugged. "I don't know, but I'm not willing to just trust his answer."

"I don't see what other choice we have, unless you want to walk up to Ma and ask her if this is her closet."

Fadin rolled his eyes and grabbed the box with their mother's supposed initials. "It's stuck shut," he said, grunting with effort.

"Let me try," Tase declared, pulling it away.

"You really think if I can't open it, you can?"

Tase yanked and pulled with no success. He glared at Fadin as he laughed openly.

"Told you."

"Well, it's probably sealed by magic or something."

"What's sealed by magic?"

Tase and Fadin jumped at the sound of Clearie's voice at the door.

Tase threw the box into the closet and Fadin slammed it shut.

Tase flung himself at the door, as the handle began to jiggle.

"It won't go back to the old closet," Fadin whispered harshly.

"What are you two doing in there?" Clearie demanded, banging on the door.

"Try leaning on it like you did before," Tase whispered back. He could feel his feet slipping and Clearie was beginning to push harder.

Fadin hurled himself backward, trying to find something, anything, that would return the closet to normal. He began to smack every plank of wood frantically.

When Tase thought he could hold the door no longer, Fadin hit a knothole and the access changed into their white closet almost instantly.

Tase backed away from their door.

An excited Pathos and a stumbling Clearie burst into the room.

Pathos jumped up and licked Tase.

Clearie simply glared from his spot on the ground. "What were you two doing?" he asked, standing up.

"Spring cleaning," Fadin answered smiling.

Clearie ignored him. "What's magic?"

"Nothing," Tase said, feeling his insides tremble.

Clearie raised his blond eyebrows. "Nothing huh? Then why didn't you let me in?"

"What do you want from us?" Fadin almost shouted. "We never come bursting into your room like this. And I'm sick of you, thinking we have something to tell you. If we did, you'd know."

Tase gasped as Pathos scratched at the knothole by their closet. He saw it changing into paintless wood and lunged forward.

"So leave us alone and get out," he screamed, pushing Clearie out the door.

"But…" Clearie started.

Tase slammed it shut and pointed at the closet.

Fadin jumped, grabbed Pathos, and pressed the knothole.

"What are you trying to do?" Fadin asked, patting the Bernese on the head. "I thought you were on our side."

Pathos merely looked up at them and let his tongue hang low.

"For your information," Clearie's voice came muffled through the door. "I was just coming up to ask if you two are hungry. We're having an early dinner because Ma's not feeling very well. She wants to know if you two would like anything or if you're still full from the picnic. Since you shoved me out of the door like maniacs, I assume it's the latter."

Tase glanced at the clock. It was almost four. He exchanged looks with Fadin and then slightly opened the door. "No, we aren't hungry."

Clearie raised his eyebrows, shrugging. He turned to go down the stairs.

Tase stopped him. "Sorry for shoving you around like that. Thanks for asking anyway."

Clearie didn't respond. Instead, he stood still for a moment and walked down the stairs.

"Nice of you, thinking he may actually be human," Fadin said, coming up beside him. "Unfortunately, he disappoints every time."

"Well, we have an excuse to be gone awhile," Tase said, turning to his brother.

Fadin looked a bit apprehensive but nodded just the same.

Tase understood why. Although he did want to find out the truth, it could mean they had to face the fact that Ma had been dishonest with them. It was, however, something that had to be found out.

They snuck down the stairs as quietly as possible and dug up the old carving with Pathos at their heels.

They made sure no one was watching, especially Clearie, as they made their way to the East Tower.

Once there, Fadin opened the door with the wooden carving.

The three of them moved through the bookcase entrance and walked up the cold stone stairway.

Tase thought it odd that both times they had come up to the attic, Pathos had been with them. At least he had been there, partly, last time. He smiled down at the old dog, grateful for the protection.

They entered the old deserted bedroom and walked to the hidden door.

Tase read the inscription aloud, and the access slowly crept open.

Tase entered the attic at a snail's pace, darting his eyes from corner to corner, trying to spot Ciaran. Yet the attic was quiet and there appeared to be nothing moving.

"I wonder where he is," Fadin said, stepping inside as well.

Tase clutched Pathos' collar and moved further in. "Ciaran?" Tase called.

There was a sudden flash of yellow and Tase bounced backwards onto the floor. He felt Pathos' collar ripped out of his hand as whiteness blurred his vision. He heard an abrupt, shrill whine, which undoubtedly came from Pathos.

Fadin began shrieking angrily. Yelping and cursing.

Tase pulled the sheet away which had covered his face and shot up, trying to see what had happened.

In the middle of the attic, a yellow, disturbed Ciaran stood atop Pathos, waving his right arm in the air, as if he were an American cowboy riding his bull. He had the Bernese on his back, tied with green string around all four paws and snout. He breathed in hard and tugged tightly on poor Pathos' restraints.

Fadin, while muttering profanities, was trying to seize the green twine and swat the house goblin away.

"No," Tase said, when he had fully taken in the scene.

"This monster will not harms you," Ciaran said in a very brave voice, "I will hang him by his toes and pull out his nasty teeth one by one."

Pathos growled and snapped through the twine at the little goblin.

"If you even harm one hair on him, so help me," Fadin seethed.

"No," Tase repeated moving in front of Fadin. "Ciaran, he isn't a monster, he's our dog, our pet."

The yellow slightly faded from the goblin's face. "Pet?" he said awkwardly. He looked down into Pathos face and cocked his head. "This teeth-filled things is your pet? He cannot be. He is not pet. Not dog. Look him eyes."

"Yes, I see his eyes, Ciaran. They are the eyes of a dog, my dog. He isn't a monster. Let him go."

Ciaran tipped his head again, thinking. "A dog? A trickster him is. No dog. Unless," Ciaran got very quiet and looked from Pathos to Fadin to Tase. "Is really your pet?" he asked.

"Yes," Tase said exasperated. "Please, let him go."

Ciaran thought for a moment, then smiled. "Of cores I let him go. I is sorry for harming your pets." He untied Pathos and stepped away from him.

Pathos shook his body angrily and stood behind Fadin. He secured his brown eyes on the goblin and kept up a low, constant growl.

"Well," Ciaran said, jumping from a stack of books onto the old rusted table. "I didn't know if I ever see you things again."

Fadin rolled his eyes.

"It's been long time."

"Yes," Tase said, glancing at Pathos' feet. "We've been busy."

Ciaran was almost completely olive-green, his little tuft of hair was again turning jet-black, and his eyes were changing back to their normal hazel.

"Busy," Ciaran mimicked. "Yes, I see you with girl outside. Pretty thing she is." He smiled and showed his ugly teeth. The goblin plopped himself down on the table and kicked his oversized feet. "So why you come back to see me?" he asked, eyeing them both.

"We had a question," Fadin said, staying close to Pathos.

"Yes?" Ciaran asked, his large ears sticking straight up.

"Whose magical closet is hidden in our room?" Tase asked, seeing Fadin obviously wasn't going to.

"Closet?" Ciaran said, allowing one ear to flop by his face. "Hidden closet? I know not," he answered to Tase's surprise.

"You don't?" Tase said, biting into his lower lip. "I thought you knew every part of this house."

"I do," Ciaran said. "But I have never heard of this hidden closet."

Tase glanced at Fadin.

"Maybe you should have a look."

Ciaran looked up at the ceiling. "Okay," he responded.

Before they had time to react, Ciaran grabbed Fadin and Tase's pinkies and shoved their heads into the floor.

Tase felt a cold sensation, a sickening feeling. He opened his eyes slowly, only to be confronted with the stairway. Yet as he looked at it, he realized that he was seeing things from above. He strained his neck and saw that his head was poking out from the ceiling.

He started to scream when Ciaran shoved a ceiling-looking foot into his mouth.

"Silence, you," he said in a harsh whisper. His entire head looked like it was made of wood, like it was made from the ceiling. Just like it had the night Tase and Fadin thought they had seen a ghost.

Tase pushed hard and spotted Fadin's head covered in the same wood-looking material.

"That goes for you as wells," Ciaran whispered to Fadin.

Fadin looked sick and closed his eyes as he peered down.

"Now," Ciaran said quietly. "Where is this closet?"

"Through there," Tase whispered, pointing with his head.

Ciaran nodded.

Tase had the most awkward sensation as they began to move. It was almost like swinging upside-down on the monkey bars, and he had butterflies in his stomach.

They entered the room and Ciaran turned to look at the closet.

"Oh, yes," he said in a whisper. "You're rights. I have no seen this closet befores. How did things find it?"

"Not this closet," Fadin said, finally opening his eyes. "This was here when we moved in. There's a different closet hidden within it."

"How do you opens this hidden closet?"

Fadin pointed with his head. "You push that knothole."

Ciaran nodded. "Okay, push it." Without warning, Ciaran lunged forward.

Tase held his breath.

Fadin tumbled to the floor, still covered in the wood-looking camouflage.

Ciaran had a hold of his hair. The little goblin, held up only by his grip on Fadin's scalp and Tase's finger, dangled in mid-air.

Tase cringed, suddenly feeling the pressure, Ciaran's weight, had put on him. He felt himself slip a bit, and saw, to his horror, his shoulders come out of the ceiling. He gulped and clutched Ciaran's whole hand.

"Steady you," Ciaran said, moving closer to the floor. He turned to Fadin. "Push it."

Fadin did as he was told, and the white closet quickly changed into an old brown door, with a "K" in the middle.

Even with the wood covering them, Tase could see Ciaran's eyes widen.

He nodded to the handle.

Fadin opened it.

Tase saw the goblin's mouth drop, and his eyes became even bigger.

Ciaran moved just a little closer and stared at the contents filling every shelf and hanger. He looked to be in almost a trance.

The sound of swift footsteps hit Tase's ears, causing him to panic.

Fadin jumped up so fast, Tase was amazed Ciaran still held his grip on him.

Tase felt like he was slipping even further out of the ceiling and could tell the footsteps were getting closer.

Ciaran yanked on Fadin's hair and nearly flung him at the closet door. "Close it and locks it away."

Fadin slammed the door shut and kicked the knothole.

The door began to change back to white.

Ciaran turned to Tase and squeezed his finger. "Pulls up," he said, perhaps a bit too loudly.

Tase didn't know how, but he tried. He yanked up with such force that it sent them flying out of the room, through the ceiling, and backside first when they entered the attic.

Pathos came leaping to them. He gave them all a slobber bath and whined profusely.

"Get your pets off me," Ciaran yelped.

Tase saw that Pathos had accidentally slobbered him up as well, trying to get at Fadin.

Ciaran's eyes were becoming a piercing yellow and his hands began to swell.

Tase jumped up and moved Pathos as quickly as he could.

Ciaran stood up and limped awkwardly over to a stack of books. He pulled out the box Tase had seen on their last visit—the box that Ciaran had ambushed them for.

"Did Pathos hurt you?" Tase asked, watching him favour his right leg.

Ciaran looked up. "No, no, I think was yanking," he smiled at Tase. "You is stronger than thing think."

"I'm sorry," Tase said, making to come nearer to him.

Ciaran held up a skinny hand. "No, no say sorry. I just think some screw came loose."

Tase cocked his head. "Screw?"

Ciaran grabbed his hurt leg, twisting and yanking it. It came off with a horrible pop.

Tase gasped.

Ciaran opened the box and pulled a little wooden leg out of it. He fit it firmly on the end of his knee stub and then stood up.

"You have an amputated leg?" Fadin asked, mouth agape. "How did it happen?"

Ciaran smiled. "Long time ago, but now not time for stories." He walked with a limp over to another pile of books in the shape of a chair and sat down.

The sound the little goblin made as he toddled was familiar to Tase.

Thump—clack—thump—clack.

It was the same noise he and Fadin had heard the night the face came out of the ceiling. The clacking part of the sound made sense now. It was Ciaran's wooden leg hitting the floor.

"That closet yous saw," Ciaran started, looking up at them, "was not a hidden one. That old brown closet was the ones that has always been there. The magicals closet, as you say, is really the white one you things use."

The boys exchanged frightened looks.

"Well then, whose closet was the brown one?" Fadin asked.

Ciaran looked up at them and shook his head. "Was things mother's."

Tase felt a strange combination of fear and satisfaction. He had been right, it was Ma's closet. But that also meant she really had lied, and there were far more secrets than they had even imagined. Tase put his arms around his middle as his stomach began to turn.

"Are you sure?" Fadin asked, clinging to Pathos.

The little goblin stood and waddled under the old broken table. He returned with a book that looked far too heavy for him to hold up.

"Looks at this," he said grunting a little, "don't takes my words for it."

Tase took the book and laid it on the table.

Fadin joined him and they turned the first page.

There, in what looked like a burn, was the same symbol they had seen all over the house. The large engraved "K."

Tase swallowed hard and turned the page again.

There, in a black and white photo, stood several young people. They looked to be in their early twenties, some perhaps a bit older. There was a large scratch on the photo, which cut off two individual's heads. One was a woman and the other was a man.

Tase looked to the right and saw, to his surprise, Ma smiling broadly and dressed in an unusual, medieval outfit. Next to her stood the same young man from the picture inside her closet. He was smiling too, and had his arm around her waist.

"Fadin," Tase said, "do you see…?"

"Ma? And that odd chap from the photo in the brown cupboard? Yep, I see them."

Tase looked above the photo and saw there was a caption.

*The Feneg*, it said in curved handwriting.

"The Feneg?" Fadin said, looking closely at the letters. "That means 'the seven,' doesn't it? I remember that from school. In our Gaelic class, I think."

Tase arched an eyebrow. "Fadin Michael O'Callaghan actually remembers something from school?"

Fadin rolled his eyes. "Oh dry up, Tase. I'm just pointing out that there are a lot more then seven people in this picture."

Tase looked down. "Yes there are. But I don't think you remember that word from school. Feneg isn't Gaelic, 'seacht' is the word for seven in Gaelic. I don't know where we heard it, but I remember that word meaning seven too."

Fadin nodded. "Weird, but we must be wrong, there's more than seven in this photo."

Tase furrowed his brow. "But look, there seems to be seven huddled around that man there with the scratched-out face. Seven men, and the others are a little spaced out from the others."

"Or they could be huddled around that woman." Fadin pointed out. "It's hard to tell."

Tase scanned the seven men huddled together more closely and stopped as a face popped out at him.

"Da," Tase cried.

Fadin looked at him. "What?"

"Look there," he pointed with his finger. "Da's there, in the seven."

Fadin looked at their father's face and blinked. "Bloody geese, it is him. That's Da."

Their father stood, red hair curling upward, scrawny and skinny, in between an incredibly tall man and a blond, handsome man. He looked very short, scrunched in the middle of all the people.

Tase looked under the caption and saw a list of names. Most he did not recognize. Tase looked at the scratched-out faces. He followed a line down to the names and found the initials D.A.

"Fadin," he said quietly, "look."

Fadin's jaw opened wide. "It is a person. But is it the man or the woman?"

"I can't tell. The name next to D.A. has been crossed out. And the letter didn't specify."

"What is Da doing in this photo?" Fadin turned to Ciaran. "What is he doing here?" He put the book on the floor so Ciaran could see.

The goblin looked at their da's face and smiled. "Your things da is

Alroy O'Callaghan?" he said, not really as a question. Comprehension seemed to be dawning in him. "I see."

Fadin looked impatient. "Why is he in this picture but not with Ma?"

"Was long time ago, before they marries each other," Ciaran smiled again, seeming very pleased to be able to give them this news.

"Who's that?" he asked, pointing to the young man next to Ma. "And who in the bloody hell is this D.A.?"

Ciaran put a hand under his chin. "Well..."

Without warning, the air around them rang with a frantic cry from below.

Tase jumped, hitting his knee on something or other.

Fadin made himself completely still, listening.

"Where are they?" Ma screamed. Her voice was muffled, but the panic in it was clear.

"Oh no," Fadin said, rushing to the door.

Tase moved just as quickly behind him. "Come on, Path. Sorry Ciaran, we'll be back soon."

Ciaran nodded. "I see you things later. No make mother too worried." He smiled and waved them on.

They rushed into the abandoned bedroom and flew down the cold stone steps.

"Wait," Fadin said as they reached the door. "What are we going to tell them? Where are we going to say we've been?"

Tase felt fear and panic rushing up inside him. "I don't know. Maybe we should go out to the tunnel and say we were outside?"

"No, that won't work. We have Pathos, there's no way he can fit."

Tase bit his lower lip. "We could say we were here looking at books." He pointed to the bookcase door.

"Us, read?"

Another panicked cry rang through the castle.

"You got a better idea?"

Fadin shook his head and opened the door.

Pathos ran out and turned the corner.

Fadin and Tase were close behind.

They came out into the hallway and bolted through the tearoom and into the sunroom.

Ma was there with bloodshot, tear-logged eyes.

Fadin turned and whispered in Tase's ear. "If only she knew what we know."

When their mother saw them run around the corner her expression changed from frantic to horrified. She was furious. In fact, she looked so enraged Tase was surprised she didn't strike them.

"Where have you two been?" she screamed. "You just disappear on me? Not a word? Just gone? Vanished? Where were you?"

Tase and Fadin just stood there, a bit dazed by her anger.

"Answer me," she screeched.

"W-we were at the bookcase. At the bookcase, reading." Tase fumbled.

"The bookcase?" Ma said, visibly getting angrier by the minute. "I checked there twice. And you expect me to believe it took you that long to come when I was screaming my head off for you? And since when do you two read?"

Fadin arched his eyebrow at Tase.

"You two are lying to me, outright lying, and I will not have that in this house. Whether it be mine or not. I am not going to raise two liars, I wont."

Tase saw Fadin's hands turn into fists.

Fadin's thoughts of anger were so strong, that Tase could feel them spilling out at him. *You are the liar. How dare you accuse us when you have lied about everything. EVERYTHING!*

Tase kept his eyes forward, hard as it was.

"I want you both to march up those stairs and stay in your room. There will be no dinner tonight, and neither of you are stepping a foot outside until you have confessed to where you've been." Ma stared at them, her electric-blue eyes afire with fury. "Do I make myself clear?" she asked.

They nodded.

Ma arched a black eyebrow and pointed towards the stairs. "Then move it."

# Chapter 8

## *Crime and Punishment*

Upon entering their room, Fadin kicked at their newly stacked bunkbeds, anger nearly boiling over.

Tase laid flat on the floor, looking like a used and beat up old doormat.

"Don't you dare kick that bed again, Fadin Michael O'Callaghan," Ma screamed from below.

Fadin, unable to fight back, stuck his tongue out, made a crude hand gesture, and threw himself on the bottom bunk. "This is so unfair," he wailed, grabbing the pillow and shoving his face in it. "Us liars. Ha—that's rich. Why doesn't she just have a look in the mirror and peek at who really needs to apologize. Oh wait, there's probably a little elf hiding inside." He kicked at one of the supporting beams on the bed, although considerably quieter than last time.

"What did you think was going to happen?" Tase asked, rolling over. "It's not like we had that great a story. And you know Clearie would have said whatever he could to get us into trouble."

"Yea, that thick tool. When is he going to stop butting in and making our life a living nightmare?"

"He isn't the only one," Tase answered, nodding towards the closet.

Fadin looked at it then tossed the pillow over his head again. "I hate this castle." He felt his stomach rumble, "And I'm hungry. Now we have to wait till morning."

"Might as well go to sleep, there's not much else we can do."

Fadin nodded, lifted the pillow, and got off the bed. "You were right, Tase," he said, looking down at the floor. "She is hiding a lot more from us than we thought."

Tase nodded. "At least we don't lie to each other."

Fadin smiled oddly. He got into his night clothes and climbed up the well-built ladder which lead to the top bunk.

Tase crawled into the bottom one.

It became very quiet and still after all the footsteps in the castle receded.

Fadin heard two sets of feet come up the long stairway and drift away behind closed doors. Large, strong feet made their way all through the bottom floor, obviously checking to see if everything was in order. Quite possibly, it was the butler, Enda. He even thought he heard light footsteps above him, Ciaran scuttling about, but he couldn't be sure.

Fadin tried to close his eyes and fall asleep, but the emptiness in his stomach kept making that impossible. He tossed and turned, trying to find a comfortable position. But every time he would, the silence became too loud, so he would shift around again.

After a long while of this, he turned to face the ceiling. He wondered if Tase was having as hard a time sleeping. Since he heard no noise, he figured not.

In order to fight the growing hole in his belly, he let his mind wander. He thought about the attic, the black and white photo, the man holding their mother's waist. D.A.

He let his mind survey the past. He saw his Da, young and smiling, coming home from work, taking him and Tase fishing. He thought about all the fun birthdays and outings. He thought about the last time he had seen his father, and the last thing his da might have seen before his whole world went black.

He thought about the woman Tase said was in the courtyard the day of the accident. He thought about Mrs. Cunningham and the woman she said had been in their yard. He thought about the terrible scream in the classroom that day. The scream that had shattered every window and glass object in the room. He could hear all the glass breaking again, he heard it as if it were in a musical tune. The shattering glass changed into a soft melody, a humming melody. Fadin let his finger move back and forth to the beat in his head. He stopped. The song was not only in his imagination, he could really hear it.

He sat up in the pitch black and listened hard. Sure enough, there was a tune being hummed or sung. It sounded very far away or very quiet. He noiselessly climbed down the latter and walked toward their door.

It was definitely louder here, but it wasn't coming from downstairs.

He moved towards the window and heard it get softer. He tiptoed back towards the door and then near the closet. He pressed his ear against the closet door and heard the tune more clearly. It was still muffled, but the sound was most definitely coming from somewhere within the closet.

He opened the door with a swift *whoosh*.

No one. Nothing. Only darkness.

Then it occurred to him. What if the song wasn't coming from this closet?

Fadin shut the door and felt around blindly. He found and pressed the knothole. The door made a slight creaking sound. The white wood turned an old blistered-brown.

Distinct words could be heard now. The melody was indeed coming from the old closet.

Fadin licked his lips and carefully grabbed the handle. He turned the knob and flung the door open.

A small light was glowing above the photo of the young man. It pointed downward as if the photo was in spotlight.

Fadin shook his head. If he didn't know any better, he'd say the photo's position had changed. He had been singing before, hadn't he? Now a simple smile played on his face.

Fadin suddenly realized it was quiet now. The song was gone, and the unbearable stillness was back. Where had the melody gone?

Fadin shook his head and looked around.

Nothing.

"I wonder who was singing," he said to himself, confounded.

"My love," someone shouted.

Fadin snapped his head back and saw the photo blinking. He stumbled backwards and the picture began to sing.

"Hello my love, what a joy to see you, what a lovely surprise,

It's wonderful to be in your presence dear, and gaze in your lovely eyes.

It's been so long since you've come to see me in this dank, old, dark room,

I wondered perhaps if you'd gone and left me to sit and rot in this tomb.

It's been so long since I've seen you flower, to bask in your lovely light,

I hope you'll never close this door again, and keep me in ceaseless night.

So that's the song I sing for you, I pray it will never end,

You'll always be a treasure to me, always far more than a friend."

The photo smiled, winked, and closed his eyes.

The light turned off, and Fadin was again in complete darkness. He stared stupidly forwards and screamed, unable to control his fright. A singing photo? A moving picture? Impossible. He slammed the door shut and backed quickly away.

"What was that?" a voice from somewhere in the blackness asked.

Fadin shrieked again and jumped, smacking the black figure behind him.

"Ouch!"

He ran towards the light switch and flicked it on. Turning, he saw Tase lying on the floor rubbing his head.

"Geez," Tase cried, looking up.

"Tase?"

"Yea, me Tase," he rubbed his scalp once more, and stood up. "That hurt."

"I'm sorry," Fadin said, not really feeling so. "But you shouldn't sneak up on people."

"Sneak up on people? I wasn't sneaking up; I was standing behind you, listening to that lovely serenade. It's not my fault that you didn't know I was there. Besides, you're the one who shouldn't get so worked up over a photo's crush."

Fadin thinned his lips. "You saw it?"

"Yea, I saw it and heard it. Boy, does he have the hots for you." Tase raised his eyebrows teasingly.

Fadin furrowed his brows. "Shut it."

"Okay, okay sorry, but I just have one question," he smiled. "How long have you and the picture been going steady?"

Fadin tightened his fist. "Shut your fat gob, this isn't funny."

"I'm sorry, I'm sorry," Tase said, picking up a pillow. "How did you find it?"

Fadin relaxed slightly. "I just opened the door, and Mr. Picture began serenading his endless love. I don't think he saw who was there, if he can even see."

Fadin could tell Tase was trying extremely hard not to laugh.

"Hum," Tase paused. He was thinking, trying not to smile, but the grin broke and he blurted out, "you always have looked more like Ma."

Fadin clenched his fist again.

Tase burst out laughing.

"Dry up, Tase. You eejit."

Tase clutched his sides and nearly toppled to the floor.

"I mean it, Tase, shut up!"

Tase stood up sighing, trying to suppress a few hiccup-like giggles.

"I'm sorry, really, sorry. Just couldn't help myself," he cleared his throat.

Fadin glared at him. "So what do you think it was?"

Tase tried not to smile. "I don't know." His voice cracked at the end. "We could always ask Ciaran, but it looked like a singing picture to me."

"No, really."

"Well, what do you want me to say?"

Fadin looked down. "I want Ma to tell us the truth."

Tase nodded slowly. "We'd better get back to bed, my stomach is growling again."

Fadin climbed up the ladder.

Tase shut off the light.

Fadin turned on his back again and stared into the blackness. Why were there so many secrets in this house?

A howl went up in the blackness and Fadin's eyes darted to the window. Maybe that dog was real after all. If that were true, then it would also mean that that dog was watching them.

Fadin shook his head. No, that was stupid, and Tase had never even seen it.

He shut his eyes and fell into a dream filled with memories, laughter, fun, and engulfed in the picture's rhyming love song.

~~~

Morning came eventually, streaming new sunlight into the world.

Fadin awoke and rubbed the sleep out of his eyes. He descended the ladder and saw Tase still bundled under his covers.

He walked quietly to the door and listened. It was still. No noise anywhere.

*Everyone must still be asleep*, he thought.

Fadin stepped away and eyed the closet. It was still paintless and brown. He walked up to it, trying to hear if there was any singing going on inside.

There wasn't.

He swallowed, turned the knob slowly, and swung the door open. He saw the picture had turned back to its original pose and was completely still.

Odd. Had it all been just some crazy dream?

Fadin raised an eyebrow and to be absolutely sure, poked it with his index finger.

"Ouch!"

Fadin jumped back startled.

"You know, You twerp,
It isn't very nice to poke people in the eye,
Even if they're pictures they have feelings too, small fry.
If you ever try to harm me like you just did again,
I'll decide to hit you back, and that'll really be the end.
So go away and shut the door,
I don't want to see you anymore.
Leave me be and let me rot,
You can't deny that you've been caught.
So go—a—way."

The picture blew a raspberry and returned to its normal pose.

Fadin stared at it, once again dumbfounded. He felt something hit him in the rear. As he turned, the door to the closet backed up and smacked him again. He moved out of the way, and the door slammed shut.

Tase shot up. "What was that?"

Fadin hit the knothole and watched it change.

"Nothing, just shutting the closet."

"Well could you be a little louder about it? I think the whole world will hear you." He slumped off the bed and stretched. "Did I hear singing?"

"Yea, apparently all that picture can do is sing."

Tase rubbed his eyes. "So that was real huh? I wasn't sure if it was a dream or not."

"Yup, it was real alright." He walked over to the dresser and grabbed a winter shirt. "It's getting colder."

Tase opened the closet and yanked down a pair of trousers. "It is almost November." He put on a warm shirt too and looked out of the window. "Ma's going to make us tell you know."

"Or we could lie," Fadin said, joining his twin at the window pane. It was raining softly, "mizzlin," Da used to call it.

Tase turned to look at him. "That didn't exactly turn out so good last time, in case you forgot."

"We were rushed. We didn't have time to think of a good story."

"Well, what story is going to be good enough to convince her?"

Fadin snapped his fingers, a lightbulb flashing on. "One that will get us into trouble."

Tase scrunched up his face. "Real smart, aren't we already in enough trouble?"

Fadin smiled. He had a good idea. He knew how to calm Ma down and be able to go outside again. It was brilliant. "Come on," he said, and led the way out of the door.

Tase pulled him back. "What are you doing?" he whispered.

"Trust me, everyone's asleep."

Tase looked worried but relented.

They made their way down the stairs, through the sunroom and tearoom, and into the hall.

Fadin held his breath as they passed Aunt Kyna's room and quietly grabbed a picture from the wall. He raced back to the tearoom.

Tase was close behind.

"What are you doing?" Tase whispered harshly.

"Don't get your knickers in a twist," Fadin whispered back. "Trust me."

He saw a small closet and led them over to it. He grabbed a blanket from inside and wrapped the picture in it.

"What are you doing?" Tase asked again.

Fadin put a finger to his mouth and grabbed a large candlestick holder. He raised it high and let it crash down upon the covered picture. The sound was muffled, but the glass could still be heard breaking.

Tase stood, mouth open.

Fadin began to uncover the broken picture.

"Are you off your nut?" Tase asked, staring at him.

"Nope," Fadin whispered smiling. "Just the opposite." He folded the blanket and put the candlestick holder back. He hid the broken picture behind some old pillows and stood back to look over his work. Satisfied, he closed the door.

Tase looked at him, eyes wide and confused. "You're mental. I wonder if all this magic stuff is getting to your head."

"What are you two doing?"

They both snapped backward to see Clearie standing in the entrance way.

Tase gasped.

Fadin smiled to himself. It was the first time he was actually happy to see Clearie butting in.

"Oh, please don't tell Ma," he pleaded quite convincingly, if he did say so himself. "We didn't mean to, it just—happened."

Clearie raised an eyebrow. "What did you do?"

Fadin turned to the closet and fumbled around for the picture.

Tase followed suit and shot him an irritated look.

Fadin pretended to tremble as he found the picture and showed it to Clearie. "It was an accident, we tried to fix it."

Clearie turned the picture over and examined the shattered glass. "Is this where you were yesterday? Trying to fix this mess?"

Fadin nodded. "We really were looking at the bookcase, trying to see if we heard voices, like you." He hadn't been able to resist, and Clearie loved that suck-up nonsense. He liked to think his younger brothers actually wanted to be like him. Right. "We were there when we knocked down that picture." Fadin began to walk back and forth, trying to appear nervous. "We came and hid in the closet, trying to fix it. We were so afraid when we heard Ma calling that we just stayed hidden. But when she started to cry, we decided to come out."

Clearie nodded. "You almost gave her a heart attack, you know," he looked back over the picture. "You have to tell her, you need to tell the truth."

Fadin hung his head and nodded.

Clearie handed back the broken picture and started for the kitchen. "It's better to do it sooner than later," he called, as he turned the corner.

When he was well out of sight, Fadin turned to Tase and grinned widely.

Tase was not smiling however, he was standing very still with a scowl on his face.

"What's the matter with you?" Fadin asked.

"Your an eejit, do you know that?"

"How? All I did is getting us out of bigger trouble."

"You lied."

"So?"

"So? So don't you think Ma will know?"

"Nope."

"How can you possibly say that? She always catches us in a flat-out lie."

Fadin rolled his eyes. "Haven't you been paying any attention lately? She isn't acting like herself, I really don't think she'll know it's a lie.

Besides, if she can be dishonest, so can we."

Tase began to shake his head, but then stopped. "Fine, but if she does find out we're lying, I'm blaming the whole thing on you."

"Fine you sissy, but she won't."

They walked towards the dining room and entered cautiously.

Clearie and Ma were sitting in their usual seats. Aunt Kyna was missing again and her spot was unset.

They both sat down quietly, not daring to look up.

The door to the kitchen opened and Pathos bounded out.

Shortly after him came Daireann with a large tray. She laughed as Pathos stood on two feet trying to get at the wonderful-smelling food.

Daireann put Ma's food down first, then made her way over to Fadin.

"Thank you, Daireann," Ma said kindly.

"Yes, thank you," Clearie, Fadin, and Tase echoed.

"You're welcome, chicks," she said, using the name for children Fadin despised. "I'll be right back with some drinks."

When she was gone and Pathos had settled, Fadin decided it was a good time to come clean. Or at least pretend to come clean.

"We're sorry, Ma," he said looking up, trying his best not to let the smell of breakfast overtake him.

"Sorry for what?" she wiped at her mouth and raised a dark eyebrow.

"For making you so worried. We just..."

"Yes?" She leaned forward a bit.

"We accidentally broke something and we're too afraid to tell you." Now that he said it, Fadin wondered if it had really been such a good idea.

Ma looked unchanged and cold. Maybe she really could tell he was lying.

"What did you break?" she finally asked.

"A picture from the hall."

"What did you do with it?"

"We hid it in the closet and tried to fix it."

"Why didn't you come out when I called?"

Fadin could tell she was trying to find holes. "We were afraid, afraid you'd be angry."

Her face changed to a look of surprise. She threw her hands up and sighed. "Oh boys, I don't care about an old picture. Your Aunt Kyna probably does, and you are going to have to apologize, but that's not what I would have cared about. I was worried sick about you. I was afraid something might have happened to you." She gazed at each of them tenderly. "You are what I treasure more then anything, don't you know that?" She paused in loving affection. Swiftly, the pause was ended and reality came crashing down, sternness taking over. "Which is why, I'm afraid, you have to be grounded for a week."

"What?" they said in unison.

"For lying," she said calmly. "I cannot permit you to lie."

Fadin felt his face boiling. Can't permit you to lie? What a load of tripe. Who did she think she was? She was doing the worst lying of all and she was doing it everyday. How could they get into trouble for it when she was the person being such a shining example?

Tase must have sensed what he was thinking, because he kicked Fadin and spoke up. "Yes, Ma, we're sorry."

She smiled at them and nodded.

Daireann came back in after a moment with their drinks. "There you are," she smiled. "Anything else?"

"No, thank you," Ma said politely.

Daireann beamed wide and returned to the kitchen.

Once the doors swung shut, they all dug in, devouring the wonderful, hot breakfast.

Fadin grinned as the sausage and bacon flavour burst into his mouth. He turned to Tase, who was gobbling it down like he had never eaten before.

After a while, Clearie looked up and turned to their ma. "When are we going to be starting school?"

Fadin winced. That was a question he really didn't want to know the answer to.

"Actually," she said wiping her mouth, "you start next week."

Fadin couldn't suppress a groan.

"Now Fadin, don't give me that," Ma said. "You've been off for nearly six weeks."

Fadin nodded. "Sorry, Ma."

She shook her head slightly and turned back to Clearie. "I've been all over this area and looked at every school. Your Aunt Kyna has helped me too, and I've come to a decision."

Fadin shut his eyes tight.

"You're going to be home taught."

Fadin's eyes shot open and he gaped at her across the table.

Clearie turned to them, finally seeming to be on the same page, and shot Fadin a wide-eyed glance.

"What?" All three said together.

"Yes, you're going to be schooled at home," she smiled at them.

Fadin still gaped at her, shocked by this news. Was she sicker then she looked?

It wasn't that he didn't like the thought of being schooled here, or that children schooled at home were weird, or that he absolutely loved going to school. It was the fact that they had always gone to school. That's just the way it was. Da had worked, Ma had stayed home and taken care of the house, and they had gone to school. That was the way it had always been. Now with everything else that had changed, he was surprised that she wanted to make another.

"But," Clearie said trying to remain calm, "we're not *going* to school?"

She laughed softly. "No, being schooled at home means you're taught at your house."

Tase leaned forward. "Well who's going to teach us?"

"A tutor I hired. Her name is Caoimhe O'Keefe, but you'll call her Miss O'Keefe."

They all looked at each other, still blown away by the news.

"When is she coming?" Clearie asked.

"Next week, and she'll have each of you sit like you would in regular school, and have you do the work she assigns." She turned to Fadin. "I don't want there to be any problems."

He crinkled his forehead. "Why did you look at me?"

She raised an eyebrow. "You know why."

He sat back, his brow furrowed.

"Now finish your breakfast, we have some work to do today."

They all leaned forward.

"What work?" Tase asked.

"Chores."

They looked at each other.

"Doesn't Aunt Kyna have servants for that?" Fadin asked.

She threw him an irritated glance. "She has workers, yes, but she is letting us stay here for free, so we need to show her some appreciation. After breakfast we are going to see what can be done."

They looked at one another again and sat back.

Fadin took a few bites of his meal and gazed up. Maybe being taught at home wouldn't be so bad after all. It would sure beat seeing Headmaster Walsh every day.

Fadin cleaned his plate, drained his cup, and stood with Tase to deposit the soiled dishes into the kitchen.

"I'll take those," Ma said, gathering the tableware. "Why don't you boys start with your rooms, I'm going to clean the kitchen."

"Daireann will never let you," Tase reasoned, shaking his head.

"Humph," Ma snorted. "We'll see about that." She nodded them out of the dining room.

Fadin shrugged and went reluctantly up the long stairs and into his bedroom.

After only a short while, with his bed still being made, Fadin heard the shrill scream of Daireann shouting from the kitchen, "Teagan, what on earth are you—no. No, no, that's my job. Get on out of here, get."

With Tase right behind him, Fadin poked his head out of the door to get a better listen.

"Everyone deserves a day off, don't they?" Ma asked.

"Teagan," Daireann sighed, "for heaven's sake, will you give me that sponge and get on out of here?"

"No," Ma stated firmly. "You get. I'm not leaving this spot. You'll have to drag me."

"Teagan," Daireann whined.

"Nope," Ma said. "Get out of here. Go take a day off. I won't tell Kyna, I swear."

"That's not who I'm worried about," Daireann sighed. "But fine, I see I can't win this argument."

Everything became quiet. Moving to the banister, Fadin watched Daireann walk by the staircase and grab her coat and umbrella. She turned, grinning widely at the castle at large. "I'll be back before Kyna gets home," she announced and shut the large door.

Fadin snorted. It wasn't fair, it just wasn't fair. How come Daireann got the day off, and he had to clean the castle she was getting paid to keep sparkling? He dragged his feet behind Tase back into the bedroom. As he started picking up rubbish from the floor, he heard a door slam downstairs and voices rose up into the cluttered room. Fadin hurried back to the banister.

"Teagan, what—what are you doing?" Enda said in his screechy voice. "Put that basket down, you know Daireann and I are here to do this sort of work. Stop it, this instant."

"No," Ma said, still stubborn. "Kyna has been gracious enough to let us stay here, and it's time to give a little back."

"Come now," Enda snorted, "yes it is kind, but you and I both know why she did it, and you—well, you shouldn't be lifting something this heavy, so just hand it over."

"No."

Fadin saw his mother holding a large basket of laundry as she walked past the stairs.

Enda followed right behind her, arms open to take the basket away. "Teagan," he said, irritated. "You know I can do this faster, now just give it here."

"No," Ma repeated firmly, "everyone deserves a break, even you. I'm fine, now get out of here."

He smiled at her. "Stubborn, always were. You're not going to take no for an answer?"

She smiled back. "Nope."

Enda threw his hands in the air. "Alas, I have nothing else to argue." He walked to the front door, donned his coat, and turned back, looking up at Fadin and Tase. "Take care of your mother, don't let her overdo it." He smiled at them, and walked out into the rain.

Fadin grumbled under his breath. What was the point in cleaning when there were maids and butlers around getting paid, mind you, to do it? It wasn't that he hadn't done chores before; on the contrary, he had done them every day in their old house, but there just didn't seem to be a reason for them here. "Ma," he called down to her, "why did you have them go? They are getting paid to do this. Why do we have to work?"

Ma smiled up at him. "Oh, come now, Fadin. There's nothing wrong with a little work, is there?" She walked past the stairs and into the sunroom.

Fadin stuck his tongue out and forced himself back to the bedroom.

So on and on the day went. It was filled with wash, scrubbing, mopping, dishes, and every other kind of cleaning. It took them all day long, and Fadin really had to wonder how just two people could keep this large castle so clean. He actually had appreciation for the little cook and large butler. He had to admit, they did a good job.

Finally, when it became dark, Daireann and Enda returned. They ranted and raved about how clean the house looked, and Daireann said, "Nothing works as good as the old-fashioned way."

Clearie gave her an awkward stare to which she simply smiled back.

They were not permitted to do any more housework, and Daireann insisted that Ma sit down. The boys were told to go and clean themselves and that dinner would be ready soon. Not long afterwards, when Fadin emerged from a hot shower, the house was blanketed in wonderful smells.

Fadin grinned. "Daireann's cooking," he nodded to Tase.

"Ah," Tase sighed. "Thank goodness, I'm starving."

Tase started to bound down the stairs and Fadin followed close behind. As they reached the bottom step, the front door began to open. Fadin and Tase froze.

The handle of the door turned, then stopped, and turned again. Finally, the door swung open, revealing a cloaked figure sopping with the rain that was now coming down in heavy sheets. The figure moved forward, hooded and muddied.

Fadin glanced over at Tase. He looked like a ghost, pale as anything.

Fadin looked frontward, wondering, could this possibly be the cloaked woman Tase had seen? He stared bravely ahead and watched as the figure began to remove its cloak. The hood went back, and Fadin let out a sigh of relief as the face of Aunt Kyna came into view.

He turned and saw Tase, too, had relaxed.

Aunt Kyna saw the boys on the stairs and gave them a half-smile. She looked very worn out and tired. Her blonde hair was a dishevelled mess, and she had mud and grime on her hands, under her fingernails, and on her face.

Without a word, she walked forward and disappeared into the long hall past the sunroom.

Fadin and Tase exchanged odd glances and then hurried into the dining room.

Ma, Clearie, and Daireann were there, Daireann setting the table and refusing to let Ma help.

"Hello, boys," Ma said pleasantly.

"Hello," Fadin answered. "Ma, Aunt Kyna's home, but she didn't look very good. She looked dirty and sick, and she went straight to her room without a word."

Ma exchanged looks with Daireann. "Well," Ma answered, "I'm sure she'll be fine. She'll probably be out here shortly." Ma smiled, trying to convince them.

Fadin shrugged. She had looked pretty bad.

Thirty minutes later, Aunt Kyna entered the dining room. She looked clean and put together, but still tired. She sat at the table and poked at the food placed in front of her.

It was an awkward dinner. Fadin felt uncomfortable and noticed she didn't say a word about the house, how clean it was. In fact, she didn't say much of anything except to check in to see how Ma was feeling.

When Ma forced Fadin and Tase to confess about the broken picture, she didn't even react. She simply nodded and said, "Oh, that's fine, fine."

Fadin looked at Tase. What was wrong with her?

Daireann, seeming to worry about her strange behaviour, asked Aunt Kyna if she wanted seconds.

Aunt Kyna just sat still as if she didn't hear her. Kyna suddenly got a spacy smile on her face and excused herself. She got up and walked out without another word. Not even a thank you to Daireann.

Ma watched her leave anxiously. "Thank you for the dinner, Daireann." Ma said, smiling at her and then rose to leave. "You boys finish your dinner, help Daireann clear, and then head upstairs, okay?"

Fadin and his two siblings nodded.

Ma smiled falsely and was gone behind the swinging doors.

"Well," Clearie said leaning back, "I'm destroyed. I don't want to look at another mop for a month."

Fadin smiled, though he wondered about Aunt Kyna's strange behaviour. He, too, was quite tired, and he leaned back as well and began to stretch. He allowed himself to yawn deeply, and then got up to give his plate to Daireann.

Tase and Clearie followed suit, and they all left and began to climb the long staircase together.

Fadin stopped halfway up.

Tase turned to him. "What is it?" he asked.

"Why don't we go and listen to see what they're talking about." Fadin nodded his head towards the sunroom.

"You two coming? Or do you like the stairs too much?" Clearie asked mockingly.

"Be there in a minute," Tase called up to him.

Clearie shrugged and closed his door.

Tase walked down the stairs and turned to him. "We'd better be quiet."

They made their way silently across the sunroom and tea room. Fadin could feel his heart beat as they laid eyes on the narrow hall.

They tiptoed up to the small door and pressed their heads against it. Fadin heard voices right away and plugged his exposed ear to get a better listen.

"...And it's just getting worse," he heard Aunt Kyna say. "They won't listen, the stupid stubborn people. You'd think the Council would know a resistance forming when they saw one."

She paused for a moment and the sounds of things being moved rang through the door.

"I mean, with all the activity going on? We haven't seen so much movement since...well, since you know when."

There was banging and a noise that sounded like something being dropped in water. A pill?

"They are far too concerned with the welfare and rights of these creatures, instead of being concerned with the safety of all the others who would be affected by another uprising."

There was another plunking sound.

"I was told I was being too nervous, too concerned. Can you believe the nerve of them? We were in the first war, the first uprising, and believe me, I do not want to be a part of a second."

Fadin pulled away for an instant. What war was she talking about? He hadn't heard of any war, at least not any she could have been a part of. He thought about the letter in the closet. Could it be connected with this war somehow?

He shook himself and quickly placed his head firmly against the door again.

This time his mother's voice was heard. "Is there any news from the Ainondall side?"

"No, nothing out of the ordinary is happening in their world, which is another reason my suspicions were discredited. You know everything that happened there last time.

"No, they seem to think that everything is just lovely and that a second tragedy could never occur. It appears to me that they have forgotten how the first uprising began. It was very similar to the subtle things being seen and done now. Little pinpricks almost, then everything exploded and The Ministry was caught with their trousers down, unable to defend themselves."

"Don't you think you may be jumping to conclusions?"

Something was slammed down.

"Not you too, Teagan?"

"Don't misunderstand me, Kyna. I agree that there is strange behaviour going on, but The King and the Council are right. We can't panic and get people in an uproar, not with the little information we have."

"The whole purpose of meeting the way we do is to discuss these matters and find a solution." Aunt Kyna said, raising her voice a little. "It isn't a monarchy, our King doesn't rule over us. For all respects and purposes he isn't a king at all."

"Yes, yes, I know, but we can't jump into anything. That is why you discuss things and then put it to a vote. Nothing should be taken lightly."

"That is precisely my point, Teagan. They are treating these issues like a bothersome fly. When these things get brought up, The Council swats them away as fast as they can."

"Give it more time, Kyna. If things get worse, I'm sure they will discuss what needs to be done."

There was a sudden bark and Fadin smacked his head into the door. He turned to see Pathos staring at him and jumped again as Tase kicked the door at the sound of footsteps.

They got up and ran as fast as they could out of the hall. They flung themselves behind the couch in the tea room and squeezed into the corner.

Fadin cupped his hand to his mouth and listened.

He heard the door open and Aunt Kyna laugh quietly. "I think someone wanted to see you," she said.

Fadin looked beside him and saw Tase staring back. Suddenly a thought hit Fadin. Where was Pathos?

"Oh Path," he heard Ma cry. "Did you want Ma?"

Pathos answered with a whine and the door was closed again.

Fadin removed his hand from his mouth and popped his head up.

The coast was clear.

They walked silently up the stairs and left their bedroom door ajar. When they were in bed, Fadin rolled over and stuck his head upside-down so he could see Tase. "Why do you think Pathos didn't follow us when we ran? He always does."

Tase shook his head. "It was almost like he wanted us to get away."

Fadin nodded. "What do you think they were talking about?"

"I don't know, but whatever it was, it didn't sound good."

Footsteps were heard, and Fadin laid himself flat on the bed closing his eyes. He heard their door open further and felt Ma kiss him on the head. He heard her kiss Tase and close the door.

Fadin turned over and buried his head into his pillow. He wondered if perhaps his mother had been talking about the magic world with Aunt Kyna, and if so, would she ever really tell them the truth? What about the letter? D. A.? There were so many questions, and they would probably never be answered.

As he let his heavy eyes close, he thought he again heard the howl of the dog, but he was too tired to get up and look out of the window. Instead, he let his mind wander and fell into a confused pool of dreams.

# Chapter 9

## *Miss O'Keefe*

The next week went by very slowly it seemed to Tase. He and Fadin were not permitted to go outside or explore the castle. They were not allowed to play board games or do anything else that may have been fun or enjoyable. Instead they were forced to read the new books that had arrived for their schooling. Some of them were actual novels, while others were textbooks that they were told to look over.

Clearie couldn't have been happier. Even though he wasn't grounded and could have left the castle if he wanted to, he spent most of his time reading as well.

Tase didn't understand it and obviously Fadin didn't either. It didn't make sense to stay inside and read when there were so many other things you could do. In fact, Tase began to feel stir-crazy by the third day.

He was doing his usual reading when he decided to take a look out of the window. He peered over the grounds and looked longingly at the grass and trees. There was no rain and the sun was out. He glanced up at the ceiling and wished desperately that they were at least allowed to explore the house. There were so many questions he still wanted to ask Ciaran.

There was a knock at the door and Tase rushed over to see who it was.

Enda beat him and Fadin to it, but opened the door wide enough so they could both see.

Aimirgin stood smiling with a parcel in her hand. There was a wonderful smell wafting from it.

Tase wished more than anything that he was allowed to be outside.

"Hello," Aimirgin said smiling. "Are Fadin and Tase home?" she asked, although she could clearly see them.

Enda smiled. "I'm sorry young miss, they are unfortunately being punished. They are stuck to the ground for a week."

Aimirgin giggled, seeming to understand what he meant. "Tell them to be good so they can come outside," she said, looking right at them. "Will you give this to them for me?" She handed Enda the parcel.

"I will miss, and thank you," Enda answered.

She began to walk away, and got her jacket caught on the potted plants near the front door. She tried to yank her sleeve away and tripped, falling backward on the stone path.

"Are you okay?" Enda asked, moving to go and help her.

"Fine, fine," Aimirgin smiled. She got up and dusted herself off. "Goodbye."

Enda waved her away and closed the door.

Tase stared at the parcel and wondered if Enda would give it to them.

As if he could read his thoughts, Enda raised the parcel higher and turned to them. "After lunch."

Whatever it was Aimirgin gave them it was delicious. It was some kind of pastry with a wonderful creamy, buttery, almost chocolate taste, but it wasn't chocolate. It was something entirely different, something much better.

Their mother didn't join them for lunch; she had gone out with Aunt Kyna for the day, so Clearie was the only one they had to share the wonderful pastry with.

He smiled wide when he saw what was being brought out to them. He turned to Daireann to thank her, but she nodded to the twins, her crimpy white-blonde hair falling in her face.

"Thank them," she said, placing a plate in front of him with her plump fingers. "Their friend brought this over."

Clearie looked at them oddly for a moment and took a large bite of the pastry. His eyes immediately became wide, and a look of complete pleasure spread across his face. "I don't think I've ever tasted anything so good."

Tase couldn't have agreed more.

On and on the week dragged. Tase noticed Fadin getting grumpier with each day. He always had a negative comment about the book he was reading. It was either too long or too boring or a number of other things.

Tase tried to get both their minds off the never-ending week by discussing, at length, what they had heard in Aunt Kyna's room. They could never come up with good enough answers, however, and Tase could only discuss something for so long.

Finally Monday came, the long awaited and dreaded day.

Tase woke up early that morning and immediately remembered what day it was. He popped his head off the pillow and slipped on his clothes. He then climbed up the ladder and shook Fadin awake.

"What?" Fadin asked squinting at him.

"Come on, get up, lazy," Tase said shaking him again.

"There's no reason to get up early. All we have to do is read and read and read…" his voice trailed off and he shut his eyes, pulling the covers over his head.

"No we don't," Tase billowed yanking the covers away.

"Hump off," Fadin shouted groping for the blanket.

"It's Monday," Tase said with an air of excitement in his voice.

Fadin's eyes shot open. "Monday?" He popped up and shooed Tase off the ladder. "I forgot," he said getting dressed. "Has she come yet?"

Tase shrugged. "I just woke up."

Fadin nodded pulling on his shirt. "Let's go."

They opened the door and saw that Ma and Clearie were already up.

Tase stared at the large clock on the wall. 6:30.

"Why is everyone up so early? Ma usually isn't up till seven."

Fadin was already starting down the stairway. "I don't know, but let's find out."

As they came off the stairway into the entrance hall, they heard their mother calling to them. She sounded like she was in the garden, so they sped off in that direction.

Tase noticed as they walked by that the rose room was open and looked like it had been recently cleaned. There was also a lovely smell coming out of it, almost as if the roses on the walls where real. But that was stupid.

They found Ma sitting alone with a cup of tea. Her complexion showed very pale on her face, more then usual, and now she wore sweaters that looked far too big for her. Her hair was stringy, as though she hadn't washed it in days, and her nails looked like they needed a trim. Although she had been in the lavatory often, vomiting Tase knew, she hadn't appeared to have lost weight, at least he didn't think she had. And even though she seemed sickly, her beauty shone strongly through.

Ma smiled at them and patted a chair to her left.

They both sat down and looked at her anxiously.

"As you know, today you start school and get off your grounding." She took a sip of tea. "I would really hate for you to be grounded again, so close to October Holiday too."

Tase furrowed his brow. Ma had said October Holiday instead of Halloween. She thought of it as a day off of school, but Tase had always thought the fact that they didn't celebrate Halloween odd. Everyone else did. They had feasts, costumes, elaborate parties, candy hunting—oh how he had always wanted to go on a candy hunt. But their family didn't celebrate Halloween, although the holiday had been invented by the Irish. And come to think of it, there had never even been a good reason. They just didn't do Halloween.

Ma eyed them with her most serious face. "I would like for you two not to have to be punished again, but," she looked directly at Fadin, "if there are any problems, I'm afraid you will be grounded for another week."

"What kind of problems?" Fadin asked.

She shrugged. "If you get mountains of homework for not trying, or mouth off to the teacher, then you won't be having any fun till it's all completed or till you learn your lesson."

Fadin raised a red eyebrow but said nothing.

"So when is our new teacher coming?" Tase asked.

Ma looked through the glass doors at the clock in the hallway. "After breakfast at about eight."

Tase exchanged glances with Fadin.

"Why are you two up so early?" she asked, looking from one to the other.

"Couldn't sleep," Fadin said standing up. "When is breakfast?"

"Half an hour."

Fadin smiled. "Can we go outside till then?"

Ma laughed and nodded. "Go on, get out of here. Vanish from my sight."

They sprang to their feet, dashed out of the house, and ran all the way to where Fadin had seen the vanishing tree, grinning all the while.

Tase breathed in the cold air, shook his messy orange-red locks, and looked up at the sky. It felt so good to be free, to be out of the warm castle and into the cold. As he stared upward, a light drizzle began, lightly kissing his face here and there. A thought suddenly occurred to him. "Fadin, do you think Da is up there?" he asked, not pulling his eyes away from the blue.

"I hope so," Fadin said coming closer. "I don't really know much about that."

A pain hit Tase in the heart, an aching pain, one of loss and uncertainty. He didn't know either, he hadn't the faintest idea, and he absolutely detested that fact.

"Maybe you should ask someone who does," a familiar voice stated.

They both jumped and Tase felt a shiver go up his spine. He turned and smiled when he saw Aimirgin standing beside the tree.

Her long dark hair blew in the slight wind. She wore a red scarf and hat and held a red parasol in her long hands. "Took you two long enough to not be in trouble anymore," she said, tapping her foot.

"We thought so too," Fadin answered with a smile.

Tase moved closer. "That pastry you brought us was wonderful."

"It was a recipe my ma made," she answered proudly. "Mcayog lolo."

"What does it mean?" Fadin asked, cocking his head.

"I don't really know, but it's delicious isn't it?"

Tase thought she wasn't being entirely truthful about not knowing what the name meant, but he really didn't care. If there was something gross in the ingredients, he definitely did not want to know what it was. He was happy being ignorant.

She smiled at them and twirled the parasol. "So, what are you doing for Halloween?"

Tase looked at Fadin, and they both shrugged. They never liked to admit that they didn't celebrate Halloween.

"Well my da and I are having a feast. My brothers are coming and we have more then enough food, so he wanted to know if you want to join us. There'll be games, sweets and a lovely fire."

Tase had images of all those wonderful things and saw himself in the middle, a part of it all. Oh how he had always wanted to be asked to a friend's house for the holiday. He looked at Fadin, who nodded hungrily. Fadin had always hated not being able to have fun on Halloween, perhaps even more than Tase. Tase just hoped Ma would let them go. Perhaps with her not being in good health, and if they did well in school, she'd let them go.

"We'd love to," Tase said, "but we have to make sure our ma isn't planning anything special." He knew darn good and well she was not. It was a lie, sort of, but the truth was too embarrassing.

Aimirgin nodded. "I figured. My da never wants me to go anywhere on Halloween. He goes through so much trouble to make it special, you know?" She smiled. "I hope you can come. Oh, would you two like to come over to have dinner tonight? I almost forgot, Da made too much food because we thought Desmond and Quinlan were coming over, but as usual something came up. I'm actually amazed you met them all at once." She made to move closer to them, but her parasol caught on the tree's bark, and her scarf had gotten tangled on the parasol handle when she had twirled it, so she was jerked backward. She made an awful choking sound at the jerk, and her long, gangly legs slid out from beneath her. Aimirgin hit the grass with a hard thump and lay flat, unmoving.

Tase rushed to her head, as did Fadin.

"Aimirgin?" Tase asked.

She blinked, and smiled up at him. Her dark eyes gleamed with the tears she was holding back. "I'm alright," she said.

Tase could hear the quiver in her voice. The fall must have hurt.

"For goodness sake, woman. I don't think I've ever met anyone who hurts themselves so much." Fadin cried.

Tase gave him a reproachful stare.

"You are alright though?" Fadin tried, catching the warning.

Aimirgin sat up and discreetly wiped away the tears that had dripped from her eyes. "Yes, I'm okay. I fall all the time, so I'm rather used to getting knocks and bruises." She smiled and tried to stand. The muddy ground was not helpful to Aimirgin's lack of grace, and she fell back on her behind.

"Here," Fadin said standing. "Let me and Tase help you up."

Tase grinned and stood as well. "Yea, give me your hand."

Aimirgin looked up, beamed at them, and took both their hands.

The ground was awfully slippery, but they managed to get her up and standing. Aimirgin began to thank them, but Tase stepped on his own shoelace and grabbed hold of Aimirgin to keep from toppling face-first into the mud.

"Oh, lord have mercy," Aimirgin laughed, holding him tight. "Don't let go, Tase, I got you."

"But who's got you?" Fadin asked, as he too began to slip.

Aimirgin stood Tase firm and then tried to steady Fadin.

"Thanks," Fadin said standing upright.

"Not a—" Aimirgin began, but as she took a step, her trouser leg caught on Tase's shoelace and down all three of them went into the thick, goopy mud.

Tase looked about. He was covered head to toe, and so were Fadin and Aimirgin. For a moment anger sizzled in his head, but as he looked at his brother and new friend, he couldn't help but giggle. He laughed aloud, holding his stomach and pointing.

Fadin burst into laughter too, along with Aimirgin.

After they finished laughing, they carefully crawled out of the mud and stood up, cleaning what they could off each other.

"I hope you can come tonight," Aimirgin said, picking the mud from her hair. She leaned over and nodded behind them. "I think someone wants you."

They turned around and saw Clearie, blond hair frizzing up in the wind, yelling at them from a distance.

Fadin's blue-green eyes rolled. "That's our brother, Clearie. He's a real fecky the ninth."

Aimirgin laughed. "Well, I'd better get going," she turned away and waved at them.

"Wait," Tase said, suddenly remembering something. "What did you mean 'ask someone who does'?"

"Huh?"

"When you first got here, I was asking Fadin if he thought my da was in... heaven. He said he didn't know, but you said ask someone who does. What did you mean?"

She smiled at him. "Ask my da about it when you come over tonight.

155

I'm sure he'd be more then happy to answer that question." She waved again and disappeared behind the trees.

Clearie could be clearly heard now, and Tase saw Pathos bounding behind him.

"Time for breakfast," he yelled.

"Okay," Fadin shouted back.

After a thorough licking from the Bernese, they began to walk back.

Tase took one last look at the woods and froze.

There was something standing in the shadows. An animal. It looked like a dog, but a big dog, much larger then Pathos. The animal blinked its brilliantly light eyes and moved further into the woods.

Tase strained to see it.

"Hey, Tase," Fadin yelled.

Tase blinked and the animal was gone. He shook his head and turned around to Fadin. He must have just imagined it, like he kept imagining the howls at night. Yea, that's all it was. It wasn't real.

As soon as they opened the door, Tase and Fadin were sent, immediately, up to shower.

"And I don't want to see one drop of mud left on you," Ma yelled from the entrance.

Breakfast was good, it made Tase feel warm.

Pathos sat at their feet and begged as usual.

Aunt Kyna was not at the table again today, and Daireann complained about her workload.

"She works far too hard, she's going to wear herself out," she fussed to Ma.

When breakfast was done, Ma told them to go clean their room, which was normal now, to comb their hair, and come back down.

The room didn't take long and they were soon in front of the mirror running their hands through their hair. They never actually used a brush. Tase stood back and shook his red hair until it lay normally, then waited for Fadin to finish.

As they bounded down the stairs, a knock was placed on the door. They both froze.

Enda came from around the corner and moved to the door to open it.

Tase heard Fadin hold his breath as the door was pulled in.

"Good morning, Miss O'Keefe."

"Good morning."

Enda stood back and Tase got a good look at the woman in the doorway.

She appeared to be in her early fifties and was short, not extremely short but still not tall by any means. Her stature was thin, which made her legs seem very long, and her high cheekbones noticeable. Her shoulder-length hair was coppery, except for one silver streak that formed on the left side of her face. Her eyes were a grey-blue, but didn't stand out the way their mother's did. Her eyes and face had something missing—a sparkle that most people had was absent. She looked as though something had robbed her of any joy, and behind her eyes hid some dark, secret pain.

She smiled up at them. "Hello," she said kindly, "Fadin and Tase?"

They nodded.

"Well, I just have to put my things away and then we'll get started."

She followed Enda into the west hall.

Fadin ran to the corner and peered after them.

"The rose room?" Tase asked.

Fadin nodded. "I didn't realize she'd be living with us."

"Well it would be kind of pointless not to. She has to be here all the time anyway."

They heard zippers, a few bumping noises, then heard the bedroom door shut. They moved away from the hall and sat on the sunroom's couches.

They heard someone walk across the entrance and saw Miss O'Keefe poke her head around the corner.

"Ready to begin?" She asked smiling at them.

Her jacket was off now, and Tase could see the dark green turtleneck she wore. It wasn't quite cold enough for that attire yet, was it?

"This way," she said, gesturing behind her.

They passed the kitchen, the dining room, the garden, and the rose room before coming to a halt at a very old-looking door. Miss O'Keefe pushed it open and revealed what looked like a classroom.

There were four desks, one obviously meant for a teacher. There was also a small bookcase, a worn-out couch, and several charts on the walls, not to mention their books laid out for them.

Tase saw Clearie sitting on the couch reading something. He looked up as they entered and put the book down.

"This is where we will be doing all of our schoolwork," Miss O'Keefe said, extending her arm.

Tase entered and nodded at Fadin to join them. It would be bad for him if he decided to be stubborn.

Miss O'Keefe showed them where they should sit and told them to open their science books. She told them to read the first two chapters of "Discovering Science" and then went to talk to Clearie.

Tase did as he was told but noticed that Fadin didn't appear to be reading. He was staring at a maths chart and didn't even bother to open his book. Tase shook his head but continued reading the chapters Miss O'Keefe had assigned.

She came back after a short while and looked at Fadin, whose book was closed. She then looked at Tase, who made sure his eyes where moving as he read along the page. She didn't say anything, but instead sat on her desk and pulled out a few papers.

Tase finished and looked up at her. He wasn't sure if he should say anything or just wait till she noticed. He didn't have to think long, however, because she got up and stood in front of them.

"You're a fast reader?" She asked Fadin, who turned to look at her.

"Yep," he answered, his voice stubborn.

She nodded and began to walk around him. "Then I suppose you could summarize the chapters for me?"

Tase stared at him. Would he try and lie about it?

Instead Fadin just smiled and shrugged. "I guess I didn't pay that much attention, maybe I should read slower?"

She smiled back at him. "Maybe." She turned to Tase. "Could you summarize the chapters for me?"

Tase nodded and did his best to do so.

He obviously pleased her because she grinned at him and not in the same way she smiled at Fadin. This was genuine. She turned and got the papers off her desk, handing them out.

Tase looked and saw it was a test on what they had just read. It was a true/false exam, and he felt confident that he knew the answers.

She told them they had ten minutes and went to check on Clearie.

When she was gone, Tase turned to his brother. "What are you doing?"

Fadin turned to look at him. "I'm just doing what I always do. Giving the new teacher a hard time, I'm sure that after a while she just won't try anymore." He smiled and turned back to the test.

Tase just shook his head. This wasn't the first time he'd done this. He liked to push the teacher's buttons and he had a well of stubbornness. No matter what was said or done, he would refuse to cooperate. This was no different, but Tase didn't think Miss O'Keefe would just give up the way Fadin seemed to think she would. No, Tase bet that Fadin wouldn't be joining in on any Halloween activities at Aimirgin's or anywhere else.

Miss O'Keefe returned and collected the tests. She graded Tase's, not handing it to him and put Fadin's back in front of him. She then stood next to Fadin, put one hand on her hip, one on her knee and crouched so she was at his eyelevel.

"What's this?" She asked patiently.

Fadin folded his arms. "A test," he smirked.

"A failed test," she said, looking at him hard. "You didn't even read the first two chapters and I don't need eyes in the back of my head to see that. I know how smart you are, I know that you can solve long maths problems as if they were simple addition, I know you are excellent at science, and I know that you can be very good in history. You are an 'A' student, Fadin, but your stubbornness makes you a failing one." She looked at him for a long while. "I know what you're doing, I've been around a long time, and I know what stubbornness can do. You think you're going to scare me into not trying anymore?" She shook her head but did not break eye contact. "It's not my time you're going to be wasting; it'll be your own. If you don't want to do school in the hours you're assigned to do it, then you can do school when everyone else is done. It's fine by me, but you won't leave this room till all the schoolwork given to you is completed. And if you think it's unfair, talk to your mother, she's the one who suggested it." She moved in front of him, put her hands on his desk, and leaned forward. "I'd like to be friends, Fadin, but if we can't, then I'll just have to be harsh with you. My first job is to be a teacher, not someone you like." She picked up the exam. "You will read those two chapters after school and complete this test with a passing grade, or you won't leave this room tonight." She nodded at him and took the exam to her desk.

"Open your history books and read chapter one." She walked by Tase and slipped him his test. "You have twenty minutes, don't worry, I know it's a long chapter. Just do your best." She winked at Tase as he looked at the big red A on his paper.

Tase smiled at her, and she walked back over to Clearie.

It went on like that all day. Miss O'Keefe would give assignments and Fadin wouldn't do them. The well of stubbornness didn't run dry, not even when Fadin saw the pile of homework on Miss O'Keefe's desk. Tase just gaped at him with hopelessness and continued his own work.

It really wasn't that hard. He didn't like the reading of course, or sitting still for so long, but the tests where fairly easy. He understood most of what he read and got almost all high marks on his papers and exams.

When the day was over, Miss O'Keefe smiled and told them, with the exception of Fadin of course, that they did a wonderful job. She gave Tase and Clearie only reading assignments for their novels, which to Tase's happiness he had already done, and told them to go enjoy the rest of their day.

Fadin was left in the school room with a mountain of work and hours left to go. Tase smiled at him sadly then left.

He shook his head all the way down the hall and glanced up at the clock. One p.m. He smelled something delicious coming from the kitchen and decided to enter.

He looked around and saw several things cooking in pots and pans. The space was very messy, and the plants that lined every shelf and counter appeared to have grown since he had last been inside.

Tase moved towards a counter and saw there was a strange clock sitting upon it. Or at least that's what it looked like. But instead of being round, like a normal clock, it was triangular and there were words on it. The only hand was a spatula and it was moving very slowly.

Tase turned as he saw Daireann stand up from behind a counter. She had a large mixing bowl and several stick-looking things. She placed it all on the counter and grabbed a large knife. She began cutting the sticks and suddenly yelped as she cut one of her own plump fingers.

"Oh, let me get you a wrap for that," Tase said, moving toward the door.

She jumped when she saw Tase standing before her and knocked over the large mixing bowl. The powdery substance in the bowl flew everywhere and the sticks were thrown to the floor.

"Boy," she said holding the cut hand to her heart, "you can't just sneak up on people." She was panting and glaring at him wide-eyed. "What are you doing in here?" she asked firmly.

"I smelled something and thought I'd have a look," he smiled and began to pick up the sticks. "I'd like to help if I can."

She looked thoughtful for a moment then stopped him from picking up the sticks.

"If you want to help," she said, "take these sandwiches to the table," she nodded at a covered plate. "Then take two of them to that stubborn brother of yours. I don't think he'll be leaving that room for a while."

Tase cocked his head. How did she know? No one had come by when they were in school. Certainly not Daireann, and Miss O'Keefe hadn't left.

He looked at her for a moment and did what she asked.

There were three place settings and one plate at the edge of the table. Tase sat the large, covered tray down, and picked out two warm sandwiches. He plopped them down and poured a cup of juice into an empty glass. He piled it all in his arms, and headed out of the door and down the hall.

He kicked the door open and saw Fadin sitting alone with a mountain of books on his desk. Fadin was looking up at the ceiling and apparently hadn't touched a thing.

Tase shook his head and came in. He nodded at the desk.

Fadin pushed the books to the floor.

"I'm starving," he said, eyeing the sandwiches.

Tase put the plate and cup down and stood back to look at him. "Why are you doing this?"

Fadin swallowed his large bite and blinked up. "Doing what?"

"This!" he stretched his arms towards the books on the floor. "This is really stupid, you know. Why don't you just do the work?"

"Because I don't want to," Fadin said stubbornly.

Tase closed his eyes and shook his red head. "Fine, sit in here all week if you want." He kicked the books and angrily went to the door. He stopped and looked back.

Fadin sat still for a moment then began eating.

Tase blew air out of his mouth and shut the door.

Aunt Kyna was, unsurprisingly, not at lunch.

Tase sat with Ma and Clearie, and thought about Fadin all alone with his books.

He rolled his eyes and suddenly remembered something. "Ma," he said looking at her, "I was wondering if I could go over to Aimirgin's for dinner tonight, and she wanted to know if Fadin and I could come over for Halloween?"

She let her eyes inspect the ceiling thoughtfully.

Tase crossed his fingers.

"Alright," she finally said, "but Fadin isn't going anywhere, at least not until he finishes his schoolwork. I would have said no about Halloween, but I'm not feeling well so I'm glad you get to do something." She looked over at Clearie and turned back to Tase. "Since Fadin can't go, do you think you could ask if Clearie could? It would be nice if you all had a friend together."

Tase looked at her and crinkled his nose. He saw she was firm and that it wasn't really a question. He looked down. "Yes, I'll ask."

"Good," she said with a smile.

Clearie looked at her then at Tase. He obviously didn't want to go, but wasn't going to argue about it.

There was an awkward silence and Tase decided to break it. "Where has Aunt Kyna been going so often, Ma?"

Her head snapped up and Tase saw something in her eyes. This was obviously a sore subject, or at least one she did not want to discuss with him. "Work," she answered quickly and in a tone that said it was an ended topic.

Tase looked down and finished eating.

After lunch he went to check on Fadin again. He had still done nothing and was bent over his desk sound asleep. The pile of books on the floor looked larger then ever and it could only increase. Tase blinked at him and wondered if he would ever stop acting this way. He didn't get his hopes up.

He walked down the hall and looked at the clock. 2:06. Suddenly, a thought occurred to him. Aimirgin didn't say whether she would come get him or what time he should be there.

He began to pace in the hall and wondered what he should do. Before he could worry too much, there was a knock on the door.

Tase flew to it, beating Enda who came up behind him. He swung the door open and saw Aimirgin standing there with a large, covered dish. A familiar smell was wafting from it and Tase licked his lips.

"Hello," she said kindly. "Can you come?"

"Yes, to both," he smiled at her.

"Great, Ta—Fai—um…"

"Tase," he said with a small laugh.

"Right, sorry, are you two—"

"No, we aren't identical twins, but we do look a lot alike. Ma says we'll grow out of it."

She nodded.

"Who's that for?" Tase asked, pointing at the dish.

"Your family, silly," she said.

"I'll take that for you, miss," Enda said bumping Tase in the shoulder.

"Yea, sorry." Tase took it and handed it over to Enda. "Well just let me grab my jacket."

He took off up the stairs and nearly ran over Pathos. The dog tried to lick him but he was too quick. He grabbed his jacket off the counter then hid the wooden K in his sock drawer. They hadn't been able to hide it in the planter since they had been grounded. He hurried back down the stairs.

He turned to the sunroom and told Ma he was leaving.

She smiled, kissed him on the cheek, and told him to be home by eight.

He agreed and was off.

~~~

Tase breathed in deeply and took in everything. A week of being cooped up had felt like an eternity.

Aimirgin noticed his strange behaviour and said she would probably be the same way. "I've never been able not to go outside," she said. "I love it in the open air."

"So do I," Tase said, looking up.

They entered the dark woods and Tase kept his eyes open. If that dog had been real, he wanted to see it again.

There was a rustle behind him and he turned.

Something big and black darted behind a tree.

"Tase?" Aimirgin asked, unsure how to react.

"Um, I just thought I saw something, that's all," Tase answered. He kept walking forward and heard the rustling again. When he turned this time, however, nothing was there. Or at least he saw nothing.

They soon reached the Hogan house and Tase saw smoke rising from the chimney. He was excited to actually be able to go into a friend's house. He really hadn't had any real friends when they lived on Little Hallow Road, and the few he had never wanted him at their house.

He followed Aimirgin in and was greeted by a rush of warm air and wonderful smells.

"Hello," Mr. Hogan said, stepping out from a swinging door. "How have you been?" He gave Tase a warm hug. "I heard you were punished, huh?" He made a smacking sound with his tongue and shook his finger playfully.

Tase laughed. He thought Mr. Hogan looked even taller than before and kinder.

"Come in," Mr. Hogan said, gesturing towards the door he had come from.

Tase followed and entered a kitchen even stranger then Daireann's.

It was small but cluttered. There were pans, cooking sheets, pots, bowls, spoons, forks, and spatulas spread all over the counter. There were several odd plants, meats, cheeses, vegetables, fruits, and breads on a round table with the same type of clock he had seen in Daireann's kitchen. There were also several photos hanging on the walls along with medals, drawings, plaques, and a clay sphere with hoof-prints on it.

Tase saw the oven was on and couldn't help but notice it was oddly shaped. Instead of being square, like most ovens, it was round and stuck out like a bubble. It was also emitting a strange, almost green smoke, and even though the light was on, Tase could not see inside.

"Who does the cooking?" Tase asked, looking around the room again.

"I do," Mr. Hogan answered, smiling.

"What?"

"Yep, I do it all. The cleaning, the wash, the cooking, and I've become pretty good at it, I must say." He leaned in. "Although it took years of practice."

Tase smiled. His da couldn't even make a sandwich without help, and he was never any good at cleaning.

"He's actually almost as good as a girl with cooking," Aimirgin said sitting in a round chair, "although he doesn't do all the cleaning alone."

He smiled at her. "She's right there, my Aimirgin, is a very big help."

He grabbed a knife and began cutting the vegetables. "So what is your mother doing with you for Halloween?"

Tase looked at Aimirgin. He hoped she had talked with him first before inviting him for the holiday.

"Nothing, she isn't feeling well."

Mr. Hogan looked up and smiled. "So you two will be joining us then?"

"I will, but Fadin can't."

"I was wondering where he was. Still in trouble?"

Tase cocked his head. "He's being, well, stubborn."

"What about?" Aimirgin asked.

"School. Ma decided she wanted us taught at home and he doesn't like the new teacher. He won't do the work." Tase suddenly felt very guilty for blabbing about Fadin like that. He shouldn't have said anything. He was his brother after all. He looked down at his shoes. "So he can't come, but would it be alright if my older brother did instead?"

Mr. Hogan smiled. "Of course, if I would have known I would have invited him as well. Do you have any other siblings?"

"A sister but she's in America. She wanted to see it before she started work here, and she's at a very fine college."

Mr. Hogan smiled. "America," he glanced up at the ceiling, "nice place to go and stay, but nothing like home. People are very different there," he bent low, "not much spice in them."

Tase grinned.

"While I finish cooking here, do you want to show him the rest of the house?" he asked Aimirgin.

"Okay," she hopped off the round chair. "Follow me."

They left the kitchen and walked back into the entrance. It was a large room with deep chocolate carpet and light yellow walls. There were couches, a fireplace, a small table, and several pictures on the walls.

"The main family room," Aimirgin said, "we're in here a lot."

She led them to the stairs at the back of the room and pointed to a door. "The bathroom, it's the only one down here."

She continued up the stairs and Tase gazed at all the pictures lining the stairway. He saw one of a pretty woman with thick black hair and black eyes. She looked a lot like Aimirgin. She was smiling and was surrounded by young boys. Tase saw that her belly was round and she held a rose to it.

"My mother," Aimirgin said stroking it, "right before she died."

Tase looked at her. "How did it happen?"

"When I was born, she barely got to see me before she became too sick to even open her eyes. She died two days later."

Tase swallowed. "I'm sorry."

Aimirgin shrugged. "It's okay, I just wish I could have known her, that's all."

Tase nodded. Even though he had lost his father, at least he was able to have twelve years with him; he couldn't imagine not knowing his parents, always wondering what they were like. Although this made him wonder about his mother. How well did he really know her?

They continued upwards and reached the second floor. It seemed to be nothing but doors. There was only a small area that was open and then more stairs to the end of the wide hall.

Aimirgin pointed. "Quinlan, Desmond, Cormick, when they stay here."

Tase heard a popping noise and jumped.

Aimirgin laughed and pointed at Quinlan's room.

"He has all kinds of junk in there, it's probably just one of his stupid play things." She nodded and they went to the second staircase.

They came to the third floor. This one still had a lot of doors but more room in the middle. In fact there was a single sofa and something that looked like a television. There was also a single window and black winding stairs.

"My room, Da's, and Colmcille's," she walked over to the staircase. "Up here is the second family room."

Tase followed her up and stared wide-eyed at the wonderful attic. There were paintings, games, a television, four sofas, a small kitchen, millions of cards, a bookcase, and a small eating table. There were also many things Tase didn't recognize—an odd scale, something that looked like a coat rack, and a long, triangular screen.

"I'm always up here," Aimirgin said smiling. "It's my favorite room in the house." She moved over to a large canvas. "My ma painted up here," she stretched her arms around the room, "all these are hers."

Tase looked at them. They were very pretty. Some were abstract, some were of landscapes, but the majority were of fanciful creatures. Elves, goblins, fairies, and several things Tase did not recognize.

"Magnificent," he said a little too enthusiastically. He could tell how important her mother's work was to her. "Absolutely amazing."

She grinned widely. "I'm glad you like them. I'm a bit of a painter myself, you know. My da says I get it from her."

Before he could respond she clasped his arm and led him back down the stairs.

Mr. Hogan was waiting for them. He asked what Tase had thought of their humble home and Tase said, very honestly, it was one of the best he'd ever seen.

The night was wonderful.

Tase couldn't remember a time when he had had more fun. At first they just talked a while because dinner wasn't ready, and Mr. Hogan seemed to know Tase had just eaten.

When dinner was finally served around four, Tase was remarkably hungry. He ogled, in awe, at the feast laid before him. A multitude of breads, stews, meats, meat cakes, and several other things he didn't know.

Tase had second and even third helpings, and when he thought he could eat no more, out came the dessert. Tase had never tasted anything quite as good. It was not the 'Mcayog lolo' that Aimirgin had brought him, but instead a sort of ice cream with a sauce on top. The sauce was indescribable, a perfect combination between sweet and tangy and it was wonderfully hot. As it ran down Tase's throat, he thought he may never be cold again.

After dinner, when Tase felt as though he might burst, they went and sat in front of a now roaring fire.

Mr. Hogan sent Aimirgin up to the attic and she brought down several games. They played one that looked like chess except the pieces did not move the same, look the same, or even resemble anything close to chess. It was more like a guessing board game, and when they had played three rounds Tase still didn't understand it any better, so they moved on to cards.

These cards had pictures of elves, dragons, and several other creatures on them. They would battle each other when the card was placed down, and a remarkable 3-D image of them popped up on the board. Tase figured it was an expensive light trick or something, and was fascinated by the game. He became very good at it and even beat Mr. Hogan once.

When they tired of playing games, Mr. Hogan asked Aimirgin to go and clean up the kitchen.

Tase immediately got up to help her, but Mr. Hogan persuaded him to stay.

"That's very nice of you, but there's no need." He patted the chair in front of him. "Let's have a little talk."

Tase sat down feeling very nervous. Had he said something disrespectful or wrong? Something rude accidentally? Did Mr. Hogan think it best he didn't hang around his daughter anymore?

Tase fiddled with his fingers.

Mr. Hogan smiled. "Don't be nervous," he said kindly. "I just wanted to answer a question I heard you had."

Tase was confused then comprehension dawned on him. This must be about his da, and where he and Fadin had wondered he had gone, when he died.

"Go ahead," Mr. Hogan nodded, "ask anything you like."

Tase fidgeted. "Well, I was just, wondering," he paused, "where do you think my da is? I mean, where do people go when they die?"

Mr. Hogan nodded but a look of sadness spread across his face. "Your ma has never told you?"

Tase shook his head. "I don't suppose she knows."

Mr. Hogan looked down, almost angry. "I suppose she does. However," he looked directly at Tase, "have you ever heard of Dia Ailín?"

Tase looked puzzled. "What's that?"

Mr. Hogan's face turned white. "Not what, who. You've never heard about him?"

Tase shook his head. "No."

"Well," Mr. Hogan said, running a hand through his hair, "this is going to be more difficult than I thought. I expected you to know more, expected you'd have some idea who he was. I thought your ma or da would have said something about him or the Xoor. I know they have it, or had it."

Tase was very confused. "I don't understand, Mr. Hogan."

"No," he answered, "I wouldn't expect you to. Nothing I have to say will make sense until you know more." He looked kindly at Tase. "But one thing I can tell you, Tase, is that your da is safe and happy. He is in the most wonderful place you could imagine, and I can tell you without a doubt, that you WILL see him again."

Tase felt tears streaming down his face, and he hastened to wipe them away. He looked up at Mr. Hogan and saw something familiar, something he hadn't noticed before. He smiled at him and suddenly felt panic rush up inside him.

"What time is it?" he yelled.

Mr. Hogan glanced curiously at the fire. "9:20."

Tase yelped. "Oh no, I was supposed to be home by eight. My ma is gonna kill me!"

Aimirgin flew out of the kitchen. "Here," she handed him his coat, "run, we don't want you grounded for Halloween."

Tase smiled at her and her father. "Thank you so much," he said wholeheartedly. "For everything."

They both smiled and waved him on.

Tase rushed through the woods, the branches scratching his face as he flew. He heard something following him, but he didn't turn. Partly for fright, and partly because he didn't care. He had to get home, he had to beat his mother noticing his absence, and he had to go back up—up to the attic.

# Chapter 10

## *Halloween*

Tase stopped abruptly at the front door. He panted and gulped until he felt calm enough to enter. He opened the door quietly and peered in.

The castle was still and only a few lights remained on.

He tiptoed inside and lightly shut the door. He looked around the corner and saw Ma lying on the couch with a book tipped to the side. He smiled to himself; she hadn't noticed he was late.

He snuck down the west hall and noticed Miss O'Keefe's door was shut tight. He passed it silently and opened the school room door. He saw Fadin still sitting there but to his amazement, he was actually doing the work. There was still a pile of books and tests on the desk, but a great deal had been done. He didn't even notice Tase looking in and continued to scribble answers.

Tase sighed and left him alone. He didn't have time for him to finish his work; he had other things to do.

He ran up the stairs, still quiet so as not to wake Ma, and bolted to his room. He flung off his clothes and pulled on a night outfit. When he was finished he fuzzed up his hair and grabbed his reading book, tiptoeing back downstairs.

He moved to his mother's limp body and lightly shook her awake.

She gasped and jumped a little but calmed down when she saw Tase's face. "Oh," she said rubbing the sleep out of her eyes, "when did you get back?"

"An hour or so ago," he lied.

She gazed around the room then smiled at him. "Why didn't you wake me?"

"You looked comfortable, besides I got some reading of my own done."

"Well," she said yawning, "I better get to sleep. Is that brother of yours done yet?"

"No, he still has a bit more."

She shook her head wearily. "Well can you get him in half an hour and have him go to bed? I don't want him down there all night. He'll be cranky in the morning. He can just finish the rest tomorrow, along with his day's work." She got up and stretched. "I'm glad you've found a friend, Tase," She said stroking his hair. "I'm going to have to actually meet her one of these days." She smiled, took her book, and went upstairs.

Tase watched till she was in her room and grabbed the wooden carving from the middle of his book. He then went to the east hall and jumped as Pathos came from around the corner. Tase stared at him, then crept past Aunt Kyna's room. It was quiet and dark, but he still didn't want to risk being heard in case she was in bed.

He walked to the bookcase and opened it. He and Pathos went up the stairway, opened the second door, and then the third. He went inside the attic and found Ciaran sitting on the broken table pulling out rotted pieces of wood.

He looked up and smiled. "Hello, thing. Where is other one of you?"

"He's downstairs," Tase answered. "Listen, I need that photo album you showed us last time."

Ciaran snarled at Pathos, the Bernese growling in return, then grinned toward Tase. "Certainly," he answered, jumping from the broken furniture.

His wooden leg clunked as he hit the timber floor, then he hobbled under the table. After a few moments he returned with the large, heavy book.

Tase took it from him and opened up to the spot where the black and white photo lay.

He surveyed the picture and spotted what he was looking for. "There," he said pointing, "who is that?"

Ciaran looked at the man in the photo and blinked. "Why thing want to know?"

"Tell me," Tase said firmly.

Ciaran gazed at him with his big, hazel eyes. "I think you thing does know."

Tase breathed in heavily. "Why?"

"You has been with this man's daughter, have yous not?"

Tase looked at Lee Hogan's picture and sighed. It was definitely him. There was no mistaking his black eyes and hair, besides the fact that he was head and shoulders taller then anyone else. He was the tall man standing beside his father. "He's got his arm around my da," Tase said, still admiring it. "Did he know him?"

Ciaran smiled. "Best friends."

Tase gulped back the lump in his throat. "Why does that picture sing?"

Ciaran cocked his head. "Whats picture?"

"The one in the closet," he pointed at the young man next to his mother, "the picture of this man."

Ciaran perked up his ears. "Is singing photo. He sings to his love and insults when bothered, but can only sing, no talking."

Tase nodded. "How do you know about all this?"

"Have been around long time, have seen much."

"Can I borrow this and take it with me?" Tase asked, pointing to the picture.

"No!" Ciaran yelled. "Must stay here."

"Okay," Tase said. "Then can I look at the book a little longer?"

"Sures," Ciaran nodded. "I must finish fixing tables, thing. You okay to look alone?"

Tase nodded.

Ciaran clunked back to the table, and again began pulling off rotted wood.

Tase stroked the photo once more and flipped to the next page. The picture had been completely scratched out, and the caption looked like it had been bitten into.

Tase arched an eyebrow and flipped the page again. He found a photo of four people. Two women and two men. The picture was black and white, and obviously very old.

One of the women was older, in her forties, with black hair pinned in a bun and light eyes. She looked mean, and spiteful, and wore a dress with spikes along the collar. One of the men, in his fifties, stood beside her. He had long, lanky black hair, and a full, delicately trimmed beard. His eyes, too, were light, and his features cruel.

Then there were two younger individuals. The young man was handsome with strong features, dark eyes and black, spiked hair. He was in his twenties and did not look particularly friendly, though he looked kinder than the other two.

Last was the girl, who appeared to be no more then seventeen. She was, by far, the most beautiful woman Tase had ever seen in his entire life. She had dark black eyes, hair that hung down to her behind, thick, plump lips, a small delicate nose, and to top it off, a beautiful figure. The girl was intoxicating. Tase swallowed and blushed. He looked away from the girl and peered down at the caption.

Trandafira, Vladimir, Gabriel, and Dominique Bojin, 1954.

Tase looked up. If he wasn't mistaken, those names were Romanian. As he looked back at them, Tase was certain they were Romanian. The strong, dark features gave it away. He wondered who they were and why their photo was up in this attic.

He shrugged and turned to the next page. There was a paper with several pictures on it. It was a page taken from an old school album, a picture of all the students in one particular class.

Tase scanned the picture and was surprised to find his mother smiling up at him. She appeared to be thirteen years old, and as he looked for her name, he found it. Tase, intrigued, looked up at the school name. Perhaps she had gone to the same school he had?

*Dragon School Oxford*, it said in bold blue lettering. Tase recoiled.

Oxford? As in Oxford, England? No, that couldn't be right, she lived in Ireland, and she had always lived in Ireland. She had been raised here and resided on this island her whole life. She was Irish, like he was, like his father was. Right?

Tase felt like his head was swimming. Too much information to process in one night. Too many secrets, too many lies.

Tase quietly tore out the picture of the Feneg. He swallowed hard and handed the book back to Ciaran. "Thanks, I'd better go. It's getting late."

Ciaran smiled. "Ok thing, see you later."

Tase called to Pathos, closed the door, and began the descent. He reached the backside of the bookcase and froze as he heard raised voices. He placed his head against the wood and listened intently.

He heard Aunt Kyna shouting and then the front door close. He recognized Daireann and Enda's voices then heard them joined by his mother's. They talked for a moment in the entrance way, too low to be audible, and then moved closer.

Tase still couldn't make out what was being said, but he knew Aunt Kyna didn't sound happy. Soon they all moved right outside Aunt Kyna's room. Tase plugged a finger in one ear and eavesdropped like he never had before.

"No," Aunt Kyna yelled. "I won't agree to something this daft, this ignorant. I won't."

"Please Kyna, be reasonable," Daireann begged. "It'll get you nowhere to fight this."

"It will make me feel at peace with myself to know, at least, I tried to stop this insanity."

"Daireann is right Kyna, just sign it," Ma said.

"You can't make any difference," Enda added, "no matter how just the cause."

Aunt Kyna snorted. "You all would sell your souls to stay out of trouble, wouldn't you?"

"Kyna, stop it," Ma yelled. "We're just thinking of you. I know you don't want to be thrown off the Council."

"Don't I? I wonder anymore. They are completely insane, lacking competent judgment and thinking."

"They just want equal rights…" Daireann began.

Aunt Kyna let out a harsh, almost mean, laugh. "Equal rights? They might as well be signing our death sentence."

"Kyna, I know and understand your concerns," Enda said, "I was right there beside you in the war, we all were. But I have to say, all the Council is doing is trying to make Ireland a safer and better place. Granted, I do not agree with many of their decisions, I mean, look at me. I look like a servant boy. But I was thrown out of Cavan-Corr for what I believe in, for what I think is right. And, Kyna, I can't go back, and I'm lucky that's all they did to me. Do you really want the same treatment or worse? "

He heard Aunt Kyna snort. "Worse? What are they going to do? Throw me in jail? For what, not agreeing with them? Please, Puceula is an idiot, I'll give you that, but he's not stupid. If he laid one finger on me, many of the Council Members would leave. I have more pull then any of you think. And what do you mean they're trying to make Ireland safer and better? Puceula is trying to make Ireland his, or whoever's he's working for. And not being allowed to question that riff-raff, when they are clearly breaking the law? How is that helpful to the safety of Ireland? Isn't our job to ask questions?"

"Well everything else aside, Puceula included, what law are they breaking?" Ma asked. "Those creatures are just trying to survive. They've done nothing wrong."

"Not yet," Aunt Kyna answered, "but just you wait, they will, they will."

Ma snorted. "How can you clump them all together like that? I know what happened in the past, I remember it clearly. But if you recall, not every member of the traitor races went to Egorov's aid. There were many who disagreed, so how can you call them all riff-raff, and claim they'll do something wrong? We have no proof." Tase could tell Ma was getting angrier. "It seems to me that you are just prejudiced to those less fortunate than yourself, and those you assume are in the wrong."

Aunt Kyna laughed cruelly. "Prejudiced? O-ho, please, Teagan, I'm not discriminatory to those less fortunate then myself. If I were, would you or your ignorant children be here?"

Ma took a deep, fuming, breath. "Let us not forget, Kyna dear, where you got all this wealth from." Her tone was spiteful.

"No, Teagan darling, I haven't forgotten. Believe me, I remember who ran away and gave all this up, often."

Ma let out a seething breath.

"I am not biased to those creatures," Kyna continued, "what I am is careful, protective of my people, and wiser from the ambush we had only fourteen years ago. Don't you remember? I will not sign any treaty of equal rights and peace to those former traitors. Whether they are now, or aren't, I won't take the risk. I will not aid in the task of putting our people in danger. If they want to throw me off the Council for that, *or worse*, then so be it!" Tase heard her stomp away and slam her door.

Three sighs went up.

"Well," Daireann said, "at least we tried."

"Yea," Ma groaned. "And she wonders why I did what I did. This, right here, is why I keep my children out of this mess."

Tase heard her walk away, followed by Daireann's little footsteps and Enda's long stride.

Tase stood, motionless and quiet, behind the bookcase for a long while. Slowly, when the coast seemed clear with Pathos by his side, he snuck out. He crept down the hall, through the tea room and sunroom, and out past the entranceway.

He had to talk to Fadin, he had to tell him what he heard. He didn't care if he did have to do more school in the morning, he would just have to buck up and do it.

~~~

Fadin's hand hurt. He had done test after test and still had many more to go. He had decided several hours ago that he would not have a repeat of tonight, and he would apologize first thing to Miss O'Keefe, although that didn't mean he wouldn't still give her a hard time.

He was actually surprised that Miss O'Keefe had been serious. He thought she would have been full of empty threats, like many of his other teachers. But as the hours had gone on, Fadin realized how true to her word Miss O'Keefe was.

He rubbed his eyes, sighed, and continued on.

*Question 21: What is the definition of...*

Fadin jumped.

The door had been flung open and Tase stood in the archway.

"What the—what are you doing?"

Tase came in, followed by Pathos, and sat in the desk next to Fadin. He breathed hard for a minute, and then stared at Fadin's desk. "Aren't you finished yet?" he asked.

Fadin shook his head in bewilderment. "Never mind that, what's wrong?"

Tase took a deep breath and accounted everything he had seen and heard, including finding Lee Hogan in the picture, and the fact that it appeared their mother had gone to the Dragon School Oxford.

When he was finished, Fadin sat back and thought. "I'm out of things for one day, and a thousand new secrets pop up," he turned to Tase. "Oxford? As in Oxford, England?"

"That's the one," Tase nodded.

Fadin furrowed his brow. "Why do you think Aunt Kyna doesn't want to sign?"

"I don't know," Tase said. "Some kind of peace treaty between Aunt Kyna's people and these bad creatures."

"Well," Fadin said, looking up at the ceiling, "creatures *Aunt Kyna* thinks are bad. It sounds as though Ma, Daireann, Enda, and many other people don't think these creatures are bad."

"Whatever it was, it sounded like she could get in serious trouble if she didn't sign."

"She'll just get in trouble then," Fadin answered, "because I don't think she's going to agree to the treaty. You said she sounded pretty adamant about it?"

"Yea, her and Ma even got into a bit of a row. I don't think she's going to agree to anything pertaining to those creatures. At least that's what she called them."

Fadin nodded. "Well, there's nothing we can do about it, I guess I'd better get back to work."

"Oh for pity's sake, Fadin, are you going to give Miss O'Keefe problems tomorrow?"

"No," Fadin answered truthfully. "I've learned my lesson. I don't want to be grounded from going anywhere again."

"Fine," Tase sighed. "Give me half the pile and we'll get it all done."

Fadin smiled. "You're the best twin any guy could have, Tase."

"Yea, yea, just give it to me, you gombeen. Maybe if you get all high marks we can both go to Aimirgin's for Halloween. Besides, I could use your help showing this to Mr. Hogan."

Fadin let out a sigh as Tase lifted up the black and white photo.

~~~

"Wake up, Fadin!"

Fadin rubbed his eyes and looked around the room. It was light out, morning, but what morning? The morning of Halloween, the day he would be able to go to Aimirgin's.

Ma had been so pleased with his finished work and the work he did the next day of school, that she decided to permit him to go to Aimirgin's

Halloween Party. The only drawback was that Clearie was still coming. Ma said it was rude to uninvite him, and since Aimirgin had come over to check if Fadin could come, she said all three of them were going or no one at all.

Fadin got out of bed and got dressed.

He and Tase went downstairs, ate breakfast, and then barreled through their school. They got all their reading and tests done, with Fadin's marks a little higher than Tase's, then paced as Clearie took his time to finish.

When they were all done, and Miss O'Keefe gave them their homework, they went and grabbed their jackets and told Ma goodbye. She kissed each of them and told them to be back by nine, no later.

Finally they were outside and Fadin breathed in the fresh air. He winced a bit as the coldness stung his nostrils but breathed deeply just the same. He glanced at Tase and saw him lift up the photo. He smiled and looked toward Clearie, who had his arms crossed and was frowning.

"Oh, what's wrong sourpuss?" he asked. "Don't you want to play with the little kids?"

"Dry up, you know I didn't want to come. I'd much rather be back at home with a good book."

"You ninny," Fadin taunted. "Why didn't you just tell Ma?"

"Why do you think? In case you haven't noticed, Ma hasn't been herself lately. I wasn't going to make things hard for her by being stubborn." Clearie raised both blond eyebrows in Fadin's direction.

Fadin heard Tase suppress a laugh.

"Well," he said bitterly, "don't make things difficult for us either. Just keep your fat gob shut."

Clearie glared at him. "Gladly."

They walked the rest of the way in silence.

When they reached the woods, Fadin became on his guard. He was going to see that dog if he could, the dog he knew was there. He noticed, vaguely, that Tase too seemed on edge. But he was so preoccupied with jumping at every noise, that he paid little attention. But the thought did cross his mind that perhaps Tase had seen the animal too.

Once they reached the Hogan House without any sighting of the black dog, Clearie didn't say more than two words. They were greeted by Aimirgin, and Clearie simply nodded.

He was sulking all right.

"I'm so glad you could come," Aimirgin said, hugging Fadin. "We hoped you'd get that schoolwork finished."

Fadin smiled, arched a red eyebrow, and looked at Tase, who had his head down. Aimirgin hugged Tase too, and then held out her hand to Clearie.

"Hello, nice to meet you. I'm Aimirgin."

"Clearie," he answered.

She grinned. "Well come in, my da and brothers have everything set up in here."

They went in the house and Fadin smiled at the wonderful smells.

He saw all of Aimirgin's brothers and watched as they placed nine pumpkins on newspapers. They grabbed three carving knives, and Mr. Hogan brought in a plate full of sandwiches.

"Hello," he said smiling widely, "I hope you like carving Jack O'Lanterns, it's one of our favorite parts."

Fadin nodded and looked over at Clearie.

His mouth was agape and he was ogling at Mr. Hogan and the immense heights of his sons.

"Good," Mr. Hogan said and gestured toward the paper-covered ground.

Fadin whispered to Tase as they separated into groups, "How do you suppose we carve a Jack O'Lantern?"

Tase shrugged. "You got me."

Fadin smiled and joined the group with Quinlan and Cormick. Tase sat next to Aimirgin and Colmcille, and Clearie went with Lee and Desmond. The three groups shared a knife and competed in making the best three Jack O'Lanterns they could.

"We always do this," Quinlan told Fadin. "It's one of the best parts of Halloween, and the team who wins gets to make the other teams' costumes for the evening. They can make anything they want, and the other teams have to wear it." He smiled wide. "I'm going to make Aimirgin a rat, she hates rats!"

Fadin laughed and helped pull out the pumpkin seeds and pulp. He crinkled his nose in enjoyment at the squishy feeling of the mush. "I've never done this before, carved pumpkins," Fadin said. "Just so you know."

"No worries," Cormick grinned, "We'll beat 'em anyway."

Not an hour later the contest was over and Tase's team had won by far. They had strung the three pumpkins together and made a long, swirling line across all three, accompanied by two fairies on each side. The light shone brightly through the carving and made the designs look even more elaborate.

Tase, Aimirgin, and Colmcille told Fadin and Clearie's teams what they wanted for their costumes and got started on the six they had to make.

Soon Fadin, Clearie, and the other four were done with their outfits and began eating the sandwiches as Tase, Aimirgin, and Colmcille finished their work.

Tase yelled as his team completed the costumes and made the others model them. Fadin winced as he saw the princess outfit Tase obviously made for him and reluctantly tried it on. He came out to roaring laughter and quickly ripped it off. He felt a bit better, however, when Clearie came out dressed as a big, pink book.

After the costume show, they all put one perfect ivy leaf into a cup of water.

"I don't understand why we're doing this," Clearie said.

"Haven't you ever celebrated Halloween before?" Desmond asked.

Fadin looked down.

"Well, actually..." Clearie began and faltered.

"The reason we do this," Mr. Hogan cut in, "is to see who will have good luck this year. Typically, you are supposed to leave your leaf in overnight, and whoever's leaf is still perfect in the morning, with no spots, will be sure to have good luck for twelve months. But since you won't be staying over, we'll check them before nine." He smiled and clapped Clearie on the back. "All right everyone, put your costumes back on, flattering or not, it's time for a candy hunt."

Everyone obeyed, some, who had girly costumes, with difficulty, and prepared to find the candy. Since there were no neighbours around besides trees, they had a candy hunt throughout the house.

Fadin teamed up with Quinlan, looked everywhere, and found bucketfuls of candy. Chocolate, sour, gummy, hard, you name it, they had it.

Everybody played except Mr. Hogan and Desmond, who had obviously been the hiders.

When everybody was finished and had torn the costumes off, they all went outside.

There was wood piled high in a round, dirt pit, right in the middle of the backyard. If you could call it a yard—it was really more like a clearing in the woods.

Mr. Hogan had apparently set it up before Fadin and his brothers had come over. He instructed everyone to stand around the wood pile, took a handful of something black from his pocket, and cleared his throat as if he were about to make a speech. "To friends and family," he said smiling, "to good times, to games, and fun. To health, to love, to warmth, and meals. To enjoyment and laughter, to candy with seals. To hope, to night, to day, to growth. To O'Callaghans, Hogans, Halloween, and toast!" He threw the black powder down and the whole pile went up in purple flames.

Fadin jumped back and gazed in awe as the fire grew and grew until it was above the house. The flames flickered with a loud "pop" and then died down until they became yellow and returned to a more normal size, though the fire was still quite high.

Mr. Hogan laughed heartily, and sat on a chair, which Fadin had not noticed, that stood close to the fire. He held his hand out and, curiously, acted as if he had an invisible line in between his fingers, and began to pull violently.

Fadin watched him intently yank and tug on the invisible string. It actually appeared as if he were pulling on something, and Fadin was sure a magic trick was on its way.

As Mr. Hogan jerked for the final time, a fiddle burst out of thin air.

Fadin's eyes popped. That was no trick.

Mr. Hogan beamed warmly and began to play the magic fiddle. The melody was wonderful and fast-paced, and made Fadin's foot bounce up and down.

All the Hogans grabbed arms and flung Fadin and his brothers into the dance, whether they were willing or not. They circled around the fire, around the sporadically planted flowers, around Mr. Hogan, and then broke apart to dance individually.

Fadin laughed and stomped his foot as Quinlan and Desmond danced like a couple.

Aimirgin walked up to Tase and held her arm out.

Tase smiled, took it, and went twirling as he clumsily lead the swinging, with no help from Aimirgin, as she stumbled on her dress.

Fadin sat on a rock and just watched, happily bouncing and swaying to the music. He saw Clearie had been taken by Cormick and laughed as Clearie was dipped like a girl. He glanced at Mr. Hogan, who had stood up as he played ferociously and laughed the most wonderful laugh, all the while.

Fadin couldn't help but feel a sting of sadness as he watched Mr. Hogan. He could never again make a memory with his father. He would never be able have a Halloween or dance around a bonfire with him. He could never just feel Da's presence again, see his face, or hear his laugh. Oh how he missed his father's bubbly laugh. Fadin smiled just thinking about it.

He felt a hot tear stream down the side of his face and quickly wiped it away. It was hard to have fun sometimes, to enjoy life, to just live it. Because part of him felt like he was betraying his father's memory by being happy. But as he looked back at the Hogan family, Fadin felt warmth enter his heart. It was okay to be happy. His father would have wanted him to. And for a split second, Fadin thought he saw his father, laughing beside Mr. Hogan. But as soon as Fadin focused, he was gone.

Fadin let his eyelids flutter, to keep back more tears, and then jumped as he saw something through the heat of the fire.

Light-green eyes were peering at him from the dark form of a dog, which stood near a tree in the shadows. And that was not all; something else was with the animal, something tall, human-formed. The tall being was cloaked in something black, something so dark that nothing of the face could be seen.

Fadin felt his heart skip a beat. Whatever was watching him was dangerous, he could feel it. But he could also feel that he was safe here, that they could not touch him here. But they were watching.

Just as he was about to stand and point out the animal and other being to Mr. Hogan, they vanished into the dark.

Fadin's concentration was broken as Quinlan grabbed his hand and flung him in to dance with the others. With no way to watch for the pair, Fadin joined the merry-making, and soon forgot the feeling of dread.

Finally, when everyone collapsed from dancing, Mr. Hogan put away his fiddle and called everyone in for dinner.

They all entered the kitchen and sat at the very long table.

Mr. Hogan brought out a dish called Colcannon. Fadin had heard of it before, it was boiled potato, curly kale, or cabbage, as it is better known, and raw onions. Many of his old friends had this meal on Halloween. It was tradition; one Fadin had never been able to partake in before.

As soon as the plates were down, everyone dug in.

There was much chatter and laughter at the table. The kitchen was warm and loud, the way, Fadin thought, their kitchen used to be. But now, whenever they ate meals in that big, fancy dining room, the meals were sad and quiet.

As they ate, Fadin, Clearie, Cormick, and Quinlan found colourful coins in their potatoes. Desmond explained, for at this point the Hogans obviously knew Fadin and his brothers had never had a Halloween before, that it was tradition to wrap coins and hide them in the potatoes for guests and children to find.

After dinner a cake was brought out. It was a sort of fruit bread called Barnbrack Cake. It was another tradition and one that involved a game. After everyone got a slice, they were told to chew carefully.

After a short while, Tase made a strange face and pulled a ring from his mouth.

"Ah, hurray," Quinlan smiled, "Tase got the ring. He shall have great happiness or a romance around the corner." He smiled and knocked Tase on the shoulder.

"What?" Tase asked.

Desmond pulled a rag from his cake and grimaced. "Well that's just great, exactly what I need, less profit."

Fadin laughed. "I don't get it."

Aimirgin pulled a coin from her fork and smiled. "It's a superstition. Every year you hide a rag, a coin, and a ring inside the Barnbrack Cake. Whoever finds the rag has a doubtful financial future. Whoever gets the coin can look forward to a prosperous year. And the ring represents impending romance or continued happiness."

Fadin grinned. "Cool, looks like you're going to be a lover boy, soon here, Tase." Fadin winked at him.

Tase rolled his eyes.

When dinner was finished and the kitchen was cleaned, they all went back outside and played Snap Apple. They were all blindfolded and had to try their best to get a bite at the apple which was suspended from a string. Fadin, Tase, Clearie, and Aimirgin had their own apple, which hung on a lower branch, and the others had one dangling from a tall sturdy limb.

After many attempts by all, Fadin finally managed to get a large bite of the apple, only to end up tripping, snapping the string, and pulling the fruit down with him. Everyone, especially Aimirgin, had a good laugh.

Next they all began peeling apples, trying to get it done in a single peel. The point, Fadin and his siblings were told, was to drop it on the floor to find the initial of his or her future intended.

Fadin failed and so did Colmcille and Quinlan. Tase and Clearie both got A's while Aimirgin and Cormick got T's and Desmond an S.

After the peeling was finished, they all went inside and sat in front of the fire while drinking hot chocolate. Fadin glanced at the large clock and saw it was nearly nine. He nudged Tase and pointed at his pocket.

"I think you should ask him," he whispered, nodding toward Mr. Hogan.

"I don't know how. I can't get him alone."

Mr. Hogan suddenly got up. "Would anyone like seconds?"

"Help him," Fadin whispered harshly.

"I'll help," Tase said standing.

"Me too," Fadin nodded, getting up as well.

The three of them walked slowly out of the family room and entered the kitchen.

"Thank you so much for everything," Tase said as they poured hot water in the six empty cups.

"Of course," Mr. Hogan said turning to them. "I'm very glad you could come."

Fadin nudged him.

"Um, I have a question," Tase said, fingering his pocket.

"Ask away," Mr. Hogan said cheerfully. "Ask away."

"Did—did you know our parents?"

Mr. Hogan's face went completely white. "No—no, of course not," he was silent for a moment, then added, "but, out of curiosity, why do you ask?"

Tase pulled out the picture, looked at it, and handed it to him.

Mr. Hogan took it and sat down as if his legs could no longer hold him. "I haven't seen this in years," he whispered, stroking the spot where their father stood. "Where did you find it?"

"In our attic," Fadin said.

"How did you get up there?"

"We figured out how to use the wooden K," Tase answered.

Mr. Hogan smiled. "Smart boys. Does your brother know?"

They shook their heads.

"Didn't think so, but then again, I didn't think you knew either." He shook his head. "Well, I suppose there's no reason to lie," he looked up at them. "Yes, I did know your parents, your da mostly. He was my best friend, my closest friend." He stroked the picture again. "That's why I reacted so emotionally when you told me about him dying, Fadin. I had no idea he had passed away, we haven't seen each other in fourteen, nearly fifteen years. As for your mother," he sighed, "I knew her, I knew her very well. My Chanel," he rubbed the ring which still sat on his left hand, "was *her* best friend. But your mother and I were never really that close. Alroy always did fancy Teagan, but she was quite taken with Faolan Hennessy for many years. The young man next to her," Mr. Hogan gestured toward the photo. "It wasn't until much later that your da and ma became more than just acquaintances."

Fadin looked at him. "Why is she lying to us? Why has she kept the truth from us for all these years?"

Mr. Hogan blinked at him. "I think I know why, but I'm not the right person to ask, I'm afraid. If you want the truth, I think you should ask your mother."

Fadin turned away. "What makes you think she'd tell us anything?"

"Oh," Mr. Hogan said, "I think you'd be surprised by how much she could tell you, and would, if you asked."

"No," Tase said, "I don't think I want—we want—her to know, we know yet."

"If she keeps secrets from us," Fadin added, "we can keep secrets from her."

Mr. Hogan nodded. "You do have a right to be angry but," he leaned forward and handed back the picture, "more lies and secrets will only keep you further apart."

Fadin shrugged. "She's the one who started it."

"Yes," Mr. Hogan said gruffly, "but you're finishing it. And like I said, she has her reasons."

Neither of them spoke.

"I'll tell you what," Mr. Hogan said sighing, "if you want to know about all this, then I'll help you learn, but," he looked at them sternly, "you can't blab about it and," he pointed his finger at them, "you have to bring Clearie along too."

"But—" they both started.

"No, no, no, no, no," Mr. Hogan said firmly. "He deserves and has the right to know as much as you do." He raised his black eyebrows. "So what do you say?"

They looked at each other.

"All right," Tase said smiling.

"We'll do it," Fadin added.

Mr. Hogan fixed them with a serious stare. "You have to realize that once you get into this, there's no going back."

They again looked at one another and nodded.

"Okay then," he said getting up. "I want you three to come to a gathering with me December 20th." He looked firmly at them. "Tell Clearie nothing of our conversation, and I'll invite him myself to the event. When you come, you'll need to bring a number of things that I will send to you by letter. Aimirgin will explain the reasons for collecting these things when we see you next. You'll receive the list a few weeks in advance, and I want you to tell your mother about the invitation the first week in December. Tell her it's a slumber party." He paced as he talked. "You'll also not want to tell her my last or first name, because I don't think she'd allow you to come here anymore. And since you *are* here, I'm assuming you haven't told her yet."

They shook their heads.

"So, you are to tell her about all this when a package arrives the day before the first of December. It will have a note attached to it and you are to follow the instructions *precisely*. Also, he said, grabbing a small bottle from a cabinet, "I want you to hold these whenever you talk about coming to this house." He handed it to them and pulled two handkerchiefs out. "It will make her, and anyone else in the room, misinterpret my name if you're asked to give it."

He bent down and put his hands on their shoulders. "This last bit is very important. When the month of December begins, and you follow the instructions on the package, you are not, and I mean under any circumstances, to leave your house, even to give me a yes or no answer, until I come to get you the morning of December 20th." He looked at them hard. "Do you understand me?"

Fadin cocked his head. "But wh—"

"Do you understand me?"

They nodded.

"Good. Now, I think it is almost nine o'clock, and I believe that's the hour in which you are supposed to return home, so," he said standing up, "let's go and check on our Ivy leaves, and then we will say our goodbyes."

The boys nodded.

As they began to walk out of the kitchen, Fadin turned to take one last look. He wanted it engraved in his mind since it seemed like it may be awhile till he saw the Hogan house again. As he surveyed the room, he saw a photo that caught his attention. It was a picture of a short, freckled, dark-red-headed girl. She was smiling, with dimples that stood out, and sparkling brown eyes. Beneath the snapshot, in sloppy lettering, was written:

*To my best friend, Aimirgin*
*Love, Aednat*

Fadin smiled to himself. Cute little girl, couldn't be more then ten.

He took a deep breath, nodded, then walked out of the kitchen and joined in on the singing that was now taking place.

When the song had ended, Mr. Hogan pronounced that they should check on their leaves, and then it was time for the O'Callaghan boys to return home.

When the three of them had hugged and shaken hands until they could no more, they left the warmth and comfort of the Hogan home, and began their walk back through the woods.

"You know," Clearie said, looking up at the stars and smiling wider than Fadin had ever seen him smile before, "I really had fun tonight. More fun than I can ever remember having." He jumped over a twisted root and beamed into the night air. "I loved that fiddle trick, it was great." He turned and grinned at them. "What a wonderful, perfectly normal family." He raised his eyebrows and walked a little ahead.

Fadin and Tase exchanged incredulous and humorous looks.

Normal—right.

# Chapter 11

## *The List, and what you shouldn't do*

"Why does it have to be December?" Fadin whined as he circled the "true" written on his exam.

"Because that's when Mr. Hogan said the party or gathering or whatever it is begins," Tase answered, straining his neck to see Fadin's paper.

"Well that's too long," Fadin moaned, and catching Tase cheating, moved further to the left.

Tase snorted and leaned back in his own chair. He looked to the door and saw no sign of Miss O'Keefe or Clearie. They were still gathering supplies for their science project.

He sighed and looked back down at his test. He tried to re-read his question, but his thoughts were constantly getting in the way.

He turned to look at Fadin and grimaced. It really was too long to wait for something so exciting. He hadn't really been able to think of anything else since their visit to Aimirgin's two weeks ago. He kept telling himself and Fadin that it was worth the wait. But now, sitting in the quiet school room with nothing else on his mind, he wondered if it was true. He wondered if going would answer all their questions. If they would see and meet something amazing. If Ma would realize what was going on and decide to stop them. This seemed unlikely however, because the handkerchiefs had worked, so far at least. When Ma had asked for Aimirgin's father's name, they had told her, and she simply stared at them for a moment. Then she said something like "peculiar name," and continued whatever she had been doing.

Tase and Fadin had tried over and over to figure out how the handkerchiefs worked, but every theory seemed highly unlikely, so they took them up to Ciaran. "I no understand how these clothes work," Ciaran had said, holding up one of the handkerchiefs to his eyes. "Me never seen these before."

"Really?" Tase asked, disappointed.

"Reallys," Ciaran nodded, handing the cloth back.

"Well," Fadin said, stuffing the handkerchief in his pocket, "can you at least tell us more about our da and Mr. Hogan? He said they were friends."

"Yes, them weres friends. They know each others long old time, since them, ten years at mostest. They be friends till the day you things mother and dadies up and left."

Tase furrowed his brow.

"Why did they leave, Ciaran?" Fadin asked.

"No one knows for certain, but it was, how you say, out of blue? One day them here, nexts day, them gone. No note, no goodbyes, nothing. You things mother had seemed unhappies for long time, though. She stayed insides, not coming out much at all. Then, one day, it seemed like you mothers convinced Alroy to goes away. He never said nothing neither, and then—poof—them gone. No ones knew where, and some peoples even had thinked thems dead. It wasn't tills two years later that Kynas received a message from you mother, saying she okay, and living far away."

"Did she tell her where she was living?" Tase had asked.

"No," Ciaran said, "she was secretive. She not say much, just that she and husband were not harms."

Fadin and Tase had debated the reason for their mother and father leaving so suddenly, and the possibility that the reason for moving, and the secrets she kept from them, could be one and the same. With no other evidence, however, they couldn't come to a reasonable conclusion.

Tase scratched his head as he once again tried to read the question on his test. It was simply impossible, there was too much on his mind. Besides all the excitement over the coming trip, and the news about their parents, there was the mystery of Aunt Kyna. She continued to be absent at meal times and was hardly ever seen coming home. How was Tase supposed to concentrate on school when all that was going on? He had to get answers.

In fact, he and Fadin had tried to get answers about Aunt Kyna and why she was away all the time. They had stayed awake all night about a week ago and waited for her to come home. But she never came. She wasn't seen at all the next day or most of the week for that matter.

The majority any of them seemed to see Kyna was on the weekends, and even that was only her coming in very late Friday night and leaving very early Sunday morning. The rest of the weekend she spent in her room. All her meals were brought to her, and any news was left on paper and shoved under her wood door.

Tase and Fadin tried their best to eavesdrop on more conversations between her and the other adults in the house, but it seemed that she was just as brief with them as she was with the children. She didn't open her door for anyone, and didn't stop long enough when she was out of her room to have a decent conversation.

Tase also remembered, as he stared blankly at his desk, that Ma was acting a bit strange lately too. She was eating many fruits and vegetables, and had new pills she took each morning with breakfast. She looked even paler than before, and had large circles under her eyes. She also was in the bathroom more than any normal person and continued to wear very baggy clothes.

Tase had begun to worry about her and wondered how sick she really was. When he brought this to her attention, though, she simply told him not to worry and that she'd be fine. He very much doubted it.

Tase looked up as the door to the school room opened.

Miss O'Keefe and Clearie walked in with handfuls of supplies.

Miss O'Keefe had a red turtleneck on today and black trousers. That was all she ever wore, a turtleneck and trousers. Tase had never seen any other kind of shirt on her. And, he had to admit, it was a little odd. Almost like she was hiding something. But what did he know? He was probably paranoid over all the secrets with his mother, and was inventing secrets where there were none. Right?

Clearie and O'Keefe moved over to the back of the room and placed everything on the sitting couch.

Miss O'Keefe turned and said, "Alright boys, you have two more minutes to finish your tests, turn them in, and then it's time to come to the back of the classroom for our science project." She smiled at them and began to set up the supplies she and Clearie had gathered.

Tase swallowed hard and looked back at his paper. He tried to focus but was met with the same swimming thoughts that made concentration impossible. He bit down on his lower lip and circled the "false" answer.

He paused in Fadin's direction and grunted, watching jealously as Fadin circled answers easily. Tase didn't understand him; he was talented in maths and almost every other subject, but he just didn't care. He would rather be stubborn and make things harder on himself than do the work that was so easy for him.

Lately, he *had* been doing the school assignments. But only so he wouldn't be grounded and kept from attending the event on December 20th. That, however, did not mean he was pleasant while doing it. He always had a horrible attitude and treated Miss O'Keefe with such disrespect, that Tase was amazed she didn't give him mountains of extra schoolwork.

She didn't, though. She just acted as if he was behaving as well as Tase and Clearie and continued to give him the normal load.

Tase supposed she was happy just to have him doing the work, although Tase wasn't sure how long that would last.

He finished marking the last "true" statement as Miss O'Keefe called the end of their time. He placed the exam, on which he was sure he would get poor marks, on her desk, and walked slowly to the sitting chair.

He enjoyed the experiment the best he could, but he couldn't help but wonder how long until Aimirgin would come and invite them over again, or if she would at all until the time came for December 20th.

When the experiment was over, Miss O'Keefe gave them their usual after-school assignments and told them to clear their desks.

As they walked out of the school room, Tase heard a knock on the front door.

He and Fadin exchanged looks and rushed forward.

Enda had, of course, beaten them to it, but they clambered beneath his long arms as he swung the door open, and peered into the entryway.

Tase's eyes widened as he was met, face to face, with a large grey wolf. His heart stopped. He could feel the animal's hot breath on his face, see every sharp white tooth, and smell the mud on his fur and paws.

The animal just stood there, silent and terrifying.

Tase, unable to control himself, looked again at the pointed teeth and saw, to his confusion, a small piece of parchment held between them.

In a swift movement that caused Tase to bolt upright, the wolf placed the parchment at Enda's feet, backed away, and looked directly at Tase.

Tase gulped.

The animal licked its lips hungrily and winked.

Winked?

Tase stared in confusion. No, it didn't wink. That was impossible. Wasn't it?

Without another moment's pause, the wolf bounded away and disappeared into the thick trees.

Tase let out a horrified breath and slumped like a slug to the floor. That wolf couldn't have been real, it just couldn't. He knew, from a lesson somewhere or other, that there hadn't been any wolves in Ireland since about 1786. How was what he had just seen possible?

He looked up at Enda, whose appearance had become quite pale. He swayed a bit, ran his hands through his silvering hair, and then bent down to pick up the small piece of paper. He clutched it and moved it round and round.

Tase saw it was blank.

Enda quivered and held the paper far from him, as if it were contaminated.

Fadin made a swipe at the parchment.

Enda had expected the attempt and raised it higher. "It's nothing," he said, sounding almost frightened. He ran his hand over his top lip, in a gesture so familiar, that Tase felt he could almost place the butler. But then, as swiftly as it had come, it was gone.

Enda turned to Tase and his brother, furrowing his brow. "Best not to tell your mother about this, I think. Wouldn't want anything strange to upset her."

Tase thought he heard him mumble something under his breath like "especially not now."

Tase arched a red eyebrow.

Enda then walked down the hall and entered the kitchen. He returned, not more than two seconds later, and continued patrolling the hallway.

Fadin and Tase glanced at one another.

"Do you think?" Fadin asked.

Without even blinking, the two of them rushed into the kitchen and peered into the waste basket.

Tase grabbed Fadin's collar as he saw Daireann coming by with a large mixing bowl. She put it down and yelped with pain as she crushed her pinkie finger. She bent down to get a bandage.

Tase, seeing her disappear behind the counter, seized the small parchment out of the waste basket.

The two of them fled the kitchen before Daireann had gotten back up, nearly falling over one another as they hit a puddle of something wet.

"Open it, open it," Fadin cried as they stopped near the rose room.

It was a completely blank page.

"Are you sure you grabbed the right one?" Fadin asked.

"Of course I am," Tase snapped, "there was only one thing in…"

Tase let his words die away and blinked down at the paper. Words were beginning to form as if they were being written right in front of him. He just stood, motionless, until Fadin took the initiative and read aloud.

"Hello, boys."

They looked at one another.

The parchment began to write again.

*"Hello? H-e-l-l-o-o-o-o? Well, aren't you going to talk to me? Hello? Should I go?"*

"Wait," Tase yelled at the paper. "Wait, wait!"

*"Okay then, I thought you wanted the list for December, but…"*

Tase shook the paper. "No, we do. Wait, please wait."

"Here, you eejit," Fadin said, grabbing the parchment. He pulled out a pen and began scribbling sloppily. *"Wait!"*

There was a moment of silence, then the paper began to write. *"Smart, I thought I was going to have to explain it to you."*

Fadin shook his head and scribbled some more. *"Who are we talking*

191

*to?"*

*"Who do you think I am?"*

Tase glanced up at Fadin who quickly looked back down. *"Mr. Hogan?"*

*"Close."*

*"Aimirgin?"*

*"Correct! You are smart."*

*"Why are you writing to us?"*

*"My da invited you to December 20$^{th}$, didn't he? So I wrote to you to give you the list."*

Fadin looked up, excitement etched all over his face.

The same look, Tase was sure, was painted all over his.

*"Yes, yes, but why contact us this way? Why not call us, just come over, or invite us over?"*

*"Well, first of all, your Aunt Kyna doesn't have a phone, didn't you notice?"*

Tase looked at Fadin. He knew they were both thinking the same thing. If Aunt Kyna didn't have a phone, then how had their mother talked to her about coming to live here, in her castle? Tase had heard her on the phone, and she had said Kyna's name. Had that all just been an act for their benefit? Or did Aunt Kyna have a phone at work?

*"Second,"* Aimirgin continued, *"this way is quicker than coming over, don't you think? And third, it isn't entirely safe to be wandering around outside right now, not with December 20th being so near."*

Tase took the pen from Fadin.

*"What do you—?"*

*"It isn't safe, it's dangerous outside, especially if... well, let's just say it's dangerous for me and my family and you and your family as well. It really isn't too smart for you two to be alone outside, and after the package arrives it will be foolish to even put a single foot out of the door without my da or his say so."*

*"What's so dangerous?"*

*"I can't explain now, not over a letter. If someone really wanted to, they could re-read everything we've been saying. Let's leave it as we all need to be careful when we go outside for now, and it's best no one goes out at night, ever."*

Fadin gave Tase a nervous glance.

*"Now,"* Aimirgin persisted, *"the list. I need you to understand a few things before I give it to you. This list will contain all the items you will need for December 20th and must not be lost. Some of the things on this list will probably seem a little strange and hard to obtain, but they are all*

*necessary and if you have a problem with one, I will be more than happy to help you. Also, all these things must be gathered by December 1st before you open the package. If you have failed to gather all the items by that time, then you will have to be content with what you do have. It is extremely important that you do not try and gather anything after the package has been opened, and it must be opened by December 1st.*

*The package will be arriving by chimney because it is the fastest way to deliver mail, or in this case, certain items. Therefore, you must be waiting at the kitchen fireplace at 8 pm on the last day of November, and grab the package as soon as it is sent through; otherwise it will be burnt to a crisp. You have ten seconds to retrieve the package or it will be lost in the engulfing flames.*

*As for the danger factor after the items are received, the rules for keeping you safe are as follows: 1) Do not go outside after the package has been received. 2) Do not drink or eat anything you have not prepared yourself. 3) Do not get too close to any mirror in the house. 4) Do not get into any large bodies of water. 5) Do not pet or follow any strange or unknown animals, even dogs. 6) Do not gather any other items from the list. 7) Do not, under any circumstances, deviate from the instructions placed upon the package. Doing so could result in serious injury, house demolition, illness, and/or death."*

Tase pulled at his collar and swallowed hard.

*"Now that that's all over,"* Aimirgin wrote, *"I will give you the list. If you need to access it at any point simply write, 'THE LIST' on this piece of parchment, and it should show up immediately."*

The paper became blank and then Aimirgin's writing could be seen again.

### The List
**1. Gather six golden hairs.** *(This one shouldn't be too hard since you have an aunt with blond hair.)*

Tase heard Fadin snort.

**2. Nine clippings of dog nails.** *(You can use your dog's of course.)*

**3. A small amount of dust from the highest place you can reach.** *(Putting it in a small container will do. The more you can get the better.)*

**4. Three doorknobs, of doors that have been used often, and have been touched by many people.** *(Pretty easy.)*

**5. Six drops of rain.** *(It's supposed to rain this weekend.)*

**6. The essence of the colour red.** *(I can help you when the time comes.)*

**7. The smell of the morning air.** *(Again I can help.)*

**8. The most precious memory you have.** *(You will have to have my help* *with that.)*

The page went blank again, and then Aimirgin's handwriting came back into view.

*"I know some of those things seem strange and impossible to collect, but I assure you they aren't. I can help you with anything you need, and if you do need to talk to me, just write. I may not answer right away because I have to see your message first, but I'll keep it close to me as often as I can.*

*"My da will be sending Clearie a personal invitation to the event on December 20th, the same day you are to ask your mother about it. Use your handkerchiefs when you do. Also, when you are gathering the items from this list, it would be wise to carry the handkerchiefs with you, they will keep anyone from asking too many questions.*

*"Last but not least, if you need any containers for the items simply write 'bottle' on this parchment, and they will be sent to you by fireplace in the kitchen, so be sure you're there.*

*"I think that's everything. Don't forget the warnings I gave you, and if you need to look them over, write 'danger' and they should pop up.*

*"So before I go, are there any questions?"*

Tase simply stood still. He had so many questions that he couldn't even think where to begin. He thought it best just not to ask instead of having to write a novel and get all his questions answered.

*"Okay then."* Aimirgin wrote. *"I guess I'll see you December 20th. Remember, if you need anything, just write."* Aimirgin added a smiley face and the paper went blank.

The hall was quiet and empty, and Tase and Fadin were alone in it, once again.

~~~

A week flew by in a flash.

Tase and Fadin spent every free moment they had finding the many items on the list. The task, however, was more difficult than they had imagined.

As soon as Aimirgin had stopped talking to them through the parchment, they went to get Pathos' nail clippings, dust from their mother's closet, and the doorknob from the same cabinet. A few days later it had rained, and the gathering of the raindrops they needed had been fairly easy. The rest of the items proved to be a bit harder to obtain.

The doorknobs were a problem. The first one had been no big deal, no one ever saw the hidden closet, but removing a knob from a door that was used all the time? Someone would notice and get suspicious. That was the last thing they needed.

As for Aunt Kyna's golden locks, Tase didn't know how they were supposed to acquire them. They couldn't just walk up to her and yank nine of her hairs out, and even if they could, how were they supposed to get close enough to her to do it? She was never home.

Tase didn't even try to think about how to get the colour red, the smell of air in the morning, and one of his memories. At least Aimirgin had said she'd help with that bit.

He certainly hoped so.

The week continued on, and suddenly it was Saturday. An especially cold and rainy Saturday at that.

Tase ran his hand through his thick, orange-red hair, and peered out of the window. There was a lot of fog and he could barely see the woods.

It was hard knowing Aimirgin and her family were so close, yet felt so far away. Tase missed Mr. Hogan, Aimirgin, and her siblings. He wished they'd invite him and his brothers over, but every time he or Fadin wrote to Aimirgin on her parchment, she never said anything about them coming for a visit. And it seemed rude to ask.

Fadin came and stood beside him, pulling on a green-striped sweater. As the neckline pulled over his head, Fadin's orange-red hair poofed from the static electricity.

Tase let out a small giggle.

"Whatcha looking at?" Fadin asked his blue-green eyes surveying the vapour-covered grounds.

"The woods," Tase sighed. "I wish we could go out."

Fadin nodded. "Me too, but Mr. Hogan said it was dangerous. I really don't see how, but…" he held his hands in the air.

"We should probably spend the day trying to get the other things we need from the list," Tase offered.

Fadin bobbed his head. "Probably, but how are we supposed to get Aunt Kyna's hair, and the rest of the doorknobs?"

Tase shrugged. "Maybe we can see if they have any knobs in the extra closets?"

Fadin began to cock his head in minimal agreement, then he stopped and snapped his fingers. "The attic. I betcha Ciaran's got loads of old knobs up there. Don't you think?"

Tase blinked. Why hadn't he thought of that before? "Good idea and it's Saturday. Ma won't worry about us if we tell her we're going to Aimirgin's."

Fadin raised his eyebrows. "Good one. That way we won't get in trouble for disappearing on her."

Tase grinned. He turned toward his sock drawer and grabbed the wooden K. "Let's go, then."

Fadin led the way out of the room, but stopped dead just a centimetre from the stairs.

Tase bumped into him, not realizing he was going to halt. "What are you—?" Tase began.

Fadin cupped his hand over his mouth, and pointed to the room down the hall.

Tase furrowed his brow and leaned to look at the room. It was his mother's room and the door was slightly open. He could see someone pacing through the small crack and heard low voices.

Fadin raised both red eyebrows and jerked his head towards the door, questioningly.

Tase nodded. He wanted to know what was going on in there too.

They crept silently towards the room.

Lucky for them, there was a place in the wall, very near the bedroom, were it indented into a curve that was about half a meter deep. There was a statue, the bust of a woman, which stood in the gap and would provide perfect cover for them as they listened in on whatever was being said.

They reached the statue and hid behind it, perfectly covered, so even if someone was standing right in front of them, they wouldn't be seen.

Tase listened hard to the low voices and realized that it was Ma and Enda in the room. It was a bit hard to hear at first, but once his heart settled from the fear of being caught, he could make out what they were discussing better.

"Something's going on with her," Enda was saying. "She's acting odd, not like herself. I mean, she's hardly even talking to us anymore."

Aunt Kyna. Tase thought. He was worrying about Aunt Kyna.

"Maybe there's nothing wrong with her, Enda," Ma said. "I mean, maybe she's just moody?"

Enda snorted. "Oh, please, moody? This is a little more than being temperamental. And you wouldn't know how she is anyway. I mean, you scarcely know her. You've never taken the time, and you don't seem to care."

Tase scrunched up his face. What? Ma barely knows her? Her own sister? What did Enda mean?

"Come on, Enda, of course I care, but I don't know. I knew her very well before—before Clearie came. But after that, she seemed to—well, change."

Tase could see Enda's head nod. "I know. She was like a different person after the war. But can you blame her? I think we all changed. But what I mean, Teagan, is that you never really tried with her again, and you don't now either. I think you partly blame her for the deaths of Glendan, Etain, and—our parents."

Tase shook his head in alarm. *Our* parents?

Fadin turned to him, eyes wide, brow scrunched in bewilderment.

"I do not. I know it wasn't her fault. And the person whose fault it was, has already been dealt with." Tase had never heard such ferocity in his mother's voice.

"Yes," Enda said solemnly, "he has. But Kyna was connected with him, and I think you blame her for not knowing what he was planning. But we were all in the same boat, Teagan, none of us knew."

Ma's voice broke, angry and hurt. "But she was married to him, for heaven's sake! She was his wife. She should have known something was wrong. And she didn't even know it was him till after—after Dia..." Ma broke down into tears.

Tase could see her through the crack, and Enda went to comfort her.

"It's all right—shhhhhh—its okay," Enda cooed.

Ma took a deep breath and nodded, signaling Enda that she was well enough not to be hugged anymore. "I do know it wasn't her fault, Enda," Ma said with hiccup-like breaths. "But I don't understand her. And do you know what I found the morning Alroy died?"

Tase felt his heart stop.

Enda shook his head. "No, what?"

"A letter, a letter from Kyna to him," Ma spat. "She asked him to come here, because she was in trouble. She asked him to leave early for work, she went behind my back and told my husband to lie to me and to come and meet her!" Ma began to cry again, but would not let Enda touch her. "Why would she do that? Why would she ask him to come here? Everything seems fine to me. And when I've hinted about the letter, she acts like she has no idea what I'm talking about," Ma's voice became raised. "And you know something, I don't blame her for Glendan, and Etain, and our parents—but I, for darn sure, blame her for Alroy!"

Enda tried to hug her, to soothe her, but she wouldn't let him. "Teagan," he tried.

"No," Ma hissed. "It's her fault. If he wouldn't have left early, then none of this would have happened," Ma sobbed as she tried to speak. "I loved him, Enda, oh I loved him so much. And I don't know what to do without him."

Tase felt tears streaming down his own face. His heart ached.

Ma just sobbed for a moment and then let out a furious sigh. "And I'm angry. I'm so angry with her for writing him, and I hate her, and I blame her, and I don't know how to stop."

Enda put a hand toward her but she smacked it away.

Ma stood. "And you know something else. I blame *you*."

Enda looked wounded, more than if someone had shoved a knife in his back. "Me? Teagan, how can you say that?"

"Where were you? Where were you that day? Why didn't you stop her from writing that letter? Why didn't you know what was going on with Alroy?"

"What do you mean?" Enda asked.

"Oh come now," Ma seethed. "I know you, Daireann, and Kyna have been watching us. I know you've been watching Fadin and Tase and have been following Alroy. I'm not stupid."

Enda blinked and anger flooded his face. He stood. "Well, if you aren't stupid then you'd realize what I've done for you. What I've sacrificed. Wouldn't you? You're right you know, we have been watching. For the last ten months, we'd been watching. We finally found you. We knew you were alive and well. We saw your family, that you were happy, and we didn't interfere. Though we would have had every right to." Enda looked at her with pain in his eyes now, a deep hurt that appeared to have never fully healed. "Teagan, you just left," he cried. "I mean all those years ago, you took Alroy and were gone. No note, no goodbye, nothing. You know how much I loved you, how much I cared for you. I'm your brother, Teagan, and you were the only family I had left, and you just disappeared on me. For heaven's sake, I thought you were dead, or worse, that Afanasii had you. Do you know that I looked for you for seven years?"

Tase saw Ma's anger subside. She obviously did not.

"Yes, that's right, seven years," Enda said. "And then, when it seemed that you were truly gone, I just couldn't anymore. I had to stop, to give up, to accept it," Enda's voice cracked with the tears he was trying to keep back. "I talked to you, I said my goodbyes, and begged that you could forgive me for not finding you, for not saving you."

Tears fell down Ma's face.

"I moved on. I came back to Kyna and Daireann and reconciled with them. I went and lived in Cavan-Corr, became a professor. You know, like Da always said I would be. I was happy, Teagan, I was okay. And then I heard a rumour that you were alive. Puceula suddenly came into power, became King Raegan's advisor, his right-hand man. And he started looking for you. So we looked too. We found you first, and used all manner of protection to be sure you were safe.

"Daireann, not me, followed Alroy. Kyna watched you and I watched the children. I stopped being a professor, I left Cavan-Corr, I protected Fadin and Tase, and I did all of it for you. Look at me, Teagan!" he yelled. "I'm dressed up in a butler's outfit, for *you*. So that you can continue to lie to those boys, who by the way, are smarter then you give them credit for. They know something's up, and I can tell by the way they look at me that they recognize me. It's only a matter of time before they put it all together. And I have to say I disagree with you on this. I don't think you should lie to them, it doesn't help them. In fact, it pushes them further away from you. Have you forgotten how you felt when Mum and Da lied to us?"

Ma was angry again now. "It looks a lot different when you're on this side of things, Enda."

"Does it?" Enda asked, incredulously. He shook his head. "Well, you've done a bang-up job so far raising them, Teagan. I mean, they don't even know who their uncle is."

"Don't you dare try and tell me how to raise my children!" Ma shouted.

"Then raise them right," Enda shouted back. "You're pushing them away, Teagan. Can't you see that? You're going to lose them."

Ma's face was livid. She raised her hand ever so slightly and then slapped him, hard, across the face.

Enda's head snapped to the side, and then he stared at her. His expression was at first, enraged, and then hurt. Tears welled up in his eyes. He tucked in his lower lip and nodded. "Fine," he said. He turned swiftly and walked out.

Tase and Fadin shrunk behind the statue as he stomped past them.

He hurled himself down the stairs and slammed the front door.

Tase turned and saw Ma standing frozen by the side of her bed. Tears tumbled off her cheeks. She turned toward the door, stomped over to it, and slammed it shut.

Tase blinked and looked at Fadin.

Fadin was clutching the statue and breathing in heavily. He stood, suddenly, and walked over to Ma's door.

Tase felt his heart stop. What was he going to do?

Fadin knocked on the door. "Ma?" Fadin asked, his voice sounding chipper.

"Yes?" Ma's voice answered through the door.

"We're going to Aimirgin's, is that alright?"

Ma sniffed and answered in a cracked tone, "Fine, just don't be home too late."

"K," Fadin said, and turned to Tase. "Let's go," he nodded, and led the way down the stairs and to the bookcase.

~~~

They met Ciaran in the attic and the little goblin was more than happy to see them.

They asked if he had any doorknobs they could borrow. Unfortunately, he did not.

"I is sorry things," he answered. "But, I knows how much yous like me picture book. You wants to looks at it?"

"Sure," Fadin said.

Ciaran brought it out to them.

Tase took it and sat cross-legged on the floor with Ciaran on his left side and Fadin on his right.

He had put the picture of the Feneg back a few days ago, and it sat loosely on the first page.

"Poors old book breaks sometimes," Ciaran sighed.

Tase hid his smile. He showed Fadin his mother's picture in the Oxford school class album.

Fadin snorted.

Then they come across the photo of the Bojins. The eerie-looking foursome with the very beautiful girl.

Fadin, too, had a hard time looking away from her.

On the next page, they found a class photo of Enda in a school at Oxford as well. The Griffin school of Oxford, it was called. He looked about fifteen, and the date was several years before the class photo of their mother.

"That's it," Fadin yelled. He stood up, knocking the book off Tase's lap. "I've had enough lies. Ma and Enda are siblings? They both went to schools in Oxford, England? What are we missing here? I mean, has everything been a lie? What's the truth?"

Tase stood and put a hand on his shoulder. "I don't know, Fadin."

Fadin shook his head. "Is Aunt Kyna even really our aunt? And who is Enda, anyhow? I know I've seen him before, and he even admitted it to Ma."

"I know," Tase nodded. "I recognize him too. But I can't place him."

Fadin shrugged Tase's hand away. "I've had about enough of this. I want the truth and if I have to go all the way to the Hogans' house to get it, then I will."

Tase moved forward. "Fadin, you can't. Mr. Hogan told us not to go outside, let alone into the woods."

"I don't really care," Fadin said. "I need answers and I'm going out there, with or without you." He pointed to the small round window in the direction of the woods.

Tase sighed and began to protest. He saw something then—something that caused him to stop. It, whatever it was, was outside. "Fadin, move out of the way," he said, rushing to the widow.

"Huh?" Fadin inched away to let Tase through and peered out of the glass with him.

Tase's heart skipped a beat.

There, at the entrance to the woods, standing perfectly still and appearing to be looking right at them, was the red-headed, hooded woman, and the large black dog. The woman was the same woman he had seen in school the day their father had died.

Fadin pressed his face against the glass. "Tase? Do you see them?" he whispered.

Tase nodded. "It's her."

Fadin moved closer to Tase. "And the dog, you see him too?"

Tase nodded. "I've been seeing him and hearing him. You?"

Fadin bobbed his head. "And that, that's her, you're positive?"

"It's her," Tase repeated.

"Who, what?" Ciaran asked. "What you things looksing at?" He crawled up Tase's back and looked down at the forest. "Yeek!" he screamed and fell backward.

"What is it?" Tase asked. "What's wrong? Do you know her?"

"Banshee," Ciaran shrieked. "Is Banshee. What shes doing outs there?"

"A Banshee?" Fadin asked. "Like the kind that warn people of death?"

Ciaran nodded. "Yessss."

Fadin turned to Tase. "I'm going."

"What?" Tase ran to him. "No, Fadin. What are you thinking? You saw what she did to the glass in our classroom. Are you completely off your nut? She'll kill you!"

"Fine, let her then," Fadin yelled. "I don't care anymore anyway. And I am not letting this opportunity slip by, hiding, when that dog and her are down there with answers."

"Fadin," Tase grabbed for his arm.

Fadin knocked him away and ran to the slide.

"Fadin, don't!"

But it was too late, he sat on the slide, pushed off, and was gone.

"Fadin," Tase screamed. He jumped for the tunnel but something caught hold of his ankle. "Ciaran, let me go," he yelped. He turned around to shoo the goblin off, but did not see Ciaran's face. Instead, he was looking at Pathos.

The Bernese had hold of his trouser leg and was not letting go.

"Pathos? How did you get up here?" He decided that wasn't important. "Let me go, boy, let me go."

Pathos growled and began pulling him away from the slide.

Tase pulled back but the dog was stronger than he'd anticipated. "Pathos, stop it, bad boy. Let go."

With impressive strength, Pathos pulled him across the floor boards and towards the door.

How could he be doing this? Tase wondered. He was over fourteen years old. But that didn't matter, Fadin was outside with that woman and Tase had to get to him. "Fadin!" he screamed. "Pathos, LET ME GO!"

"Hee-yah!" screamed a loud voice.

Tase turned and saw Ciaran jump on top of Pathos and poke him with a slightly sharpened piece of wood.

Pathos gave a slight yip and dropped Tase's trouser leg. He turned and growled at the little goblin.

"Runs, thing," Ciaran screamed as he fought Pathos off. "Save brothers."

Tase turned away and ran head-first for the slide. He heard Pathos' jaws almost clamp around his trouser leg but miss, as Tase went hurtling down into the dark, twisted tunnel.

The slide hurt his face and stomach. It had been a poor idea to go head-first, but he had to get to Fadin. As he slid, he felt scratches and bruises forming on his face and hands. He felt the tunnel get hot and heard the same yelling voice he had heard before.

"Let me out, you old hag!"

The slide gave a great lurch. Tase flew upwards, crashed back down, and within a matter of seconds, burst into light and slammed into the soft mud. He didn't wait long enough to wipe the mud from his eyes. He ran as fast as he could out of the bush cover. He looked to the right and saw Fadin, wet and mud-strewn, walking towards the animal and the hooded woman.

"Fadin!" Tase screamed. With all his might he rushed forward. He couldn't let Fadin get too close, they'd kill him.

Fadin didn't look behind him at the sound of Tase's scream, nor did he stop. He kept moving forwards and held out his hand, as if he was going to touch them.

Tase's eyes widened. His heart pounded with fear. If that woman could break glass with a scream, what could she do with a touch? Not to mention that enormous dog. "Fadin, no!"

The woman held out her hand as well and moved forwards a little.

The dog growled angrily.

The woman's face was still covered, but her cherry-red hair tumbled freely out of her hood. She opened her hand wide, offering it to Fadin.

Tase was nearly next to him, but he wouldn't be at his side soon enough to stop him. "Leave him alone," he cried.

The large dog began to back away, growling ferociously.

Tase watched it. Why would it back up?

Fadin reached forwards, a centimetre away from touching the woman, when CRASH!

Something large and snake-like broke out of the ground between them. It hurtled in the air, twisting and turning, and then came down with a thud.

Fadin, seeming to break from some sort of trance, screamed.

The snake-like-thing wiggled and sprang at him.

"Fadin," Tase yelped.

Fadin turned and tried to run away, but the twisting thing grabbed his foot and pulled him forwards. "Tase," he cried.

The snake-thing was pulling him towards the hole it sprang from, trying to drag him underground.

Tase screamed in determination and leapt for his brother. He hit the ground with a hard thud, but managed to grab Fadin's hand. "Hold on,

Fadin, just hold on," he cried. He pulled and yanked, but the snake-thing had Fadin too tight, he couldn't pull him loose.

The thing heaved firmly forward, but Tase stuck his feet deep in the mud and stopped it from dragging Fadin any further.

"Tase," Fadin sobbed, "don't let go."

"I won't," Tase promised, but he felt tears streaming down his face as Fadin's hand began to slip away. Everything was just too slippery, and the rain was not helping.

There was a low grumble from the earth, and the snake-thing shuddered. CRASH. More twisting, slithering things broke from the mud, and Tase realized that they were not snakes, they were roots, tree roots.

The roots fell on top of Fadin and curled around him. They began dragging him forwards once more.

Fadin cried out with pain and fear.

Tase held on, but felt himself being pulled forwards as well.

Another grumble escaped the muddy ground and something large, bigger than the roots, crashed through the earth. It was a large, weasel-like animal with dirt-coloured skin and large black fangs. It pulled itself out from the sludge and shook like an oversized dog, flinging the muck everywhere.

Tase stared at it, eyes wide and disbelieving, heart beating like a drum in his chest. He felt his body lock in place, and his feet stick even firmer in the earth.

The roots that appeared to be from a tree wiggled and writhed, cleaning the mud away from their bodies, and Tase saw that the roots were actually attached to a large animal's behind. The root-things were its tail. The animal roared and snapped its tail in the air.

Fadin and Tase were hurtled upwards with it.

Fadin shrieked.

Tase shouted and clutched hard to Fadin, but it was no use. He was slipping away.

"Tase," Fadin cried trying to hold on, "no, don't…"

Too late. Fadin's hand slid away, and Tase felt the butterflies in his belly as he began to free-fall. The ground was too far away. When he hit it, it would be all over, he'd crack his head and drown in the mire, while Fadin would be dragged underground and lost forever.

Tase yelped and closed his eyes, preparing for the impact, when he felt something hit him from the side. He rocked and hit the ground, but lightly compared to what it would have been. He shot his eyes open and saw the wolf, the one that had been at Aunt Kyna's door, standing in front of him with a bit of his shirt in its mouth.

"Are you okay, Tase?" It asked.

Tase jumped backwards, startled.

"I said are you okay?"

Tase recognized the voice. And as he looked into the animal's eyes, he saw Desmond. The wolf was Desmond. "De—Des?" he asked, stupidly.

The wolf nodded. "I'll explain later." The wolf, or Desmond, growled and rushed toward the giant mud-weasel. He barked and bit at the large root tendrils, sending mud and blood flinging this way and that.

Tase suddenly saw Colmcille, Cormick, and Quinlan appear from the woods. They all held weapons of some sort and were flinging them about.

Cormick held an axe, and green sparks were flying from it, as he sliced in the direction of the monster. The roots reacted and tried to twirl around him. He hacked at anything that came too close and continued to beat the green sparks in the animal's direction.

The green sparks hit the animal and it screeched in pain and anger.

Quinlan jumped in the air and hacked at a root-tail with his sword, causing the weasel to scream and send more of its tail to attack. One of the tendrils managed to wrap itself around Quinlan, who held his sword high and chopped at it.

Desmond continued to bite at anything he could get his teeth into and jumped away from the animal's large, mud-covered claws which continued to try and strike him.

Colmcille rushed to his brother's aid and fought the numerous roots that grabbed at any part of his body they could. When he was free he took his spear and stuck it in the giant thing's side. Bursts of green gushed out of the wound as well as thick red blood.

The animal cried in agony and dropped Fadin into the muddy pool that had now formed. It shrieked and snapped its jaw toward the Hogans, but backed away, finally receding into its hole, disappearing. Its ugly head was the last thing to be seen.

Tase, without thinking, ran forward to the spot where Fadin had fallen.

*Don't let him be dead*, he prayed. "Fadin? Fadin?" he cried. And then he spotted him.

Fadin sat in the mud, eyes open, wiping away the blood and gunk from his mouth.

Tase jumped on him, flinging Fadin and himself back into the mire. But he didn't care, Fadin was alive.

"I'm okay, Tase, really," he said patting him on the back. "Can I, um, get up now?"

Tase released him and sat up. He suddenly remembered their saviors and turned.

There the wolf stood, shaking its body as if it were trying to rid itself of excess water. Suddenly its fur began falling away like dirt, and human hands, feet, and a face could be seen beneath the mane.

Tase allowed his mouth to drop open as Desmond looked up at him from the spot on the grass where he was crouched. He was naked except for the hair that still covered his bottom half.

Quinlan ran to his side and handed him a cloak.

Desmond took it, stood up, wiped the remaining fur away, and, along with his brothers, helped Tase and Fadin up.

"So," Desmond said, pulling two large towels from a pocket in the cloak.

Tase couldn't help but notice those towels were far too large to fit in anyone's pocket.

"Would you two care to explain why you're outside when the rules clearly told you you were not allowed?"

Tase looked about, startled. He had completely forgotten about the Banshee.

She was nowhere to be seen.

Tase turned and whispered to Fadin. "She's gone."

Fadin looked for her as well.

"Hello?" Cormick said sarcastically. "Is anybody home? We asked you why you risked your necks and ours?"

Fadin shook his head. "First of all, what the heck was that thing?"

Desmond sighed. "That thing is not important. What is important is that you broke the rules. Rules that were put in place for a good reason—to keep you safe, not to stop you from having fun."

Tase and Fadin looked at him in earnest.

"Oh," Desmond grumbled, "well if you must know, it was a Lithian. A creature that spends most of its life in the dirt, with root-like tails that can attach to trees and other plants. Most of them are on our side, but some went bad after the wa—well, that's for my da to explain."

"After the what?" Fadin asked.

"Never mind that," Quinlan said. "We want to know why you were even out here in the first place."

"Well," Fadin said, "we—we saw a Banshee outside, the same one we saw when—"

"A Banshee?" Quinlan asked, obviously disturbed.

"Yes," Tase nodded. "The same one we saw the day our father died, and this big black dog."

"You had a Banshee scream at you the day your father died?" Desmond questioned. "Are you sure?"

"Yes," Fadin answered.

The Hogan boys exchanged glances.

"And you're sure the one you saw today was the same one?" Cormick asked.

Tase and Fadin again bobbed their heads yes.

"Why?" Fadin asked. "Is that a bad thing?"

"I don't know," Desmond said, "but it's not good. Alright," he said, putting his arms around their shoulders. "Go inside, wash up and use this." He handed them an ointment. "It will help with the pain and cover the cuts and bruises, so no one will know something happened. Stay inside and do not, for any reason, come near these woods again. Do you understand?"

"Yes," they answered in unison.

"Good. We will come to get you when it's time for December 20th. Alright?"

"But Desmond," Fadin said. "How did you know we were in trouble? And how did you turn into a wolf?"

"All in good time," Desmond answered. "But it's dangerous out here. Get inside and we'll explain everything next time."

Tase clutched Fadin's arm and they limped back towards the castle. When they reached the door, the Hogan boys waved to them and disappeared into the trees.

They snuck inside, rushed up to the bathroom, and slammed the door.

Tase bolted it and began to take off his shirt. "You know something, Fadin," he said as he removed his muddy and blood-soaked trousers.

"What?" Fadin asked, turning on the shower.

"You are a real pain in me hole sometimes," he held his trousers and flung them at Fadin playfully.

Fadin grinned. "Yea, well, at least I'm not a dead pain."

Tase laughed. "Maybe I'd be better off if you were." He fuzzed Fadin's hair and knocked him into the shower.

# Chapter 12

## *The Kyna Incident*

The ointment Desmond had given them soothed and covered the many cuts and bruises Fadin and Tase had, but it did not make them disappear. Tase could still feel their soreness when he touched them.

By the time they were done with their shower, Ma was downstairs, Kyna had left for work, Daireann had lunch prepared, and Enda was alone in the garden.

No one said much at lunch, in fact no one said much that evening or the next day. Ma and Enda would not look at each other, and Aunt Kyna was as distant as ever. The only uplifting soul in the whole castle appeared to be Daireann, and her attempts at making the mood lighter failed miserably.

The night after the monster had attacked, Tase and Fadin received a message from Aimirgin.

The little piece of parchment shook as she wrote to them.

She reprimanded them over and over for going outside, breaking the rules, and being so stupid.

They apologized profusely, but it didn't do much good. They asked if she knew anything about why they would have seen a Banshee and a black dog, and she said she didn't.

But she did say her father was concerned and was trying to find a reason.

After that, they didn't hear much from Aimirgin that week.

They tried to gather the remaining items on the list but had little success. And as the days went by, Tase realized they were running out of time. They had hardly four days until the package arrived, and nothing seemed to be getting done. But Tase really couldn't blame them. They had just been attacked by a mud monster, and had found out that the butler was actually their uncle. How much could you handle in a week?

But time was still short, so they decided to spend the next two nights completely devoted to finding the doorknobs and getting the hairs. What would they say if they were caught? Tase didn't know.

So the two waited till midnight then snuck down the stairs. They searched everywhere for extra doorknobs, in closets and cupboards, in nightstands and the attic, they even dug in the kitchen trash, but there were no knobs to be seen.

"Maybe we should just take a pair off the doors," Fadin whispered, pulling his hand from the smelly bin.

Tase shook his head and leaned against the cabinet. "I don't know." A plant fell off the counter and hit Tase's head. He cursed as he felt the sore spot it had left, and placed it quietly back on its shelf.

"Hey," Fadin yelped, lunging forward, "look at that!"

Tase turned and stumbled backward as the spot where he had been leaning began to glow.

Fadin opened the cupboard and cried with excitement. "Look at this, you won't believe it." He grabbed Tase's arm and shoved him inside.

Tase had to squint because the glow was so bright, but once his eyes adjusted he felt his mouth drop. The small cupboard was full to the brim with hundreds of golden doorknobs, and the small cabinet had changed into a room bigger than the dining hall.

Tase felt a sharp kick in the back and Fadin whispered. "Someone's coming."

He felt panic rise up in his chest as he grabbed two knobs and quickly shut the cabinet. He scarcely sat behind the counter when the door burst open.

Enda strode in and glanced about the kitchen. He tapped his large foot and grunted in suspicion as he moved across the tiled floor. Unfortunately Tase and Fadin had forgotten to pick up the trash they had dug through, and Enda began to walk right toward them.

Fadin knocked Tase in the arm and nodded towards the door.

Tase raised his eyebrows in agreement and they bolted for the exit.

Enda turned and saw Tase's leg before he left the kitchen and bellowed after them. Once in the entrance, Fadin grabbed Tase by the collar and dragged him into the tea room and behind the couch. He covered both their mouths as Enda fumbled in after them.

Enda looked around the room then quietly walked towards the East hall.

Fadin didn't waste the precious distraction, and yanked Tase from behind the couch and back up the stairs.

The next day Enda was more on alert then ever. Jumping at every noise and checking out the window every ten minutes, it was obvious that he hadn't slept at all. This strange behaviour did not cause him and Ma to talk, although Fadin thought it might have.

Enda didn't stop to rest all day or all the next night. He seemed convinced they had an intruder, but it didn't appear that he had told anyone.

Fadin and Tase waited till two in the morning that evening to sneak out and steal Aunt Kyna's hairs. But Fadin still nearly knocked Tase over trying to get his head back in the door before Enda saw him.

"Better wait till tomorrow night," Tase said lying on his bed. "Besides, Kyna should be coming home tomorrow. It's Thursday and she always comes back Friday night."

Fadin climbed onto his bunk and flopped down. "Where do you suppose she is all this time?"

Tase shrugged. "Work?"

"Some work," Fadin said moving around. "I wonder where she sleeps."

"I don't know but at least she sleeps here on the weekends. How are we supposed to get her hairs anyway?"

"We have to sneak into her room."

"With what? We don't have a key and Enda, or Uncle Enda, never leaves them out of his sight."

Fadin sat up. "Maybe we can ask Aimirgin for help."

He climbed off his bunk and opened their sock drawer. He pulled out the crumpled piece of parchment and a pen.

Tase got up to look over his shoulder as he wrote.

*"Aimirgin, we need your help."*

The paper remained blank and still.

*"Aimirgin?"*

*"WHAT?"* The paper shook a bit and there was a fleeting shade of red.

*"We need your help with the list."*

*"Do you know what time it is?"*

*"Yea it's late, but we need something, something we can open doors with."*

*"They've already invented that, it's called a key."*

*"Ha ha. I mean we need something that can open a door we don't have a key to."*

*"Fine, you two need to go down to the kitchen fireplace at six o'clock tomorrow. I'm sending you something that can unlock doors, but be careful with it. You don't want to lose it or accidentally cut yourself."*

*"Thanks."*

*"Yea."*

*"Okay, well goodnight then."*

No answer.

*"Goodnight."*

*"GOODNIGHT!"* The paper shook, a flash of red filled it, and then it was blank.

When they awoke the next morning it was quiet downstairs, nothing moved and no one was around, not even Pathos. They moved silently toward the kitchen and opened the door slowly. As they walked in, a burst of red filled the kitchen and a bright green knife lay in the fireplace.

Fadin leaned down and grasped it in his hands. "This is going to open doors?"

Tase moved towards it. "That's what she said," he took it and swung it about. "Neat."

Fadin grabbed it back and began to thrust. "I don't see how this is going to help us but…"

They left the kitchen and went back to sleep, too tired from their attempt last night to stay awake.

When they woke up later, the house was buzzing with noise.

To Fadin's surprise, Ma and Enda were talking again.

They both sat at the kitchen table, chattering away; Ma still looked sickly, but not as depressed.

"Good morning," Ma smiled.

"Morning," Fadin grinned.

He and Tase sat down and ate breakfast in awe of the newfound kindness between Ma and Enda.

Whatever had happened, it had worked, and Fadin didn't really care what it was.

After breakfast they said they were going outside, and spent the rest of the day in the attic with Ciaran.

They looked in the old photo album and found more pictures of their mother. One of them was of her with four other people.

There was another girl, who appeared younger than their mother, and two boys. One older, one was possibly younger than Ma. Fadin and Tase did not recognize the three but they did see Enda. A much younger and handsomer Enda, but it was him all the same.

The unknown individuals had black curly hair and blue eyes, except for one of the boys whose eyes were the most stunning hazel that Tase had ever seen. The hazel-eyed boy looked as though one of his eyeballs was permanently stuck to the left, like a deformity of some sort.

The photo was titled *"Glendan, Enda, Dubhlainn, Teagan, and Etain 1985."*

Tase touched the face of the older-looking boy.

"Who do you think they are?" Tase asked as Fadin pulled out another album from under the broken table.

"I don't know." Fadin opened the book in his lap and cried out.

He pointed at a large, black-and-white photo of two people who looked very familiar.

"Is that—?" Tase started.

"Yea, Aunt Kyna, and look at this," Fadin pointed to the man beside her, "He was in that picture with Ma."

Tase looked at his photo and spotted the cockeyed young man. "It is him. Hey, Ciaran." There was no answer. "Ciaran?"

"He does that a lot, probably just looking through old junk," Fadin said matter-of- factly.

Tase stared at the picture in which the couple did not look very happy. He read the caption above it.

*Dubhlainn and Kyna 1987.*

There was a distant slamming sound and the two of them looked up.

"Kyna's home," Fadin said.

They shoved the albums back under the table and ran down the stone staircase. As they entered the tea room, they heard shouts.

"No, no I won't."

"Won't? Won't what, Kyna?" Tase recognized his mother speaking.

Fadin gestured toward the couch and they hid behind it.

"I won't," Aunt Kyna yelled.

"Please, Kyna, you must get some rest," Daireann said nervously.

"Do they think I'm crazy? Have they gone mad?"

Enda spoke next. "Daireann is right, you need to sleep."

Kyna made no attempt to respond, she instead walked through the tea room and into the hall.

Tase heard the others sigh and walk off in all directions.

He turned to Fadin, who was smiling widely.

"It will be easy to get the hairs if she's so tired she can't even talk straight," Fadin grinned.

Tase couldn't disagree.

They climbed out from behind the couch and listened. Everyone seemed busy so they crept down the narrow hall. To Tase's surprise, the door to Aunt Kyna's room was open.

The boys looked at one another and slowly went inside.

The room looked more like a pigpen than a bedroom. It was horribly dirty and clothes were sprawled out everywhere. There were papers flung in all directions, plates upon plates of food filled each corner, and the floor was sopping wet.

They spotted Aunt Kyna at once, sitting at what used to be a vanity table. Now it looked more like Miss O'Keefe's school desk with mountains of paperwork. She was reading a very long piece of parchment and mumbling to herself.

Tase thought she looked rather mad.

Fadin ducked low and crawled silently to where she sat.

Tase followed suit, cringing when his hand smashed a several-days-old salad.

Fadin nodded to a brush sitting at the end of the vanity table.

From the prickled side of it, Tase saw several golden hairs.

Fadin moved slowly, careful not to knock into Kyna's chair. He reached up and tried to grasp the handle, but at that moment, Kyna grabbed it and began running it through her matted hair. Fadin recoiled and sat still as Kyna stood up, still reading the parchment, and began to make her way around the room.

Tase had to dart out of the way to avoid being kicked by her. He saw one of the papers sitting on the floor.

*ACT OF UNISON AND PEACE TO THE HALF-BREEDS AND OTHER DISCRIMINATED CREATURES*

Tase picked it up as Aunt Kyna continued to circle the room.

*Fourteen years have passed since the Great War, many things have been resolved and Ireland has become a far better place. Yet the discrimination of creatures like werewolves, vampires, ghouls, orcs, trolls, giants, mulks, harpies and others, has not. Therefore it is the opinion of King Raegan that a treaty should be signed to form peace between the Dalbach and these outcast creatures. This act of friendship and compassion could heal and unify Ireland, and bring it into a new and peace-filled era.*

*Sincerely,*
*Puceula Lynch,*
*Adviser to The King*

Suddenly, Kyna screamed a horrible, earsplitting screech.

Tase jumped.

Fadin knocked his arm on the vanity table.

Kyna grabbed at her head and pulled out chunks of golden hair. "No, no I won't. You can't make me, you can't make me."

Tase stared, horrified, unable to move.

She screamed again and pressed her hands over her ears. "Won't, won't, won't, I will not listen, you can't force me!" She stumbled across the bedroom and knocked several things over.

Tase clambered alongside Fadin and they hid themselves behind her bed as she began rocking back and forth.

"She's off her nut," Fadin whispered.

"I can't hear you," she wailed in a sing song voice, "I ca-a-an't."

"Kyna," came Daireann's high-pitched cry. "Enda, help me."

The tall figure of Enda appeared in the cluttered little room.

At his entry, Kyna let out another horrified scream. She began banging her body against the walls and crying out, "Stop it, stop it, no, I won't, I'll never."

"Kyna, stop this, this instant," Enda bellowed in his screechy tone. He reached out and grabbed for her but she dodged him.

"Shut up," she screamed and pulled out yet another chunk of hair.

"Kyna," This scream of terror was from Ma.

Tase saw her black hair through the cracks of the bed.

"Enda do something, stop her."

Again, Enda reached for her, and this time he managed to seize her arms.

She screamed louder than ever and struggled to get loose from his grip. She kicked and jerked, sending more items plummeting to the floor.

"Get out, get off me. You can't make me sign it. I won't do it, do you hear me? Let me go, let me go!"

"No, Kyna," Enda tried, "stop this, we're trying to help."

She screeched and kicked at Enda's sturdy legs.

Daireann attempted to grab the flaring feet, but was hurled backwards by a powerful lurch.

"Kyna, stop this nonsense," Ma cried. "We want to help you." Tase watched as she approached her with something sharp in her hands. It looked like a syringe of some kind.

"No," Kyna screamed. She lunged towards Ma.

Enda could not hold her back.

Before he could react, she had grabbed the sharp thing and plunged it into Ma's neck.

Tase shouted, but a sudden flash of light caused him to cover his face and drown his scream. The whole world seemed to swirl and fall away into an endless pool of brightness. Then it receded, turned to colour, then sound, and he was back in the tiny room.

Kyna stood silent and still with a blank look on her face. She swayed for a moment, then crumbled like paper to the floor.

Enda, who had been staring off into space, moved forward to Ma, who was also in a heap on the ground.

"I'm fine," Ma said standing up, "check Kyna." She turned to the doorway. "Thank you, I don't know what would have happened if you hadn't have been here."

Tase looked toward the entrance and let his mouth fall open.

Miss O'Keefe was standing in the doorway, a dagger held high in her hand, pointing it towards the spot where Kyna had been standing. "It was nothing," she said, lowering the small dagger. "You sure you're alright?"

Fadin knocked into Tase's head and gaped with eyes wider then saucers.

"Yes," Ma replied. She bent down and helped Daireann up.

Miss O'Keefe flicked her dagger, and the room began to clean itself. Blankets folded, broken objects were repaired, and the food plates stacked themselves.

"What was that all about?" O'Keefe asked, moving towards the bed.

"She doesn't want to sign the peace treaty," Daireann said, dusting herself off. "She won't do it."

Miss O'Keefe made a swooping motion with her knife, and one of the papers flew into her hands. "She still hasn't agreed to sign? Foolish and utterly stubborn woman. Doesn't she realize who she's dealing with?"

"Apparently not," Ma said.

"Well then, enough's enough," O'Keefe said firmly. "She'll sign the bloody thing tomorrow."

Enda snorted, "If only it were that easy, Caoimhe. We've tried to reason with her, but she won't do it. She is adamant about standing against the act. She thinks the half-breeds and others named in the treaty are untrustworthy. Can you believe that? After having me, *me*, live inside her home. Doesn't she realize they're no different?"

Tase furrowed his brow. What in heavens name did he mean?

"Well, in her defense," Daireann said, "there are many half-breeds and like creatures that have gone to the dark side."

"Some," Enda agreed, "but not all. That's like saying all dryads are a bunch of idiotic peace nuts who won't lift a finger in times of need."

Daireann snorted. "In that case you'd most often be right."

"The point is, Daireann, she's being racist. Lumping groups together, labeling them."

Miss O'Keefe sighed. "Typical, most Dalbhachs do label, most of them unaware they are doing it. But no matter. This has gone plenty far. She'll sign that peace treaty, even if I have to climb on top of her and force her." Miss O'Keefe shook her head and added, "Thick as a ditch."

No one said anything.

Daireann covered Kyna up and followed Enda and Ma out.

Miss O'Keefe stopped at the doorway and turned around.

Tase could have sworn she looked right at them, but she simply nooded and left without a word.

Tase didn't move and neither did Fadin. They just sat silently for what seemed like hours.

Tase lifted a hand to his throbbing head and swallowed hard.

He couldn't believe it, Miss O'Keefe, the home school teacher? She was magic? She had stopped Kyna's fit? She had saved their mother?

But now that he thought about it, why was he so surprised? His mother and father had lied to him his whole life. Aunt Kyna didn't appear to actually be his aunt. Enda had turned out to be his uncle. Mr. Hogan was his father's best friend. There was a goblin living in the attic. And a big black dog and hooded woman were stalking him and his twin. Why should this surprise him? Nothing was normal here, nothing.

Tase rubbed his aching skull as it swarmed with the overwhelming information. He jerked abruptly as Kyna shifted in her sleep.

Fadin tapped him on the arm and nodded towards the doorway.

Tase agreed and slowly followed behind.

Fadin, as he was crawling towards the exit, looked down at a clump of blonde hair on the floor.

Tase wrinkled his nose at it. How could she have pulled that much hair from her own head?

Fadin picked it up and stuffed it inside his pocket.

Tase shuddered and continued to creep out of the now silent room.

~~~

Once outside, Fadin tried to make sense of what he had just seen, and led them into the tea room.

Tase stopped, mid-stride, and pulled out a small, crinkled piece of parchment from his trousers. "It was shaking in my pocket," Tase exclaimed. "It was glowing green too."

"Open it," Fadin said, making a grab for it.

"I tried," Tase answered, "but I can't."

"Let me see," Fadin said. He took the paper in his hands and tried to pull it open, but his fingers became numb and limp. He grabbed it with both hands, but the parchment slipped from them and fluttered to the floor. "What's wrong with it?" he asked, trying again to pull it open, but it fell from his grasp a second time.

"I don't understand," Tase cried, grabbing at it. "I can't even pick it up now."

The paper began to tremble and glow with a bright green light.

"We have to open it," Fadin almost shouted.

They both reached for the paper.

Fadin cringed. The moment he came in contact with it, his fingers felt as if no bones existed in them.

The parchment rumbled harder, glowed greener, and then began to ring.

Again and again they tried to get a hold of the little article, but it was no use. Soon the parchment began to smoke and the ringing became almost unbearable.

"What are we supposed to do?" Fadin yelled, covering his ears.

The parchment burst into green flames and a loud voice echoed through the room.

"Get away from the mirrors, I'm coming over, no time."

There was a loud *BANG,* and Aimirgin stood in front of them covered in red powder. "I said get away from the mirrors!" she yelled.

Fadin looked behind them, and saw a huge mirror only centimetres away.

"Sorry," he said.

He and Tase stepped away.

"Follow me," she ordered, obviously not willing to explain why she was there.

They made their way to the entrance and peeked around the corner.

She turned to them and whispered something into her hand. She lifted her hand up, blew green dust in their faces, and clapped loudly.

"Quiet," Fadin whispered, "Enda will hear."

Aimirgin sprinkled the dust on herself. "No he won't," she said loudly, "because only you can hear and see me, and only I can hear and see you."

"What?" Tase asked, still whispering.

"Never mind that," she snapped, "we have work to do."

"Work, what work?" Fadin asked. He arched a red eyebrow.

"We have to get the last things on your list. The package is arriving early, and December 20th has changed to December 12th. We don't have much time."

"Why did—?"

"I don't have time to answer your questions now; I can explain it all later." She looked at a small device on her wrist. "We have barely half an hour before the package comes, so let's get to it." She nodded to the stairs, her long, ebony hair fluttering with the movement of her head, and lead the way to their room.

"Do you have anything red?" she asked, as they reached the bedroom. She scanned the area.

"Yea," Tase said, opening the dresser, "here." He held up a bright-red-coloured sock.

"This will do," Aimirgin said, taking it. "Won't be the best colour, but…" She took out a small hose-like object, fastened one end to her mouth and the other against the sock.

Fadin cocked his head. And what was that going to do?

Aimirgin sucked in hard through the tiny hose. Immediately, colour began to drain from the cloth starting at the top and ending on the bottom. When the sock was completely grey and dead-looking, Aimirgin, with her cheeks looking as though they could burst, pulled out a small bottle and breathed into it.

Red filled the minuscule container in a swirling gas-like substance.

Aimirgin sealed the bottle and handed it to Fadin.

"Keep this safe," she said, pointing a finger at him. "Now, as for the smell of the morning air, I think it's obvious that we are going to have to skip that bit, we don't have enough time, and it was only for comfort anyhow but we can focus on your memories."

Fadin moved closer. "How exactly are we supposed to gather these memories?"

"Like this," Aimirgin said, pulling out dark gloves.

They were black with white tips on the ends of the fingers. On the left one, there was a small bottle attached to the wrist area.

Aimirgin slipped them on. "These give me the power to help remove a memory. Some people can extract a memory with their bare hands and their own magic, but I'm too young. These here are very expensive, and only very few people are allowed to have them." She arched her eyebrows menacingly. "Meddling with memories can be a dangerous thing, you know."

Fadin heard Tase gulp. "Dangerous, huh?"

"Yea, sort of," she smiled at him, "I was exaggerating to scare you a little. Don't worry, it doesn't hurt—much."

Fadin swallowed hard.

"Let's do you first, Fadin," she said moving closer.

Fadin bit his lower lip.

"Now," Aimirgin began, putting both hands on the sides of his head. "I want you to think of the happiest you've ever been, the most content, the most peaceful, and then make it real. Make it so that you feel as if you're back in that memory, and it's all happening for the first time. I want you to be there, understand?"

Fadin nodded.

"Good, now close your eyes."

As soon as he did, Fadin saw bright lights bouncing off the silvery ocean, the sun rising over the water, fish jumping to catch their next meals. He could hear the birds crying, the waves crashing, and his father's voice, strong and kind, whispering to him.

"Slowly, boys," Da said, touching Fadin's shoulders, "easy, easy does it. Don't lose him, keep him where you want him, Fae. Careful T, careful, easy with the yanking."

Fadin looked over and saw Tase, a much younger and skinnier Tase, standing beside him clutching a large pole.

"Good, very good, give him a little slack, that's it. Careful, easy, almost, nearly there, WHOOPS!"

Fadin watched as the large fish on younger Tase's pole broke free and snapped the line. The power of the large pole sent younger Tase flying backwards, and snapped Fadin's line, releasing the fish on his hook.

"Oh no," Tase wailed, "I ruined it and Fadin's as well!" The younger Tase flung himself to the ground and began to cry.

Feeling slighted by the loss of his own fish, Fadin began to ball along with him.

"Now, now," Da said, "no crying over lost trout." He bent down and grabbed both their chins. "There's plenty of fish in the sea, so what if two got away?"

Fadin smiled and wiped his tears.

Tase followed suit.

"That's my boys," Da laughed. He scooped them into his arms and they giggled along with him. "My right arm," he bellowed, "and my left." He swung them around and around in the growing sun, laughing, smiling, and full of life.

Then the scene began to fade, much to Fadin's disappointment. It dwindled, sparked, and was gone.

"Ouch," a horrible pinching feeling began in Fadin's ears, and was moving to his head, now his eyes.

"Hold on Fadin," Aimirgin was saying, sounding under strain herself. "Just one—more—got it!"

With a horrible jerking pain, Fadin felt something make his eyes open, and felt as though an invisible force was pushing on them, squeezing them, as if trying to make them pop. Then Fadin saw something blue float away from his eye, and float into Aimirgin's little bottle. As soon as the blue thing entered the glass, it became foggy and blurred pictures appeared randomly in the case.

"Is that?" he asked, pointing at the bottle.

"Yea," Aimirgin nodded, "your memory."

"But," he looked at the miniature pictures as they replayed the scene he had just witnessed in his head, "Will I get it back? I mean—I am really fond of that memory, I actually forgot I had it."

Aimirgin smiled. "You do have it," she said kindly. "This," she shook the bottle, "is only a mirror image of your memory, a copy if you will. The original is still up here," she touched his forehead, "safe and completely intact."

Fadin touched his head as if he could feel the memory swirling inside him.

"Your turn, Tase," she said, moving towards him.

"Wait a minute," Tase said, backing away. "I don't want to. I change my mind."

Fadin cocked his head. "What? Why? It's not that bad."

"No," he put his hand up in an attempt to block out Aimirgin, "don't."

Aimirgin gaped at him, her black brows furrowed. "What's the matter with—?" She stopped and turned to Fadin. "Wait, is there a mirror in this room?"

Fadin looked at her. "I don't—think—so," he answered a little incredulously. "But what's wrong with Tase?"

"Are you sure?" Aimirgin asked.

"I don't—"

"Then look for one," she snapped.

Fadin raised his eyebrows but obeyed. He dug through the dresser and looked through the closet but found no mirror. "I couldn't find any."

Aimirgin kept her dark eyes on Tase. "Look under the bed."

Fadin eyed the bed and dropped to the floor. He peered under and sure enough, a piece of glass no bigger than his pinkie lay face up on the hard ground.

"There's one here," he said reaching for it.

"Don't touch it!" Aimirgin yelled, but too late.

Fadin had his hand clutched over it and was staring down at his distorted reflection.

*"You fool."* A high-pitched whisper said.

Fadin flinched and tried to let go, but he couldn't.

*"Magic and Dalbhachs? Singing pictures and goblins?"*

Fadin lay, transfixed on the mirror. He no longer had any desire to let go, to get away. He was mesmerized by the voice that seemed to be speaking directly in his ear, and longed to hear what else it would say.

*"Secrets, so many secrets. Why has no one ever told you these things? Why have you been kept in the dark? Does no one care? Does no one love you?"*

Fadin swallowed and stared harder at the piece of glass.

*"I know you have thought these things and you were right. No one does care. They hate you because you are a useless, non-magic being who can do nothing but uncover truths—truths you were not supposed to know. Your parents lied to you your entire life. Your new friend lied to you and her father lies to you. Your aunt is not your aunt, the butler is your uncle, your teacher is a magician, and who knows about the cook. And how about your father? He's dead, isn't he? And why is that?"*

Fadin felt a horrible sinking feeling as the room began to spin.

*"You know the truth. The truth is your father killed himself for shame of you. You have no magic powers, you are not special. He killed himself for the awful realization that you would amount to nothing. That, my dear boy, is why they all lie to you."*

Fadin felt the hot tears stream down his face.

*"But don't cry. I can help you. I won't lie to you, or betray you, or be disappointed in you."*

A hand, white as snow, appeared in the mirror.

*"Take my hand boy, take it, and I will show you the real truth. I will bring all your secrets to light."*

Fadin looked at the thin, scabbed, long-nailed fingers.

*"Take it, and I will answer all of your questions. Nothing will be denied you."*

Fadin trembled, unable to move.

*"Take it. Take it."* The voice pleaded.

Fadin moved his hand forward.

*"TAKE IT."*

"No, Fadin!"

He blinked and looked behind him.

Aimirgin had hold of his feet and was trying to pull him from under the bed. "Don't listen, don't believe anything he says. He's a liar."

Fadin shifted his eyes to the bit of mirror, the hypnosis broken, and made to put it down.

An awful screech broke from the glass, and Fadin saw, to his horror, a long, white hand come through.

"Fadin," Aimirgin screamed, "get out of there!"

He crawled backward as another hand reached out. Then the top of a scabbed head, two enormous red eyes, and a small disfigured body crawled out from the mirror.

Fadin screamed as the small frog-like thing ran at him.

"Pull me out," he yelled as the little creature got closer and closer.

Aimirgin yanked at him but not quickly enough.

The frog mutant had jumped and attached himself to Fadin's face.

Fadin yelled and screamed, trying to prise the creature off, but it was no use.

The thing had suction fingers and had stuck itself fast.

Fadin flung himself from under the bed and tried again to pull the creature off. It wouldn't budge. He rolled and smacked the front of his head on the floor, trying to beat the thing off him. Fadin suddenly cried in terror as he felt something slimy and hot crawl down his throat.

*"You're mine!"*

Fadin tried to scream, but no sound would come. He kicked and flailed, scratched and pulled, but the creature would not budge.

"Don't move," he heard Aimirgin yell.

He stopped trying to prise the thing away and lay as still as he could. He felt the hot thing move deeper into his throat and thought he might gag.

Something cold and wet was unexpectedly poured all over him, and the thing on his face began to scream. The hot something in his throat recoiled and the suction on his face loosened.

Fadin pulled at the creature and this time it let go.

Fadin coughed and gasped for breath as the frog-like creature fell to the floor.

It writhed and screamed and new cuts could be seen appearing on its thin, white flesh. Then, shaking violently, it crawled under the bed. It turned and looked at Fadin. It gave him a horrifying glare, screeched at him, and vanished beneath the mattress.

Fadin doubled up and retched. He felt all the remains of the hot thing leave his throat and the sick feeling in his stomach dissipate. "What," he asked, wiping his mouth, "was that?"

Aimirgin pulled out a small rag and dropped it on the vomit. It immediately cleaned the floor and made the vomit disappear.

"Well," she said, picking the rag back up, "it was a Glomhan. A mirror-dwelling creature that feeds off of people's voices. They try to trick you into taking their hand and making you afraid or heated enough to scream. Then they stick their tongue down your throat and suck out your voice."

Fadin shuddered and put a hand on his neck. "Where did he go?"

"Back into his mirror, I suppose. He shouldn't bother anyone for a while, he's too injured."

Fadin ran his hand across his face and looked at the clear liquid. "What was that stuff you poured on me?"

"Tears," she said holding out a small flask, "Glomhans can't stand tears. They burn their skin."

Fadin groaned and felt his stomach jerk. "Where's Tase?" he asked, suddenly remembering his brother.

"Oh," Aimirgin said, running a hand through her long raven hair, "I almost forgot."

They turned and saw Tase crunched in a corner, shaking.

Aimirgin moved to him and bent low. She placed an olive-skinned hand on his forehead.

"What's wrong with him?" Fadin asked, kneeling beside her.

"The Glomhan tried to work on him first, but Tase was too far away. He could hear the creature's voice, and I think that's what frightened him." She pulled out a small pastry and tried to give it to Tase. "Eat this. It'll help you feel better."

Tase shook his head violently and closed his eyes.

"Will he be alright?" Fadin asked, taking the pastry from Aimirgin, and trying to show it to Tase.

"He'll be fine," she said. "He just needs to eat this, and then he'll be perfectly alright."

"Come on, you thick wanker," he said holding the sweet up, "just eat this."

Tase shook his head and shivered. "No, I can't."

"You can, just take it."

Tase flung his head harder. "No."

Fadin raised his eyebrows. "Fine, then I'll do it for you." He grabbed

Tase's head and crammed the pastry into his mouth.

Tase tried to spit it out, but Fadin kept his hand cupped over his mouth.

"Swallow it." Fadin said.

Tase tried to pull away.

Fadin covered his nose. "Swallow."

Tase crinkled his nose and then gulped.

Fadin released him at once, and jumped backwards as Tase wretched all over the floor. "Yuck!" he backed away and covered his nose. "I thought it was supposed to help him feel better."

"It did," Tase said, picking his head up.

"You have to vomit after coming in contact with a Glomhan," Aimirgin said, dropping the rag on the floor. "It's the only way to feel right again."

Fadin screwed up his face and looked at the watch-type thing on Aimirgin's wrist. "So how long do we have till the package comes?"

She jumped and looked at the device. "Oh, suck a dragon's wing," she turned to Tase. "Think of a happy memory and do it quick, we barely have ten minuets left."

Tase raised his red eyebrows, and clamped his eyes shut.

"Make it real," she said, putting her now-gloved hands on Tase's head. She peered down at the watch object on her wrist and shook her long tresses. "Make it as though you are back in that memory, and it is happening for the first time."

A blank look spread over Tase's face and he smiled broadly.

"Good," Aimirgin said, "he's already got it, shouldn't be long now."

She shifted the position of her hands on his head. Aimirgin began to screw her face up in concentration. Her body locked, her jaw clamped shut, and her hands shook with intensity.

Tase screwed up his face in pain as something blue began to almost pour from his eyes.

Aimirgin continued to shake and began to sweat as the blue thing came nearer and nearer to the jar on the end of her left glove.

Fadin looked on in awe. As much pain as it had been to be the one giving the memory, it looked as though it was equally as painful being the one to receive the memory. He was just glad his turn was over.

The blue thing filled the jar on the end of Aimirgin's glove, and she moved her hands away from Tase's head, looking exhausted.

Tase opened his eyes and rubbed them. "Ouch. That was weird," he looked at the bottle in which pictures were now appearing. "How do you do that?"

"I don't have time to explain," Aimirgin said, panting a little. She put both bottles on their dresser. "We have to get down to the kitchen or we'll miss it." She led them to the door, turned around, and pointed. "Take care of those. It's very important not to lose or break those memories."

Fadin and Tase nodded, and they all clambered down the stairs.

Aimirgin asked them to show her to the kitchen, but when they got there they heard Daireann and Enda inside.

"What do we do?" Tase asked, moving away from the door.

"They can't see or hear us, remember?" Aimirgin said. "All we have to do is create a distraction while the package comes through."

"How are we supposed to do that?" Fadin asked, red eyebrows raised.

"Knock something over, spill something, make noise, I don't know, use your imagination." She put her head against the door. "It will be coming any minute. Now listen, me and Tase will retrieve the package while you do something to get their attention. Got it?"

"But…" Fadin began.

"Good, now let's go." Aimirgin opened the door and they all ran inside.

Enda, who had been talking angrily, looked over in the direction of the entrance. "What was that?" he asked, moving closer.

"Probably the dog," Daireann said. "He always pokes his cute little head in here. I give him scraps sometimes."

"I don't know," Enda said looking around the room.

"Oh, stop being so paranoid, Enda. No one's in here."

Aimirgin pointed towards a large frying pan. "Knock it over," she said. "Be sure to move out of the way though, they may not be able to see you but they can still feel you."

She moved towards the fire with Tase.

Fadin moved closer to the pan. He came just within reach when the kitchen began to glow red.

"Now," Aimirgin yelled.

Fadin knocked the pan to the floor and spilled a bag of flour.

"Oh no," Daireann wailed. "I had it all ready too."

"Don't worry," Enda said, bending down with her, "I'll help."

Fadin jumped to the side and jerked as Tase grabbed his collar and pulled him out of the kitchen.

"Got it," Aimirgin cried, holding up a large, wrapped package. "Come on." She led them back into the tea room and handed the package to Fadin.

"Alright, now you have everything you need, but you have to step on it a bit. Like I said, the time of the gathering has changed from December 20th to the 12th, so you have to work hard. All the instructions are in that package, all you have to do is follow them exactly. Do not deviate from them in any way, understand?"

They both nodded.

"Since the gathering has been moved closer, you need to start on the instructions tonight and when you aren't working on it, keep it hidden somewhere dark," she glanced at her arm. "Alright, I have to go, but one last thing. You are to ask your mother about coming to our house for a sleepover on the tenth. That same day, Clearie will receive a letter asking him to come as well. After Clearie gets the letter, the three of you are to go and ask your mother. Take care of yourselves and stay away from mirrors. And no going outside," she scolded. "Oh, and take this." She flung a small piece of parchment at them and Tase caught it.

Raising her hands over her head, like a great statue, she vanished in a puff of red smoke.

Fadin stood still for a long moment, then looked down at the bulk in his arms. It was neatly wrapped in brown paper and, now that he really felt it, was quite heavy. He shook it and heard a little rattling. "To open or not to open, that is the question," he said, turning to Tase.

Tase did not smile.

Fadin cleared his throat and put the package on the floor. Shaking slightly, he slowly began to unwrap the paper. Beneath it was a silver-coloured pot with a square lid taped to the top. Fadin pulled it off and peered inside.

It was full of tiny bottles, plant-like things, a bit of wood, and a tightly wrapped scroll.

A sudden flicker of green caught Fadin's eye and he looked up in alarm.

"What was that?" Tase asked looking around.

"I think," Fadin said, unsure of himself, "I think the magic Aimirgin used just wore off."

Tase put a finger to his mouth and tilted his head. "Someone's coming."

Fadin lurched upright and listened. Sure enough, he heard footsteps coming from the stairs. "Let's go," he said, picking up the silver pot.

Tase gathered the paper and the lid.

Quietly they walked to the sunroom and listened as Ma, from the sound of her footsteps, hit the bottom stair and turned towards the kitchen.

Fadin nodded his head, and they both dashed up the stairs and into their room. When the door shut, Tase crawled under the bed and pulled out the small bit of broken mirror. "We don't need any more visits from this little gowl," he hissed. He then opened the window and threw the glass out. He stood, unblinking, at the window for a moment. "So what's in it?" he asked, turning to Fadin.

"Bottles and this stuff," Fadin said, pulling out two limp, plant-like objects and handing them to Tase.

"Yuck," Tase rubbed his hand on the floor, "they're slimy." He dropped them on the bed and leaned forward to look inside the little pot. "What's that?" he asked, pointing at the scroll.

Fadin pulled it out and stroked the dark-blue wax sealing it. "Instructions?" he broke the blue seal and unrolled the parchment.

*Dear Fadin and Tase,*

It read in sloppy handwriting.

*I am entrusting this dangerous package and job into your hands. I cannot stress enough how important it is to be careful when acting on the instructions I have given you. Besides being careful with what you do, you must be aware and not allow yourselves to get caught. Be sure that when you are not working on this project, you hide it somewhere safe and dark where no one is to stumble upon it accidentally.*

*I am sure that you will succeed and we'll be looking forward to seeing you on the 12th.*

*Sincerely,*
*Mr. Lee Hogan*

Fadin saw a small green hand pointing to the end of the paper.

"Do you think that means anything?" Tase asked pointing to it.

Fadin touched the little hand and a bubble appeared above it.

*"FLIP ME."*

Fadin flipped the parchment over and saw more writing.

### Keik: The Traveling Potion

*These instructions shall help you to create the perfect traveling potion. Not only will it get you from a to b but it will also protect you from enemies, take you to places you've never been before, and offer destinations that can help with your goal. There's no going wrong with a Keik potion, so get ready, get set, and brew!*

Fadin smiled and continued reading down the paper.

### INGREDIENTS

*1 ball of goat saliva*
*3 melted gold doorknobs*
*9 golden hairs*
*4 table spoons Blood Fungus juice*
*2 diced Limp Roots*
*3 tears*

*15 dog nail clippings*
*A pinch of dust*
*6 drops of rain*
*The colour red*
*2 memories*

Tase let out a groan. "We still have to get the hairs. Why did we have to forget?"

Fadin smiled. "We didn't."

Tase tilted is head. "What do you mean?"

Fadin reached inside his pocket and pulled out the clump of hair Aunt Kyna had yanked from her own head.

"When did you grab that?"

"On the way out," Fadin said, "looks like I'm a smart one."

Tase rolled his eyes. "Why don't we keep reading."

Fadin smirked and looked back down at the paper.

## INSTRUCTIONS

*Put the caldron on the small piece of wood provided. There is no need for a match, it is self-lighting and will only cause heat to its caldron.*

*Put in doorknobs and allow them to melt. It should take up to twelve hours for them to melt completely and purely. They must be stirred every four hours to ensure they are melted thoroughly.*

*When they have become complete liquid, bring to a boil and let it stew for three days and nights in complete darkness. Do not disturb, not even to check.*

*On the morning of the fourth day, add the hairs, Blood Fungus juice, and rain. You will find these in the bottles that are labelled with their contents.*

*Bring this to a boil and then freeze overnight, preferably in the night air but for this time, in the freezer.*

*Remove in the morning and add saliva and dog nails. Bring to a boil and then let cool. It will harden to a stone-like substance in about five minutes and is to be kept in the dark for five more days.*

*On the fifth night, remove the caldron from the secluded area and dice the Limp Roots with the green dagger. Be sure to cut them nice and thin with none of the top tufts attached. When they are diced properly, add to the pot along with the dust, and allow three of your tears to fall on the stony surface. It should liquify instantly and then must be stirred twenty times: five clockwise, ten counter-clockwise, two clockwise, three side to side.*

*When stirring is completed, place the bottle with the colour red very near the surface. The colour should enter the pot and become one with the liquid.*

*This brings the Potion to its last and final step and is now completed. Deposit the mixture into the three extra bottles provided.*

*The potion should be kept safe and away from any eyes. It should not be taken out until the 11th, the day you will come and stay the night.*

*Also, keep your memories hidden and prepare to bring them with you when you come.*

*Follow the instructions, stay safe, and whatever you do, **do not drink**!*

Fadin whistled loudly. "We'd better not hash up, huh?"

Tase stared at him, wide-eyed. "What if we do?"

"What? Come on, Tase, it's all laid out for us right here. How could we mess it up?"

"This isn't funny, Fadin, don't you remember the warnings Aimirgin gave us?"

Fadin looked at him blankly.

"You're a Fecky the Ninth sometimes, you know that?" Tase said scowling. He sighed and recited, "Do not, under any circumstances, deviate from the instructions placed upon the package. Doing so could result in serious injury, house demolition, illness, and/or death."

Fadin furrowed his brow. "Did you memorize it or something?"

"You plonker," Tase yelled, smacking his arm. "Don't you get it? This is serious. If we mess up, this could be the end."

"The end of what?"

Tase held his hand up again.

"Alright, alright, I get it. I know it's dangerous but freaking out about it isn't going to help."

"Making jokes won't help either."

Fadin looked down at the silver caldron. "You really think we could ruin it?"

Tase peered into it as well. "I hope not."

"Well," Fadin said pulling out the wood, "there's only one way to find out."

# Chapter 13

## *The Thing in the Well*

"One, two, three, four, five, stop, change direction. Now, one, two, three, four, five…" Tase rotated his shoulder and released the spoon in his hand. "My arm hurts already."

"Oh stop complaining," Fadin answered. "It isn't that hard."

"Really? Why don't you try it then?"

"No, it's your turn; I already had to shed two tears for you and dice up the Limp Roots."

"For me? You mean for us."

"Right," Fadin said looking up from the instructions, "for us, if you really think this traveling potion or whatever it is will help us. Seems to me that we're just making something for Mr. Hogan."

Tase looked into the pot and its orange substance. "So what if we are? It's not like we've done anything else for him and he is the only person who's told us the truth. Besides," he looked towards the bunk bed," you didn't do so great with the Limp Root dicing."

Pathos lifted his head and looked at Fadin as if he were waiting for an answer. He had been with them nonstop since the package had arrived, and didn't even sleep with Ma anymore.

"Please," Fadin said, looking at the bed then at Pathos. "It wasn't my fault, how was I supposed to know they could do that?"

"Well the name 'Limp Roots' might have given you a clue."

"That's a good one, Tase, I mean since you were so smart and warned me. I am just so sorry. I should have listened to your advice since you figured it out so quickly."

Tase glared at him. "Okay fine, so I didn't know what they did, but this," he pointed to the bed, "I did warn you that I heard something."

"No, you said you thought you heard something."

"Yes I did, and I told you to put the pot away, but no, you had to keep going. Now look at the mess we got ourselves into. No wait, correction, *you* got us into."

Fadin looked towards the bed and laughed. "Yea well, I think a little trouble was worth the look on his face and watching him plummet to the floor like a rock. Wham!" Fadin slammed his fist into his hand.

"It isn't funny, Fadin. Clearie is unconscious and I'm almost positive he saw something." Tase looked at Clearie's limp form on the bed. The juice from the Limp Roots had caused him to pass out. Fadin had accidentally squirted it on him when he walked in.

"Oh, Aimirgin said he'd be fine when we wrote to her. And so what if he did see something? He can't prove it, all he can do is guess, besides he'll have all the answers he wants in three days."

Tase smiled. "Yea, three days. It's felt like forever."

Fadin nodded. "I wonder what we'll see there."

"I don't know, but I can't wait."

"Me neither, I wonder if it's safe to go in large bodies of water at Aimirgin's?"

"Huh?"

Fadin looked at the floor. "Nothing."

"Wait," Tase said leaning forward, "why would you want to know that?"

"No reason."

"There's got to be a reason. Come on, spit it out."

Fadin looked at him. "Well, since the hooded woman and Glomhan incident, I've —well, I've kind of been afraid of mirrors and anything else Aimirgin warned us about."

"Like what?" Tase asked, now smiling.

"Like," Fadin looked at the ceiling, "like large bodies of water, okay?"

"You mean you haven't taken a bath since Aimirgin was here ten days ago?" he smiled and started to laugh.

"Shut your gob, Tase. It isn't funny. I'd like to see how you react when a frog-monster shoves his tongue down your throat."

Tase closed his mouth and tried to stop the last few hiccup-like giggles. "Okay, okay, I suppose you're right, but how have you cleaned up?"

"I'd rather not say."

"Come on, Fadin. I have to know."

"Just drop it, alright?"

Tase smiled and shook his head. "Well, I think it's safe to assume that it will be fine to take a bath at Aimirgin's. I doubt any Glomhans would enter their mirrors."

"Yea," Fadin said, "you're probably right." He looked down into the pot and poked it with the spoon. "You know, I've been thinking about the Glomhans, and I wonder if everyone who's mute doesn't have a voice because a Glomhan sucked it out."

Tase thought about this for a moment. "I don't know, I suppose that could be true."

"Yea, I bet it is, and I wonder whether or not Glomhans can make you lose your voice when you get sick. I remember plenty of times when my voice went away because of the flu. I always thought I felt something hot in my throat the night before."

Tase raised his red eyebrows. "I doubt it, a lot of normal humans lose their voice with the flu, and I think it's just from being sick."

"Yea, well I doubt that Glomhans don't go after normal humans. Why wouldn't they? Humans without magic or knowledge of them seem like a better target than people who know they exist and how to fight back."

"I suppose that's true. What if they really are the cause of losing your voice? That would mean that all those times when we got sick..."

"Ma knew what was really going on and decided to lie to us again, yea," Fadin said bitterly.

Tase looked at him then down into the pot. "I wonder if she ever told us the truth."

The sound of movement caused them both to jump.

Tase looked behind him and saw Clearie beginning to stir.

"Hurry," Fadin said, gathering up the pot. He kicked the knothole and the white closet vanished to be replaced by the old wood one.

They thrust the pot and instructions into the closet, slammed it shut, and kicked the knothole a second time. Then they walked towards the bed and stood over Clearie as he opened his eyes.

"What, what happened?" He sat up and began massaging his neck.

"Fainted," Fadin said sitting next to him. "Fell like a rock."

Clearie looked at him. "Fainted?"

"Yup, out of nowhere too. You walked in, then 'bam' hit the floor."

Clearie arched a blond eyebrow. "I passed out, just like that?"

"Yea," Tase said trying to sound convincing, "just like that."

"Why?" Clearie said, turning to him. "Why did I pass out?"

"How should we know?" Fadin asked.

Clearie looked from one to the other. "That doesn't make any sense."

"We didn't say it did," Fadin answered. "We just told you what we saw."

"Right," Clearie stopped, rubbing his neck. "I just passed out for no reason when I came in your room, even though I have absolutely no history of ever fainting."

"That's right," Fadin smiled at him.

"What little liars you are."

"Liars?" Fadin repeated. "How did we lie? We told you what we saw."

"Give me a break. Do you think I'm stupid?"

"Well," Fadin said looking up.

"Oh dry up, Fadin. That is the worst story I've ever heard."

"I'm sorry you feel that way."

"You're sorry I feel that way? Oh come on," Clearie stood up and looked around the room. "I know you're lying. I know there's something else going on."

"Careful," Fadin said, "you just got past the hearing voices incident."

Clearie glowered at him.

Tase could see his temper rising.

His left eye electrified into a brighter blue, while his right became a more violent shade of purple. "I never heard any imaginary voices," he yelled. "I heard you inside the walls somewhere."

"Yea, that's really normal," Fadin mocked.

"Don't deny it. I recognized your voices and they were coming from the walls—no—from the bookcase."

Tase swallowed hard. Clearie was too smart for his own good.

"I could hear you and then Pathos came bounding out of nowhere, and you two showed up coming through the front door. There must be a second exit to wherever you were."

"Give me a break," Fadin said, standing as well. "We just came in from outside."

"Sure you did. You seem to think I'm a real eejit, don't you? But I know you're hiding something, something big, both of you." He glared at Tase now. "I know I heard you in the bookcase, I know you were hiding something in this room when you tried to lock me out." He moved closer to Fadin and jabbed a finger in his chest. "I know you had something in here when I walked in today, and I know you had something to do with my passing out, if that's even what really happened. You're both liars, and I'm going to figure out what you're hiding."

Fadin got so close to him that they almost touched noses. "Try all you want you mentaller, you'll never figure it out."

Clearie's eyes brightened. "Watch me." He turned on the spot, walked out, and slammed the door.

Tase let out the air he had been holding in and sat on the bottom bunk. "Now what?"

Fadin shook a defiant fist at the door and slumped next to Tase. "It doesn't matter, we don't have to keep all this a secret from him for much longer." He flung himself backward and stared up at the wood. "It's a good thing Mr. Hogan made us have him come to whatever's going on December 12th. I don't know how much longer we could have kept lying to him." He sighed. "Clearie's smart, too bloody smart."

Tase began to nod his head in agreement, but stopped and sniffed at the air. "Do you smell that?"

Fadin sat up. "Smell what?"

Tase crinkled his nose. "That. That smoky smell."

Fadin sniffed the air, then stood up and smelled around the room. "What is that?"

"I don't know, but it almost smells like something's..." Tase turned to the closet and stared at the small cloud seeping from under the door. "The potion!" he yelled. "It's the potion, hurry." Tase ran and kicked the knothole.

The door swung open and an explosion of white smoke filled the room.

*"Cloud and smoke,*
*Your potion's broke.*
*My closet you fill,*
*You are trying to kill!"*

Tase ignored the singing picture and grabbed the pot.

"Ouch," he leapt away from it, shaking his hands.

"Is it hot?" Fadin asked.

"Cold," he said, trying to fan away the smoke. It was filling his lungs and he began to feel light-headed.

"Open a window," Fadin said. "If Ma sees this, we're dead."

Tase moved away from the closet and, coughing now, yanked open the window.

The room began to clear and Tase saw Fadin holding the pot with what used to be his shirt.

The shirt was beginning to freeze in places and was shattering like glass. Fadin plopped the potion on the floor and hopped away from it, shaking his hands and screwing up his face. "Bloody monkey snogging gack," he cursed, prancing around the room. "Oh, that was bloody cold," he hopped up and down for a few moments then leaned over the pot and peered in.

Tase looked down at it too and saw that the colour had changed from bright orange to pale grey. He fanned away the last bit of smoke and touched the spoon still protruding out of it. "The spoon's still warm."

"Oh, is it? Well good for the spoon, 'cause I don't think my hands will ever be warm again." He screwed his face up in pain and rubbed his hands together.

"What do you think went wrong?" Tase asked.

"I don't know, maybe we weren't supposed to stop in the middle of stirring? Where were you with that, anyway?"

Tase thought but he couldn't remember. Everything that happened with Clearie had wiped from his mind how many times he had stirred the potion. "I don't know."

"What do you mean, you don't know?"

"I can't remember," he felt panic rush up inside him. "I can't remember how many I've done!"

"Calm down, Tase, we'll figure it out."

"What if we can't? Remember what Aimirgin said? Household demolition and/or death."

"Please, I bet she said that just to scare us."

Tase could see the worry in his eyes despite the brave act. "Sure, that's a great thing to joke about. A really hilarious prank. What are we going to do?"

"Well, I do remember you just started, because you were already complaining about your arms."

"Yea, that's right, but how many times had I stirred it?"

"Um, I remember you did the first five clockwise, but I don't know how many you did counter-clockwise."

"Five?"

"No, I think three, or four? I don't know."

Tase looked hopelessly at the potion.

"Seven?" Fadin continued guessing. "No, six, six for sure."

Tase looked up at him. "You're absolutely positive?"

"No," Fadin answered shaking his head, "I'm not, but it's my best guess."

Tase swallowed. "You want to finish it?"

"No, I think you should. You started it and maybe you aren't supposed to change stirrers halfway through. Better to be safe then sorry again."

Tase closed his eyes and took a deep breath. He peered into the grey liquid and clutched the spoon.

"Seven," he gulped, "eight," the spoon was becoming heavy, "nine," he looked up at Fadin, "ten."

He stopped and looked down at the potion. It was still cold and grey and nothing appeared to have changed.

"Are you sure it was six I already stirred?"

Fadin shrugged his shoulders.

"It is ten counter-clockwise, right?"

Fadin reached in his pocket and pulled out a small piece of paper. He scribbled on it with a minuscule pencil and held it out to Tase.

*Ten counter-clockwise, two clockwise, three side to side."*

Tase nodded and looked back down into the pot.

"Should we stir it clockwise?" Fadin asked.

Tase didn't answer. Something wasn't right, he could feel it.

Pathos came and stood beside him and Tase patted him on the head.

Tase looked into the dog's dark brown eyes, and a sudden feeling of absolute surety came over him.

He moved forward and reached for the spoon, turning it counterclockwise.

"What are you doing?" Fadin asked.

"I know, I don't know how, but I know that I didn't stir it six times, I stirred it five."

"You remembered?"

"No, I just know."

"Tase, I'm not so sure…"

"Well, I am."

He held the spoon tight and with a grunting effort, he moved it round the pot once more. The small basin gave a sudden lurch. The cold ice melted off it and the grey liquid burst into a bright orange.

Fadin sat with his mouth wide. "How did you?"

"I don't know," Tase smiled, "but I was right."

He clutched the spoon again and stirred it twice clockwise. The pot's contents seemed to be becoming denser with each stir, but Tase didn't stop. He held the spoon tight and moved it side to side once, twice, three times.

The pot gave another little jump and the orange substance glowed brightly. A wonderful-smelling steam floated from its surface and Tase felt himself becoming light-headed.

Fadin grabbed the bottle of red and held it close to the orange surface. The red substance flowed into the liquid and caused the whole potion to smell sweet, like roses.

"Let's bottle it up." Fadin said smiling.

Tase nodded and tipped the pot as Fadin brought the little bottles close.

The liquid fell directly in the container's small hole, it never spilled out and the stream of potion stopped once the bottle was full. Fadin pulled out the second, then the third, and once they were all full to the brim, the few drops of potion left in the pot vanished.

Fadin put the bottle safely in their top drawer and closed it quietly.

"You did it, Tase," he said, turning to him. "If you would have listened to me, this castle would probably be gone now."

Tase smiled. He was right, for once in his life Tase had been the smarter one.

Fadin grabbed his head and scratched it with the top of his knuckles.

Tase laughed and pushed him on the bunk.

They rolled off it and onto the floor, smacking one another with playful force.

"Boys."

Tase sat up and shoved the leftover contents under the bed.

"Boys?" Ma's voice called again.

*"Mama's calling,*
*You'd better be going,*
*She'll know you're stalling,*
*Unless you'll be showing,*
*The potion you've hidden,*
*The pot that was smoking,*
*She'll give you a chidden,*
*You'd better be going."*

Fadin glared towards the picture, slammed the door, and made it turn white. "I really hate that picture," he said with a scowl.

They bounded down the stairs and saw Ma standing in the entrance. Her arms were folded and she was wearing her usual, very large, sweater. She smiled as they hit the bottom step and ran her hands through their red hair.

"Time for dinner," she said sweetly. "Oh, and Miss O'Keefe and Aunt Kyna are joining us tonight, so please," she looked from one to another, "no fighting."

Tase nodded and looked at Fadin, who threw him back a glance, meaning, "She should tell that to Kyna."

They all entered the dining room and sat at the table to which an extra chair had been added. No one besides Clearie was at the table yet, and he gave them a cold piercing stare.

The door to the kitchen swung open and Daireann, dressed in her usual apron, with her white-blonde hair put up in a bun, stumbled in with a large tray full of bread.

Behind her came a smiling Miss O'Keefe. She was dressed in a blue turtleneck and jeans. Her copper hair hung down to her shoulders and her white streak framed the side of her face. She held a tray full of drinks and was laughing happily with Daireann.

"Sit down, Caoimhe," Daireann said with a giggle, "you've been enough help."

The entrance to the room burst open and Aunt Kyna entered, looking as angry as ever. Her golden hair was brushed silky smooth. Her green eyes were framed in brown, her lips clad in pink. She wore a lovely green gown with long flowing sleeves, which made her look like royalty. But the scowl on her face made her appear a villain. "Yes, Caoimhe," her voice was cold, "you've done plenty, I'm sure." She sat herself down and glared at Miss O'Keefe.

"Thank you, Daireann, I think I will sit." Miss O'Keefe said kindly. She threw Kyna a cool glance and moved to the open spot next to Clearie.

Tase sat, tight-lipped, looking around the table.

It was quiet and cold, the way it had been since Aunt Kyna's breakdown. Actually, since the day she had woken up from her fit.

Someone had constantly been with her for two days straight, in case she did wake up, and was not cured.

Tase and Fadin made it part of their business to sneak around the room when not working on the potion. But for those first two days, there was nothing to report. The third morning, however, was a different story.

Tase had woken up to a scream, and he and Fadin rushed down the stairs and hid behind the couch so they could listen in.

Tase heard Kyna yelling at someone to let her up and stop talking nonsense.

Then another voice, who Tase recognized as Miss O'Keefe, yelled back that Kyna was ill and shouldn't try to go back to work.

Then Ma, Enda, and Daireann showed up. They all tried to calm Kyna down but she would listen to none of them until they "let her off the bed."

After a small cracking sound, Kyna stomped out of her room and into the hall.

"Be reasonable, Kyna." Ma said. "You aren't well."

"I'm not?" Kyna hissed angrily. "I look just fine to me, besides being tied up in a bed for three days."

"Kyna," Miss O'Keefe said, her anger as evident as their aunt's.

"No, I don't want to hear it from you."

"Who will you hear it from then?" Miss O'Keefe asked.

There was silence.

"You aren't stupid, Kyna, but sometimes you sure act daft. You know as well as I what happened in that room was no simple sickness."

Tase could see Kyna's face through the crack in the couch. She stared like a deer caught in the headlights at Miss O'Keefe.

"What was it then?" she asked.

Tase saw Miss O'Keefe arch an eyebrow. "A purposeful and planned attack against you. But you already knew that. Why else were you trying to stay away from all of us? Having your meals in your bedroom, not speaking to anyone for more then a second, not letting a soul get a good look at you? Did you think you could beat it?"

"I thought, I hoped I was being paranoid."

"Please, with Puceula Lynch at the Kings side? You know as well as I that he serves another more powerful master, no matter how high on the throne he is."

"So you think it was him then?" Daireann asked.

"Of course it was," Enda said sharply. "The entire peace act had to be his idea, at least his real master's, anyway."

Tase saw Miss O'Keefe nod. "You were the only one holding out against the new peace treaty Kyna, he had to make you sign it somehow. I think he put a spell or hex of some kind on you. It wouldn't be too hard, just slip something in your drink or food. What he wasn't counting on, however, is how strong a fighter you are. You wouldn't let him win."

"I won't let him win," Aunt Kyna said forcefully. "You're all speaking as though I've decided to go along with this ridiculous treaty. As if I've given up."

"You have," Miss O'Keefe said.

"Oh really, say's who?"

"All of us," she stepped closer to Kyna and looked her right in the eye. "If Puceula can, and knows how to get at you, then what's to stop him from doing it again?"

"My vigilance."

Miss O'Keefe rolled her grey eyes. "There is no way you can avoid another run-in with Lynch, he'll figure out that the hex hasn't worked, and he'll find another way to make you sign it. It's better for you, for all of us, that you stop fighting and sign it now."

"I won't, I won't let him win. I won't agree to some stupid treaty that will single-handedly put us at the mercy of these creatures."

"You really think one person's going to stop it? And let's say you do, Kyna. Let's say, for argument's sake, you stop this one, do you think he won't just make another treaty? Or won't simply eliminate the problem altogether?" Miss O'Keefe stepped closer. "You think he won't suspect the rest of your family? You think he wont track them down? He will, and he'll use the tentacles he's got locked into the King to do it. He'll make up a reason to arrest them, or worse. Just so he can get them and the problem out of the way."

Kyna stared at her, obviously lost for words.

"They won't give up that easily, Kyna, and they won't hesitate because of children. Besides that, let's be completely selfish. You think he won't kill you? He will, and then where will we be? You were a great warrior in the first war, and if a second is indeed coming, we will need you again." Miss O'Keefe held up a folded piece of paper. "So sign it."

She did sign the treaty. She placed her name on the dotted line and agreed to be more careful wherever it was that she worked.

She came home on time, ate meals with the family, sat with them. But she wasn't the same Aunt Kyna Tase had met a few months ago. She was abrupt and cold. She didn't talk much anymore and always had a snide remark for Miss O'Keefe.

This particular meal was no different from the meals they had had recently, except for the fact that Miss O'Keefe chose to dine with them.

The way this dinner was going, however, Tase suspected it would be the last one she'd be joining for a while.

He and Fadin didn't say much the whole meal. They simply finished their dinner, cleared their plates, and left the very awkward table.

"She certainly is a stubborn one, isn't she?" Fadin asked.

Tase gave him a sarcastic glance but said nothing.

"Hey, you want to go visit Ciaran for a bit? We haven't seen him for a while. Maybe we can find some more pictures of Da? Or this D.A.?"

Tase thought for a moment. "Alright, why don't we take the bottles of memories to him? He may be able to tell us how Aimirgin extracted them in more detail, and what they're for."

So they hurried up to their room and found the small bottles.

When they reached the bookcase, however, Pathos stood blocking their way.

"Move it, boy," Fadin said, continuing forward.

Pathos snapped at him and growled furiously.

"What's the matter with you?" Tase asked. "Come on, Path, move over."

The Bernese stood firm and growled angrily.

"What do we do?" Tase asked.

Fadin looked up at the ceiling. "Maybe we can find another way."

"What other way?"

"Come on."

They ran from the hall and up to their room.

Pathos followed closely behind and as soon as he was through the door, Fadin slammed it shut.

"Can't follow us now," Fadin said with a smile.

The dog scratched and barked but Fadin didn't seem to care.

Tase wanted very much to go and see Ciaran, so although he did feel a bit guilty about locking their dog in the room, he followed Fadin back down to the bookcase and up to the small attic.

Ciaran was sitting on the broken table and looked up as they entered the cluttered room. "Hello things," he said standing up. "How has been?"

"Good Ciaran," Tase said, "You?"

"Goods too. I finds more photos of father for you. Lets me get." The little goblin clunked down his book-made-stairs and vanished beneath the old wood.

"Sure is to the point," Fadin said.

"Heres they is," Ciaran said, holding a small pile of thick paper. "Father when was in school."

"What school did he go to?" Tase asked, taking the picture. "Is there one around here?"

The photo was old and scratched. Tase saw his father standing next to a very tall dark-haired boy, Mr. Hogan.

Alroy was very short, skinny, gangly, had large, orange-spiked hair, and very baggy clothes. He couldn't have been much older than Tase and Fadin were now.

"Was a school here, gone now," Ciaran said.

Fadin took the stack of pictures and they all sat, quietly admiring each of them. Whenever Tase or Fadin would ask a question, Ciaran would answer. He would explain the photos and where they were taken. He seemed to know so much about their father and when he was young.

They found photos of birthdays, of swimming, of picnics. They found photos of Ma and Da together, when they were just friends. They found a photo of Ma with Saoirse and Da by her side. There were dozens of them, and Tase admired each and every one, locking them away in his memory.

"How long have you lived here, Ciaran?" Tase asked, after a lengthy description of the picture in his hand.

"Oh, long time," the goblin answered. "Much before you things was borns."

"But have you lived up here your whole life?"

"No, no. I lived in castle one time, long ago."

"Really? Did my Da know you? My ma?"

The goblin looked up at the ceiling, "I wouldn't say they know me, but they did meet me."

"Would they remember you if they saw you?" Fadin asked sitting up.

"No," Ciaran answered, "I don't thinks they would."

Tase nodded and sat silently thinking about this. It was odd to be sitting with someone their father and mother had met. A goblin they both had seen before, someone else who had lived in this castle.

Tase flipped through more of the photos, and found one that had been completely scratched up.

"Who's this?" Tase asked.

"Oh, meant to throws that ones out," Ciaran said, making a grab for it.

Tase looked down at the caption.

*For the one who lead us, sacrificed for us, died for us, and made us live again. For the one who gave us hope, who gives us life, who hands us victory. In loving memory of Dia Ailín, the savior of all Erin.*

Tase put the picture down. "Dia Ailín?"

"What?" Fadin asked, looking at the picture.

"Remember when I told you Mr. Hogan said something about a man named Dia Ailín?"

"Yea, and you said he didn't make any sense."

Tase shook his head. "I think I just figured something out."

"What?" Fadin asked.

"D.A. is Dia Ailín. It's him. The person who the letter is about, the person who is scratched out in all these photos. The person the crest is for. D.A. is Dia, and Mr. Hogan was going to tell me about him. He *is* going to tell us about him."

Fadin blinked. "Da knew this Dia? Didn't Mr. Hogan say he was a savior or something like that?"

Tase nodded. "Yea," he looked back down at the picture. "Why do you think his face is scratched out in all the pictures of him?"

"I don't know," Fadin said. "Maybe not everyone liked him and thought of him as a savior." Fadin looked at his watch. "Wow, we've been here a long time," Fadin said standing. "It's nearly one in the morning."

Tase jumped to his feet. "Do you think Ma—?"

"No," Ciaran said smiling, "she thinks you things are asleep."

"What? How would you know?" Fadin asked turning to him.

"I makes sure of it. Puts a fake door in fronts of room. Looks like things are sleeping in beds and mother would not check."

"How did you do that? And how do you know she wouldn't check?"

"Magic ofs course, and the spell makes people only look, no goes in."

Tase stared at the big-eared creature. He looked harmless, small, unthreatening, stupid even, but he wasn't. He had managed to fool their mother when they hadn't even given her a second thought.

"That was really smart, Ciaran." Tase said smiling at him.

"I's know," he said smiling back.

A sudden thought came rushing back to Tase. "Ciaran," he said digging in his pocket, "I have something I want to show you." He pulled out his small bottle of memory. "I was wondering if you could look at this."

He handed it to the goblin, who snatched it up eagerly.

"Memory?" he asked, shaking the bottle.

"Yes, my memory."

The little goblin grunted and shook the vial again.

The container burst into bright blue, and a scene began forming inside. Tase saw the memory of the last time he had seen his father. He saw him

243

laughing at the breakfast table, reading the letter from Saoirse, getting up, gathering his things, touching the carved spot by their old front door, smiling at him, telling Tase he loved him, and then vanishing through the door, to be gone forever.

The scene dwindled, faded, and was swallowed in the blue smoke.

"More is there?" Ciaran asked, shaking the bottle again.

"No, that's it." Tase said. "I was wondering…"

"Are you sure there no more?"

"I'm sure," Tase said, watching him shake the container harshly. "But I wanted to know…"

"Listen," Fadin said standing, "I hear people moving downstairs."

Tase became quiet. He did, indeed, hear the sounds of people moving around. It wouldn't be long till their mother called for them.

"We have to go," Tase said, snatching the bottle away from Ciaran. He headed for the door.

"Wait thing, you cannot go that way."

"Why not?" Fadin asked holding open the door.

"Dog is out and light-haired brother is with him."

"Clearie is with Pathos? How did he get out?"

"Scratch hard and opens door. Light-haired thing is waiting at bookcase for you. You cannots go that ways."

"Fine, we'll take the tunnel," Fadin said, moving away the half-a-pan cover. "Come on, Tase."

Tase fallowed Fadin, and stood at the entrance to the tunnel. "How did you know, Ciaran? How did you know Clearie is waiting for us?"

The little goblin's ears shook and his eyes grew even wider. "I know this castle betters than anything in it. I hear things no thing else does. Brother makes noises, pet thing scratches loud. Ciaran, puts it together. I knows this castle."

"Come on, Tase," Fadin said impatiently.

Tase stood and looked, unblinking, at Ciaran for a moment longer, then nodded to Fadin, who pushed himself off and slid down the dark tunnel.

Tase followed suit and was soon gliding down the dark hole after him. Almost immediately he felt something was wrong. The tunnel began to shake and tremble. He felt it become hot then suddenly cold. The floor beneath him trembled more violently, and abruptly broke away.

He heard himself cry out for Fadin as he fell from the slide. He hit something cool and wet and sank through it to the bottom. He realized, as his feet hit the ground, that he was in water, water that was near freezing point.

He kicked off the floor and burst into the nipping air. He gulped for breath and tried to reach for the hole he had fallen through. As he did, the realization of what was happening hit him. The small hole he had tumbled through was closing, and the metal was far too close to the water. So close, in fact, that there wouldn't be any air left once the hole was sealed.

Tase screamed for help, but the metal was too fast. It closed itself up and Tase barely had time to take one large breath.

He pounded and kicked, fought and screamed, but it was no good. The tunnel wouldn't budge and Tase could feel reality slipping from him.

The cold and lack of air was making everything around him hazy, as if he were in a fog. He felt the cold seep into him and felt his lungs begin to give out. He tried to fight it but it was no use, he was going to die, alone, frozen, drowned in water, under a secret tunnel in a magical castle.

Just as he began to accept his fate and let reality glide away, something yanked on his arm and pulled him further down. Something warm touched his lips and breathed into his mouth.

Tase felt his lungs expand with fresh air and he stared motionless at the creature in front of him.

His vision was blurred from the water but he could tell the creature was female. Her long green hair flowed around them and her eyes were the lightest shade of blue he had ever seen. She hissed something at him then pulled his arm hard.

They soared through the water at a speed Tase had never thought possible. As abruptly as they had begun, they stopped, dead. And the creature turned to him and punched him in the gut.

Tase felt all the air leave him and his head again become light. Before he had much time to reflect upon what happened, the creature swam upward and shoved his head into an air pocket. There was only enough for one good breath, but Tase took it. Once the air was gone, the creature yanked him under and they were off again.

Twice more she did this and each time Tase obeyed. He let his air out and took new air in. He didn't know where they were going or what she intended to do with him, but he had very little choice. The only thing he did know was that his body was shaking violently and he didn't know how much longer he could stand the cold. As this thought rushed through his head, however, the creature began to swim upwards. This time she moved much faster and Tase saw light above them.

She picked up incredible speed and just as Tase saw the surface, she let go, and he watched as she was lost in the dark as he continued to fly up.

His head broke the surface and he gulped in the cold air. He could feel himself sinking so he grabbed on to the stone around him.

When he felt the ability to look around, he saw that he was in some kind of well, and that the top of it was covered by a large stone lid. The only light in the circular hole was the moon, which had managed to peek through the cracks.

Tase suddenly became aware of a noise that had been growing steadily louder. He quieted his breathing and listened.

"Tase," someone was screaming hysterically. "Tase, where are you? Answer me, you stupid plonker."

It was Fadin, and Tase could tell that he was bawling. His voice cracked with each horrified yell and he was taking great hiccup-like breaths.

"Tase, Tase. Where are you? Tase!"

"Here," Tase yelled, "I'm here." He felt the cold taking over his body, and was having a hard time keeping his grip on the rocks.

"Tase? Tase, where are you? Are you in the tunnel?"

"No," Tase screamed, his teeth chattering, "I fell through, I'm in some kind of well."

"You fell? What well? There's not a well around here."

Tase surveyed his surroundings. "Yes there is, and I'm in it. It might be hidden but it's definitely here." He closed his eyes as pain surged through his body. Something other than being in the cold was wrong, but he couldn't pinpoint it. He felt as though thousands of needles were pricking his skin, and his legs were now completely numb.

"Okay, so there's a well. I can't see it, so I need you to keep yelling."

"I'm here," Tase screamed. "Here, over here." He called out over and over until he heard a loud bang above him.

"Ouch," Fadin shouted. "I think I found it."

"You did," Tase said thankfully. He couldn't feel his waist now, and the numbness was spreading fast.

"I'm going to try and move this, just hold on."

"Don't worry," Tase said, his teeth sounding like a motor, "I'm not going anywhere."

Fadin grunted and yelped. He moved the lid little by little, and slowly moonlight hit Tase, making the dank well brighter. As the light filled the round tomb, Tase saw that the stones had a word etched into them. Every single stone had the same word carved into their faces, the same word that was carved into the walls of the round room near the attic.

X-O-O-R.

Tase tried to think what it could mean, but the cold and numbness were too much, he could hardly even breathe.

Finally the lid slipped from the top.

Tase looked up, shivering, into the tear-stained face of Fadin.

"Give me your hand," Fadin said, bending down.

Tase tried, but could barely move. He felt himself slipping further into the water and the numbness spreading to his chest.

"I can't reach," he gasped in desperation. "I'm slipping."

"No, just reach. Come on, Tase, reach!"

Tase tried but as he moved his arm up, he fell and completely submerged himself in the water. He tried to swim upward, but he had no strength left. He could hear Fadin screaming and he tried again to swim up, but it was no use. He was sinking and there was nothing he could do.

All of a sudden, he felt something hit him from beneath, and he flew out of the water, over the well, and over his astonished-looking twin. He felt the thrust of the push fade and he watched, as if in slow motion, as Fadin got closer and closer.

He fell right on his brother and they both hit the ground with a thud, Tase on top of Fadin's warm body.

Tase lifted his head and peered nose to nose into his brother's face.

"What was that?" Fadin said, half-laughing. "Are you okay?"

But Tase did not feel okay. He felt sick and the numbness spread now to his face, and he watched as the world around him grew dark.

"Tase?" He could hear Fadin yelling, "Tase hold on, just hold on."

He could not hold on. He was slipping away, and now Fadin sounded like a faint echo in a place full of silence and peace. He watched the world swirl into a dark mist, as all feeling left him. He felt warm, happy, he didn't have a care in the world. Then everything went black.

# Chapter 14

## *The Problem with Clearie*

Fadin sat, watching the limp form on the bed, his leg shaking uncontrollably and his nails becoming shorter with each bite.

He gazed breathlessly as his brother's chest moved slowly up and down as if he were afraid it might stop altogether.

Tase lay bundled to his chin in the old cobweb-covered bed. His face was whiter than the sheets, and his skin colder than ice. His chest moved so slightly that Fadin had to stare at the blanket for a few moments before he could be sure his breathing hadn't ceased.

He felt an overwhelming sense of guilt and panic as he sat in the old room hoping and praying that he would see Tase's eyelids flutter open.

He hadn't been able to think when Tase had lost consciousness. He had panicked and yelled for anyone to come. Luckily, the castle was too thick and no one heard, for Fadin realized what trouble they would both be in if their mother found out where they had been.

He had considered using the small piece of paper in his pocket to contact Lee Hogan, but he was too afraid that Mr. Hogan would be upset because they were outside. They had, after all, been warned repeatedly about that.

Before he had to think too hard however, a small voice had called to him.

When he turned, he saw Ciaran standing by the hidden tunnel. He told Fadin to bring Tase to him, so he obeyed. The little goblin touched Tase's forehead and mumbled something Fadin had not been able to understand. The small creature then nodded and, with a movement that Fadin couldn't see, placed his brother in the tunnel and managed to make the slide pull them up into the dark old attic.

Now he sat in the bedroom, which once must have been beautiful, but currently lay in dust-covered ruins, watching for any signs of life within his brother's motionless body.

Fadin turned as he heard the familiar "clunking" that told him Ciaran was coming over to them.

He watched as the goblin hobbled over with a tray containing a rag, a bowl, a small vial, and a tray of something steaming. "How is the thing?" Ciaran asked. "Wakes up at all, has him?"

Fadin shook his head.

"No worries," the goblin said with a smile. "Thing will be ups soon, you see."

"Thanks," Fadin said, biting his nails again. "What happened to him?"

"Mean water babies," Ciaran answered, putting the tray down.

"Mean what?"

The goblin looked up at him. "Small muirín, little water fitheal, baby vejvaim, water baby?"

Fadin simply stared dumbfounded.

Ciaran scratched his large ears. "How many water things you know?"

Fadin crinkled his forehead. "Um, I know there's fish…"

Ciaran pointed a skinny finger at him. "Yes, fish. Mean half-fish, half-thing, like you."

"What?"

"What is you called?"

"Fadin."

"No, not name, what creature you called?"

Fadin furrowed his brow, thoroughly confused. "You mean a human?"

Ciaran jumped up and down. "Yes, yes, mean part-human, part-fish."

"A mermaid?"

Ciaran nodded. "Yes, muirín, but little," he made his hands no longer than a pencil. "Very small baby fish-human. Spike things on back, and they like to pull things like you down to the coldest water. They have wet mouth stuff, "he spit on the ground and pointed, "that makes prey lose feelings in body. Then baby—how you say—mermaid, pull prey down and chomp." He made large crunching sounds.

"So those things were trying to eat Tase?"

"Yes, trying to eat."

"Will he be okay?"

"Me thinks so. He will get better. Just have to give fix drink and bites no bites."

"Give him what?"

"Bites no bites."

"Whats 'bites no bites'?" Fadin asked cocking his head.

Ciaran held up the steaming things. They were green cookies, with square bits sticking out here and there. He picked one up and took a large bite, "Bites," he put the cookie down, "no bites."

Fadin blinked and looked at the green 'bites no bites'. "You know, I really don't think green cookies are going to help Tase at all."

"Will help, and so will fix drink."

"Fix drink? What is that?"

Ciaran furrowed his brow, obviously trying to find the right word. "Meed-i-son?"

"Medicine?"

"Yes, that, medicine. I give to thing's brother and he will gets well." Ciaran put his cookies down and dipped the rag in the bowl, rung it out, and placed it over Tase's eyes. Then he picked up the small vial and pulled the lid off. "You thing help hold brother's mouth."

Fadin got up and opened Tase's mouth.

"He wills fight this medicine, so we have to keep him mouth open, understand?"

Fadin nodded.

Ciaran held the bottle above Tase's mouth and began to let the liquid fall.

As soon as it hit his tongue, Tase's eyes shot open. He thrashed and kicked trying to get up and in the process knocked the tray over which sent the water and cookies crashing to the floor.

Fadin held tight and kept him down.

Ciaran let the last bit drain from the bottle, then helped Fadin make Tase swallow the strong-smelling medicine.

After a short fight, Fadin saw Tase's throat move and he signalled for Ciaran to let him go. They moved away.

Tase shot up, spitting and wiping his tongue with his hands.

"What," he said, standing up and hacking, "was that?"

Fadin, feeling the horrible worry leave him, smiled and jumped on top of Tase.

"What's the matter with you?" Tase asked, when Fadin released him from the tight hug.

"Don't you ever fall down a well again, got it?"

Tase stared at him, obviously confused. "Alright, I won't."

Fadin nodded then turned to Ciaran. "Will he be okay now?"

The goblin nodded. "Okay now."

"Thanks, Ciaran," he turned to Tase, "we better go, Ma's been awake for awhile and it won't be long now till she comes looking for us."

Tase nodded and they turned for the door.

"Wait," Ciaran said, "did thing lose his bottle? Him memory?"

Fadin looked at Tase, who fumbled in his pocket.

"No," he said smiling, "still got it."

Fadin thought he saw Ciaran grimace, but he couldn't be sure, for the little goblin was grinning wide now.

"Good, you things be careful, and stay away from water. Dangerous to be around right nows, water baby season."

"Water what?" Tase asked.

"I'll explain later," Fadin said. He opened the door and they snuck down the stone stairs as quietly as they could. Once at the bookcase, Fadin placed his head against the door. "I don't hear anything," he whispered.

"Open it then," Tase whispered back.

Fadin pulled the small handle and the wood swung in. As the hall came into view, Fadin saw something that made his heart stop. On the floor in front of them lay Pathos and, to his horror, Clearie.

Clearie's mouth was open and his eyes popped, as big as saucers. "I," he said slowly, "I knew it!"

Fadin jumped at him but missed.

Clearie began to dart down the hall. "Ma," he screamed.

"Get him," Fadin yelled.

Tase jumped on Clearie's back, knocking him to the floor.

"Ma," Clearie shouted even louder. "Ma I found—"

But Fadin was on top of him now and had his mouth cupped. "Dry up, you bloody eejit."

Clearie kicked and mumbled, but there was nothing he could do.

Fadin racked his brains for an idea and suddenly one lit up in his head. "Listen to me, you thick tool. If you don't do what I say, then you'll be sorry. Do you remember that pot you saw in our room? Well that was real, it's a potion we're making and it puts you in a deep sleep. We did it before, remember? And that was an accident. If we gave it to you on purpose, who knows when you'd wake up. Plus it gives us the power to..." he thought quickly for something to scare him, "to control your body when you're really in dream land, so don't give us a reason to use it."

Clearie stopped struggling and became very quiet.

"Good," Fadin said catching Tase's eye. "Now I'm going to let you up, but you'd better be quiet, or I'll put that potion in your mouth so fast, you won't know what hit you."

He nodded to Tase and they both slowly got off the limp body.

Clearie just lay on the floor for a few moments, then turned slowly to them. "How?"

"It's a long story, Clearie," Tase said, "one we don't have time for right now."

"Yea," Fadin said giving him a hand, "so why don't you get up and stick with us. We can't trust you alone anymore."

"Oh really? And what does that mean? Are you going to read with me? Bathe with me? Sleep in my bed? Be in the bathroom when I used the toilet?"

"If we have to," Fadin said. "Whatever it takes."

Clearie glared at them.

"Alright," Fadin said, as Clearie stood up from the floor, "I suppose we'd better..."

But he let his voice fall away as a knock echoed through the castle.

"The tenth, it's today," Tase said smiling at him.

Fadin grabbed Clearie's arm, and together the four of them and Pathos ran to the door.

Enda turned, as they bounded around the corner, with one eyebrow raised and a small envelope in his gloved hands.

Fadin pushed Clearie forward. "It's for us, right?"

Enda furrowed his bushy brow. "Yes, but how did..."

"Lucky guess?" Tase interrupted.

Clearie gaped at them.

"Go ahead, Clear," Fadin said warningly, "open the nice envelope. We don't want our little talk forgotten, now do we?"

Clearie sneered as Enda handed over the letter. He pulled at the top and let a small piece of parchment land in his open hand.

"Dear Clearie, Fadin, and Tase," he read grimacing, "I would like to invite you all for a sleepover at my house tomorrow night. We will have games, food, music, and stay up all night long. Then the next morning, we will go and explore the woods with my father. We would love to have you come, please respond A.S.A.P. Signed, Aimirgin."

Fadin looked at Tase, who smiled broadly.

"That sounds… nice," Enda said, sounding suspicious. "That's from your new little friend, right?"

"Yup," Fadin answered, eyeing him suspiciously. He always tried to figure out where he had seen him before, but it never worked.

Enda nodded slightly.

"Well," Tase said, bouncing on his tiptoes, "we'd better go and ask Ma, huh?"

Clearie stared blankly, obviously not sure what to make of the invitation.

"We should," Fadin said, grabbing Clearie's arm. "Thank you, Enda."

The butler, or their uncle, rather, looked as though he wanted so say something else, but he simply shook his head and walked away.

"Where do you think Ma is?" Tase asked.

"I don't know, upstairs?"

"No," Clearie said, yanking his arm back, "she's in the dining room. I was supposed to go and get you two for breakfast."

"Oh, well, let's eat then…" Fadin started.

Clearie snorted. "Too bad it took you so long. Breakfast is over, it's been over for half an hour. Now Ma's worried sick and is sitting in there with Aunt Kyna, who we know is acting crazy, and you two have been playing around in the walls!" He glared at them. "I highly doubt we are going to be attending any sleepovers at Aimirgin's or anywhere else. In fact, I'd be surprised if you two weren't grounded again. For a month this time."

Fadin felt all the hope and excitement drain out of him. It couldn't be, they couldn't be in trouble, and they couldn't miss the event December 12th. The thing they had been planning for and hoping for. The thing they had talked about every day for over a month. Why did they always have to get caught?

Tase turned to him, the same look etched on his face. "What are we going to do?"

Fadin thought hard of something they could tell Ma, something to calm her down and allow them to attend the sleepover. He bit his nails and scratched his head, trying to find some answer. Then it hit him, the bulk in his pocket.

"Tase," he said, pulling the handkerchief out.

"Do you think they'll work like that?" Tase asked, removing his own.

Clearie looked from one to the other. "What will work? What are those?"

"Worth a try," Fadin said, ignoring Clearie's questions.

Tase nodded and clutched Clearie's arm. "Just don't say anything."

"Yea," Fadin added, "just keep that big gob of yours shut."

Clearie threw them both dirty looks.

When they entered the dining room, Fadin was surprised to see not only Kyna with their mother, but Miss O'Keefe as well.

Kyna was stroking her raven hair, while Miss O'Keefe was bent low, as if whispering to her.

As soon as they came in, however, the scene changed.

Their mother looked up and all the sadness and despair left, only to be replaced by a fire Fadin hadn't seen since their last grounding.

Perhaps there was going to be no December gathering for them after all.

"Where have you two been?" she demanded.

Fadin clutched the handkerchief in his pocket tight. "Exploring, around the house."

She looked away from them and let out a horrible giggle. "What a load of tripe."

Fadin winced. He had never heard his mother speak this way to them before.

She looked at them again. "You really expect me to believe that? You expect me to believe that all this time I've been calling you, looking for you, worried sick about you, that you've simply been exploring the house? Do I look dense to you, Fadin?"

He turned his eyes to the floor. "We didn't know you were looking for us."

She snorted. "It seems you never do. Clearie, where did you find them?"

This was it. It was all over. Clearie would tell her exactly where he found them, and then life as they knew it would be gone forever.

Fadin clamped his eyes shut and squeezed the handkerchief with all his might.

"I-I found them in an old closet, upstairs somewhere."

Fadin's eyes shot open. What did he just say?

"It was full of old clothes and junk. They really couldn't hear anything in there, and they were all the way in the back of it. I really don't think they heard you, Ma."

Fadin looked up and stared at him, mouth gaping. Was he hearing right? Clearie was defending them?

"They really couldn't hear me, Clearie, are you sure?"

Clearie looked at his mother, his blond hair falling in his face. "I'm sure."

Fadin clamped his mouth shut. Bloody hell, Clearie may have actually gotten them out of trouble.

The fire in Ma's eyes seemed to die and she sat limp in the chair. "I'm—I'm sorry boys," she looked back at the table. "I suppose I just, overreacted." She lifted the small cloth she was holding to her face again. "Just stay where you can hear me next time," she said trying to hold back tears, "alright?"

Fadin nodded. "Yes, Ma. I'm sorry we gave you a scare."

She nodded and held the cloth to her face.

"Um, Ma," Tase said, surprising Fadin. "We actually wanted to ask you a question."

"What is it?" she asked looking up at them.

"Well, Aimirgin, our friend, she uh, wrote us this letter, and we were wondering if we could go?" He handed her the letter.

She looked it over quickly, then glanced up from it as if in deep thought. "December 12th... is anything going on that day, Kyna?"

Fadin watched her carefully.

She appeared to be thinking too. "I don't think so."

Fadin saw Miss O' Keefe grimace as if she was trying hard to remember something.

"Don't remember," Fadin whispered, "Don't remember."

"Yes," Ma said looking at them again, "It would be fine for you to go. Just be back at a decent time the day after. Remember, Clearie's birthday is New Year's Eve, and we have things to prepare." She smiled at her oldest son.

Fadin looked at them all, astonished that they were being allowed to attend. "Alright," he said, trying to contain his shock and joy, "Thank you, Ma. We'll um, just be going now."

"Don't you want any breakfast?" she asked. "I know you two haven't eaten."

"No," Tase said smiling at Fadin, "we aren't hungry."

They left the dining room and walked silently until they reached the entrance.

"What was that?" Fadin asked Clearie, once they were sure there was no Enda around.

"Well, I don't exactly want to be given a sleeping potion, do I?"

Fadin arched a red eyebrow.

"Don't read into it," Clearie scowled.

Fadin folded his hands and looked up. "Thank you, Mr. Hogan, thank you so much." He turned to Tase. "Can you believe it?"

Tase smiled. "They really do work, and I think I figured them out. All you have to do is squeeze them and decide exactly what you want them to do." '

Fadin pulled out his handkerchief and looked at it. "Yea, that's what I did, and they couldn't figure out what was taking place on the 12th."

"What is taking place on the 12th?" Clearie asked, looking from one to the other nervously.

Fadin grinned. "Oh, you'll see." He pulled the small piece of parchment and tiny pencil from his pocket.

"What's that?" Clearie asked, peering over Fadin's shoulder as he wrote.

"None of your business," he said with a smile. When Clearie did not move away, he added, "just writing Aimirgin a response."

"How are you going to send it?"

"Already did."

"What?"

"She said she'll pick us up tomorrow at six in the evening."

Tase grinned and looked up. "Anything else we need to bring?" .

"Just some extra clothes is all."

Clearie waved his hands in the air. "What are you talking about? Where are we going, how could you have sent her a response, and how could she possibly have answered you already?"

Fadin put a hand on his shoulder. "Its alright, it will all make sense soon, my son."

"Hump off," Clearie shouted.

"Come, come now Clear, you don't want to make us angry do you?"

He glared at Fadin but didn't say a word.

"There's a good boy," Fadin said, patting Clearie's head.

Pathos barked.

"Not you Path," Fadin said smiling. "You're not the only dog in this castle."

Clearie's large ears turned pink.

"Well, I think we'd better head up to our room so we can make the necessary preparations. And Clearie," he said in a commanding voice, "you can sleep on the top bunk tonight. No reason to take any risks, right?"

~~~

Tase sat on the sofa in the sunroom. His leg shook uncontrollably and his wrist was hurting from the pressure of his head. He looked up at what he thought to be someone at the door, but unfortunately it was just the creaking of the floorboards as Enda moved about upstairs.

He looked at Fadin, who was staring out of the window again. Fadin sighed as nothing happened and made a circle around the room.

Clearie sat, looking nervous, on the couch opposite Tase. He was biting his fingernails and fidgeting with his backpack. He had acted this way since the invitation had arrived the day before. He was anxious, constantly jumped at every noise, and hardly spoke at all. Now he seemed even worse and refused to look at either of their faces.

Tase sighed and lifted his eyes to the ceiling, then to the small watch on his wrist. "It's already 6:14. I wonder what's keeping them."

"I don't know," Fadin answered, again peering out of the window, "but I can't take it much longer."

"Neither can I," Tase agreed. He let his leg bounce faster and glanced up the stairs. He wanted to go. He wanted to leave and get to Aimirgin's. He had been feeling antsy all day and was constantly worrying that their mother, Kyna, or the other adults would remember what was taking place on the 12th and try to stop them. It had to only be a matter of time, and each moment they spent in the castle was like the ticking of a bomb. Anything could set it off, and Tase felt that if they didn't leave soon, something surely would.

In fact, Aunt Kyna had come up to them twice earlier that day. She had appeared to want to tell them something. But as soon as she came near, she would forget whatever it was she wanted to tell them and walk away looking confused. Tase figured it was the handkerchiefs keeping her from remembering, and was ever grateful to Mr. Hogan.

Tase picked his head up as the sound of water hit the window.

"It's just the rain," Fadin said pacing.

Tase sighed and patted Pathos next to him.

The Bernese yawned and laid his head on Tase's lap.

Tase turned to Fadin. "Do you think," he gestured toward Clearie and lowered his voice, "anything will attack us?"

Fadin moved closer and whispered back. "With Mr. Hogan next to us? The man's a giant." He smiled and shook his head. "I don't think we have anything to worry about."

There was a knock on the door.

Pathos barked.

Tase felt a jolt of excitement rush up in his chest as he heard Enda coming to answer it.

"We got it!" Tase and Fadin yelled.

They beat him to the door and opened it wide.

There, standing in dark blue cloaks, stood Aimirgin, Colmcille, and the large grey wolf, or, as they now knew, Desmond.

"Hello," Aimirgin said, a wide smile on her face. "You all ready to go?"

"Yea," a shaky voice said behind them.

Tase turned and saw Clearie holding his backpack nervously.

"Hello," Colmcille said to Enda. He shook the rain off his long black hair, which was slung in a low ponytail, and held out his hand.

Enda, refusing to touch his hand, nodded his greeting, and turned to Tase and his brothers. "Your mother's not feeling well, so she said for you three to go on. Be careful though, and be sure to take your coats."

"No need," Colmcille said smiling. "Got three here already." He pulled three identical blue cloaks from a pocket somewhere on him.

Enda put on a fake little smile and pushed a stray lock of gray hair from his face. "Well, be careful then."

Tase stared at him oddly. Enda was suddenly acting very parental. If he didn't already know the man was his uncle, he may have been suspicious. But, knowing what he knew, it made Tase feel good that Enda was worried about them.

"Okay," Fadin said moving out of the door and grabbing a cloak. "See you later Enda, Path."

Tase looked back at them then followed Fadin out. "You coming, Clearie?"

Clearie stared at Desmond the wolf.

"Don't worry," Aimirgin said. "He's quite tame, I assure you."

Tase couldn't suppress his smile.

Clearie looked up at her, smiled feebly, and, taking one last look inside the castle, stepped out and joined the group.

Colmcille handed him a cloak.

Clearie quickly put it on, not taking his eyes off Desmond.

"Good," Colmcille said smiling, "we better be off. Keep close and don't wander away from the group." He nodded to Enda, who again smiled weakly, then lead them away from the door.

The night was cold and the rain hit Tase hard in the face. He pulled the cloak tightly around himself and closely followed Colmcille and his small lantern.

The wolf, Desmond, walked beside Colmcille and seemed to be looking for something. He crept low to the ground and constantly moved his head in all directions. He paid the others little attitude besides looking back at them now and then.

Tase shuddered as they entered the woods. The trees loomed over them and seemed scary in their leafless form. His last brush with the woman and the black dog came flooding into his mind. He was very grateful to have the Hogans with them.

He noticed Fadin looking in all directions. Obviously, he was trying to spot the black dog, who always seemed to loom here.

Tase decided to look for him too. As he turned his head to the right, he thought he saw light green eyes glaring from the inky blackness. He held his breath and watched as the eyes moved in the same direction they were walking in.

A stray beam of light from Colmcille's lantern hit the area of forest where the eyes dwelled, and Tase saw, to his horror, that the eyes did indeed belong to the black dog.

The animal noticed the light and darted further into the darkness.

But Tase could still see his eyes. Tase quickened his pace so that he was in step with Aimirgin. He thought of telling her what he had seen, but he didn't want to scare her, and besides, Desmond scared off that giant dirt weasel easily enough. How bad could one black dog be?

"Is your brother alright?" Aimirgin suddenly asked, nodding to Clearie.

Tase looked and saw that he was very pale and his wide eyes were staring blankly ahead. "He accidentally walked in on us," Tase said dropping his voice, to be sure Clearie couldn't hear, "creating the potion."

Aimirgin nodded. "I see. Does he know anything?"

"Not really," Tase said watching him. "I think he's just scared since Fadin threatened him with the potion."

"What?"

"He had to. That little snitch would have run out to Ma in an instant if we didn't have something to keep him quiet. We told him it would put him in a deep sleep," Tase smiled. "It worked too, he hasn't said a word."

Aimirgin looked over Tase's head. "I hope he isn't too frightened."

Tase let out a snort. "Well if he is, I wouldn't worry. I'm sure he'll recover."

Aimirgin gave him a reproachful look.

"Almost there," Colmcille shouted.

Tase looked ahead and saw the Hogan cabin coming into view. He could see several tall figures standing outside. As they got closer he saw they were the remaining Hogans.

Mr. Hogan and his sons came to meet them with umbrellas and towels.

"Come in," Mr. Hogan said. "Hurry along, come on."

Tase noticed that he was glancing in all directions as well, and was all but shoving them through the front door.

"Wait a minute, Da," Colmcille said. "I want to show Fadin and Tase something."

"Hurry it up then," Mr. Hogan said, moving Clearie inside. "It's not safe to be out here."

Colmcille waved his father away. "So, you wanted to know how he can do that, right?" he said, pointing to Desmond the wolf.

Tase and his twin nodded vigorously.

The grey canine moved close to them and with a violent shake, allowed the hair on his body to shed. It fell to the wet floor like water and within a few seconds, Desmond could be seen kneeling on all fours where the wolf had been. He was naked except for the hair that remained on his bottom half.

Colmcille handed him a cloak.

After putting it on, Desmond shook the remaining hair off and stood next to Tase and Fadin.

Tase felt the confounded look on his face. He knew the wolf had been Desmond, but it was such a shock to see him change. It was like having fairytales come true. "How did you do that?" Tase asked, wide-eyed.

"Yea," Fadin said. "What are you? A werewolf?"

Desmond laughed. "No, werewolves don't turn into regular wolves. They are a mutation between the two."

"Then are you a half-werewolf or something?"

"No," Desmond giggled, "neither. What I am, was an accident actually. I was—well, how to explain it to you? Ah, I know. Have you ever heard of wolfsbane?"

Tase cocked his head. "Isn't that a flower?"

"Yes," Desmond nodded, "It is. I'm not sure if you know this or not, but many of the werewolf, or lycanthrope myths—"

"Lycanthrope?" Fadin asked.

"It's the word they use for werewolves in Greek. Or Lycans, as they themselves prefer to be called."

"You know a werewolf?" Tase asked, astonished.

"Well, I know of them. And I have met one before, yes."

"Wow," Tase said in awe.

Desmond smiled. "Anyhow, as I was saying, wolfsbane is the root of many Lycan myths. The most common story goes, if you wear, smell, or eat wolfsbane on the full moon, you'll be turned into a Lycan."

"Is that true?" Fadin asked.

"No," Desmond laughed. "Its ridiculous, but nevertheless, wolfsbane does indeed have Lycan properties. It can, in some cases, reverse the effects of a werewolf bite."

"So you do turn into a werewolf if you're bitten, like in movies or books?" Fadin questioned.

"Well it's not exactly like the movies. You do have to be bitten yes, but you don't automatically turn into a werewolf if you simply receive a bite. If that were true, then the world would be overrun by Lycans." Desmond ushered them a little closer to the house. "You see, it's not accidental like books and TV portray it. A Lycan doesn't become bloodthirsty, turn into its mutant form, and accidentally turn someone into a werewolf. They do become bloodthirsty and kill accidentally, but humans cannot be turned Lycan by such an attack. A Lycan has to bite when in human form, and then feed the bitten individual its own blood.

"This can sometimes happen unintentionally, by instinct, a natural survival instinct. The Lycan in question can be overrun by its wolf side and, without thinking, bite and feed another being its own blood. By the time the werewolf realizes what it is doing, it's too late. But that only ever happens with newly turned Lycans. Like in my case."

"But I thought you said you weren't a werewolf?" Tase argued, confused now.

"I'm not," Desmond repeated. "But by all accounts I should be one. You see I was bitten and fed the blood of a newly turned Lycan when I was eight. An accident if there ever was one, but nevertheless, it happened. I should have turned, but my race—I mean, my family, seems to have an unusual resistance to the werewolf toxin. My parents decided to try and treat me with wolfsbane. The plant did work, it stopped me becoming a Lycan, but, unfortunately, not enough was known about the flower. While it does stop certain Lycan qualities, it adds some of its own. I was cured of my illness, but I received some wolf traits, like having a lot of body and facial hair. I also acquired the ability to turn into a wolf, which at first was uncontrollable, but as I've grown I've learned to command it. In a way, I am much like a half-Lycan. But I am lucky in the fact that I do not crave blood and have full control over my changing."

"Wow," Tase breathed, "that is so cool!"

Desmond smiled. "You think so, huh?"

Fadin nodded. "Oh, yes. Can you change for us again?"

Desmond and Colmcille laughed.

"Okay, but just once more."

"Hey," Mr. Hogan poked his head out the door, "It's not safe out here, and it's raining. You've been outside long enough—come inside this instant."

Desmond smiled, "Alright, Da." He put his hands on Tase and Fadin's shoulders, "I'll show you again tomorrow, okay?"

Tase grinned.

Desmond and Colmcille lead the way in.

Tase looked at Fadin, who mouthed, "I love this family."

Tase smiled as the warm feeling in the pit of his stomach spread throughout his whole body. "So do I," he whispered, looking up at the sliver of moon he could see through the cloud cover. "So do I."

# Chapter 15

## *The Winter Fair*

"Get up, Fadin!"

Fadin sat bolt upright, his vision blurred from sleep, his heart pounding. "What, what is it?"

"Time to go. The Hogans, me, and Clearie are already up and dressed."

Fadin looked down at his sleeping bag then met Tase's eyes.

"What? Why didn't you wake me sooner?"

"I tried," Tase said. "We all did, but you were being a sleeping princess."

Fadin jumped out of his bed on the floor and ripped open his backpack. He found the shirt and trousers he was looking for, undressed, and pulled them on.

"Hurry up, you little dope," Quinlan said bounding in the living room. "You're sleeping the day away." He smiled and knocked Fadin in the shoulder.

"I'm up, I'm ready," Fadin said shoving on his shoes. "Let's go."

"Hold on now," Quinlan said flinging himself on the couch. "Why don't you wait for the rest of us?"

Fadin looked at him, then at Tase, and saw they were still in their night clothes.

"Those were some nice knickers though," Quinlan said, making an OK sign. "Lovely."

"Why, you little eejit," Fadin said throwing a pillow at his brother.

Tase dodged it and broke into laugher along with Quinlan.

"Oh you have to admit, that was a good one," Tase giggled.

Fadin snorted. "Ha ha, very funny, now why don't you get going, you muzzy?"

Tase smiled then grabbed his own backpack.

"Morning," Mr. Hogan said, walking into the room. "Fadin, dressed already?"

"Yea," Quinlan said, "he couldn't wait."

Mr. Hogan smiled. "Well maybe you should get your lazy bum up and do the same. Your brothers and sister are dressed too."

Quinlan smiled and rolled of the couch. "Be back in a tick." He bounded out of the room then disappeared up the stairs.

"Got your potion and your memories?" Mr. Hogan asked, turning to them.

"Yea," Tase said, pulling his bottles out from the backpack.

"Good, keep them in there and don't lose them."

Fadin looked around the room. "Where's Clearie?"

"In the kitchen," Mr. Hogan answered. "He's helping Cormick set up for breakfast." He handed Fadin and Tase their blue cloaks. "I dried them; they should be nice and warm for our trip."

Fadin took his and stroked it. He hadn't noticed how soft it had been the night before. In fact, now that he thought about it, he had hardly even been wet or cold when they had arrived at the Hogan's cabin.

"All we have to do now is eat, gather our packs, and we'll be off," Mr. Hogan said, glancing about the room. "And I suggest you eat heartily, we've got a long walk ahead of us."

Fadin did eat more then his share. It was hard not to. The black pudding, bacon, and bread were to die for. In fact, everything the Hogans made was amazingly delicious.

When they were all finished and the dishes cleared, they left the warm house and travelled out into the morning air.

Mr. Hogan and Desmond lead the way, while Colmcille and Cormick took turns beating on one another. Quinlan talked with Clearie, who seemed a little more normal then he had the night before, and Aimirgin talked with Fadin and Tase.

"We'll be there in half an hour," Mr. Hogan said. "That'll put us at 8:30. Perfect." He turned and smiled, then continued to lead through the dead-looking forest.

The hike was cold but nice. The sun was out and Fadin could see through the forest clearly. He constantly looked for the black dog and his red-headed friend, but he saw neither. Perhaps they were afraid of Mr. Hogan?

After about ten minutes of not seeing any sign of the two, he decided to join in on the conversation with Aimirgin and Tase. They discussed the Glomhan in their mirror and the Water Baby incident.

Aimirgin shook her ebony head at Tase for falling into the well. Her dark eyes twinkled with disapproval, and she even stumbled when trying to explain the dangers of being in a large body of water so near to this time of year. Water Babies, according to her, were very dangerous; their favorite meal was human children. She concluded that the well must be completely infested with them since Tase had lost all feeling in his body so quickly.

"So, Aimirgin," Fadin grinned, running a hand through his orange-red hair. "Where are we going?"

Aimirgin shook her dark head. "Nope, I'm not telling you. We'll be there soon enough."

"Oh, come on. Can't you just give me a hint?"

"Okay," Aimirgin smiled, "there's the hint." She pointed with her olive-skinned hand directly in front of them.

The sky suddenly became grey and Fadin snapped his head forward.

A very dense fog lay directly in their path. It rolled and twirled, blocking out the sun and whatever it was that waited for them further in the forest.

"We're going in there?" Fadin asked, looking at Aimirgin then Mr. Hogan.

"Everyone in a straight line," Mr. Hogan said.

They obeyed and fell behind one another.

"Now," Mr. Hogan continued, "when you go through the barrier, follow the person directly in front of you. Do not turn to one side or the other, do not go back, walk completely straight. Once you're through, don't stop, keep going till you're clear of the mist or someone's bound to run into you." He looked at them all. "Understood?"

They nodded.

"Alright then, follow me."

He walked directly into the thick cloud and was gone.

Next was Desmond, then Cormick and Colmcille. After them went Quinlan and Tase, Clearie, and then it was Fadin's turn.

He walked forward, stared into the swirling fog, took a deep breath, and walked through. Everything felt light and wet. He couldn't even see his hand in front of his face. He moved forward and stretched his hands out, so as not to run into anything.

Suddenly, there was a low rumble that came from Fadin's right. He paused. Should he turn to face it? Should he run left, or just go back? But then Mr. Hogan's words came back to him, "Do not turn to one side or the other, do not go back, walk completely straight." Fadin gulped. He furrowed his brow in determination and kept going forward. The rumble became louder and it turned into a growl, but Fadin did not stop. He kept walking onward.

He began to get a little panicky as the mist seemed to stretch on forever, but then, just as he decided he would turn back, light peeked through and sounds. He began to see shapes, movement, and the way out. Butterflies and relief danced in his stomach as he pushed back the light sheet of fog that was left. He took a deep breath, let excitement completely take him over, and stepped out of the swirling, twirling vapour.

~~~

Fadin stood just outside the giant cloud, dazed, confused, and in complete and utter shock.

Elves, goblins, trolls, large reptiles, horse-men, furry animal-like creatures, things with wings, beings with horns, huge ears, and multiple eyes, all moving, laughing, eating, playing, and existing, in the clear cool meadow before him.

There were food stands and shopping trolleys. Tents and huts filled with things to buy. Musicians, storytellers, and salesmen lined the narrow walkways.

Fadin jumped as an enormous, long-necked reptile stepped not a centimetre from his face, and moved directly down the centre of one of the narrow aisles. A small puffy thing rolled close to its feet, keeping time with the long footfalls.

To the left, Fadin noticed an almost cat-like creature sitting on a small stool playing a fiddle with several other bizarre beings. To his immediate right, a small blue thing was selling what looked like jewellery, trying to interest passerby in his merchandise.

Fadin blinked, trying to clear his head. This couldn't be real, this just couldn't. It was like stepping out of reality and into one of Clearie's books. Besides the creatures that were here, which were indeed impossible, the meadow itself looked like something out of a book, or even out of the dark ages. The whole plain was covered in carts and tents that looked like they belonged in the time of knights and kings, when women only wore pretty dresses and awaited their princes to rescue them from a dragon-guarded tower. In fact, now that Fadin looked, he saw women only in long flowing dresses, made of silk and other light material.

Fadin's head was swimming. He just couldn't grasp this, it was all too magnificent to believe.

"Watch it," he suddenly heard Mr. Hogan say. Mr. Hogan put a hand on his back and moved him out of the way before Aimirgin burst through the swirling mist.

Aimirgin stumbled, not surprisingly, and took out a small, nine-legged creature as she fell. "Sorry, sorry, so sorry," Aimirgin bumbled.

Fadin gaped up at Mr. Hogan and watched as he stretched out his long arm. "Welcome," Mr. Hogan said happily, "to the Dalbhachs *uair* a year, winter fair."

Fadin, feeling dizzy, looked up into Mr. Hogan's face, but jerked away as he noticed Lee did not look like himself. His neck looked very long, much longer than any normal person's. His eyes were most certainly darker, they could by no means be mistaken for the brown Fadin had taken them for, because they were the deepest shade of onyx he had ever seen. His neck, arms, and hands were covered in odd markings, almost like a giraffe's spots, and his ears were pointed at the tips. When Fadin looked down, he saw that Mr. Hogan wasn't wearing what he had thought to be dark shoes, but instead had cloven hooves for feet.

Fadin turned and looked at Cormick, Desmond, Quinlan, Colmcille, and Aimirgin. They all had the same changes.

Fadin felt his heart pound faster. This was not possible.

"Don't be afraid," Mr. Hogan said.

Fadin glanced to his right and saw Clearie and Tase huddled together, wide-eyed and confused.

"We aren't the humans you took us for," Mr. Hogan explained gently. "We're Farógs. Creatures who, well, don't exactly belong in the human world."

Fadin pulled further away and stared at them. "Why couldn't we see the way you really were before?"

"Because we hid it," Aimirgin said. "Our kind often lives among humans, we just don't show them our true appearance."

"We have a certain ability that allows us to control what we look like to others around us," Desmond said, moving closer. He was still very hairy, but the changes in him were identical to the rest of his family.

"We only did it so we wouldn't frighten you," Mr. Hogan said. "Would you have come near us if you saw what we really look like?"

Fadin raised his eyebrows and again gazed at them all. They were the same people, the same family. They were still the kind neighbours they had been, the people who had, by all standards, taken them in and told them the truth. They just looked a little different, that's all.

"Well," Tase said moving closer, "I guess that explains why you're all so tall then?"

Mr. Hogan smiled. "Yes, that explains it."

There was a sudden horrified scream from behind them.

Fadin turned, startled, to see Clearie shaking and staring, horror-struck, at everything around him. "What's going on?" he yelped.

"We're at a magical convention, you big dope," Fadin mocked. "Can't you see the fairytale creatures around you?"

"How? How is this possible? How do you—how did they?" Clearie stumbled over his words.

"Ma's been lying to us, Clearie," Tase said, walking to him. "Her, Da, Aunt Kyna, Enda, Daireann, even Miss O'Keefe. They all know about this stuff. Look," he pulled out a piece of paper from his backpack. "That's Da and Mr. Hogan."

Fadin smiled. He remembered how he had stolen that picture before they left. He thought it'd be a good idea to have some kind of proof when they broke the news to Clearie. It seemed to have been a good idea, so far.

Clearie took the picture and gazed at it.

"They were friends, Clear, best friends," Tase said, looking at the photo over his brother's shoulder. "Ma's been lying. Her and Da lied to us this whole time."

"But," Clearie said, tracing the picture with his finger, "how did you find out?"

"We found that wooden carving," Fadin said. "You know, the one you smashed to bits."

Clearie looked up. "I knew it. I knew there was something odd about that thing."

"You were right," Tase said. "We found it and used it to open the bookcase."

"Then we met Aimirgin," Fadin said, nodding to her. "And we found that picture of Da and Mr. Hogan. It all just sort of, fell into place."

Clearie handed the photo back to Tase. "So this," he looked at the large meadow covered with strange creatures, "these, they're our people?"

"Yes," Mr. Hogan said, "and I thought you all deserved to know where you came from. Where you really came from."

"And Ma," Clearie said, "she doesn't know? I mean, that you know about all this?"

"No," Fadin said, "and we aren't going to tell her either."

Clearie nodded and stared at the ground. "So what is this place?" he asked, looking up at Fadin then Tase.

Fadin smiled. "I don't know." He turned to Mr. Hogan. "This is a...um...magical fair?"

"You could say that," Mr. Hogan said. "We all gather here once a year in the winter. Its fun, social, and we get to buy a lot of things that aren't in normal stores."

"Cool," Fadin said, looking out at the many trolleys. "Can we have a look?"

Mr. Hogan grinned widely. "Let's go then." He led the herd down the first aisle.

Fadin, Tase, and Aimirgin moved ahead of the group, gawking and pointing at this and that.

Fadin saw a stand selling makeup that put itself on, rings that talked, mops that cleaned by themselves, and shoes that tied on their own. There were dozens upon dozens of carts with food and even a tent where large trolls hammered weapons.

Above the tent, where the large creatures were hammering away, was an old tattered sign. It looked to be written in two different languages—one Fadin had never seen, and the other was English. It read:

***Prices for Weaponry: Spear****: colour of hair* ***Bronze Hilted Short Sword****: two childhood memories* ***Falcata****: four fingernails* ***Iron Long Sword****: colour of eyes* ***Broad Sword****: eleven elf hairs* ***Ring Pommel Broad Sword****: two gold doorknobs* ***Flail****: two grams of rain* ***Dagger****: two centimetres of dust* ***Dirk****: colour red to the second falley* ***Bow****: ten tears*

People in the crowd didn't seem too interested in the swords and other weapons, but many of them were congregating by a small stand with a large-eared creature who was yelling something.

"A clock, a cookbook, and a memory all in one," the creature shouted. "If you get an idea for a recipe it will write it down for you. Open it later, and there it is, the recipe that simply popped into your head. All you have to do is say it and the Clookory will remember it for you." He held up the

270

same small, triangular clock Fadin had seen in both Daireann's and Mr. Hogan's kitchens.

"When you're racking your brains for something tasty and you're drawing a blank, the alarm will sound. Just open it up and see a new recipe. If you make adjustments so you make the meal your own, it will save them for you.

"Plus this little beauty comes with a built-in timer. Just make your meal and it will set itself. And if you have a big family, the Clookory can even make you a food schedule. Never have to worry what's for dinner again, simply open it up and there is the plan.

"Whether you're an expert cook or can't even melt butter, the Clookory's right for you. Buy one now, impress your friends, and you'll never have to order magic meals again. Take one now and we'll even throw in a second one for free!"

"That actually does work that," Mr. Hogan said, coming up behind them. "I haven't had to plan for dinner in over six months."

Fadin smiled and turned his head to another loud voice, one that was obviously trying to drown out the Clookory salesman's.

"Come on up and take a seat," a furry creature was yelling. "We'll snap a photo, it's really neat. Instead of sitting dull and snoring, this one sings so it's not at all boring. We take the pic and add a spell, get a sample of your voice, and all is well. If your voice is terrible, it will sing with bliss. If your singing is lovely, you just can't miss, this one-time offer two for free, if you just buy one now, what a minuscule fee. So come on over and see the new fad, the one fourteen years ago that we all had. With prices like these you can't say nay, come on now, we're practically giving them away!"

Tase nudged Fadin with his elbow.

Fadin nodded. Now they knew where the annoying picture in their closet came from and why it constantly sang.

"Oh," Aimirgin cried, spotting a makeup stand selling lipstick that made girls' lips swell to a larger size. "I'll be right back."

Fadin rolled his eyes. "Girls."

Tase smiled.

"I'm going to check that book stand out," Clearie said, walking over to a large dusty trolley.

Tase looked at the tent near the book stand. "I want to have a closer look at those swords."

Fadin watched as everyone walked off in different directions, then saw something that caught his own eye.

A large, long-bearded creature was holding up a small box and passing it out to the men walking by. "Stache-a-grow! Come on up and try some, folks. It'll make your hair grow so fast you won't know what hit you. Put it on your face or your head and within ten minutes you'll have all the hair you want. Cheaper than potion and more efficient too. Just try it on and take a look, you simply can't go wrong."

Fadin walked near the stand and peered into one of the several mirrors on the sides of the cart. He felt his face and imagined what it would look like if he had hair there.

"Sorry, boy," the creature said spotting him. "It's only for those who are old enough to grow their own beard, and those who can actually reach the counter. Not for little boys like you."

Fadin snorted and turned quickly to walk away.

Smack!

He bumped into something hard.

"Ouch," someone wailed.

He looked down and saw a small girl rubbing her forehead.

"Oh, I'm sorr—"

But the girl scrunched up her nose and sneezed directly into Fadin's face.

He saw something small and brown fly toward him. He closed his eyes tight.

"Sorry 'bout that," the girl said. "They're always comin' off."

Fadin opened his eyes and saw something moving on his nose. As he looked closer, he saw it was a small dot. A freckle. Several freckles in fact.

"These are yours?" he asked, blinking at the small girl. She looked familiar somehow.

"Yea, they like to escape. Me da says they'll grow out of it, but I don't know, because his snake still climbs up on his face at night, and he's never stopped doin' that."

"What?"

"Me da, he has a snake tattoo. Doyle, he calls him. Never listens to a thin' he's told."

"And this tattoo, it moves?"

"Of course it moves, silly, what else would it do? Did you really think a snake would stay still on a Geartú?" she asked with a shake of her dark red head.

Fadin stared. "A what?"

"You know, a Geartú, a Gear, or Get." She looked at him and furrowed her brow. "Have you been livin' under a rock? What, have you been raised by an Ainondall or somethin'?"

"Huh?"

"Hi, Aednat!"

Fadin turned and saw Aimirgin walking towards them. Suddenly, who the girl was came crashing into Fadin's memory. She was the little girl in the picture on Aimirgin's fridge.

The girl kept her large brown eyes on Fadin. "Hi, Aimirgin."

"How've your sisters been?" Aimirgin asked, standing next to them both.

"Good I suppose, they're around here somewhere," she waved her hand nonchalantly. She was still staring, unblinking, at Fadin.

"I see you've met Fadin."

The girl looked startled. "You know this Ainobhach?"

"Don't call him that!"

"Well he is," Aednat said, moving so close to him that Fadin felt her breath on his face. "He doesn't even know what a Geartú is. If that's not an Ainobhach, then I don't know what is." Her short hair fell in her eyes and Fadin saw that her ears spiked in four places.

"That's a horrible thing to say, Aednat Mykaela Aislinn."

The girl scrunched up her face. "Come on," she said whistling. "Get away from that Ainobhach."

Suddenly, the little brown dots shuddered and flew from Fadin's face onto hers.

"He is not," Aimirgin said folding her arms.

"Well then how come he doesn't know anythin'?"

Fadin suddenly entered the conversation, feeling defensive. "I know things," he said, standing straighter.

"Oh really," Aednat snorted, standing on her tip-toes so she was nearly the same height, "then what is a Fitheal?"

Fadin didn't say anything.

"That's what I—"

"It's a goblin," Fadin said with a sneer. He folded his arms in satisfaction and thankfulness at knowing Ciaran.

"Well," Aednat said standing flat again, "that's an easy one."

"Enough," Aimirgin growled. "He's my friend and he came with our family, so be nice Aislinn."

Aednat crinkled her nose. "Fine Hogan, but tell me the truth. Is he Ainodall?"

"You know it's against the law to bring them here."

"Did I ask you what the law says?"

Aimirgin made her eyes into small slits. "He's not."

Fadin looked from one to the other as they stared.

"Fine," Aednat finally said, "then was he raised by one?"

"So what if he was?"

"Well then he doesn't belong here, and that would make him an Aino…"

"Don't you dare call him that again," Aimirgin spat, stretching to her full height, which towers over little Aednat. "For your information, he wasn't raised by an Ainodall, he was raised by one of the most powerful Dalbhach families Ireland has ever known."

Aednat arched one of her dark-red eyebrows.

"Teagan Kavanagh."

Aednat's eyes looked as though they could pop from their sockets. "He's a Kavanagh?" She looked Fadin up and down. "You mean they're back? Teagan and Alroy, after all this time, they've come home?"

Fadin flinched at the sound of his father's name. It was still hard to hear other people talk about him, people he hadn't known had been a part of his father's life. A life Fadin and his brothers had never really known.

"Well," Aimirgin said, seeing Fadin's reaction, "Teagan's back."

"You mean her and Alroy split up?" Aednat threw her hands in the air. "Oh, boy! I think she about broke every boy's heart in Glas Cavan, at least that's what me ma says. Did you know—"

"Shut your gob. They didn't split up, Aednat." Aimirgin said, her voice harsh. "He—he's d—"

"He's dead?"

Fadin turned around to where the deep voice had come from. There was no one there.

He furrowed his brow. "Who said—"

"My brother—my baby brother. He—he's gone?"

Fadin looked down at his feet and saw a tiny man standing in the middle of them. The man reached no higher then Fadin's knee. His body was rotund and squatty, his hair was orange-red and thinning at the top, and when Fadin looked into his face, the small man reminded him of his father so much, that he had to fight away tears. He looked very similar to his father, except for the fact that his eyes were blue, not the chocolate brown of his father's, he had a thick beard, and this little man wore glasses and had quite a high-pitched voice.

"He's dead? Alroy?" The little man asked, gaping up at them. "Someone answer me!"

"Yes," Fadin said bending down, "he's dead."

The little man's eyes began to fill with tears. "You, you're his son, aren't you?"

Fadin heard footsteps behind him. "Yes, and so are they." He turned and pointed at Clearie and Tase who were walking toward him.

"So are we what?" Clearie asked.

"You're Alroy O'Callaghan's sons," the little man cried. "My brother's sons."

Tase looked at Fadin.

"How did he die, my brother?"

Fadin tried to swallow the lump in his throat. "He died in an accident. A car accident."

The little man nodded then covered his face and began to sob.

"Lorcan," Another little red-haired man ran under Aimirgin's feet. "What is it Lorcan? What's wrong?"

Fadin felt his heart stop. Lorcan? The man his father went to work with? The only coworker he had ever heard his father talk about? This was him? This was his uncle?

"My brother," the first little man sobbed, "Alroy. He's dead, Feidhelm, he's gone!"

The tiny man called Feidhelm patted Lorcan on the shoulder while, Fadin noticed, fighting back his own tears. He was taller then Lorcan, and much leaner. His hair was also red and spiked high. His eyes shone a deep green, his nose sat long on his face, and his chin was lined with a small beard.

Lorcan looked up and shook his head. "I knew there was something wrong, Feidhelm. I knew it when Alroy didn't show up for work. I knew it since he's been missing, but I just hoped…" He had to stop for his sobbing, "I had hoped that he and Teagan had decided—decided to run again." He sobbed even louder, and Feidhelm had to help hold him up.

"We all did, Lorcan, we all did."

Lorcan pointed to Fadin and his brothers. "That's them, Feidhelm, that's his boys. Clearie, Fadin, and Tase."

Fadin stood up and looked at his twin. "You knew about us?"

"Of course we did," Lorcan said, taking huge hiccup-like breaths. "We knew all about you and your sister. Your father was so proud of you all."

"You saw him?" Tase asked bending down. "I mean, you've seen him recently?"

Lorcan nodded and wiped his face. "He had been working here in Glas Cavan for almost five years now."

Fadin felt the colour drain from his face. "He had been coming here every day, for *five years*?"

Lorcan nodded.

Fadin took a deep breath. His father had been working at the bank for five years, it made sense. But what a liar. And what about Mr. Hogan? He had said he hadn't seen him since his da and ma had left. He had lied too?

Fadin turned to Aimirgin, his temper boiling. "You liar!"

The colour drained from her face. "What?"

"You and your father. You both lied!"

"No, Fadin, we didn't."

"Yes you did, your father told me my da hadn't been back here in over fourteen years."

"No he didn't, he told you he hadn't seen him in over fourteen years, and he hasn't. We didn't know he was back."

"Sure you didn't. And I suppose it was just an accident that you found me by the hole in our castle?"

"It was, Fadin, honest."

"Liar!"

"Fadin," Tase said, moving between them, "maybe they really didn't know."

"Don't be a blind ape, Tase. Of course they knew."

"No, they didn't," Feidhelm said. "It was a secret. He didn't want anyone but family to know," He patted Lorcan on the back and let him stand on his own. "I'm his cousin, second cousin to you, I suppose." He held out a small hand. "Feidhelm Forest Malone."

Fadin felt his cheeks burning and the tears beginning to fall from his eyes. He didn't know what to believe anymore. Everyone lied, his mother, his supposed aunt, even his deceased father had lied about everything he thought had been true. He couldn't trust anyone.

Tase looked at him with an understanding frown, then nodded at the small red-haired man with his tiny arm outstretched. When Fadin made no reply, he bent down and shook Feidhelm's hand with his pinkie.

"I'm Tase." He shot Fadin a glance.

Reluctantly, Fadin wiped his face, then shook Feidhelm's hand as well. "Fadin, and that's Clearie."

Clearie made no attempt to greet the little man.

"It's wonderful to finally meet you all," He said with a smile. "It's just a pity your father couldn't be here too."

Lorcan pulled out a small handkerchief and after blowing his tomato-like nose, nodded in agreement. "Yes, I couldn't be happier to meet you boys, or happier that your mother is finally back and ready to tell you all the truth."

"Well," Fadin said, trying to keep his voice calm, "she is back, but as for telling us the truth...I have to say she's in short supply. Fresh out, actually."

Lorcan looked up at them, obviously surprised. "Oh, she hasn't...how are you here then?"

"The Hogans brought them," Aednat said. "I suppose he thought they deserved the truth." She looked at Fadin and gave him a weak smile. She no longer seemed upset or ready for a fight.

"Yes, he did," Tase said, removing the single tear that had escaped his eye. "He's been the only honest person we've known."

Lorcan nodded and moved his eyes over all of them. "I'm sorry you didn't know the truth."

"I'm sorry we didn't know our father," Fadin said coolly.

Clearie glared at him. "We did know him, just not all of him. I'm sure that he had a good reason to—keep things from us."

"Sure," Fadin snorted, "whatever makes you feel better, Clearie."

Tase knocked him with his elbow and shook his head. "Enough, Fadin."

Fadin bit his lower lip and stared at the ground.

"So," Tase said, "what um, what are you anyway?"

Lorcan seemed to perk up at this question. He pushed his glasses up his face and bowed so his nose nearly touched the ground. "A Leprechaun, my dear nephew. Lorcan Tristian O'Callaghan."

"So, that means we're half Leprechaun?" Clearie asked, putting a hand to his forehead as if he had just become aware of a pain there.

"It does indeed, my good nephew."

Fadin picked his head up. "How was our father so tall then?"

Lorcan shook his head. "I don't know, freak of nature, happens sometimes. And we have a bit of giant blood running through our veins, although, it's been several times removed. I suppose it just decided to show up in Alroy. Although by human standards, he wasn't tall at all."

Fadin nodded.

"Well," Lorcan said breathing in deeply, "since we have the privilege of meeting each other, and since I don't know the next time I'll get to see my nephews, would you mind if I spent some time with you? Got to know my brother's children, the boys he talked so much about?"

Fadin looked at him and smiled. "No, Lorcan, I think we'd all like that."

He smiled back broadly. "Then why don't you follow me, I know all the best trolleys, and can get you outrageously cheap prices."

"Sure you can, Lorcan," Feidhelm joked. "Even though you don't have a single friend at the fair who didn't know me first?"

Lorcan let out a sarcastic laugh. "Ha, that's rich, considering I work in Cavan-Corr."

The little Leprechauns lead the group down one of the long aisles of trolleys, carts, and tents.

"Fadin," Aimirgin said, grabbing hold of his arm and pulling him aside,

"I'm sorry if you thought, if you felt…"

"No," Fadin said shaking his head, "I'm sorry, Aimirgin. I should have realized you and your father wouldn't lie to me." He fixed his eyes on the ground. "Tase was right, you know. Your family have been the only people who have ever been honest with us."

Aimirgin touched his shoulder. "I'm sure your mother will tell you, in time."

Fadin glanced at her incredulously. "Maybe, I hope so."

She tried to give him an uplifting smile. "Well, we'd better follow them, huh?"

Fadin nodded but turned back when he noticed Aednat, the little red-headed girl, walking the other way.

"Hey," he shouted to her, "aren't you coming?"

She turned around and grimaced. "Didn't want to break up a family reunion, seein' how it's so complicated and all."

Fadin smirked. "I don't think it could get any more complicated than what you already saw."

She smiled, cute dimples standing out on her freckled cheeks. "Alright then, I suppose I can tag along." She ran up and walked next to Fadin. "I'm sorry for callin you an Ainobhach."

"That's okay," Fadin said, "I didn't know what it meant anyway." He furrowed his brow. "What does it mean?"

"Well, it means you were raised by, act like, or are, an Ainondall."

"And what's an Ainondall?"

"Well, technically it means ignorant, gullible, and blind. But we use it as a name for, well, non-magic humans or other creatures."

Fadin nodded. "Oh, so what does Geartú mean?"

Aednat scrunched her face in concentration. "I think it means, amputate and tattoo. I'm not sure though, because we learn what new creature's names mean every week and that one was a while back."

"Where do you learn it?"

"School, of course. Don't Ainon—I mean, humans, go to school?"

"Obviously they do. How else would we—um—they, have cars and things like that?"

"Cars?"

"Yea you know, the things on wheels. They use keys and gas?"

Aednat stared.

"Oh," Fadin said folding his arms and staring down at her, "so now who's the one who doesn't know anything?"

She shook her short, dark-red hair and glared at him. "Well how am I supposed to know about Ainondalls and what they do? I am only ten, and most Dalbhach schools don't teach that stuff till we're eleven."

"Sure they don't."

"That's right, they don't. And if you knew anythin', then you would know that, wouldn't you?"

"Say whatever you want Freckles, but I know the truth."

"What truth?" she spat, her little freckled face becoming flushed.

"That you," he patted her on the head like he would a dog, "don't know anything."

"I do to!"

He simply smiled to himself and moved in to see why Tase and the others had stopped.

"Look at those fancy ones," Feidhelm was saying, "bet they cost a pretty dragon feather."

"Yea, or more then that," Aimirgin said, leaning over the cart to touch something.

Fadin moved in close enough to see several beautiful carpets laid out across the cart's counter. "What are they?" he asked, leaning over to stroke one.

"Magic carpets," Lorcan said, "can help you get around when you don't have a potion on hand."

The carpet gave a little shudder as Fadin touched it.

"What about brooms?"

"Brooms?" Feidhelm laughed. "No, we don't use brooms around here. We mostly use potions, spells, or Orthanach dust. Only occasionally will you see a Dalbhach or other creature riding a magic carpet, but never a broom."

"Why? Don't they work?" Tase asked.

"Oh I'm sure they do, but we just don't care for them, too much to carry around and too dangerous. In fact, about thirty years ago we did have a big broom market, but I guess we Irish don't know how to fly 'em because we had all sorts of terrible accidents, so the King banished them."

"The King? You mean Ireland has a king too?"

"Yea of course we do, the Dalbhach side anyway. King Raegan, at the moment."

"Why not a Prime Minister like the humans?" Clearie asked, now tuned into the conversation.

"Well actually," Lorcan said, turning so he could look at them, "he's more like a Prime Minister. He really isn't a king for all respects and purposes, but we just never got rid of the title. He, like a Prime Minister, is the head, but then comes the deputy Prime Minister or Advisor to the King, and then the Council of Ministers, or as we call them, The Council of

Princes. The Council is who handles all the day-to-day rules and problems, the king and his advisor handle anything big or something that concerns all of Ireland. In fact if I'm not mistaken, Kyna, your aunt, is on the Council."

"Kyna is on the Council of Princes?" Tase asked.

"Yes, she is. I'm surprised she's stayed on for as long as she has, actually. She doesn't agree to or bend to the will of others very well. As a matter of fact she just got into some trouble for not signing the new peace treaty, I believe. I noticed she wasn't at work for a while, and I know Puceula, the Advisor to the King, had a lengthy and heated discussion with her."

"Yea, we kind of heard about that," Fadin said catching Tase's eye. "Aunt Kyna, was freaking out about signing some kind of paper. It took our ma and three other people just to calm her down. She was completely off her nut."

"Ah, a hex," Lorcan said nodding. "He gets them every time with that. Old Puceula is far more cunning and dangerous than anyone gives him credit for. The other Council Members and I decided just to sign the thing and get it over with. Not like fighting about it would make much difference."

Clearie looked at him. "You're on the council too?"

"Yep, and so is Mr. Malone here," he nudged his cousin in the shoulder.

"What did our da do?" Tase asked.

"He worked at the bank," Lorcan said with a grin.

"Well at least when he told us he was going to work at the bank he was sort of being honest," Fadin said sarcastically.

"Son of a Troll," Lorcan gasped. "It's Devi. Oh, no. He's been trying to get me to raise the price of Ogre Pellets for the last two weeks."

A large, round-headed, heavily built creature with milk-white skin and tiny pink eyes came stomping towards them.

"Hide me quick," Lorcan yelped. He ran under Aimirgin's skirt, just before Devi came stomping into the middle of their group.

"Watch it, you big oaf," Feidhelm cried. "You nearly crushed me."

"Sorry, Malone," The gigantic creature said in a voice so deep Fadin could feel the rumble in his toes. "Have you seen O'Callaghan anywhere?"

Fadin almost answered in reference to his last name, but clamped his mouth shut as the word, yes, nearly escaped his lips.

"Nope, I haven't, Devi," Feidhelm answered.

"Well it's very important that I speak with him, so if you see him, will you let him know that I…" he noticed Clearie staring at him and began to shake. "What are you looking at boy?"

"What are you?" Clearie almost shouted.

Devi gasped and jolted backward. His head shook and then his eyes disappeared with a horrible "pop," leaving two small, gaping holes.

Clearie yelped and nearly knocked Tase over. "Oh no. Did I kill him?"

Lorcan peered from underneath Aimirgin's dress and sighed. "No, you didn't kill him, unfortunately. You just scared him."

"I scared *him*?" Clearie snorted.

"Come on now, Devi," Lorcan said, climbing up the enormous creature. "Come out, no one was trying to hurt you." He pounded on Devi's skull. "Wake up, you big fool!" He sighed again and turned to the rest of them. "Ogres are always doing this you know, they act all tough and frightening, but they're the biggest scaredey-faeries I know," he pounded on the Ogre's skull again. "Oh, well, it's going to take me a bit to get him out of this state, why don't you all go and get a snack and meet me back here in twenty ticks or so?"

"Alright, Lorcan," Aimirgin said. "Come with me, I know some good food stands."

Fadin moved with the rest of the group but felt something tug on his sleeve.

"Wait a minute, Fadin," Aednat said grabbing his arm.

"What you want, Freckles?" he asked with a smirk.

She put her hands on her hips and glared up at him. "Just to prove to you that I do too know thin's, I want to show you the best tastin' food trolleys around here. Trolleys that even Hogan doesn't know."

"Oh really?" Fadin said folding his arms. "And how would you know about them and not her?"

"Because me father works in the Cavan-Corr Market, and he knows everythin' there is to know about good sellin' items."

"Fine," Fadin said, "take me then, Freckles."

She turned up her nose and led him in the opposite direction of the others.

Fadin smiled to himself. He thought Aednat was a funny little girl, fun to be around and to tease. He had to keep himself from laughing at the way she strutted through the food aisles, and how she nearly ran into a few people because her head was held so high. Nevertheless he didn't doubt that she could show him a good food stand, and then perhaps he could show off to the others next time they came here or somewhere like here.

"There you go," Aednat said coming to a halt. "That is the best snack trolley in the entire fair."

She was pointing to a crumbling cart with a rusted sign that held several minuscule bags of small nut-shaped things.

"That?" he said blinking at her. "Are you mental?"

"What? Is little Fadin afraid of tryin' somethin new?" she said in a mock baby voice. "Is he ready to admit he doesn't know anythin'?"

"Absolutely not," Fadin said stepping up to the cart.

"Hello there," said a large creature with tusks, popping up from behind the snack stand.

"Hi," Fadin said staring at Aednat, "How much for a bag of—of whatever this is?"

"You want a bag of my Mayog Xukk Clape?" The creature asked, mouth wide.

"Yes I want a bag of your Maka lacka cacka or whatever it's called."

The food salesman beamed at him. "Well my normal price is an elf hair, but since you are the first customer of the day, and such a fine-looking young man, I'll change my price to three red hairs instead."

Fadin put his hand up to his head and yanked out three of his own orange-red hairs. He handed them to the tusked creature.

"Oh thank you, little master," the creature smiled. "And here is your Xukk Clape, as promised."

Fadin took the bag of old nut-looking things, and stood in front of Aednat.

"Well?" she said folding her arms.

Fadin took a large handful, looked at it, crinkled his nose in disgust, and shoved it in his mouth. To his surprise, the nut-like things were very good.

"So?" Aednat asked, smiling.

"Alright, I'll admit it, they're good. But that doesn't prove anything."

She smiled even wider. "Oh, we'll see what it proves."

He took another large handful. "Yes, we will."

"Fadin."

He turned and saw Aimirgin laughing hysterically with Tase, Quinlan, and Colmcille.

"Put that down, Fadin," Aimirgin laughed, "Don't eat that, don't eat any more."

"Why?" he asked, mouth full.

"Because you're eating Dragon Butt Scales, you idiot," Quinlan cried, throwing his head back with extreme laughter.

The food salesmen ducked behind his stand.

Fadin stared at the bag of nut things and dropped it, spitting out the mouthful of butt scale he had left. "Oh," he cried grimacing at the hysterical Aednat, "you, you little…"

"I told you I knew thin's," she cried, "I told you and this," she had to pause for her laughter, "this proves it, you Dragon Dung Mouth."

Fadin glared at her, but a smile played on his lips. He had to admit that was good, too good. Little freckle face could be sure that something quite fun would be coming her way very soon.

~~~

The rest of the day was wonderful.

Although Fadin was still upset about the Aednat incident, he let it go when they met up with Lorcan and Feidhelm.

The two Leprechauns finally managed to get Devi's eyes from the inside of his skull to the slots of his nose, which they considered good enough. When Devi was sent on his way, the large group went and shopped around the little stalls, tents, and trolleys.

Tase found a deck of cards that really did disappear, no tricks involved.

Clearie got a novel that contained over twenty different chapter books, including stories such as: The Fairy Who Couldn't Fly, Hoblin the Goblin, The Three Golden Princesses, and The Elf Who Made a Wish. The book was a good buy, four tears, and though it carried so many stories, it was only the size of a pencil in length and width.

Aimirgin bought the swelling lipstick, which made her already plump lips look like a blowfish, in Fadin's opinion anyway.

Aednat got talking emerald earrings for her mother.

Quinlan, Cormick, and Colmcille got a bottle of Stach-a-grow.

And Fadin, though begging for a bottle of the Stach-a-grow, decided to get a box of exploding marbles instead. Which, in all honesty, were quite fun and only cost him ten eyelashes.

When the shopping spree had ended, Mr. Hogan treated them all to a nice meal, one which Fadin made sure was approved by Aimirgin.

The meal was wonderful, the best Fadin could remember having in a long time. Sitting with the Hogans, whom he now loved, and the new uncles which he was beginning to know, along with the spicy little freckled girl by his side, made his heart feel light. He could almost feel the weight being lifted off his shoulders, and the constant anger, which he carried with him all the time, beginning to fade.

When all was said and done, and the sun was beginning to set behind the now darkening clouds, it was time to say goodbye.

"I loved spending time with you today, boys," Lorcan said hugging their necks as they bent down. He pushed his round glasses back up his small nose. "I don't know when I'll be able to see you again, because I'm going to be busy for the next few weeks or so in Cavan-Corr Ministry, but I want you to write me at least once a week. Give your letters to Aimirgin. I know she knows where I work."

"Yes," Feidhelm said shaking their pinkies, his dark green eyes twinkling. "Send us both letters. We'd love to hear from you. And I have a son of my own who I'm sure would love to meet you. He isn't exactly what you'd expect for a son of a Leprechaun, but—well I'll just have to let you meet him."

"Take care of yourselves, boys," Lorcan winked, "And Happy Christmas!"

"Happy Christmas," Fadin and his brother's wished back.

The two red-headed men bowed and with a snap of their small fingers, were gone.

"How did they do that?" Clearie asked.

"Leprechauns," Desmond said, "have a little magic all their own."

"Well I guess I'd better go too," Aednat said sighing. "Me Da and sisters will be lookin' for me now." She looked sorrowful.

"It was nice seeing you, Aislinn," Aimirgin smiled giving the little dark-red-head a hug.

"You too, Hogan." She smiled at Fadin, Clearie, and Tase. "It was nice meetin' you all. I hope to see you soon."

"Us too, Freckles," Fadin smiled.

She smiled back and disappeared into the now bustling crowd.

"Well," Mr. Hogan said, putting a hand on the twin's shoulders, "ready to go?"

Fadin looked back over the darkening meadow, taking in the last bit of magic it held, before he knew it would be gone forever. He nodded. "Yes."

"Alright, you boys pull out those bottles of potion."

"What potion?" Clearie asked.

"This one," Tase said handing him a bottle.

"Yea Clear," Fadin grinned, "the one that kept your gob shut when you found out about us and the attic."

Clearie rolled his eyes and took the bottle from Tase.

"Good, now I want you to add your memories and drink it, all of it, when I count to three. I want you to think of the outside of my home as soon as it's in your mouth, and only my home till it's over, understand?"

"Till what's over?" Fadin asked uncorking the glass vial and adding his memory.

"You'll see," Quinlan laughed. "Just don't think of anything but our cottage, or who knows where you'll end up."

"Okay, on my count," Mr. Hogan said, "One…"

Fadin looked down at the slimy liquid.

"Two…"

He took a deep breath, brought the vial to his lips, and thought of the Hogans' little house.

"Three!"

With a horrible jerk Fadin watched as the world flew away from him. The pressure made his limbs ache as if they would tear away from his body, and his head was spinning. His stomach became sick, and out of the blue the world came back into focus, and they were at the Hogan cottage.

"Wow," Fadin said, toppling to the ground and feeling that his hair was sticking up on end. "What a ride."

"Yea," Clearie said stumbling, "a ride that you die on." He leaned forward and heaved sick all over the grass.

Tase staggered over to Fadin and laughed as he tripped over a small rock.

Abruptly, several puffs of red smoke appeared, and all the Hogans stood around them.

"Fun huh?" Quinlan asked, patting Clearie on the back.

"Oh yea," Clearie said sarcastically, "loads." He leaned forward and puked again.

"Well as soon as Clearie is feeling better," Mr. Hogan said touching his shoulder, "I think we should all head inside. There's something I want to talk to you boys about before you go."

# Chapter 16

## *D.A.*

Tase and the others entered the warm cottage, took off their cloaks and packs and washed their faces and hands. It felt good to Tase to clean up a bit after the long but thrilling day. He could feel the effects all the excitement and emotion had had on him, and was looking forward to the night, when he could lay his head down on his fluffy pillow and sleep.

When everyone had begun to settle in, Mr. Hogan asked all of his children if they could leave him alone with Tase and his brothers.

They agreed and soon it was only the four of them in the little living room.

Tase felt nervous. He wondered what Mr. Hogan could possibly want to talk to them about. Was he angry? Did he feel that they were ungrateful for all he had done for them? Had Tase or his brothers said or done something wrong? Or was this the talk he had been waiting for? Was this, finally, going to be the moment when Mr. Hogan would tell them about the mysterious D.A., Dia Ailín, the person who seemed intertwined with their mother's and father's pasts?

Mr. Hogan smiled at them, obviously trying to calm their nerves.

His kind smile, though warming, did not help Tase relax.

Mr. Hogan stood and walked around the sofa, stopping to stand before them all. His eyes fell directly on Tase.

He had to suppress a little shudder.

"Do you remember, Tase," he said, beginning to pace, "a while back now, me and you having a talk about a man named Dia Ailín?"

Tase nodded. He had been right, here it was, the subject he had wanted to talk about since the day he had found out what D.A. stood for. He realized he could hardly breathe, and had to make a conscious effort to do so.

"Well," Mr. Hogan said, continuing to pace, "I think I can safely say that you two probably know something about him. Seeing how you figured out I was your father's friend, and learned that your mother hasn't been entirely honest with you about who and what you are. So, before I say anything else, what do you know about him?"

Tase looked at Fadin, willing him to speak for the both of them.

Fadin took the hint. "We do know a little about him, yes, but only really that he went by D.A., he was a leader of some kind. Ma, Da, and you knew him, he lead a group of seven people, men, we suspect, called the Feneg, and we know that his initials keep popping up all over the place. Like on this, for example," he pulled out their father's golden crest and handed it to Mr. Hogan.

Mr. Hogan's eyes widened. "Where did you find this?" He sounded breathless.

Tase eyed him suspiciously, "In our Da's office the day he died."

Mr. Hogan stroked the crest and let his mouth fall open. "Then I was right, they did take it, and the car crash—it was no accident."

"What?" Tase, Fadin, and Clearie all shouted at once.

Mr. Hogan put the crest up on the mantle. "That thing, is very dangerous boys, and very powerful. It holds the power to unlock something that is both magnificent and terrible, and if your father left it out for you to find, which, no doubt in my mind, he did, then he was expecting something to happen that day. Your Da knew or suspected that he would die, and he left that for you boys, because he wanted you to know the truth."

Tase felt his heartbeat quicken. "So, you don't think the car crash was just an accident?"

Mr. Hogan shook his head. "No. But before we get into all that, which I do have a lot to tell you, we need to talk about this," he grabbed the crest, "and him." He pointed to the initials D.A.

Tase swallowed and pushed himself deeper into his chair.

"Well, for you to completely understand where this, very real, power came from, I think I need to tell you an old Dalbhach story." He moved to the mantle and picked up an old tattered book. "The truth of this particular story," he said, flipping through the pages, "has been debated, and I can't tell you if all of it is accurate or not, but there are definite truths in it." Mr. Hogan put on a pair of reading glasses, and began to scroll down the page. "Thousands of years ago, when the earth was still new, a great demon named Indomitus arose from the deep, where he had been kept prisoner by the light. He escaped the light's grasp and fled to the nearest land he could find, and in so doing, came to the Emerald Isle.

"He found that he had the ability to manipulate creatures to his will and turn many into followers of his own. He terrorized the people of Ireland, killing many, kidnapping some to become his servants, and trying to make himself king, so he could rule the whole Emerald Land, and then stretch out his hand and take all the world along with it.

"The light, seeing the blackness in the demon's heart, did not like this, and knew that if he ruled the earth, then it would fall. So the light went to the elves, wisest and fairest among all beings, and chose a warrior to fight Indomitus.

"The warrior went and tried to smite the demon down, but Indomitus only turned him to the dark of his powers, and gained more strength. So the light went to the Nymphs and tried yet again, but that warrior too, was turned to the dark. And so, on and on the light tried, as Indomitus sucked all the power from each race and became more and more powerful, until he nearly had enough magic to take the world as his own.

"It looked hopeless, with nowhere left to turn. But there was one race the light had not tried. The race of man. Weakest among all races, easily corrupted, easily destroyed, but with a strength no other race had. The strength of persistence, when no magic was found. And so, the light decided to create a man who indeed did have magical powers, a Dalbhach, to take the powers of Indomitus and rid him from the world."

Tase swallowed. This had to just be a fairytale, it sounded far to fantastical to be real in any way, but he did find himself leaning forward to hear the outcome of this Dalbhach.

"So the light created a boy, raised him, and taught him, made him more powerful than any man had ever been, and for a time, it looked as though there was hope. The boy the light created turned into a man capable of healing illness, destroying the dark followers of Indomitus, and even bringing back the dead."

Tase felt his heart flutter at the thought. Bring back the dead, bring back his father. But he quickly shoved the thought out of his mind. Doing such a thing was impossible.

"The time to face Indomitus drew near," Mr. Hogan said, "but unfortunately, the pride of man has never been matched, and the Dalbhach went to face him, filled with pride in himself, believing he was truly the greatest and most powerful thing in all creation."

Tase unintentionally looked over at Fadin. That sort of sounded like him and his teacher problem. If he had great powers, what would Fadin do with them? Well, at least he'd be on Tase's side. Tase smiled at the thought, and refocused on Mr. Hogan's words.

"Indomitus was filled with pleasure seeing the Dalbhach come, knowing his power was the final piece for him to take over the world. And when the Dalbhach reached him, they fought, long and hard. The Dalbhach was truly powerful, he matched Indomitus' strength in nearly every way, and finally struck him to the ground. Victory was near, but the pride of the man caused him to leave himself exposed before the final blow, and the demon seized him. He began to take his power, draining the man's life as he did so. Hope was fading, but the Dalbhach, remembering all he was taught, gave his powers up to the light, to counter the attack, and in so doing, created a force which sucked both their powers and combined them into a single object. A book."

Tase crinkled his nose. A book?

"Indomitus tried to grab the book, but he was weak, and the light, powerfully with the Dalbhach, would not let him gather any strength. The light gave one last bit of magic to the man, and with it, he began to flee, to destroy the book. But before he could go Indomitus cursed him, binding his life to the life of the book, and forbidding him to ever touch it again. The curse was put upon him, but the light held it back for as long as it could, so that the Dalbhach could hide the book, forever.

"The Dalbhach named the book, the Xoor, and hid it in the only place the demon would not look. The race of man. He created six keys to unlock the book, and gave them to six human families, one of which hid the Xoor itself."

Tase shifted in his seat. A book? Really?

"Indomitus, weak, powerless, but determined, searched Ireland over for it, but never found it. And then the Dalbhach, doomed for his pride, was made to walk the earth forever, until one day someone would destroy the Xoor, setting him free of his curse." Mr. Hogan closed the book and removed his glasses, as the words of the story still hung in the air.

Tase swallowed. The tale just seemed too fantastical, too much like a dark fairy-tale, or a legend to make children obey their parents. It couldn't be real. "Mr. Hogan," he said squirming in his seat, "I liked the story and all, but what did it have to do with us, or Dia?"

Mr. Hogan bent down so he was at eye level with him. "Everything."

Tase leaned back.

"You see," Mr. Hogan said standing, "whether or not it was a demon, and whether or not there was a Dalbhach, there is, in actual fact, a book. The Xoor is real, the six keys are real, the human families are real, and the dark power in that book is extremely real. You see this?" He held up the crest.

"Yea?" Fadin said.

"This is one of the six keys that unlocks that book, and your mother belongs to one of the six families who were given the job of protecting it. The most important family, perhaps."

Tase let his eyes grow wide. "You mean the family who kept the Xoor hidden?"

Mr. Hogan nodded. "Precisely."

Tase felt his head spinning.

"Wait," Clearie said, putting a hand to his forehead, "our mother was supposed to protect this book? The Xoor?"

Mr. Hogan stood up. "Her and her family. The Kavanaghs have always been the protectors of the Xoor, since the very beginnings of their family. They were honored, trustworthy people long ago, but as the years went by, the generations began to deteriorate. Your family became obsessed with power and with the Xoor, it corrupted them, in fact, all six families became corrupted and warped as the years stretched onward. They turned from upright, peace-abiding humans, into Dalbhachs of the dark arts. Each one falling in its own time. And the cycle was only broken with your grandfather."

"Our grandfather?" Tase asked. He had never really thought about his grandparents before, for he had never even seen pictures.

"Yes," Mr. Hogan said, "your grandfather was a good man, he didn't desire power or fame. He desired what was right and just, and he turned away from the dark power of his family. His brother, Brian, hated him for turning from the dark arts, and they were always at war with one another. But your grandfather, Declan, never faltered."

"And, what happened to him?" Fadin asked.

"To answer that," Mr. Hogan said, "I need to tell you exactly what happened fourteen years ago."

"You mean," Tase said, sitting erect, "why our parents ran away?"

Mr. Hogan nodded. "But first, you have to realize that your family, the Kavanaghs, were nearly destroyed. The complete facts of what happened, I'm not sure of, but what I do know is that every single member of the six families, the key families, were murdered in a single night. Everyone, except for your grandfather, grandmother, Ma, and her siblings."

"Who murdered them?" Clearie asked, visibly quivering.

"I don't know. Your grandparents would never say, and neither would your mother. But, needless to say, your grandparents fled for their lives. For many years they were gone, until they felt it was safe to return. Finally, when your mother was thirteen years old, they came back." Mr. Hogan smiled to himself. "I remember the look on your father's face when he saw your mother for the first time."

Tase smiled. So they had met when they were thirteen. He could just picture it, his father, young, scrawny, short, with curly red hair that stuck up on all ends, beaming at their mother, who must have been beautiful, even when she was so young.

"Did she like him?" Tase asked.

Mr. Hogan laughed. "No, she liked another boy, and hardly paid attention to your poor father at all. But that's another story. Right now, I need to talk to you about Dia."

Tase felt his heart leap.

"Now, something you should know, is that when the Xoor was created, some of Indomitus and the Dalbhach's magic, spilled out onto another. The being it hit was a human slave girl, who made a prophecy. She professed that many years from then, the darkness would return, and all of Ireland, once again, would be oppressed. She told of a man, a very powerful man, who would come and save Ireland from the darkness, and would smite it with all his power. The Dalbhach, when going to hide the Xoor, met this girl and wrote her prophecy in the book before putting it into hiding."

"So this prophecy," Fadin said, "people must have known about it."

"Yes," Mr. Hogan nodded, "many people did, and they told and retold the story in their families, generation after generation. The story was never lost. But thousands of years later, after the destruction of your family, and after your grandparents fled, the Xoor was found. Your grandfather completely forgot about it in his escape, and left it, unprotected." Mr. Hogan sat on the sofa opposite Tase and his brothers and leaned forward. "Dia was born in a village not far from here, a village which no longer exists. He was born to a poor, insignificant family, but he was noticed right away. He had amazing talent in magic, and could do many things other Dalbhachs could not. When he was eleven, Dia was sent to the king, King Raegan, who had heard of his talents. On his way, Dia passed your grandparents' castle, and asked to go inside. There, he found the Xoor, hidden away high in the towers, and brought it to the king."

Tase blinked, remembering suddenly the room upstairs, the round room that led to the attic. Wasn't that word, that was scratched all over the walls, X-O-O-R? It was, he remembered. Someone had known it was there, and had become obsessed with it, carving the name everywhere. Tase shuddered thinking about a crazed man or woman up in the room, scratching the word over and over.

He shook his head and leaned in further to listen.

"King Raegan, though a good man, was, and is, weak and foolish. He knew at once what the book was, and remembered the stories of the power it held. He had every Dalbhach in Ireland try and open the book, but it was no use, the book was sealed, and the keys lost. In his fury at not being able to achieve the power of the book, he announced, in a decree to all of Ireland, that the book was a fake, not the book of legend, not the Xoor. The fool, who sent it to every corner of Ireland, alerted every dark force who had been searching for the power. He basically told them where the book was hidden and how to get it. And in so doing, he began the chain of events that caused the Great War."

Tase swallowed. So it was the king's fault? What an eejit to blab to all of Ireland about the book. No wonder there was a war. He shifted in his seat and listened eagerly for Mr. Hogan to continue.

"Many years passed. Dia grew up in the castle, taught by many great men, and became a very well-known figure in Ireland. Well, in the magical world, anyway."

"I knew him, your father knew him, in fact, we were both part of his inner circle of friends. The Feneg, as you called us, Fadin. The Seven. Being with Dia was unexplainable. He was the best and kindest man I have ever met, and for a while, life was good, peaceful, wonderful. And then the clouds set in."

Tase shivered.

"A strange man came to Glas Cavan. A Russian man named Afanasii Egorov, who was very good at manipulating. He introduced himself to King Raegan and soon had a place by his side. No one really thought much of it at first. We didn't pay much attention. But little by little, he began to take over. He started to thrust his will upon the king and manipulated the king into doing whatever he wanted. He threw many innocent, but powerful, people in jail, he tore apart villages in search of, what he said, were stolen riches. But what he was really searching for was the Xoor, and Dia recognized it at once.

"King Raegan had all but given himself to Afanasii, except for the place in his heart and mind that he kept for the queen. She was the voice of reason, and begged her husband to throw Afanasii out. After much pleading, the king decided he would listen to his wife and rid himself of his new advisor. Unfortunately, the night before Egorov was to be sent away, the queen went missing, never to be seen or heard from again."

Tase bit his lip. How awful. Even if this story sounded too crazy to be real, it was still sad. How awful for the king to lose his wife, even if he was a blubbering idiot.

"The king was never the same once the queen went missing," Mr. Hogan said, shaking his head. "He gave up his will to live, and gave nearly all his power to Afanasii, which is when things really became awful.

"Men, women, and children were all slaughtered by his hand. Elves, Fairies, Mer-folk, and other creatures of the deep went to stand by his side. Some, afraid to face him, others, power hungry, and wanting revenge. His forces doubled and tripled, and soon, all of Ireland was overrun by his followers.

"Panic spread quickly, and the few brave souls who had fought for their homes and families, lost all hope and fled. I myself was terrified. I took my wife and children and prepared to leave. I was ready to find someplace safe to hide away, and leave Ireland to its fate. But Dia would have none of that."

Tase felt his insides jump a little with excitement.

"He called a meeting of all who were willing to stand up against Egorov. There were very few, but among them were your mother, your mother's family, your father, Kyna, Enda, Daireann, me, and your teacher, Caoimhe. I think there were barely a hundred in all. A hundred against several thousand. The odds were hopeless. But Dia said we should fight, fight for our freedom, and if we lead the way, others would follow.

"I was petrified, how could we possibly fight the force of Egorov and hope to win? It was absolutely impossible. But I trusted Dia and so did many others. So we agreed to fight with him. And so began the war."

Tase was nearly falling off his chair. He had to know what happened next, why would his mother leave? With Dia leading the fight? And obviously they had succeeded, because Afanasii was nowhere in sight. Why had his family run away?

He let his leg bounce up and down as he listened.

"It was awful. The battles were bloody and full of loss. Many died, many were captured, tortured, or turned. But Dia was right, others joined our ranks, and though we were still outnumbered, with Dia on our side, we gained strength. We destroyed several fleets of his soldiers and broke into many prisons, freeing captives, and stealing supplies. We hid away beneath your family's castle and had protective charms and spells around it, so that Afanasii could never find us. We gained ground each day, and victory finally seemed feasible."

Tase's heart fluttered with exhilaration.

"And then," Mr. Hogan's face fell, "the unthinkable happened."

Tase's heart sank. "What happened?" he almost shouted.

Mr. Hogan looked up. "One of our closest friends, one of the Feneg, betrayed us. Your uncle, your mother's brother, Dubhlainn, turned on us and joined Afanasii behind our backs. He told him how to break our spells, and showed him the way. He lead Afanasii, and a huge fleet of troops to the castle, catching us off guard. If it hadn't been for Kyna, who somehow saw the army coming and warned us of their arrival, we all would have been slaughtered. But there was still no time. Nowhere for us to turn, nowhere to run. We were going to die. But Dia, once again calming the panic, told us all to get inside. I assumed we were going to barricade ourselves inside, and fight to the bitter end. But once everyone had gotten into the castle, Dia slammed the doors shut, locking us in, and him out."

Tase bit his lip. He could see where this was going.

"I remember watching it happen," Mr. Hogan said, looking unseeingly into the fireplace. "I watched from the round window in the attic. I saw Afanasii and his troops come forward. I watched Dubhlainn stand by Egorov's side as they beat Dia, and tortured him, trying to cause us to come out, to fight. But we could not. Dia's power was too great, and we could not unlock any of the doors, nor break any windows."

Tase could see Mr. Hogan's memory was a thousand miles away. He was re-living the nightmare, seeing it again before his very eyes. And Tase, though he obviously had no memory of the event, could see it occurring in front of him, too.

"Finally, when Egorov had had enough fun," Mr. Hogan continued, "he killed Dia. He killed him in front of us all. And then left his broken body in the dirt, and walked away."

Tase slumped back in his chair, a sense of despair in his stomach.

"Well," Fadin said, irritation in his voice, "couldn't Dia have stopped them if he wanted?"

"Of course," Mr. Hogan said, "but his sacrifice was the most powerful magic of all. Afanasii could not touch us once Dia gave up his life to keep us safe. Any other spell would have left the castle open for Egorov and his troops to have their way with us. But Dia gave up his power, his life, to keep us protected, and nothing could harm us. If we chose to go and fight him, we could die, but we could no longer be turned to the dark arts, or be a slave of his will. We were safe, and nothing but sacrifice could have done that."

"Well did you go and fight him?" Clearie asked.

Mr. Hogan laughed. "Of course we did. After we buried Dia, we gathered together and decided to storm the King's castle. If we were going to die we were going down fighting."

Tase sat up again, eager to hear the end of the tale.

"We made it to the castle, we broke down the doors, killed many of his followers and made it all the way to the floor beneath Afanasii's chamber, when we were stopped. There were too many of them, and we couldn't seem to break through their ranks. But one of our own, one of the Feneg named Fintan, somehow slipped past the enemy and made it up to Egorov's bedroom." Mr. Hogan paused and looked away from the fireplace, and back into Tase and his brother's faces. "I did not see it happen, for I was battling with one of Afanasii's worst followers, the Bojin girl, Dominique. But from what Fintan told us, he battled with Egorov—"

"Wait," Tase said, interrupting Mr. Hogan, mid-sentence. "Did you say Bojin?"

"Yes," Mr. Hogan nodded, looking confused, and surprised. "You know the name?"

"Yes," Fadin cut in.

"We do?" Clearie asked, staring at his brothers stupidly.

"How?" Mr. Hogan asked, looking from Tase to Fadin, and back again.

"We found a picture up in the attic," Tase answered. "It's an old black-and-white photo with four people in it. I remember one of the names was

Dominique, the young, very, very, very *pretty* girl." Tase blushed as he realized how many times he had said the word very.

"You have a picture of them up in your attic?" Mr. Hogan asked sounding concerned.

"Yea," Fadin nodded, "there's loads of old junk up there and mountains of pictures."

"But you have a photo of Vladimir, Trandafira, Gabriel, and Dominique, all four?" Mr. Hogan's voice sounded panicked.

"Yea, why?" Fadin asked, shrugging.

"Because I've only ever heard of one photo that exists of the four of them. And last time I saw it, it was sitting up in Afanasii's chamber. A few days after the siege on the castle, it disappeared. And now, somehow, you have it."

Tase gulped. "What do you think that means?"

"I don't know," Mr. Hogan said, shaking his head. "But you boys be careful what you poke around in. You never know what's waiting to be discovered, and how dangerous it can be."

"But it was just a picture." Fadin said.

"But you have no idea what kind of powers that family has." Mr. Hogan said sternly. "They are the most powerful Dalbachs, with the exception of Dia, that I have ever seen. They are immersed in black magic, and are cold and cruel. They have no respect for life of any kind, and kill anyone and anything that threatens what they want. Hundreds of children, babies, were murdered at the hand of Trandafira. Her and Vladimir, the elder two, are *really* brother and sister, though they often pass as a couple. She is a year older then he is, and they are heirs to one of the greatest castles in Romania. Or at least they were. The castle was destroyed many years ago, and they moved, along with two younger Romanians, to Ireland. The young man, Gabriel, and the young woman, Dominique, are in no way related to Vladimir and Trandafira, or to each other. They call themselves family, but are only bonded by black magic. But the bond is very much stronger than any you could imagine.

"The woman, Dominique, though very beautiful, is extremely deadly, and merciless. She has naiad blood in her veins, and though it is several times removed, she still has great power over men. And not only that, but the Bojins used a very old and very powerful magic to give her unthinkable powers. The thing they did is so horrible, that it is said they no longer posses their souls."

Tase shuddered.

"So, just so you understand, she may be beautiful, but she is dangerous, and she is forever locked in the body of a seventeen-year-old girl, though she may well be ten years older than I am. They are ageless, timeless, and ruthless. You never know what spells they put on things that belonged to them, so be careful with that picture, boys. You don't know who could be watching."

Tase swallowed hard. "So they sided with Afanasii?"

"Yes," Mr. Hogan said darkly, "they did. And as I was saying, while Fintan broke into Egorov's chamber, I was battling with Dominique, so I didn't see what happened."

Tase settled back in his chair, showing Mr. Hogan that there would be no more interruptions on his part.

Mr. Hogan cleared his throat and continued. "From what Fintan told us, he fought with Afanasii, but his power was too great, and he nearly killed him. But, just as Egorov was about to succeed, Fintan swore he saw Dia standing behind him. The hope that brought Fintan caused him to strike Afanasii in his side, piercing his heart. Some force that Fintan did not recognize flowed out of Afanasii's wound, through Fintan's sword, and into Fintan himself. It drained both of their powers, until the sword burst with a force that was so powerful, Afanasii was hurled from the highest window.

"Fintan, though weak, climbed to the broken glass and tried to see where Afanasii had fallen, but he could see nothing. Just glass here and there on the ground, no sign of the dark leader.

"When the sword had been destroyed, and Afanasii hurled out of the tower, the spells he had put on many of his followers broke, and they turned and fought with us. So we overthrew the followers of Afanasii, killing all but a few dozen, and the Bojins, who fled into the west. When we found Fintan, he was passed out, and it took several days before he was well enough to tell us what happened. By that time, it was hopeless to search for Egorov, for he was long gone."

Tase realized he was chewing his nails and stopped abruptly.

"It took some time to clean up the mess Afanasii had created, but after a while things began to go back to normal, or at least, as normal as things can be after something like that.

"In the beginning, many people said they saw Dia walking in the forest or passing them in the street, but I never saw him. I could feel him though, as if he never really left, and I still feel as if his spirit is with me today, but of course, that could just be me wishing, but I don't think so.

"As for Afanasii, no one has heard from him or seen him to this day. Nor has anyone heard of or seen the Bojins. Their castle, which lies far north of here, is abandoned and has not been occupied since they vanished. And though they seem gone, I know they're not. They're out there somewhere, and so is Afanasii."

"But," Tase said, unable to control himself, "couldn't Afanasii have died from his wound, or from old age?"

Mr. Hogan shook his head. "No, not from old age. And if he escaped, which he did, he couldn't die from his wound either. For you see, Afanasii was no man, he was," Mr. Hogan paused, "a vampire."

Tase's heart leapt into his throat. As if Afanasii hadn't sounded bad enough just being a human. Now Mr. Hogan tells them he was a vampire? A vampire! A blood-sucking, lightening-quick, coffin-sleeping vampire. Tase's heartbeat thudded in his ears as Mr. Hogan continued.

"There are very few ways to kill a vampire, especially one as powerful as Egorov, and I don't think Fintan discovered a new method. No, Egorov is still alive somewhere."

"He was a vampire?" Fadin asked, eyes wide.

"Yes," Mr. Hogan nodded. "And because of that, your mother became frightened for her safety and her children's safety. She had your sister already, you realize, and when she and your father left, she was pregnant with you, Clearie. She didn't want you to grow up here, I suppose. Always afraid if you would be safe. So they left. And I—I never saw your father again."

Tase let out a long breath and felt a shiver go up his spine. So that's why they ran away. It made sense now, but it didn't make things any easier, or the feeling of betrayal by his parents any less severe. She had kept everything from them, even if she did have the best intentions.

"So you see," Mr. Hogan said, snapping Tase back to reality, "I don't think your father's death was an accident. In fact, I know it wasn't. I suspected foul play before, but knowing now that your da left this key for you to find, tells me that he knew something was going to happen to him."

Tase felt tears welling up in his eyes, but abruptly pushed them back. This was no time for crying.

"You see, I have always been looking for your mother and father, but I have never found them. When I heard family had moved back to Kavanagh castle, I sent Aimirgin to check and see who it was."

"So she wasn't just there by accident that day?" Fadin asked.

"No," Mr. Hogan answered. "I figured your mother and father had never seen my daughter before and wouldn't recognize her. So she went to see if your family had come back. And when she came home with the two of you, and told me your last name was O'Callaghan, I nearly passed out."

Tase thought back to when he had met Mr. Hogan. He understood now why he had suddenly gone so pale.

"Then, when we were on our picnic, and you told me your father had died, and Fadin expressed how hurt he was, I myself became overcome by

300

grief. I had no idea Alroy had died, my best friend. That's why I was so emotional. It was a complete shock to me. I would have walked you boys home myself, but I was so grief-stricken that I just needed to be alone and cry for your father."

Tase could no longer keep the tears back and as he looked at his brothers, he saw tears pouring from Clearie's eyes, and Fadin, fighting with all his might, to keep the water puddles from spilling over.

"When the knife of grief had subsided a little, I began to do some digging. I looked into your father's car accident, and found it to be very odd. The humans couldn't explain it, and at first, neither could I. But as I investigated more, the more I realized that someone, or something, not of the human world, caused your father's car to crash. It was either one of Afanasii's followers or Afanasii himself. He wants that key, he wants the Xoor. He knew your father had the key and somehow, he thought, your family had the Xoor. But it's been lost to us since the war, and we always assumed the Bojins had it, but seeing this makes me think otherwise."

"So why wait to tell us this till now?" Fadin asked. "Why lie about being our father's friend? Why pretend to be human, when you are clearly not?"

Mr. Hogan eyed Fadin, incredulously. "Why? I thought it'd be obvious. What would you have done if I would have blurted out everything to you that first day? What would you have thought of me if I had walked up to your aunt's castle, looking like this, and yelling about being your father's best friend? Huh? You would have run away screaming. You would have thought me crazy, and would have been frightened of me. Not to mention, something like that could have caused your mother to run away again."

"Then why did you come to us and not our mother?"

"Because, though I care about your mother, I think there's more she's not telling, and I don't want her to leave, to take you away. Don't you understand? When I realized your mother had told you nothing, I took it upon myself to teach you, to warn you of the dangers in this world, to protect you. I am keeping my dearest friend's sons safe, as I would want him to do for my children. And besides that, Fadin, Tase, Clearie," he said each name with a tenderness that made more tears well up in Tase's eyes, "I love you. I love you more than you could fathom or understand. I love you like I love my children, as if you were my own sons, and if your sister ever comes here, I will love her that way too. I would rather die than see any harm come to you, and you are in danger."

Tase shuddered. "What do you mean?"

"I've heard that you've seen a Banshee on more then one occasion, and you keep seeing a black dog, right?"

Tase and Fadin nodded.

Clearie looked thoroughly confused and frightened.

"Well, Banshees only come before a death and they are very rare. They usually only come if black magic is involved, and if you have seen her more then once, then something worse than I could have thought is out there, waiting for you. Something that wanted your family back here, something that killed your father."

Tase felt the panic rush up to meet him. "Then shouldn't we leave? Shouldn't we run?"

Mr. Hogan moved close to them and kneeled so he was eye level with them. "No. Your father must have known who was doing this and he didn't run. He knew he couldn't get away, which means whatever it is, it's extremely powerful. Your da knew where your mother would go, and he wanted her here. He wanted you all here because he knew I would help protect you, and so would Enda, Kyna, Daireann, and Caoimhe. There is safety and strength in numbers, and you are safer here, with us, than anywhere else you could possibly run to."

"So you'll stay with us? You'll protect us?" Tase asked, grabbing Mr. Hogan's arm.

"I'll never leave you boys. You understand? Never."

There was a sudden scream from somewhere in the kitchen, "Mail call!"

Mr. Hogan turned and stood. "What? But the mail already came this morning."

Tase and Fadin exchanged glances.

Desmond came from inside the kitchen, holding a large green scroll. "Da," he said, his voice falling, "it's from the ministry."

Mr. Hogan took it and tore it open. He read the scroll quickly and abruptly rolled it up. He stood, completely still for a long moment, as if he were deciding something. He looked from Tase, to Fadin, to Clearie, and then turned to Desmond and Aimirgin, who appeared suddenly behind him.

"Da?" Aimirgin asked, in a timid voice.

"Start packing," Mr. Hogan barked. "Aimirgin, go into my room and get my suitcase ready."

"What?" Fadin burst, outraged and horrified.

Tase felt an awful lurch of fear burst into his chest and apprehension sink into the pit of his stomach. "W—what did the scroll say?" he stammered, feeling the rumbling panic begin to take over.

"I can't tell you," Mr. Hogan said, bending down and putting a hand on each of their shoulders. "If I told you, that could put you in more danger. But what you can know is that I have to be gone for a little while."

Tase felt like he was going to throw up. That was the worst thing he could possibly think of happening, short of his mother dying.

"What do you mean you have to be *gone*?" Clearie screamed. "You just said you'd never leave us!"

Mr. Hogan looked at them all sorrowfully. "I'm so sorry boys. I really am, but I honestly have no choice. And if I choose to disobey, I will be putting you in further danger."

Tase's head was spinning. What could possibly cause them danger if Mr. Hogan stayed with them? This was all too much, Tase could not handle it.

"You're putting us in further danger by leaving," Fadin cried.

Mr. Hogan hugged all three of them up tight.

Tase clutched onto his shirt, taking in the smell. How could this be happening? Mr. Hogan was the only thing that took away the sting of his father's death. He wasn't da, but he was like a second da. How could he be losing another father? He just couldn't do it.

Mr. Hogan released them, and then took Tase's face in his hands. "I love you," he then took Fadin and Clearie's faces in his hands, "I love all of you. But things are getting more risky and I cannot disobey this order. I will come back. Do you understand me? I will come back to you, all of you. But you have to listen to me. Do not come looking for me. Do not come into the woods. And do not come back to this house."

Tase cried openly now, this was just too awful, this had to be a nightmare.

"Whatever is after you is out there now. It's watching. My magic can protect you as long as you stay inside the castle grounds. But if you wander off, you're on your own." Mr. Hogan stood. "Desmond, take the boys back to the castle. Do not let them leave your sight until they are inside. Understand?"

Desmond nodded. "Come on, come with me," he said, huddling the boys together and pushing them toward the door.

"I'll come back as soon as I can," Mr. Hogan said, standing in such a way, that it appeared as though he was hugging himself. "Oh, and boys," he added, moving a little forward, "do not tell your mother about all this yet, I want to be back before she realizes you know the truth, in case she decides to leave."

Tase nodded vaguely, his head still swirling.

"Be safe," Mr. Hogan whispered, his voice sounding as if it might break.

Tase looked back as he was nearly shoved out of the entrance. He peered into Mr. Hogan's raven eyes and saw tears forming there, and

Aimirgin, openly bawling at his feet.

A fresh wave of nausea crashed over him, as the realization of what was happening began to thoroughly sink in. And with that, the large wooden door was shut and Tase was taken away, away from the only place he had felt safe since the terrible accident, since his world had been turned upside-down. He found himself wondering if he would ever see Mr. Hogan and his children again. The possible answer to his question made his soul sink.

# Chapter 17

## *Waking Nightmare*

Fadin was running. Running through the forest, trying with all his might to get away.

But his pursuer was fast. So fast, in fact, that he was nearly on top of him now, when he had been meters behind only a few seconds ago.

Fadin gulped in the cold air and tried to will his legs to go quicker. "Run, run," he cried, grinding his teeth. Sweat dripped from his brow and he could taste its saltiness as it ran into his mouth. Fadin swung his head around, taking a peek to see how close his hunter was. He gasped, the dark figure was only centimetres from his face. Fadin screamed, and pushed his body even harder, but it was no use, the dark figure grasped his ankle and sent him flying towards the damp earth.

Fadin hit the mud with a sickening *crash*. He bolted himself upright as soon as his head hit the floor and turned around.

His pursuer stood above him, dark, as if in shadow, laughing happily. "Oh, did the poor baby fall down?"

Fadin tried to stand, but he could not, his legs were stuck. "Get away from me," he cried.

"Get away?" the dark figure asked. "Please, Fadin. What fun would that be?" The dark man rushed forward with the speed of lightening. He was at Fadin's neck before he could blink, and his teeth sank into Fadin's skin like a knife into butter.

Fadin screamed in pain and horror as he felt blood dripping down his back.

"Delicious," the dark figure purred as he backed away, licking his lips.

In that moment, Fadin realized who he was. "Egorov," he yelped.

"In the flesh," the dark figure bowed. "And since you're such a clever boy, perhaps I'll tell you why I'm here."

Fadin struggled to move away, but his bottom half was numb. There would be no running.

"You and your family have been particularly knotty," Egorov stated. He began prancing back and forth and made a popping sound with his lips. "I want what's rightfully mine, what you...*stole*...from me."

Fadin stared at him, confused.

"Where's the book, little Fadin?" Egorov growled. "Where's the Xoor?"

"I—I don't know," Fadin stammered, feeling the fear pierce his heart.

"Oh, really?" Egorov laughed, "You know, that's exactly what your daddy told me. And do you know what I did to him?" Egorov stepped aside to allow Fadin to peer behind him.

Fire, hot and terrible, suddenly burst into Fadin's vision. The flames licked the air, and small explosions resounded from somewhere inside the upturned car that lay in a broken heap in front of him. Fadin, with a sickening realization, saw his father trapped inside the crashed vehicle, screaming, begging to be let out.

"Help me, Fadin," he shrieked, "help me, save me!"

Fadin's eyes widened in shock and horror. A scream escaped his lips that felt like it shook the entire earth with its pain and hatred.

"I burned him alive," Afanasii purred, still watching the blaze, ignoring Fadin's cries, "and if you don't tell me where its hidden..." he trailed off, and turned swiftly around.

Fadin gasped at his appearance.

Egorov had long white fangs that stuck out from his mouth, blood-red eyes, bat-like ears, a hideously ugly face, wings, and horribly long claws. "I'll *burn* you, *too!*"

Fire erupted from the ground and rose around Fadin. He screamed as he began to smolder. His skin blistered and his lungs filled with smoke. "Help me," he screeched, as his hand began to melt, "*help me!*"

~~~

Fadin snapped upward, panting and breathing hard. All he could see was red for a moment and he began to panic. But blackness started to creep into his vision, and he could suddenly feel the warm mattress beneath him and see the outline of his room. He sighed with relief and fell back on his pillow. It had only been a dream.

"Fadin?" The voice of Tase was unmistakable.

"Yea."

"Are you alright? You were screaming."

Fadin breathed in deep, calming himself. "I'm fine. Just a dream, that's all."

Tase was quiet for a moment.

Fadin heard rustling and then the creaking sound of the ladder. A second later, Fadin saw Tase's head pop up from the small opening of the bunk-bed's railing.

"It didn't sound like *just* a dream," Tase prodded.

Fadin looked up at the ceiling. *It wasn't*, he thought.

"I know it wasn't," Tase confirmed the unspoken answer.

Fadin flicked his eyes to his twin's face, and sat up. "How come you can do that sometimes? Hear what I'm thinking?"

Tase shrugged. "I don't know. I don't exactly hear it, I feel it. How can you?"

Fadin thought back to the few times when he could feel what Tase wanted without him having to ask. "I don't know. Maybe it's just a twin thing."

Tase nodded and plopped himself on the mattress. "I know what you're doing. You're dodging talking about your dream. But I won't let you." He moved closer. "It's the same one, isn't it?"

Fadin sighed. He had been having the same dream over and over for the past 13 weeks. Ever since Mr. Hogan and his family had left, the nightmares were a regular nocturnal companion. "Yea," he nodded, "the same one."

Tase inched closer. "I'm sorry," he said, "I know what it feels like to watch Da die."

Fadin shuddered. He had almost forgotten that Tase had had nightmares when they first arrived at the castle. His, too, had consisted of Da being burned alive. "Thanks, Tase," Fadin said, wanting to dismiss the conversation he knew was coming. "I'm okay, though. It's just a dream, and I'm tired."

Tase looked at him, incredulously. "You're tired?"

Fadin nodded, though it was a lie. "Yea, I'm tired, so I think I'll just go back to sleep." He laid down and pulled the covers over his body, hoping Tase would become upset and go back to bed.

Tase just sat there for a while, obviously thinking.

Fadin felt him finally get up and heard him climb back down the ladder, and crawl into his own bed. Fadin could hear him muttering to himself angrily.

When Fadin was sure Tase wouldn't come back, he began to cry silently. It wasn't okay for Tase to know how frightened he was, how horrified. Because *he* was the brave one, and if he began to panic, how would Tase handle it? Tase had been having a hard enough time losing Mr. Hogan without Fadin's emotions adding to the equation.

Fadin covered his mouth as his sobs began to turn into moans of pain. Everything was wrong, everything was out of place, and ever since Mr. Hogan had left, nothing and nowhere felt safe. Especially not sleep.

Ideas of betrayal and lies had started to fill Fadin's head as the days had stretched into weeks. It had been over three months, it was now the beginning of March, and there had been no word, no sign, no hope, nothing. The Hogans had just vanished and things at the castle had begun to go quite wrong.

Animosity seemed to seep from the very walls of the castle, for fighting was a regular pastime now. Enda and Ma, Kyna and Caoimhe, Enda and Daireann, Ma and Kyna, Daireann and Caoimhe, they all fought, all the time. It had started two weeks ago and had not stopped. It was as if they couldn't help themselves, they had to argue and be mean to one another. The only one who never fought back was Caoimhe, although she was often the object of name-calling and one-sided arguments. Only Fadin, Tase, and Clearie got along, and that was new, for it had always been that Fadin and Tase fought with Clearie. But ever since they had all learned the truth about their pasts, they were bonded together, especially with all the hatred in the air now.

At least Christmas had been alright and Clearie's birthday. Though, much to Fadin's, and he was sure his brother's, disappointment, Saoirse had not been able to come home for the holidays. Her expenses were more than she could handle, and she had no money to come and see them. Ma couldn't offer any funds for it was not her money to give, and she was not about to ask Aunt Kyna for help.

Fadin had felt his heart sink at the news, he had wanted Saoirse to be there so badly. Perhaps she would know what to do, how to find the Hogans, or find a way to make Ma tell them the truth, the whole truth. But she had not come and Fadin found himself wishing, more and more as the weeks dragged on, that she would somehow show up at the front door. But that was a fantasy.

Besides all the hostility inside the castle, there were the things that lurked outside that kept Fadin's nightmares coming, and alive even in the daytime. Dark shadows lurked in the forest, trees moved, creatures howled in the night, the water baby population increased significantly, and the black dog paid more frequent visits to the edge of the forest. The dog watched them when they got the mail, were up in the attic, were out by the tunnel. He only ever disappeared from view when an adult was with them, but as soon as the grownup's presence was gone, he was back at the edge of the brush, staring with those piercing eyes.

All of the odd happenings had begun to get the best of Fadin, though he hid it well from his brothers. He began to wonder how close Egorov was, how determined, and conversations about him never ended. Fadin often brought up the fact, or the fear, that vampires could be roaming the earth, and that perhaps Egorov was not the only one with a grudge against their father. He would stop vocal conversation there, but his mind took the idea much further. What if vampires learned where they were staying? What if they were waiting for Mr. Hogan's magic to wear off? What if they found a way in? Everyone would be slaughtered, or worse, turned. Fadin could think of nothing more terrible than becoming a monster, especially something like Egorov.

All of these things were terrible and overwhelming, yet another concern had leapt into Fadin's mind. Ma seemed to be getting sicker. She constantly wore clothes that were too baggy, and was in the bathroom all the time. Fadin had almost forgotten that she'd been ill, with everything else going on. But lately, the sickness had been getting more apparent, and Fadin began worry. But what could he do? Nothing, only fret about what would happen next, and pray she'd be alright. She had to be alright. And as long as she was sick, there was no way to approach her for the truth.

As Fadin lay in his bed, allowing his mind to wander the past weeks, he began to realize that something had to be done. Somehow, Mr. Hogan had to come back, or Fadin had to find him. If the Hogans stayed gone, it was obvious; everything was going to fall apart. Something Mr. Hogan had done, or just his very presence, had kept the peace in the forest. But now, with him gone, that peace had disappeared, and the woods were becoming more and more alive with whatever it was lurking there. If someone didn't take action, it would only be a matter of time till the forest no longer obeyed Mr. Hogan's last command. Someone had to do something.

With that thought, Fadin drifted off to sleep determined and void of the idea of Egorov and the horrible burning car.

~~~

"Are you mental?" Clearie cried, staring wide-eyed at Fadin.

Fadin rolled his eyes, looking about the old, dusty attic. It appeared exactly the same as it had 13 weeks ago. He and Tase had not been up to the attic for a long time, and with the magical world feeling so far away, it seemed a good place to visit. This was also Clearie's first time seeing the top story.

"No, I'm not mental, I'm tired. Tired of sitting around here waiting for something to happen. We talk about it all the time, about Afanasii, the black dog, the hooded woman. We know they're out there. Mr. Hogan told us they are, and if we just sit here waiting, we are easy targets."

"Exactly," Tase yelped, folding his arms. He didn't seem thrilled with the idea either. "Mr. Hogan told us it's dangerous outside. He told us what's out there waiting. If we go into those woods, we *are* easy targets. Mr.

Hogan told us to stay inside, and we've seen what can happen when we disobey. I personally don't need to see it again."

Fadin shuddered a little at the memory of the great tree-root weasel that had tried to drag him underground. He shook off the recollection and focused on the task at hand. "I've thought a lot about this. I've been thinking about it for the past week, ever since that black dog has stopped coming around. And don't you shake your head, Tase, because I know you've noticed he's been gone too."

Tase let his arms drop to his side. "That's beside the point, Fadin. We know, all three of us, that there are other things out there besides the dog. In fact, we've even heard them."

"Not lately," Fadin pointed out. Ever since the night he had decided to take matters into his own hands, things had become quieter. The forest was no longer filled with howls in the night, and the black canine had stopped showing up at the woodland edge altogether.

"So?" Clearie, asked. "That doesn't mean they're gone. That means they're tired or sleeping, or off for a short break. Things like that don't simply disappear."

"And you know so much about it, do you?" Fadin challenged.

Clearie did his best to tower over him and ran a hand through his blond hair. "Obviously more than you do."

"Things, things," Ciaran, the little goblin, suddenly cried, popping up from behind the broken table, "what's this alls about?"

Clearie turned his eyes to the goblin and let his mouth drop open. "AHHH!" he screamed. He pointed at Ciaran, screaming and backing up, stumbling over books and old furniture.

Ciaran, startled by the outburst, began screaming also and crouched low on the table.

Clearie hit an old couch that was still rather sturdy and toppled over it, smacking his head on the floor, stopping his screaming.

Fadin blinked. He had forgotten that Clearie and Ciaran had never been introduced. Whoops.

"Clearie?" Tase called, moving towards the couch.

Fadin followed.

Clearie popped up and stared, his blue and purple eyes wide. "W— what in the bloody hell is that thing?"

Ciaran, who had been huddling on the broken table, stood straight up. "Thing?" he cried, his ears and fingers becoming yellow.

"Uh oh," Fadin said, turning to Clearie, "now you've done it."

Ciaran yelped and stomped on the table. "I not thing, you thing, you stupids two-coloured eyes wingless fairy."

"What?" Clearie said, standing.

Ciaran jumped off the table. "You hears me, blondy boy. Hows dare you calls me a thing, I is a Fitheal, a greats Fitheal ats that."

Clearie looked at Ciaran and furrowed his brow. "And what the heck is a Fitheal?"

Ciaran's entire body turned yellow. "A goblins, you little devils!"

"What did you call me?" Clearie asked.

"Hey, Clearie," Fadin said standing between him and Ciaran, "maybe you should shut your gob, huh?"

"Shut my gob? What about, him?"

"I shuts your gobs for you," Ciaran growled, walking forward.

"Whoa," Tase said, standing in front of Ciaran, "let's not fight, okay?"

"No okay, I no likes this two-coloured eyes. You makes him leaves," Ciaran grumbled.

"He's our brother," Tase said, trying to calm the little goblin.

Ciaran looked from Tase, to Fadin, to Clearie. "Grrr..." he growled, trying to control his shaking. His colour began to fade back to its original olive green. "Fines," he said, once he was completely back to normal, "I nots kill hims, but I donts have to likes him, neithers."

"And I don't have to like you," Clearie hissed.

"Obviouslys," Ciaran shouted.

Clearie turned away from the goblin and glared at Fadin.

"What?" Fadin asked.

"You know what. Thanks for keeping me in the dark on this one."

Fadin raised an eyebrow. "Sorry, I didn't exactly think about it, with everything else going on."

"Well you should have," Clearie pouted, "what are we now? A family of liars?"

"Hey," Fadin said, getting close to Clearie's face, "Watch what you say."

"Oh, what's the big Fadin going to do? Pound me?"

"You'd be surprised," Fadin threatened.

"By what? Your stupidity? Because I was surprised by it with your little plan. How thick are you?"

Fadin clenched his fits together.

"Calm down," Tase said, putting a hand on Fadin's shoulder.

Fadin backed away and glared around the attic, trying to blow off steam. He had thought this would be a good place to convince his siblings of his plan, to prove to them why it was important to take matters into their own hands. But Clearie and Tase were not taking his idea as he had planned. This clearly was going to be harder than he thought.

"So," Ciaran said, jumping up on the broken dining table. "Lets me see if I understands." He began to pace back and forth, allowing his large ears to flop up and down as he walked. "You things," he pointed to Fadin, "wants to goes into woods, to Hogan home, and proves that he is…" he paused and held his hand in the air, questioningly, "still theres?"

"Yes," Fadin nodded. "I want to go into the woods and see if the house is abandoned or not."

"I repeat," Clearie said, his purple eye becoming more violet, "are you mental?"

"Oh, dry up, you scaredy cat," Fadin growled. "I know you both have to be thinking it too."

"No, Fadin," Tase said, "we haven't. We believe Mr. Hogan. If, and I mean, *if*, we go out there and go to their house, it will be empty. We will have gone outside the castle boundaries for nothing, and put ourselves in danger when Mr. Hogan clearly told us not to go into the woods. He told us he can't protect us from what's inside the forest. I don't want to see what that means."

"So you're telling me you don't find it odd, how long they've been gone? How strange it is that they haven't sent a letter? A postcard even?" Fadin lets his arms flop to his sides. "And Mr. Hogan is supposed to love us? He sure has a funny way of showing it."

Tase shook his head. "Of course it's odd. I don't like it, but I know, and you know, that Mr. Hogan does love us. He told us what he was doing was to protect us, to keep our family out of danger. He wants us to be safe."

"Safe?" Fadin laughed. "Then he shouldn't have left."

Clearie growled under his breath. "You are so stubborn sometimes. Do you know that?"

Fadin smiled sarcastically. "Yea, I do actually. Do you know you're a real eejit sometimes?"

Clearie ground his teeth together and made a fist.

"Okays, okays," Ciaran cried, stepping between them. He came up only to Fadin's knee, but he put his hands on both boys' legs, attempting to hold them back. "No fighting. Understands?" Ciaran asked.

Neither Fadin nor Clearie backed away.

"Looks," Ciaran said, gazing up at the two of them, "I haves answers for you things. K? I have a ideas."

"And what is that?" Fadin asked, not taking his eyes off Clearie's face. He was sure he knew what Ciaran would say, "stay heres, be safe." The little eejit. He would, of course, side with Tase and Clearie. They were the smart ones after all, right?

"You things should go."

"What?" Tase and Clearie said in unison.

It took a minute for the words to click into place in Fadin's mind. "Yea, what?" he asked, now understanding what the little goblin had said. He looked down.

Ciaran still had his hands on both their legs, though Clearie and Fadin weren't even looking at each other anymore. He looked up at them with his large, hazel eyes, and let out a deep breath. "I think you things should go. Should checks. That way, Fadins is satisfied, and you things know for fact toos. It can'ts hurt, and that way, you know if them gone or nots."

Fadin blinked. He couldn't believe what he was hearing. "Really?"

"Reallys," Ciaran smiled.

"Wait a minute, wait a minute," Clearie said. "First of all, it can hurt," he threw Ciaran a nasty look, "and there are things out there that want to kill us. Second of all, Mr. Hogan told us to stay here, and going into those woods would be strictly disobeying an order."

Fadin snorted. "An order made by someone who thought they'd be back by now. Why should we keep it?"

"Because it will keep us safe," Tase said.

Fadin felt the blood rise into his face. "Well you know what," he backed away and walked over to the round window so he could look out, "I'm going out there. You two can either come with me, or you can stay here." He turned to look at them. "It's up to you."

Tase stared at him for a long moment, arms crossed, stubbornly set in his way. He finally sighed and let his arms fall away. "Fine...I'm with you, but if we get into trouble," he raised his hand and pointed a finger at him, "it's all your fault."

Fadin grinned in spite of himself. "Clearie?"

Clearie shook his head. "Well if you two are going, I can't very well stay behind, can I?"

Fadin shook his head. "No, I suppose not."

"So," Clearie said, looking out of the round window as well, "now what?"

"Now," Fadin said, turning towards the tunnel, "into the woods we go."

~~~

The forest was dark, and even though he was determined, Fadin did feel a little frightened.

Everything was still and quiet. Unnaturally so. No birds sang, no mice or other furry animal scurried on the ground. It was...well...dead.

"It's awfully quiet out here, isn't it?" Clearie said. It wasn't really a question.

"Awfully," Fadin answered anyway. He let his eyes dart from one tree to another, half expecting to see the black dog following. But there was no sign of him or anything else, for that matter.

Fadin cringed at the crunching sounds the leaves made as they walked. They sounded like glass breaking with everything else being so still. If something was following them, it would take no great talent to seek them out. He was happy the Hogan cottage wasn't far away.

"Tell me something, Fadin," Clearie said, hopping over a fallen tree, "what exactly are you expecting to find out here anyway? Do you really think you're going to find the Hogans living happily in their little cottage? And if so, would that make you feel better? And if they're gone, what then? Will *that* change the way you feel now?"

Fadin felt a twinge of pain in his chest. He wanted the subject dropped. "I don't want to talk about it."

Clearie nodded sarcastically, his blond hair shimmering in the small amount of light that peeked through the branches. "Yea, good decision. I mean we're only out here for you, but hey, you don't want to talk about it."

"Dry up, Clearie," Tase defended.

Clearie grumbled.

Fadin turned to look at Tase, surprised.

Tase grinned. "Fighting won't help," he jumped over a small hole in the ground then caught up with Fadin. "Just so you know, I think this is really stupid, but..." he trailed off for a moment, "I understand why you have to see." He raised his orange-red eyebrows perceptively.

"Oh," Clearie cried, "help. My foot's bloody stuck."

Fadin turned around and saw Clearie, one leg knee-high, trapped in the mud.

Tase furrowed his brow hopelessly, and dropped back with Clearie, helping him get his foot unstuck.

Fadin rolled his eyes and twisted to look towards the Hogan cottage. He froze.

In the distance, shining with the dim light of the sun, long ebony hair flowed behind a girl, running through the trees.

He blinked and squinted, trying to get a better look. "Aimirgin?"

"What?" Tase asked.

Fadin paid no attention. He began to move forward, to follow the long hair. Could it be? Could they be back? Or never have left? "Aimirgin?" he called again.

"Fadin?" Tase said, questioningly.

Fadin picked up his pace. He didn't want to lose her.

"Fadin?" Tase cried, more desperately. "What are you doing?"

But Fadin wasn't listening. He began to run, following the long, shimmering hair. It flowed, as if in slow motion, through the dead-looking forest, like a magical wave of charcoal silk.

"Fadin!" Tase called, his voice sounding far away and panicked.

Fadin didn't care. They'd be fine and he couldn't just let her go. He had to find out. "Aimirgin," he cried yet again, although he didn't really expect an answer.

The girl began to move faster.

Fadin too, picked up the pace. He was flying through the forest, moving so fast, that everything appeared a blur. He began gaining on her, and he pushed his feet to bound even more rapidly.

The long hair looked even silkier as he got closer, but the girl's face was invisible to him, and she darted in and out of trees in a confusing fashion, which kept him from being in step with her.

Suddenly the girl darted sharply to the right, nearly tripping Fadin.

Fadin had to stop and turn himself around to follow.

The girl now had more space between them.

Fadin worried that he could not keep up much longer when out of the blue, the Hogan cottage appeared. Fadin screeched to a stop, and stared in awe at the familiar building. He breathed in heavily as he stood, blinking up at the house that once looked so friendly and inviting. Now it looked as dead as the forest around it. The flowers, which had been sporadically planted here and there had all wilted, the green tendrils that had climbed the cottage walls were now brown, and the windows that once boasted of warmth were now dark and cold. Even the paint looked faded.

One thing, and one thing only, showed signs of possible life. The front door stood wide open, swinging in the slight wind, inviting Fadin to step inside.

He felt a shiver go up his spine. Perhaps he shouldn't. But then, wasn't this why he had come here?

Fadin gulped and moved forward. He stepped slowly towards the door and paused when he reached the threshold. He took a deep breath, looked into the blackened entranceway, and marched inside.

The interior was as dead-looking as the exterior. Everything was dark and empty. The family room was devoid of furniture and pictures, and the floor was covered in leaves from the door being open and wind making the forest floor dance. Water stains, from the many rains that had come and gone in the past months, marked the carpeting as well.

Fadin sighed and looked at the open, worn-out door. They must have forgotten to shut it in their haste to leave. That was the only explanation.

One thing was for certain, no one had been living here for a long while.

Emptiness suddenly filled Fadin's stomach, and a hole, huge and painful, punched through his chest. He slumped to the floor and allowed the sobs and gasping of breath to wash over him. There was no stopping it anyway.

What had he expected to find? That they would be here? Waiting for them? And if they had, would he have been happy? Or angry?

Clearie was right, what was the point? This had been very stupid.

He covered his face and cried into his hands. The emptiness was overwhelming, and the sorrow was greater then he had imagined. He missed them, all of them so much, but mostly he missed Mr. Hogan. He had been so much like a father to him, so much like his own da. He had been their father's best friend as well, and now he too, like his beloved da, was gone.

Was it fair that he had to lose two fathers? What had he done to be punished like this? And who was doing it? Dia? That was a good person to blame. The supposed savior of the world, right? That sounded good, blame him. He deserved it. This had all happened because of him anyway.

"If you had just never come," Fadin yelled to the nothingness, "my parents would have in no way been in any stupid war, and they would both be alive right now. But no, you just had to show up and ruin everything!" He screamed the last words in hiccup-like sobs as the tears poured out freely. There was no stopping the waterfall now. He curled into a ball and just let the emotions come. He had been hiding them for so long, it almost felt good to be sad.

"Fadin!" someone screamed in a voice that was all too familiar, but sounding as though it was quaking.

Fadin ceased crying immediately and snapped his head up. "Tase?"

"Fadin," the voice cried again. It sounded almost dream-like, and shuddering at the first and last syllable. "Fadin, help."

Fadin stood up. "Tase?"

"Fadin, help us please!" Tase's voice was filled with terror.

"Tase? Where are you?" A sudden wave of nausea crashed over Fadin and he had to grip onto the wall to keep from toppling over. Everything started to spin and a flash of light seemed to transport him somewhere else.

Fadin opened his eyes and found he could somehow *see* Tase, standing, frozen, with Clearie beside him, staring at something out of Fadin's sight. He couldn't move, he couldn't talk, all he could do was watch as the vision, or whatever it was, played foggily in front of him.

"Stay," Tase said, holding his arm in front of him, "just be a good dog, and stay."

Deep and angry growling could abruptly be heard somewhere off to the right.

Fadin made himself look there, and saw, to his horror, the black dog, massive and deadly, snarling with large, red-stained teeth that glistened in the dim light. The animal had eyes so light, they nearly appeared colourless, and his fur was as black as midnight, making the contrast startling.

Tase backed up slowly, bending down to pick up a stick. He held it out, nonthreatening, in front of him. "Stay," he said again.

The animal barked and leapt forward.

Tase and Clearie screamed in unison.

Tase's twig snapped as the animal landed on top of him, but the dog had not been aiming for Tase. He bit down on Clearie's leg and pulled with immense force.

Clearie yelped in fear and pain as the dog dragged him along the forest floor, away from Tase, and into the deep trees.

"Clearie," Tase screamed. He rushed forward trying to keep up. "Fadin, where are you? Help!"

The vision swirled and blurred into a fog. Fadin gasped and he was suddenly back in the empty room, alone except for the slight wind that played at his red hair. He shook and crumpled to the floor. He gasped for air and the strength to stand. He knew what he had seen had either just happened or was going to happen soon. He had to get up; he had to get to them.

"Get up," he yelled at himself, "get up." And with that, he stumbled to his feet, out of the door, and began to stagger through the woods.

~~~

"Fadin?" Tase screamed after his brother. But it was too late, he could no longer hear him. Tase saw his red hair dart behind a tree and disappear into the woods.

"What is he doing?" Clearie cried, trying to yank his leg out of the muck.

"I haven't got the slightest idea," Tase answered. He looked back at Clearie and his mud-stuck leg. "Give me both your hands," Tase said.

Clearie stuck both arms out.

Tase seized them, stood, and began yanking.

"I can feel my leg moving," Clearie informed.

"Good," Tase grunted, "try to use your other leg to push yourself out."

Clearie nodded, and pushed on the firm dirt with his good leg.

Tase could feel the progress being made. He looked down and saw the entire leg nearly exposed. The only part left was the foot. "Almost there,"

Tase grumbled. He gave one last hard pull, and Clearie was free.

"Thanks," Clearie said, shaking his foot to get the mud and grime off.

"Yea," Tase accepted inattentively. He looked through the woods, trying to spot Fadin, but he was nowhere in sight.

"That caffler, I can't believe he just left us," Clearie whined.

"Me neither," Tase said, feeling a little nervous. Why would he leave?

"Maybe we should head to the cottage? What do you think, Tase?" Clearie looked at him questioningly.

Tase nodded vaguely. "Yea, maybe we should." He turned to head toward the Hogan's house when a low grumble filled his ears.

Clearie froze. "Tase? Tell me that was your stomach."

Tase gulped and looked behind him.

There, standing tall and menacing, was the black dog. His eyes were so illuminated that they looked white, with only the faintest hint of green. He curled his mouth into a sneer, and Tase saw that his teeth were stained red from something, or someone, he had recently eaten.

Tase swallowed hard. *Fadin.* He thought. *Fadin, help.* He looked about the woods, racking his brains for something he could do, something he could put between them and the large canine.

The dog began to move forward.

*Fadin, help us please.* Tase called in his mind. He held up his hand, trying to keep the dog as far away from them as possible.

Clearie quivered behind him, keeping himself out of the hound's view.

"Stay," Tase said to the animal, "just be a good dog and stay." He backed up slowly and spotted a large stick on the ground. He bent to pick it up, and held it out in front of him like a weapon. "Stay," he repeated.

The animal was having none of that. He barked, a deep and horrifying sound, and leapt forward.

Tase screamed in terror and he heard Clearie cry out too.

The animal landed on top of them and Tase felt something break. He wondered if it was his arm or neck, and the pain hadn't caught up with the shock of it yet. But then he saw the twig, half of it sticking out from under the animal, and realized that his bones were fine.

Clearie suddenly shrieked in pain.

Tase snapped his head backward, as far as the weight of the animal would let him, and saw that the dog had Clearie's leg clamped in his mouth.

The animal pulled with impressive force, dragging himself and Clearie off and over Tase. The animal continued to haul him along the ground and into the deepness of the woods.

Shock made Tase's eyes feel like they would bulge out of their sockets. He jumped to his feet. "Clearie," he called, and began to sprint towards his brother, trying with all his might to keep up. "Fadin," he called in desperation, "where are you? Someone, help!" He bounded with all his might towards Clearie and the animal, and began to gain.

"Tase," Clearie screamed. He was thrashing and trying to turn around. His hands clawed at the dirt and trees, making scratch marks along the ground.

"Clearie," Tase called back. He breathed heavily and dug his heels into the earth. He was close enough now to almost touch Clearie's hands, but if he stopped to bend down, he'd lose them. So Tase flung himself forward, into the air. He landed at precisely the right spot and clutched Clearie's hands, which curled around his own.

The sudden addition of weight caused the dog to lose his grip on Clearie's leg, and he stumbled backward.

Tase, eyes wide with fear, tried to stand Clearie up. "Come on, come on," Tase pleaded.

Though Clearie tried, his leg was too badly wounded for him to put weight on it, and he cried out in pain as he attempted to stand. "Oh, I can't, Tase!" he screamed in panic.

Tase looked toward the spot where the animal had fallen and saw, to his terror, the dog leaping into the air right for them.

Tase yelped and lugged Clearie backward with all his might in an attempt to dodge the large animal.

Something brown and hefty suddenly struck the canine mid-jump, and sent him flying backwards.

Tase spun himself around and saw a large, mud-covered, weasel-like creature growling at the dog. Its behind had root-like tendrils snaking here and there, acting as its tail. The root-like tail snapped like a whip in the black dog's direction.

Tase remembered, without much effort, that the creature was called a Lithian. He remembered the Lithian he had run into with Fadin, the one that seemed intent on killing him. But this one appeared to be protecting them. Tase didn't understand it, but he moved toward the large weasel-creature, putting as much distance as he could between the dog and Clearie.

Clearie looked up at the Lithian and shrieked.

Tase clamped a hand over his mouth, not in the mood to explain.

The black canine got up from its beating, and darted back towards Tase and Clearie.

The Lithian growled and snapped its tail toward the dog.

The canine dodged the blow and barked furiously. He paced back and forth, trying to find an opening so he could spring.

A shrill cry caught Tase off guard. He snapped his head off to the right and saw something running towards them.

The Lithian growled and yipped, as a knife flew from whatever was running at them, and stuck into its side.

Tase gasped and looked to see what had thrown the weapon.

Thick black hair flowed through the trees, glistening in the soft light. Suddenly the hair stopped not a meter from them. It blew wildly in the soft wind and parted, revealing a beautiful teenage girl with pale skin and midnight eyes. Her figure was as beautiful as her face—thick, plump lips, elegant nose, curvy hips, and long legs. She was cloaked in an ebony silk dress with her whitish feet bare.

Tase, enthralled by her beauty, nearly let Clearie fall down so that he could be nearer to her, but he snapped back to reality as, with a shock to his conscience, he realized who she was.

Dominique Bojin, the beautiful but deadly girl from the black-and-white photo. The girl Mr. Hogan had warned him about.

Tase trembled and clutched Clearie tighter. He tried to yank him away, but his brother was becoming heavier by the second.

The Lithian snapped his root-tail towards Dominique, but she whipped out a knife and cut part of it off.

The Lithian screeched and held its head up to howl as blood poured from the wound.

"Go," Dominique suddenly cried to the hound.

The black canine lunged forward in obedience.

Tase screamed, fear seizing every part of his body.

The dog hit them, throwing Tase and Clearie backwards into bushes and rocks. Tase panicked and tried with all his might to right himself, but his terror caused him to stumble and trip.

Clearie tried to crawl away, but became as still as a statue as the canine came within centimetres of them, snarling and biting.

The animal licked his lips and opened his mouth wide.

"Ahee," someone cried.

The canine was unexpectedly flung backwards into a tree by something long and pale.

Tase blinked and stared in front of him.

A woman, tall and lean, stood before him. Her frame was so thin, he would have thought her an extremely tall child if he had not seen her face. And her face was indeed lovely, not the same erotic beauty of Dominique, but a pure and innocent exquisiteness. Her face was dawned with a flattened nose, dainty lips and astounding eyes, for whenever she glanced this way or that, they changed colour like crystal in the light. Her head was crowned with white curls and her forehead bore a beautiful opal horn.

Tase felt himself have to make an effort to breathe in her presence. She seemed so glorious that it was hard to look at her for long.

The horned woman turned away from him and glared in the direction of Dominique and the dog. "Haway," she yelled, "haway shrom here, Dominique. Hi whorn you. Lehave now."

Tase swallowed. This woman was very brave to demand the Bojins to just go away. He snapped his head to see how Dominique would react to this.

The black dog ran to her side, as Dominique threw her head back and laughed. "Avay? You vant me to go avay? Vell let me tell you somting, my horned feind. I, and my companion here, are going novhere." She smiled wide and the white of her eyes filled with inky blackness, giving her a demonic look. Her hair began to fly in all directions and her lips parted.

Tase backed up instinctively, and he even noticed the Lithian take a step away.

Dominique closed her pure black eyes and folded her hands together.

The horned woman stood, crouched, as if ready to lunge forward or catch something being tossed at her.

With a burst of wind, Dominique opened her eyes and held her hands in front of her mouth. She blew into them, like she was sending a kiss on the wind, and fire erupted from her fingertips, flying towards the horned woman and Tase.

Tase yelped and jumped backwards, sending Clearie tumbling again to the ground.

The horned woman stood tall, holding her long-fingered hands before her, and seemed to catch the blaze. She gripped it, with merely a centimetre of air between the fire and her skin, and suddenly shot it back at Dominique.

The canine winced backwards, but Dominique laughed widely. She hit the ball of fire nonchalantly with her hand and sent it flying into a tree.

The tree went ablaze and completely burned to a crisp in under a second.

Tase gulped.

Dominique yipped like a wild animal and held her hands to her hips. Knives exploded from her hair and rose around and above her. With another yip, they shot forward.

The pale woman touched her horn and a translucent shield burst before them.

The knives hit the barrier and fell on the ground.

The tall, horned female took a step forward and neighed like a horse. She shook her long white locks and then snapped her head towards Dominique.

Light shot like an arrow from the horn towards Dominique and the canine.

Tase saw her try and stop the light, but it was too powerful.

It hit the dog and Dominique like lightning. They sped backwards and hit several trees, cutting them down with the force of the blow.

Dominique shot up, obviously attempting to fight back, but her head was bleeding. She touched the red liquid and hissed like a cat in their direction.

The pale female neighed again and stamped her hoofed feet. "Haway," she repeated. "His not your sime yet."

The black canine growled furiously.

Dominique hissed again. She shot a dark glance at Tase and Clearie, and pointed with her index finger and pinkie finger towards them. "Dis is not over." She glared at the horned woman, "not by a long shot." She smiled at Tase and Clearie, "I'll be seeing the tvo of you, very soon." She swiftly backed away into the shadows, stepping lightly so that not even the leaves crunched beneath her feet.

Tase swallowed as she and the black dog disappeared.

The horned woman turned first to the Lithian. She walked to him and hummed something while she touched the knife in his side.

This caused him to yelp thunderously.

The pale woman patted him and quickly yanked out the weapon.

The Lithian cried out and then licked the horned female with a long black tongue.

The horned woman smiled and pointed to the mucky hole the creature had burst from.

The Lithian nodded and crawled, noisily, back into the earth.

Tase just sat next to Clearie with a dumbfounded expression painted across his face. His legs ached, his arms burned, and his face felt like it had scrapes all across it, but he barely noticed the pain. All he could do was stare, bewildered and fear-stricken. The shock had not worn off.

The horned woman looked at Tase and Clearie. She made her way gracefully towards them. She bent down low and touched Tase's face. "Go home, Taseling," she said.

Tase opened his mouth in surprise, for when she spoke, her mouth did not open. She was communicating with him in his mind.

She touched Clearie's face, and Tase heard her say, "Stay inshide the castle. Is not shafe here."

Clearie nodded.

The woman smiled at them, backed away, and took off, running like a wild stallion, into the trees.

Tase let out the breath he had been holding and stared off into oblivion, trying to let his mind catch up. That had been completely mental, and impossible, but it had happened. Evidence of the battle was all around him. Broken trees, upturned earth. It had been real. Impractical as it was, it was real.

"Tase, Clearie," a familiar voice called.

Tase didn't register the words at first, and still sat, blankly gazing at the forest.

"Tase, Clearie, where are you?" the voice screamed.

Tase blinked, and looked in the direction of the shouts.

Fadin, red and wet with perspiration, came bounding out of the trees. "Tase, Clearie," he cried, "you're okay." He looked around at the clearing that had been created, and back to his brothers. He obviously noticed the cuts and bruises on Tase, because his face became concerned. "What happened?"

Tase looked at him blankly. He made himself stand up and walk over to him. Fury suddenly took over, and he made his hand into a fist.

"Tase?" Fadin asked, unsure.

Tase picked his arm up and punched Fadin, right in the nose.

Fadin howled in pain and shock. "Oh," he grunted, and covered his nose in his hands as he crumpled to the floor.

Tase shook his arm as it stung from the powerful blow.

Fadin pulled his hands away, and glanced at the red liquid running down his fingers. "What was that for?" he asked angrily.

Tase turned to him, livid. "What was that for?" He stamped towards him.

Fadin backed up.

"Do you see this?" Tase spun about, holding his arms out to the disaster around them. "Do you see that?" He pointed to Clearie's bitten and bloodied leg. "This, is all your fault! Huge black dogs, giant weasel monsters, horned women, a crazy teenage girl, all fighting over us. If you hadn't have been a complete eejit, and talked us into disobeying Mr. Hogan, we'd have been fine. But oh no, you had to come out here and see for yourself. Well I hope you're satisfied, because *we*, "he pointed to Clearie and himself, "were almost killed. And by the way, thank you so much for leaving us to *die* while you ran off to chase shadows or who knows what. Thank you for that, it just put the icing on the cake." Tase flared his nose in anger. "So that," he pointed to Fadin's nose, "is payback. And let me tell you, *that* was nice of me."

Fadin's expression fell. He got a strange look on his face, and nodded. "I'm sorry. You're right."

All the anger left Tase in a flash. This was not the response he had been expecting. Something was wrong. "Fadin?"

"You were right, you know. The both of you. I'm sorry for bringing us out here, it was mental." He looked up at Tase. "I found the cottage and it was empty, just like you said it would be. No one is there or has been there. They're gone, Tase. They're really gone, and look at what's happened." He nodded to Clearie. "We had better get out of here, you two can explain everything inside." Fadin stood up and walked over to Clearie.

Tase stood still for a minute, stunned.

"I need your help, Tase," Fadin grunted.

Tase stumbled over to him, and helped get Clearie up.

"Ouch," Clearie whined. "Oh, careful for my leg."

Tase and Fadin propped him up with their arms and shoulders.

"You okay, Clearie?" Fadin asked.

Clearie nodded. "I can make it back like this. But um, just out of curiosity, how are we going to explain this to Ma?"

Tase looked at them.

Fadin was covered in dirt and blood was dripping down his face.

Clearie had sticks and muck in his hair, his face was bruised from being dragged along the ground, and his leg looked like it had been ripped apart.

Tase glanced down at himself and saw he was covered in sticks and mud, had cuts on his hands and legs, and his clothes were badly torn.

"Um…" Tase said, unsure how they could dodge the truth.

"We can say that we went exploring into the woods." Fadin answered. "We'll tell her Tase and I got into a fight, and that your leg got caught in an old hunting trap, Clearie."

Clearie nodded his head in approval. "That'll work."

Tase raised his eyebrows. "If she buys it."

"Well, it's better than telling her what really happened," Clearie pointed out.

Things were silent for a long moment, then Clearie added, "You know what this feels like?"

"What?" Fadin asked, propping him up a little higher on his shoulder.

"Like a dream but when you're awake?" Tase tried.

Clearie nodded. "Yea, except not a dream, more like a nightmare."

Fadin sighed, "Yea, I hope Ma buys the story, or else the two of you are going to be committed."

Tase shook his head and smiled at Fadin. A sudden feeling of love and appreciation swept over him as Fadin grinned back, the blood on his face beginning to thicken. "Thank you, Fadin."

Fadin eyed him, taken aback. "For what?"

Tase laughed, what was he thanking him for exactly? "For existing," he decided.

Fadin raised his eyebrows. "You must have hit your head or something. But..." he knocked him on the back of the skull, "you're welcome, Tase. Anytime."

Tase giggled.

Fadin and Clearie joined in, and together, they hobbled towards the castle, to their doom with their mother, and out of the gloomy, dead forest.

# Chapter 18

## *Time for Truth*

The story about the hunting trap seemed to go over pretty well, Fadin thought. Granted, he and Tase had been yelled at and grounded, but since they had no desire to go outside anyway, it really didn't matter.

Clearie's wounds were dressed by Miss O'Keefe, who apparently, on top of being a teacher, was also a skilled nurse. To Fadin's astonishment, his leg was not broken, but it did have to be wrapped, and he was ordered to either be in bed or in a chair throughout each day. Embarrassing as it was, he needed help to get cleaned up, so Tase and Fadin's job, also a part of the punishment, was to help him shower each morning.

Fadin's nose healed quickly, leaving his eyes black and blue for only a few days.

Tase's scrapes and bruises didn't last long either. But time, at least to Fadin, seemed to drag on forever.

~~~

March turned into April.

The sadness and the hole that lived in Fadin's chest from the emptiness of the Hogan house lingered, and the fear of what had happened in the woods held on without loosening its grip. The nightmares did not cease, in fact, they worsened. There was not a night when Fadin did not wake up screaming, seeing Afanasii and the flaming car. Now his father was accompanied by Mr. Hogan, and they both burned in the inferno, calling out to Fadin for help, who was useless to do anything.

In the waking world, things had changed. Kyna got into a horrible argument with Ma, packed her bags, and left. She hadn't been home in two weeks, and besides the concern for her safety, things at the castle were quiet. The arguments seemed to have stopped, and everyone was being kind to one another again. It seemed to Fadin that Kyna had been the cause of all the animosity, and in her absence, there was peace.

Well, peace for everyone except Fadin.

~~~

April turned into May.

There was still no word from Aunt Kyna and absolutely nothing from the Hogans. Nine days since May had started, and not one word. Something was wrong, Fadin could feel it.

Not only had there been no word, but there had been no sign of life inside the woods. No black dog, no howls in the night, not even the breeze seemed to move the trees anymore. Everything was dead.

There seemed to be no hope left, not for Fadin. He felt that with the death of the forest, so the possibility of the Hogans returning died. There was nothing to look forward to, well nothing except for June 12th, his and Tase's birthday. They would be turning thirteen, teenagers. But, as exciting as that should be, birthdays seemed a thing of the past, something unimportant now.

Fadin lay in his bed, gazing up at the ceiling, letting all this twist and turn in his brain. The hole in his chest had not gotten smaller, and the memory of the empty house seemed to sink into his stomach, never leaving.

The sudden sound of quick footsteps caught Fadin's attention, and he sat up to listen.

Someone was running down the hall. They hit a wall—no, a door—and swung it open. The door was slammed shut and the sound of retching could be heard.

Fadin crinkled his nose. Ma.

She was not getting better. She was pale as a ghost, constantly covered up in gigantic sweaters and bulky blankets. Enda and Caoimhe fussed over her a lot, and popped her full of vitamins and healthy things to eat. None of it was helping.

Fadin heard the toilet flush and the footfalls of Ma as she made it back to her room.

"I think she's getting worse," Tase said from the bottom bunk.

Fadin leaned over the railing, and saw Tase's blue eyes looking up at him. "Yea," Fadin agreed. Thoughts of death, truth, and the Hogans swarmed in his head again, almost becoming unbearable.

The handle of their door began to twist unexpectedly.

Fadin, out of habit, flung himself backwards and pretended to sleep.

The door opened and someone walked inside.

"You don't have to pretend you're sleeping, it's just me," the voice of Clearie informed.

Fadin sighed and sat up.

"Did you hear Ma just now?" Clearie asked.

329

"Yes, we did," Fadin nodded. He moved towards his ladder and hopped to the floor.

"It's definitely not getting better," Clearie said, shaking his blond locks.

"No," Tase said bleakly, "she isn't."

Afanasii, Dia, the war, Dominique, Aunt Kyna, the black dog, Ma's illness, and the Hogans' strange disappearance all flooded Fadin's thoughts. Every part of him seemed to be consumed with wanting answers, not satisfied with the things he knew. It had been too long, far too long for the Hogans to be gone, and the hole in his chest confirmed his fears. Something was very wrong, and Fadin had had enough. "I can't take it anymore," he yelled.

Tase and Clearie turned to him in surprise.

"What?" Tase asked, looking confused.

"It's been five bloody months," Fadin growled, "something's wrong, something's very wrong, and I want to know what it is. I'm tired of being in the dark."

"Fadin," Clearie said, but Fadin interrupted him.

"No, I don't care. We have to find out what happened to them. This isn't right."

"What do you want us to do?" Tase asked. "You saw what happened last time we interfered. Look at Clearie's leg."

Fadin glanced down.

His leg was still bandaged up, though it had healed significantly.

"I know what happened last time, but it's been almost half a year and we haven't heard anything. Not to mention the fact that that black dog has seemed to have vanished. You two have to admit that something isn't right."

"Really?" Clearie asked sarcastically, "I had no idea." He took a step forward, "Look Fadin, I know something isn't right, but last time we disobeyed Mr. Hogan, we were almost killed. We'd be mental to try something else."

Fadin laughed crazily. "We'd be mental?" He walked in a small circle, and turned to look at his brothers, "I'm already mental. I have nightmares every night, I can't stop thinking about Afanasii and the Hogans. And I just can't stand this not knowing anymore. The way I look at it, and I have looked at it a million ways, is that the Hogans either lied to us and betrayed us—"

"No, Fadin," Tase started.

Fadin held a hand up to him, "—or, they're in serious trouble. Either way, we'd be eejits not to find out."

Tase looked angry now. "Look Fadin, Clearie and I feel the same way, but...have you completely forgotten about what happed in the forest? Or what Mr. Hogan told us? We were almost *killed*. Maybe if you had been the one dragged along the ground or thrown meters in the air, you'd be more cautious. But let me tell you something, you are not going back out there because I'm not letting you. It's suicide."

Fadin shoved the hand Tase had placed on his shoulder away, and stomped to the window. "I know we're not going back out there. I wouldn't risk what happened twice. But I am going to find out what happened to them, with or without your help."

"And how are you going to do that, smart one?" Clearie asked.

"I'm telling Ma what we know."

"What?" Clearie and Tase shouted.

"No, Fadin, she's sick," Clearie growled.

"Exactly," Fadin snorted. "She's sick, and we don't know how sick. I can't tell you how many times I wish I could have asked Da about the crest before he left that morning. How I wish he could have told us the truth. But he never did, he died, and I am not making the same mistake with Ma. I'm getting *her*, not Mr. Hogan, to tell me what happened. I want the truth, all of it, before it's too late."

"Fadin," Clearie tried.

But he wasn't listening. Fadin ran forwards and opened the door.

"No, Fadin don't," Tase yelled, "You'll make things worse." Tase grabbed a hold of Fadin's arm.

Fadin pushed him away and ran down the hall.

"Fadin," Clearie shouted, angry.

Fadin didn't care, enough was enough. It was time for the truth. He put his hand on Ma's door knob and began to turn it. "Ouch," Fadin yelped. Something had hit him on top of his head. He turned to Clearie and Tase, "Throwing things won't stop me."

But they weren't looking at him. They were staring up at the ceiling.

Fadin followed their gaze and saw Ciaran's big-eared head sticking out from the ceiling above. He had to suppress a cry of shock, though this was hardly an abnormal event anymore.

"Psst!" the goblin whispered. "You things, all you things. Comes up to my's home. Must tells you something. Come, come, quick." Ciaran's head vanished.

Fadin gawked at his brothers for a moment.

They all dashed down the stairs.

Fadin paid attention to nothing but his feet and the possibility of news about the Hogans.

"Whoops!"

Fadin looked up. He tried to stop, to put the brakes on, but the force of gravity kept him running, and he hit Enda with incredible force, as the butler, or his uncle, placed his foot on the first stair.

The tray in Enda's hands went flying. Soup, juice, and vitamins fell all around them, and Enda slammed into the floor.

"Oh, I'm sorry," Fadin said, trying to help pick up the broken glass.

"Don't bother," Enda said. "I can clean it faster." He tried to sit up. "Ow," he yelped.

"What's wrong?" Fadin asked.

"My back, oh! I think I've cracked or bruised something."

Tase's eyes widened and he blinked at Fadin.

Fadin fidgeted. He wasn't about to leave Enda lying on the floor but he desperately wanted to get to the attic.

"Stay here," he said, getting out of the juice puddle and running to the rose room.

Miss O'Keefe was there, sitting on her bed, reading something or another. She had half-moon spectacles on and wore a deep gray turtle-neck. Her hair lay flat around her face, as always, and her eyes seemed to be intently scrolling the page.

Fadin thought for a moment. Why would she wear a turtle-neck in May? It was spring for goodness sake, wasn't she hot? But the gravity of the moment swept him up again. "Help," he said. "Enda fell and hurt his back. He can't get up."

Miss O'Keefe sat up and removed her reading glasses. "Where is he?"

"Here, in the entrance," Fadin said and dashed back down the hall.

Miss O'Keefe was right behind him, and she leaned down once she spotted the accident. She put her hand under Enda's neck.

"Can you move?" She asked him in her deeper voice.

He shook his head. "No, no I can't."

"You've killed him," Tase moaned, putting both hands on his head.

"No, not killed," Miss O'Keefe said, feeling Enda's ribs. "Bruised, perhaps."

Enda moaned as she put her hand on his spine. "It's alright Enda, I'll fix you. It really isn't that bad."

"Not that bad?" Enda wailed. "I can't even pick up by bloody arm. Ouch!"

She had touched another part of his spine. "It really isn't that bad. Boys," she said, "I want you to go and fetch Daireann for me, alright?"

"I can stay here and help..." Clearie began.

"No, I want you to help your brothers."

"But it's not that..."

"Go," she said firmly.

Clearie didn't ask again.

They ran down the hall and into the kitchen.

Daireann was obviously making lunch.

"We need your help," Fadin said. "Enda's been hurt."

She dropped her spatula. "Hurt? Oh no, is he okay?"

They started moving down the hall as they talked.

"I think so, Miss O'Keefe's with him."

As they rounded the corner, Enda was standing. He looked fine; in fact, better then fine, he looked great.

Fadin stared.

"Told you it wasn't that bad," Miss O'Keefe said smiling.

"But he couldn't even move," Clearie said.

"Guess she was right," Enda answered grinning.

"So you're okay, En?" Daireann asked.

"Never better."

She smiled. "Guess you boys got yourselves all worked up for nothing, huh?" She said putting a hand on their shoulders. "Well, I better finish that pudding," she smiled then walked back down the hall.

Tase shook his head. "But you couldn't move."

Enda just smiled and kept picking up the broken glass.

"Why don't you boys carry on with whatever it was you were doing," Miss O'Keefe said. "I can help him."

Fadin gawked, thoroughly confused. "Okay then."

He grabbed Tase's and Clearie's arms and lead them through the tea room into the narrow hall. If she wasn't going to answer their questions, then there was no reason to waste time standing still.

"How was he, okay?" Clearie asked once they were sure no one had followed them.

"Isn't it obvious?" Fadin asked. "She used her magic. Remember that day when Aunt Kyna flipped out Tase?"

Tase nodded.

"She must have used whatever power it is that she has."

"She is magic? How does that work anyway?" Clearie asked.

"I don't know. No one found it fit to tell us that bit," Fadin answered, pulling out the wooden "K" and fitting it with its counterpart.

The bookcase rumbled and opened.

"Let's go."

They entered the stone stairs, the forgotten room, and then opened the attic door.

Ciaran was sitting on the broken table waiting for them. His wooden leg was removed and he was biting his fingernails.

"What tooks you things so long?" he asked sounding very nervous.

"Sorry, we ran into a bit of trouble," Fadin said.

"Ran, funny you think you are thing? This is no times for joking."

"What's wrong, Ciaran?" Tase asked.

"This wrong," Ciaran said handing him a torn piece of parchment.

Fadin looked over his shoulder and read the big, bold print.

*Ministry in uproar.*

He scrolled down to the actual story.

*The Ministry in Cavan-Corr is in a shambles. The new peace treaty has caused much division within the Council of Princes and has even put a gap between the king and the people.*

*The decision to have the council sign the new act without even announcing the plans to the people has caused many to worry about the king's sanity. In fact, there has been talk that our King has ruled for long enough. The people seem to think it's time for a new ruler.*

*As of yet, the council has not stated its opinion, with the exception of one individual. Council Member Kyna Kavanagh.*

*Earlier this morning, Mrs. Kavanagh made a public statement in Cavan-Corr Market that she and other council members strongly disagree with what is happening at the Ministry. She claimed that it is time for Cavan-Corr to move on and choose a new ruler, one who in her own words, "is sane, logical, and an actual leader, not a sniveling buffoon."*

*The Ministry Guard arrested Mrs. Kavanagh for slander and for speaking about Ministry Matters without the permission of the king. Mrs. Kavanagh was then thrown in Cavan-Corr Penitentiary to await a trial on a later date.*

*Now we, the people of Cavan-Corr, must ask ourselves, what do we believe in? What do we think? Do we agree or disagree with Mrs. Kavanagh? And lastly, do we sit by and watch as the Ministry crumbles? Or do we get up and do something about it?*

*-Argonne Nugent*

Fadin backed up and looked at Ciaran.

"Aunt Kyna is in jail?" Clearie asked, taking the paper away from Tase.

Fadin thought about the contents of the letter. Cavan-Corr, where had he heard that name before? Mr. Hogan. He had told them that was the secret city the followers of Dia had built during the war.

"What does that mean?" Clearie asked, still talking about Aunt Kyna.

"It means you in troubles," Ciaran said, putting his wooden leg back on.

"What?" Tase asked. "Why would we be in trouble?"

"Kyna is your sister-mother. That mean you things coulds get into trouble for what she said."

"Why would they be angry at us? We didn't say it," Fadin said.

Ciaran shook his head. "No matters. Stills you her relations and if king or advisor is angry enough, they comes here next."

Fadin looked at his brothers.

"Are you sure about this, Ciaran?" Clearie asked him.

"Positives," Ciaran said nodding vigorously. "They will comes."

"But I don't think they even know we're here," Tase said. "Didn't Lorcan say that Da working in the bank had been a secret? How would they know we're here?"

Ciaran snorted. "Because you things' so-calls friends tells them."

"What?" Fadin said turning to him.

"The Hogan things," Ciaran said. "Everyone's talking. They say that run away mothers is back with sons. Peoples become angry, they no like to hear that. They say they want O'Callaghan's gone. They say that you things is troubles."

"What did the Hogans say?" Tase asked.

"I no hear," Ciaran said looking away.

Fadin could tell he was lying. "What did they say Ciaran?"

"I no remember."

"Come on, Ciaran," Clearie said. "We can tell you know."

Ciaran looked up at them with his big hazel eyes. "I may misunderstand you knows."

"Just tell us," Fadin said.

"I think them say they no understands. They no understand why mother had leave or why she come back now. They say you family is trouble and was better when was gone. Them say they stay in Cavan-Corr, not come back till you go home. But maybe was someone else, is hard to see from where me hide."

Fadin looked away. So, they weren't in trouble, they just didn't want to see Fadin and his brothers anymore. They had left for good. He had known five months had been an awfully long time.

"How did you hear all this?" Clearie asked.

"Remembers how me has been gone lot."

They nodded.

Ciaran hadn't been around much since the incident in the woods. "Well mes been going to Cavan-Corr. Ever since peace paper, peoples been going nuttsy. So me thinks I should have look. I sneak in the rocks and no one sees me. I listen to what they say and takes papers when I can," he nodded to the piece of parchment in Clearie's hand.

"What do you mean you sneak in the rocks?" Fadin asked.

"You know, rocks, bigs, round, grey..."

"No, I know what rocks are, Ciaran. I'm talking about why would you sneak in the rocks. Why not hide behind trees or bushes?"

"Trees no grow underground," Ciaran said cocking his head. "Does they?"

"Underground?" Clearie said. "You mean Cavan-Corr is underground?"

"Ofs course. Where else it be?"

Fadin threw his hands in the air. "And Mr. Hogan didn't think this important to tell us, why?" He sat on the floor and hung his head. "I'm tired of not being told the truth."

Ciaran hobbled over to him. "I sorry thing. I wish somethings I could do's to help."

"You already have Ciaran. You helped us the most."

Ciaran gave him a weak smile.

"Now what?" Clearie asked looking at the piece of newspaper again.

"Now," Fadin said standing. "We go talk to Ma."

"About what?" Tase asked moving in front of him.

"About all this," Fadin moved his outstretched arms in a circle.

"I don't think that's such a good idea, Fadin," Tase said.

Clearie moved forward. "Neither do I, I mean she's been really sick."

"And I think she's going to be a whole lot sicker if a bunch of Ministry Guards show up at this castle, because of Aunt Kyna, without her even understanding why."

Tase looked at him then whispered. "Do you think what he's saying about them coming for us is true?"

Fadin glanced back at the little goblin fiddling with his wooden leg.

"Why would he lie?"

"Me would not lies," Ciaran said, obviously hearing Tase's feeble attempt at whispering.

"We didn't think you would," Fadin said. "Now when do you think the people from Cavan-Corr are coming?"

"Oh, me not know. I just thinks they are. If Kings Raegan is upsets with aunts, then he most likely sends people to you things."

"Would they arrest us?" Clearie asked.

"Me not sure. I think no. They may takes in for questions, but if they finds good reasons, they may take you to go see aunt. And me no means for a visit."

Fadin nodded. "Thank you, Ciaran. I think we'll go have a little talk with our mother now."

"Wait! You things gonna tell mother you knows. Knows about magic and others things?"

"That's right," Fadin said looking at his brothers.

"Wells, then can things makes a promise to me?"

Fadin turned to look at the wide-eyed Ciaran. "What?"

"Cans you makes me a promise?"

"What kind of promise?" Tase asked.

"When you things tell mother, please no tell her bouts me."

"Why?" Clearie asked.

"Cause some Dalbhach not like goblins living in attic. Kyna not even know me here. I no want to have to finds nother home."

"Well of course we wont tell her then, Ciaran. We won't tell anyone," Fadin said.

The little goblin smiled. "Thanks you, Fadins."

Fadin smiled. That was the first time Ciaran had ever called him by his name.

"We better get going. We have no time to waste."

They walked over to the old door but Fadin stopped before leaving.

"Thank you for always telling us the truth, Ciaran."

The goblin smiled wide. "Always."

Fadin smiled back and left the room.

Once out of the bookcase, Fadin could hear Daireann and Enda whispering nervously. As he rounded the corner he saw they had a large newspaper in their hands.

"Do you think they're reading about Aunt Kyna?" Tase asked.

"No doubt," Fadin answered.

He walked closer to them, making sure they didn't hear or see him; it wasn't too hard for they were completely distracted by the newspaper. Fadin moved behind them and glanced down at the page.

"What you reading?" he asked.

Enda and Daireann jumped.

"Oh, Fadin," Daireann said, "nothing, nothing at all."

"It didn't look like nothing."

"Well it was," Enda answered harshly.

"It looked like a newspaper," Tase said standing next to his brother.

"Yea," Clearie said joining them, "What was the title? The Cavan-Corr Post? I've never heard of it."

"Neither have I," Fadin said smirking up at them.

"Well," Enda said staring down at the three brothers, "this is a big place and I wouldn't expect you to know the name of every newspaper in the country."

"Yes, but I thought the local newspaper was called The Killeen Times," Fadin said.

"Well then, I suppose you were mistaken."

"Were we?" Fadin said. "Imagine that."

Enda eyed him suspiciously. "What are you getting at?"

"We want to talk to our Ma," Fadin said folding his arms.

"Yes, we need to tell her something," Tase added.

"Well, I'm sorry but you can't. She isn't feeling well so she's upstairs in bed," Enda informed them.

"Then we'll go upstairs and talk to her," Tase smiled.

Enda looked at him. "No, I'm sorry, you won't."

"Won't we?" Clearie asked, folding his arms as well. "She is our mother, you know, and I think we should be allowed to talk with her."

Enda looked from one to the other.

Fadin saw panic in his eyes.

"Sure you are," Enda nodded, "but you aren't going now. Like I said, she isn't feeling well."

"She really isn't," Daireann added looking equally as uneasy.

Fadin stood firm. "Well I think she's well enough to talk to us and what we have to say is very important."

"I'm sure it is but whatever it may be, it will have to wait till she's a little better."

"A little better?" Clearie said. "She's been sick since we got here and she's only getting worse, never better. If we wait till she's better, we may never get to talk to her and it will be too late."

"Please boys," Enda said standing in front of the stairs, "leave her be and let her get well."

"I don't think I will," Fadin said getting very near Enda. "Let us through."

"No."

Fadin moved even closer. "What was in that paper, Enda?"

Enda just looked at him. "News."

"News about what? Huh? News about maybe someone named Kyna."

This startled Enda for a moment and he put his arms down so there was a narrow way up the stairs.

"How would you know?" He asked staring.

Fadin took his chance. He rushed forward and managed to fit through the small gap. Enda turned immediately and tried to grab Fadin's legs but Fadin was too quick for him. He dodged the grasping hands and flew up the stairs.

"Wait!" Enda yelled. "Fadin wait!"

Fadin saw his mother's room and ran for the doorknob. Before he could reach it, he felt large hands on him. Somehow Enda had managed to get up the stairs.

"Put me down!" Fadin cried.

"Not till you swear to leave your mother alone. She's sick."

"She seemed just fine to me when I saw her the other day."

"No she didn't, she looked worse than the day before. You know she's sick so why are you doing this?"

"I have to tell her something," Fadin groaned trying to wiggle away from Enda's grip.

"Tell her what?"

"Yes," a feminine voice said, "tell me what?"

Enda released Fadin and they both turned to see Fadin's mother standing in clothes much too large for her. Her hair was a mess and she looked far too white.

"Tell me what?" She repeated.

Miss O'Keefe came from behind her and put a hand on her shoulder. "I think you should get back in bed, Teagan."

"I'm fine and being up can only do me good, right?"

"If you feel you can." Miss O'Keefe answered.

"I do." She looked at Fadin. "Come on." She kindly gestured towards her room. She looked over the railing and smiled at Tase and Clearie. "You two come up here as well."

Fadin swallowed and glanced back at his brothers fumbling up the stairs, following his mother into her untidy room.

The large rectangular space was messy but still pretty. There were two windows, both draped, and several lovely pieces of furniture along with the room's own bathroom.

Fadin watched his mother sit down on the unmade bed and pat it to indicate he should sit also. Fadin did and looked back to see his brothers come through the doorway. They too sat down and stared at their mother.

Even though he couldn't see them, Fadin knew Daireann and Enda were standing just around the corner listening intently.

"So what is it you wanted to talk to me about?" Their mother asked.

Fadin felt his throat was dry and his palms became sweaty. He wanted to tell her, more than anything in the world now, but when it came down to it, he was afraid. Afraid of upsetting her, afraid of what else he may find out, afraid she may call him crazy and deny everything.

"Well?" She said looking from one boy to the next.

"We…" Fadin started. His voice fell away. He was nervous, so nervous that his foot was shaking. He had to tell her, he had to. "we…we know, Ma."

She seemed unchanged. "Know what?"

"Know about everything, about what you've been keeping from us."

There. Fadin saw it. Her entire face changed into almost a state of panic. If she had looked sick before it was nothing compared to what she looked like now. It was almost as if she was seeing a ghost.

"You know?"

"Yes," Fadin said, "we know everything."

Fadin watched his mother wring her large sweatshirt. "How long have you known?"

"Almost the whole time we've been here."

"That long?"

"Yes."

"Why didn't you say anything to me?"

This question infuriated Fadin. Why didn't they say anything to her? What about her? Wasn't it her place to say something? She was the one who lied, she was the one who had been keeping all the secrets, and she wanted to know why he hadn't said anything?

He stood up now. "Why didn't you?" he snapped.

"I was afraid."

"Afraid of what?"

"Your father had just died Fadin, I didn't think you could handle it."

"I couldn't handle it?" He glared at her. "Please, after everything we've been through, the least thing you could have done was be honest with us. And why did it have to wait till da was dead? Didn't you ever feel like telling us before then? Or did you two just think you could keep it a secret forever?"

She looked confused now. "He didn't know, Fadin."

What? Fadin was really confused now. Their da didn't know? He had come to work here almost every day for the past few years. What was she talking about?

"What?" Fadin said looking at her.

"He never knew Fadin. He hadn't the slightest idea."

Fadin turned to his brothers who were staring at her with the same dumbfounded expression. They didn't have the faintest idea what she was talking about either.

She noticed their faces and looked equally confused. "Why are you all looking at me like that?"

Fadin turned back to her. "I want to hear you say it," he said firmly. If she wasn't talking about being magic, then what was she talking about? "We deserve to hear it from you," he yelled.

She looked startled. "Okay," she said. "I'm pregnant."

Fadin felt like he just got whacked with a ton of bricks. He sat down next to his brothers and stared at her. "You're what?"

"I'm pregnant, Fadin." She looked at each one of them.

Fadin looked at his brothers whose eyes were wide and mouths open.

She stared at them. "You said you knew. Why are you all looking at me as though this is the first you heard about it?"

Because it is, Fadin thought. It all made sense now. Why she had been so sick, the vitamins, the baggy clothes, always vomiting. She had been pregnant this whole time and she had lied about it. A brand-new fresh lie. Fadin wondered if she could ever really be honest with them.

"I guess it's just the shock of hearing you say it." He said looking down at the untidy covers.

His mother looked hard at him and suddenly it looked as though a light bulb had gone on. Her eyes looked fearful and when she spoke, her voice quivered a little.

"You weren't talking about me having a baby, were you?"

Fadin looked up at her. "No Ma, we weren't."

Her eyes became large but she simply nodded and stared down at her sweater. "I see." She was quiet for a few moments, then she looked up at all of them. "How much do you know?"

"Enough to know you have never been honest with us our whole lives." Fadin said, feeling now not anger but pain at this simple fact.

Tase moved closer to their mother and stared deep into her eyes. "Why, Ma?"

Fadin watched tears form as she grabbed a hold of Tase's chin. "Oh my darlings, I do not know where to begin."

"How about at the beginning," Clearie said, "that seems like a good place to start. Or even when you and Da left Glas Cavan, and why it is that you only left a note."

She looked at him. "How did you know about that? To my knowledge there is nothing in this castle to tell you your father and I only left a note."

"Well Mr. Hog—"

Clearie stopped. Fadin had given him a warning look. They didn't want to get Mr. Hogan into any trouble for telling them things their mother wouldn't want them to know.

Fadin looked back at his ma. Too late. Comprehension was dawning on her.

"Oh," She said smiling now, "Not Free Sogan, or Mee Frogan, and not

Tee Gogan," she shook her head and stared at them all. "Lee Hogan, that's whose daughter you've been playing with, that's who your little friend Aimirgin is. Now it all makes sense." She smiled to herself. "You've been using a Orthanach cloth haven't you? I should have known, all those times I used one on my own parents."

"Don't be angry Ma, he didn't tell us much, we found out most of it from the attic."

"The attic? How did you get up there?"

Clearie pulled out the little wooden "K." "With this."

She took it and smiled. "I haven't seen this in over fifteen years." She looked at Fadin. "What exactly do you know?"

"Well, we know you lived in this house when you were young, we sort of found that singing picture in your old closet." Fadin watched her smile. "We know Aunt Kyna is not your real sister, We know Enda is your brother, we know Da and Mr. Hogan were best friends, we heard some about Dia Ailín and the war, and we know you and Da left shortly after telling no one and leaving only a note."

She nodded. "Well," she patted the bed, making the boys move closer to her. "There is still a lot to tell, and some of it will have to wait till you're a little older but," Fadin saw her grab their father's jacket from the nightstand, "the reason we left, your father and I, was to protect you. All of you. We didn't know we were going to have you twins but we wanted to get away from here, away from Glas Cavan. We didn't know what was going to happen with Afanasii or if he was going to come back. Your father and I made a hard decision, we decided to cut all ties to our families and friends to try and protect you and your sister.

"We never told you anything because we were afraid you'd be curious, and I couldn't bear to see my children get hurt. We thought it was the right thing to do— to keep you all away from this, from the chaos and hurt."

Fadin felt tears streaming down his cheeks. "It isn't all bad though, Ma, we have met some really nice people—Mr. Hogan and his family, we even met Da's brother and Feidhelm, his cousin."

Their mother smiled. "Oh, Lorcan and Feidhelm. Yes, they are good people and you're right, it isn't all bad. But I, we, weren't willing to take the risk to show you the good in case you got hurt."

"But isn't it our decision to make whether we want to take the risk or not? Da did when he came to work here in Glas Cavan."

Their mother nodded. "Yes, you're right. It is up to you and your father did decide to take a risk in coming here. In fact, he took the ultimate risk and I sometimes have wondered over these past nine months whether his car crash was really an accident or not."

Fadin swallowed hard. "You think someone killed him on purpose? So does Mr. Hogan."

He watched his mother shake her head. "That doesn't surprise me. And I, well, I don't know."

A thought popped into Fadin's head. "Is Aunt Kyna really our aunt?"

"Yes and no," Ma said. "She's your aunt by marriage. She was married to my brother, Dubhlainn."

Fadin felt a rush of panic. "The same Dubhlainn who betrayed Dia?"

Their mother nodded. "Yes, I am sorry to say. He was my younger brother by one year, then came Glendan three years older, and then Etain, the youngest sister."

"Where are they all?" Clearie asked.

"Here on the grounds, buried with the rest of my family. I am the only Kavanagh left. Everyone, including my cousins, aunts, uncles, grandparents, parents, and even my very distant relatives, were killed during the Great War."

Fadin watched tears stream down her face. He knew it wasn't just the war that had killed them.

"Please don't be upset with me for keeping all this from you," Ma sobbed, "I know it was a mistake now, but I just wanted to protect you and keep you safe. You boys are my whole world and I don't know what I'd do if I lost you three as well." She covered her face and began to sob.

For the first time in his life, Fadin looked at her not as his mother, but as a woman who had loved them and their father with all of her heart, even if that meant she had made some mistakes. It was odd to him but he was no longer upset with her. He loved her and even though he didn't agree with many of the choices she had made, especially the choice to lie to them, he understood why.

Fadin moved closer to her and hugged her tight. He felt his brothers move forward and hug her too. He felt the tears on his face but this time he didn't care and didn't want them to stop, they weren't sad tears after all. They were tears of joy and satisfaction at finally having his mother back, the mother they had known all their lives.

Fadin opened his eyes and looked in the corner of the room. He saw his father there smiling broadly, tears on his cheeks, and hands on his hips as he had always done when he was pleased with something. Fadin blinked and he was gone but Fadin knew he had been there and he was happy his boys knew the truth—happy they could all be a family again, even if he couldn't be there with them.

The boys moved away from their mother and Fadin felt the round belly under the very large sweatshirt as he released her from his tight hug.

Their mother wiped her face and smiled at them all. "I love you boys more than life itself, do you know that?"

Fadin grinned, "Yes we do, Ma."

She opened her mouth to say something but stopped. Her face went frighteningly white and she looked as though she might faint.

"Enda!" Fadin screamed.

Enda popped his head in from around the corner.

Fadin looked at him. "Something's wrong."

Enda moved towards their mother. "Teagan?" he said watching her cautiously.

She looked at him then her eyes rolled back and she fell backward on the bed.

"Daireann!" Enda screamed. "Get Caoimhe!"

Daireann's footsteps could be heard rushing down the stairs.

"Will she be alright?" Clearie asked getting up.

"Teagan?" Miss O'Keefe asked entering the room.

"She just collapsed, Caoimhe." Enda said looking up at her.

Miss O'Keefe bent down and felt their mother's forehead. "She's fine," she said smiling.

Fadin let out a sigh of relief.

"She just overdid it. We need to let her rest, I think today's the day." She turned to Daireann, who was wringing her plum little hands. "Can you get her some soup, Daireann?"

The little cook nodded and walked quickly away.

Caoimhe turned to Fadin and his brothers. "I'm afraid I'm going to have to ask you three to leave this room. I really don't think you want to be in here when your new little brother or sister comes."

Indeed, Fadin did not. He, Tase, and Clearie got up and left the room as Daireann ran past them with a bowl of soup.

They made their way down the long stairs and sat in the sunroom, listening to the rumbling noises upstairs.

"Well, now we have a new little brother or sister to look forward to." Clearie said jokingly. "Hip, hip, hooray."

Fadin smiled at him.

A new brother or sister. He wasn't sure he liked the idea of that but what could he do? The baby was coming, probably today, and then there would be a new little one to feed, play with, and take care of. Ha, hip, hip, hooray indeed.

He really couldn't be angry though. He finally knew the truth and their mother had told it to them. He knew there was more to the story and he'd be sure to ask her, but for now he was happy and content with the fact that they had gotten some answers.

Fadin suddenly remembered that they hadn't gotten the chance to tell their mother about Aunt Kyna, although he was sure now that Enda and Daireann knew they would be on the lookout for Ministry Guards. They should be in safe hands, he hoped.

He looked over at Tase who smiled at him. Fadin was glad he had a brother like him. No matter how much had changed since they got to this castle, and how many new secrets came up, Fadin did have his brothers— brothers he could count on, brothers he could trust. Whatever came their way he would have Tase, and even though things became crazy around them, he and Tase would remain the same. No one could take away what they had and no matter what happened, they would be there for each other.

Knock! Knock! Knock!

Fadin and his brothers jumped.

"Was that the door?" Clearie asked visibly shaking.

"I think so." Tase said. "Do you think it's them?"

Knock! Knock! Knock!

"Should we check?" Fadin asked, looking at Tase then Clearie.

"Well they'll come in even if we don't answer the door, right?" Clearie said with a trembling voice.

Fadin nodded. "Right."

"Then nothing for it." Tase said standing behind Fadin.

Knock! Knock! Knock!

They all moved toward the door together. Fadin peered up the stairs as they entered the foyer. The door to their ma's room was shut.

Knock! Knock! Knock!

Fadin put his hand on the knob, Tase pressing against his right shoulder, Clearie on his left. He turned the handle, held his breath, and pulled.

He looked down first at the dirt-covered, tattered, worn-out, old shoes. Next at the stained jeans tore at the knee and high thigh. Then the long, grime-covered nails and the shirt full of holes and one sleeve ripped short. His eyes found the mouth, slightly open and caked in something red with small white feathers here and there. And last at the piercing green eyes and the thick, black, matted hair, and feathers spread throughout the knotted curls.

Fadin stepped back and stared into the face—cold, frightened, angry.

"Saoirse?" He said, looking into his sister's green eyes as the pupils expanded then shrank.

She turned her gaze to him and asked in a gruff, deep voice very unlike her own, "Where is she?"

"Who?" Fadin asked breathless.

Her hands flexed and her nails looked even longer.

Fadin stared at her, heart pounding. She locked eyes with him and sneered.

"Where is she? Where is Ma? She's got some explaining to do."

Fadin felt his heart stop. How was she here? Where did she come from?

Why did she look so dirty? And what did she know that she thought their mother should explain? Fadin didn't know but he was sure he was going to find out.

His mind played quickly over all that had happened that year. He had gone from living a normal life in a normal city knowing exactly who he was and feeling sure about everything to living in a castle filled with magic and secrets and no longer knowing who he was and feeling quite unsure about everyone and everything around him. He had spent most of the year searching for the truth, and upstairs with Ma he had finally gotten it, at least part of it, and he felt that one chapter in this new life had ended. However, seeing Saoirse at the door looking the way she did he quickly understood that a new chapter was beginning, and that things in this new life were much more complicated than in the old one. One thing and one thing only was Fadin now certain of . . . his story was far from over.